THE COLD EYE

THE DEVIL'S WEST, BOOK TWO

THE COLD EYE

LAURA ANNE GILMAN

SAGA PRESS

LONDON SYDNEY **NEW YORK** TORONTO NEW DELHI

SAGA PRESS
AN IMPRINT OF SIMON & SCHUSTER, INC.

1230 AVENUE OF THE AMERICAS, NEW YORK, NEW YORK 10020

Text copyright © 2017 by Laura Anne Gilman
Jacket illustration copyright © 2017 by John Jude Palencar
SAGA PRESS and colophon are trademarks of Simon & Schuster, Inc.
For information about special discounts for bulk purchases, please contact Simon & Schuster Special Sales at 1-866-506-1949 or business@simonandschuster.com.
The Simon & Schuster Speakers Bureau can bring authors to your live event. For more information or to book an event, contact the Simon & Schuster Speakers Bureau at 1-866-248-3049 or visit our website at www.simonspeakers.com.
The text for this book is set in ITC Galliard Std.
Manufactured in the United States of America
First Edition
2 4 6 8 10 9 7 5 3 1
Library of Congress Cataloging-in-Publication Data
Names: Gilman, Laura Anne, author.
Title: The cold eye / Laura Anne Gilman.
Description: New York : Saga Press, 2017. | Series: The Devil's West ; 2
Identifiers: LCCN 2016029456 (print) | LCCN 2016038640
(eBook) | ISBN 9781481429719 (hardcover : acid-free paper) |
ISBN 9781481429733 (eBook)
Subjects: LCSH: Teenage girls—Fiction. | Devil—Fiction. | Magic—Fiction. |
BISAC: FICTION / Fantasy / Historical. | FICTION / Fantasy / General. |
GSAFD: Western stories. | Fantasy fiction. | Occult fiction.
Classification: LCC PS3557.I4545 C64 2017 (print) | LCC PS3557.I4545
(eBook) | DDC 813/.54—dc23
LC record available at https://lccn.loc.gov/2016029456

IN MEMORY OF

JUDITH SHAPIRO KRUPP,

WHO HELPED A THEN-TEENAGED ME

DISCOVER MY HOME IN THE SF COMMUNITY.

WITHOUT HER, THIS BOOK (ALL MY BOOKS)

WOULD NOT HAVE EXISTED.

1937-2016

Northern Wilds

Unclaimed Lands

Junction

Flood

De Plata

The Mother's Knife

SPANISH PROTECTORATE

THE DEVIL'S
WEST

0   200   400

Miles

THE DEVIL'S WEST, BOOK TWO

THE COLD EYE

PART ONE
UNCERTAIN GROUND

There was a well-ordered murmur to the saloon in Flood that evening, some combination of chairs scraping and glassware clinking, laid against the *flickerthwack* of cards against felt, and the self-assured calls of the dealers. Marie cast her gaze around her domain, confirming that all was well, then moved through the crowd to stand behind the dealer at the main table.

"Gentleman in the far corner wishes to have a word with you when you're done dealing for the evening."

She waited until the boss nodded, the barest hint of a chin drop, and moved along to the next table, a smile on her lips, eyes bright and alert. The carmine she'd rubbed on her cheeks had been replaced by the flush of warmth and hard work, the ache of ankle and hip joined by the soreness of elbow and knee. It was entirely possible, Marie thought, that she was finally growing too old for this.

A dry snort behind her gave the boss's opinion of that, and her smile warmed for a heartbeat.

Still and all, there was no gainsaying she'd earned her aches. Five tables full, and Iktan busy at the bar, her people coming and going in a well-choreographed dance. She should feel satisfied. She did feel satisfied. It was near impossible for her not to take satisfaction, being who and what she was, when things went well and needs were gratified.

But her ankle and hip ached, and her elbows and knees were sore, and she worked to keep her smile in place as she nodded to strangers and placed warm hands on the shoulders of regulars. The responsibilities of the Devil's Right Hand were hers: the gathering-in and the granting, ensuring that all who came to him were noted and heard.

"We dance to his tune," she'd told Izzy. So you put your smile on and left the aches until later.

"Cardsharp at Jack's table," Molly said as she passed, her tray filled with empty glasses needing refills or cleaning. "Black-haired gent in the kersey weave. He's not started cheating yet, but he has a look about him."

Marie slanted a look in that direction. "Give him one more drink and have Iktan settle his tab," she said. Cardsharps came regular, either to see the devil deal cards or to test themselves on his table. She'd seen the boss spend all evening with one, the two of them grinning like a pair of schoolboys as the stakes grew higher and the cheats wilder, all other games abandoned until they ended with a bottle between them after hours, talking until dawn. But to come with intent to cheat others . . . The devil ran an honest game, and an honest house, and she'd sweep out any who tried different.

In the end, the cardsharp went quietly, with a rueful grin that might have amused another woman. Marie forgot him before the door'd snicked shut on his heels, busy with her responsibilities until the last *flickerthwack* of cards was laid to rest, the last bootheel sounding on hardwood, and all that was left was the whisper of slippers and the sighs of bodies loosed from jumps and hair down from knots in the rooms upstairs. The boss disappeared into his private office, and Iktan whistled soundlessly as he cleaned the last of the glassware and stocked up for the night, the kitchen silent and dark.

"Marie?"

She would say the quiet voice startled her, save she'd been expecting it for at least a week now. Rosa: the others had likely elected her, from the way she shuffled forward, hesitant and determined in her night-wrapper, arms crossed against her bosom.

Marie placed her glass of whiskey down on the bar, hearing the glass clink wetly on the hardwood and watching with amusement as Iktan lifted the glass to swipe under it with his cloth, replacing the glass more quietly.

"Have you . . . have you heard anything from Izzy, recent? I was just wondering; she's been gone so long, and so sudden . . ."

Overnight, Rosa meant. One evening the girl was among them, clearing drinks and smiling at the players, one of a handful of girls under the boss's protection. One evening she was there, and the next dawn she was gone. "On the devil's business," they'd been told, and nothing more. Because if they needed to be told, they had no need to know.

None of them had seen the quiet depths to that one girl, the hunger they lacked; none had understood the skill they thought could be learned, and not simply trained when it appeared.

"She'll be home to us soon," Marie said, and her smile was all that was comforting and sincere, even as she wondered if she lied.

Isobel had been riding alone for three days, two to her destination and one heading back, when she first heard the whisper.

She reined the mare in, listening. In the months since they'd left Flood, she'd learned to sit relaxed in the saddle, aware now of the grass and rocks under Uvnee's hooves, the distant, steady chitter of insects and the calls of birds, the rustle of the breeze coming cool from the northwest, and the clear, quiet hum of the Road ahead of and below her. But this was something new.

They'd been skirting the western edge of the Territory for weeks, the bare rock and hints of snow on the high jagged peaks to her left still strange to her prairie-born eyes, but she could sense nothing wrong here, could hear no alarm in the breeze or the birds, see no cause for her skin to prickle or the pit of her stomach to tighten.

Another might have dismissed the whisper as discomfort, sweat and dirt itching her skin. Despite the brim of her hat shading her eyes, her jacket rolled and tied to the back of her saddle, the early summer sun was strong, leaving the fabric of her skirt and blouse damp with sweat. But Isobel née Lacoyo Távora was no longer the green girl she'd been, newly made Devil's Hand, with no idea of what that was or what it meant.

And Isobel had heard whispers before. Not a voice, not a word, but a sensation, curling not within her ears but inside her bones, and it rarely brought pleasant news. But always before, Gabriel had been with her, his steady presence a comfort, his experience a guide. That was why the boss had chosen him, to mentor her while she learned.

She was alone now, Gabriel waiting back at camp, a day's ride on.

The whisper came again, skitter-cool under her skin, scraping and pulling her, until she nearly swayed in the saddle.

Two days' ride out, two days' ride back. She dared not divert her course. If she was late returning, Gabriel would worry.

Isobel stiffened her spine against that thought. She was the Devil's Hand, his proxy in the Territory, and her Bargain did not allow her to ignore a call for aid, no matter its source. She licked her lips, rubbed her left palm, with its black-lined sigil, against her skirt, and adjusted the brim of her hat, and when she spoke, her voice was firm.

"Yes."

The whisper yanked her forward, knees pressing Uvnee off the trail they'd been following, hooves clattering on rock, up over a long, narrow rise northwest of where she'd meant to be, the tug-tug-tug a steady ache until they crested the rise and could see what waited for them.

A sudden shock of *wrongness* flashed in her bones and rocked her back into her saddle, making her reach instinctively for the long knife sheathed above her knee. But even as she did so, Isobel knew that the *wrongness* was not a threat to her, and nothing a knife could defend against.

Uvnee shifted, clearly wanting to be gone. Isobel calmed the mare and forced herself to study the scene below her, nostrils flaring to catch the hint of anything more than decay in the air, her ears alert to noise from above or behind. But she was, save for Uvnee, alone.

Alone, save for the buzzards who lifted their heads to study the newcomers as she rode closer, and then, once it was clear she had no interest in chasing them from their meal, dropped bald heads to their grisly business once more.

Corpses. Hillocks of flesh, draped across the grass, white bones showing through here and there where the buzzards and foxes had already been.

She felt bile rise in her throat. Not at the sight or smell of dead flesh—any delicacy she'd been born with had been extinguished, if not from her years living under the devil's roof, then certainly in the past months of riding the Road—but from the sheer *waste* of it all. The buffalo carcasses had been shorn of their hides and horns, but the flesh had been left on the bone, rotting under the sun.

Anger did not replace the disgust but fitted itself alongside, curling along her spine, making her head dizzy. This was wrong, it snarled. This was wrong*ness.*

"What a blasted waste."

Isobel's knife was ready in her hand even as Uvnee spooked sideways, her hooves scraping against stone. The man who had spoken did not react to the threat, his gaze resting on the piles of flesh below them. He was slight-built, dressed in a rider's long oilcloth coat, worn brown boots on his feet, and a battered hat on his head, the skin of his face and hands sun-brown and spotted.

She knew him, although she had never seen him before.

"Jack."

"Hand."

He met her gaze then, the lines of his face etched around a thin mouth, and stone-grey eyes deep-set under the shadow of his hat's brim. A Jack. Men—and some women—who'd sat down at the devil's table and wagered more than they could afford to lose. Sworn for seven times seven and seven again, to serve the boss until their debt was cleared.

"Even dumb beasts are given mercy denied me," he went on, returning his gaze to the scene below.

She glanced at the slaughtered remains. "You call that mercy?"

"I felt their death, felt them return to the wind and bones." He flexed his fingers, the knuckles crackling loud in the silence between them. "The quiet of death is a dream, and I am not allowed to sleep." He exhaled, as though summoning words, before she could speak in turn. "Will you kill me, Hand?"

She knew, the way she knew what he was, that he had not served his term. And he knew, even as he asked, what her answer must be.

She realized she was still holding the knife in her hand, and slipped it back into its sheath. "Did you see who did this?"

The Jack shook his head. He had no cause to lie, even if he'd dared. "I felt it. A day back, p'raps more. It drew me, same as it drew you." The lines in his face pulled taut. "That much power, he resents it being gone."

The near-insult to the boss offended her, but something thrummed under her skin before she could rebuke him, shimmering along her bones to pool hot and sharp in the palm of her left hand. She didn't bother to look down, merely stretching her fingers as though they had cramped. The sigil etched in her palm pulsed once in response and then subsided, leaving her cold despite the sun still high overhead.

"All right," she told the mark, the sensation, the anger. "All right. I know."

Had it been their deaths the whisper warned of? The buffalo were no obligation of the devil's, no matter what the Jack said. The Territory's medicine was none of his concern or handling. But there was no arguing with the sigil: it demanded her attention, demanded her action.

"May I have your leave to go, Hand?"

She nodded; she had no use for him here.

The Jack's boot heels scraped stone underfoot, heavier than Gabriel's steps, the movement of a man accustomed to walking, not riding, two steps, five, and then gone. And then it was only her, and the buzzards, and the silent heaps of scraped bone and rotting flesh. And the pulse of demand in her left hand.

Isobel could not fix this, could not erase the insult given, and from the smell of the bodies, the killers were long gone, and she was no tracker, to follow and find them.

Gabriel could have done it, most likely. But Gabriel wasn't with her. Five days back, they'd ridden into La Ramée, only to learn that a post rider had collapsed off his horse, near death with dysentery and not yet recovered, his post undelivered.

Gabriel had volunteered to take the packet on to the next waystation. "It's good you be seen doing things like this," he'd told her. "Solving problems that aren't life-shaking, give 'em confidence the devil's looking after them, even way out here."

Isobel was reasonable certain that the Left Hand hadn't been meant to ride as a post-rider, but she'd a letter of her own to send back to the boss, anyhow. Two birds with one stone, Marie would say, and Isobel was aware she'd a strong streak of the practical in her.

Practical, and aware of the burden of duty and obligations. Something had drawn her here, just as it had the Jack. Unlike him, she was not constrained to wait on specific orders.

Isobel slid off Uvnee's back, her boots crunching lightly on the dry grass, and tucked the reins up, then walked closer, trusting the mare to stay where she was. Up close—closer than Isobel had ever been to one of the beasts, living, and closer than she'd ever thought to be—their size was even more impressive. She counted seven bodies, although the churned-up grass indicated that there had been a few more. Four were full-grown, three were calves, smaller than ponies, their pelts sparse and untouched, their thick skulls broken by the bullets that killed them.

Isobel had seen a great herd only once, but the wonder of it lingered in her own bones, the way it had caught at her, stilled her heart and breath with the drumming of thousands of hooves, holding her captive until the beasts had moved on. Buffalo did not merely live within the Territory; they were *part* of it, the power flowing from the earth into their hearts and returning through the pounding of their hooves, much as water found its way through stone.

That much power, he resents it being gone. "He" being the boss. But the buffalo were no part of him, no obligation of his, any more than the wind or the rain or . . . or magicians. Their medicine was not one the boss could touch or use. Why would it concern him?

The sigil in her palm pulsed again, the deep black lines stinging as though she'd grasped a handful of berry-bramble. She flexed her fingers, telling it to wait, to be patient.

Gabriel had told her that buffalo hunts began with offerings to appease the spirits of those killed, that every part of the animal was used, that waste would offer insult and ensure that none of the beasts gave of themselves to those hunters again. Buffalo pelts were prized, but so too were the meat, the horns, the tail, the bones . . . not left to bloat and rot under the sun.

This . . . this was nothing short of desecration. The word came from nowhere, the taste of it like ashes and dry bread on her tongue, and the bile churned again.

The ground needed to be cleansed.

Isobel went back to the mare and rummaged in her saddlebag, her questing fingers resting briefly on her journal, the leather binding worn soft at the corners now, before pulling out a winter apple, slightly mushy but still edible, and a handful of loose salt, crumbled from the stick no Rider went without. Almost an afterthought, she reached for the canteen slung over the saddle, hearing the water slosh inside, then went back to where the bodies lay.

The buzzards shifted as she approached, moving away but refusing to relinquish their meal entirely. She placed the apple on the ground, drawing a half-circle of salt around it, then splashed some of the water, soaking the grass where blood had dried. Salt to cleanse, and offerings of grazing and water to appease. There should be smoke, and a better offering, but this was all she had.

"I'm sorry," she said to them, her gaze touching on each beast in turn, memorizing their shapes, even their smells. "You should have been better honored, in your death. I—" She hesitated, unwilling to promise a thing she was not certain she could perform. "I will carry your memory with me. I will honor your gifts, although they did not come to me."

She couldn't promise any more, not faithfully. But as the words left her mouth, one of the buzzards lifted its bald head and swiveled its neck to look directly at her, and a burning chill touched her face, even as the sting in her palm faded.

Something had heard her, and accepted her promise.

Isobel made camp that night soon after the sun fell below the horizon, stopping only when it became clear she would not reach the Road before full dark.

The stars were bright, the low moon waxing crescent, and Isobel paused while burying the remains of her dinner to appreciate the way their light echoed against the darkness, silent counterpoint to the occasional howls and hoots rising from the land.

She had been raised under a roof, and the first few nights on the Road, the vast open space had unnerved her beyond the telling, the sweep of stars brighter than any lamp, the sheer *emptiness* of the land a weight pressing her down into the ground until she could barely breathe.

Slowly, over weeks, that sensation had faded, until the open air became familiar as walls and windows, the light of the stars and the passage of the moon the only comfort she needed, the emptiness filled with the less-subtle noises of the night, the howl and barks of predators, the flutter of wings as soothing as the sound of slippers in the hallway.

But that night, she missed Gabriel, his low voice telling stories of how Badger pulled first man from stone, or Buffalo created the plains, or teaching her to identify an animal by the flick of its tail, or a plant by the turn of its leaves. She missed the sound of his breathing as he slept across the fire from her, the snort and mumble when he dreamed. She missed the collective sighing and grumbling of his horse, Steady, and Flatfoot the mule when they were picketed together with Uvnee.

Even the Jack would have been welcome company, simply to feel another person nearby.

"Foolishness," she told herself, startling a stripetail that had crept close to see if she'd left scraps for it to scavenge. She kicked the ground to discourage it, and it fled.

Unwilling to sleep just yet, Isobel took her journal out, wetted her pencil, and wrote down what she had seen, how many bodies and how they had been butchered, what had been taken and what had been left, and a description of the hollow where she'd found them, the shape of the hills from where she'd stood. The boss might want to know. More, she had promised to remember.

When she slipped the journal back into her pack, her hand touched something else, not cloth, that crinkled under her fingers. She'd almost forgotten about the letters. Two waxed envelopes had been at the postal drop, one addressed to a Matthew Smith someplace called Tallahatchie, and one . . .

And one for Gabriel. The envelope had been battered at the edges as though it had traveled a long way, but his name was written in clear script on the dun-colored envelope. Master Gabriel Kasun.

You didn't meddle in another's business in the Territory. You didn't ask questions you'd no need the answers to. She left the envelopes where they were, refusing to indulge any curiosity in who might be writing to her mentor, and lay down, pulling the blanket more closely around her shoulders. Sooner she slept, sooner she'd be on her way again, sooner she wouldn't be alone.

Wake, Hand.

Isobel couldn't move. Nothing bound her, nothing held her down, but she could not convince her limbs to lift, a soft indolence encasing her as securely as if she were swaddled like an infant.

Wake, Hand.

The voice was insistent, the shape of it poking, prodding. "I am awake," she tried to tell it, then realized that she wasn't. She was dreaming, and the voice needed her to wake.

Her eyes opened, the stickiness on her eyelashes evidence that she had been asleep for several hours. The belly-rounded sliver of the moon was sinking, the stars beginning to fade, and she estimated, groggily, that it was a few hours before sunrise. The coalstone glimmered faintly within its circle of rocks, and she could hear Uvnee shifting, but it was a peaceful, sleepy shift; whatever had woken Isobel had not disturbed the mare or roused her to defense.

What had woken her?

Gut feeling made Isobel turn her head away from the coalstone, scanning the dark air next to her for the shadow of a snake, its tongue flickering secrets; a native stepping quietly through the night; a demon lurking, intent on mischief. But there was nothing there save grass. Nothing came visiting tonight.

You must go.

Her bedroll was packed away and the coalstone cooled before Isobel realized she had been directed to do so. She paused, drawing a sharp, shocked breath. An owl called twice in the darkness, and she waited, half-expecting a third call that never came. If an owl called three times in the night, it meant medicine was being worked. Two calls, it merely hunted unsuspecting mice.

Beyond that, there was only an echoing silence, the night creatures stilling, the dawn birds not yet singing.

An empty space in the world, through which other voices could be heard.

Go.

It did not feel the same as what had drawn her to the slaughtered buffalo. That had been a feeling, a pressure, a pull. This was . . . like the boss, when he used a particular tone, but nothing at all of that warm, familiar voice. There was nothing human in this at all, and it would not be refused.

Isobel finished breaking her simple camp, waking Uvnee and replacing her blanket and saddle with a soft apology. "We'll make up breakfast later," she said as she mounted. "We need to be on our way now."

The sigil in her palm remained cool in her skin, the black lines invisible in the darkness, and yet she knew the way she knew things now that the whispering voice was a summons she could not refuse.

Was it about the buffalo? The spirits of the dead lingered until they were laid to rest, protected. Did the spirits of animals do the same? She had made a promise . . . Was she now being driven to satisfy it?

"Boss?" She knew he couldn't hear her. The devil might have long ears, but there were none that long, to cover the breadth of the Territory; she was months from home, and he had more to do than listen for her.

Uvnee snorted, her warm breath almost visible in the chill air, and turned her head to nip at Isobel's skirt, as though asking why she'd been woken and saddled if they weren't going to go anywhere. Isobel patted the mare's neck with the hand not holding the reins, reassured by the solid warmth of muscle and flesh. "You're right," she said. "I'm sorry."

She buttoned her jacket and tucked the fabric of her skirts under her legs, then gave the mare the signal to move forward, both of them keeping their eyes on the grass in front of them: traveling in the dark was always dangerous, and the grass could hide any of a dozen threats, from gopher holes to snakes, to ground suddenly wet and slippery from a hidden creek.

The stock of her gun, a new acquisition in La Ramée, rubbed against her leg, but its presence gave her little comfort. Gabriel was the sureshot of the two of them. She could hit things most times out of ten, but not always, and she'd never yet had to shoot at a thing that went on two legs.

Only a fool would be riding before dawn, alone, driven by a whisper in the dark. But her life was not her own. She kept riding, north and west of where she'd planned to go, farther away from the campsite where

Gabriel was waiting, until the sky began to shift from black to purple, and from purple to streaky red ahead of the sun.

It was full dawn when Isobel rode over yet another low, undulating hill and saw a narrow river cutting through the shallow valley below, the outline of a small farmstead a little ways uphill from it, on the other side. Her destination?

No answer came, either by whisper or sigil-burn.

There were three buildings set in a grassy clearing: two square, low-roofed houses and a barn set around a trampled-down center. Beyond that, there was what looked like an icehouse, half-hidden under the turf, the buildings weathered from both winter's wind and summer's sun, doors shut and windows shuttered.

Cautiously, she rode Uvnee into the creek, the water splashing at her boots, soaking the mare's legs, Isobel's gaze slipping from right to left and then back again, waiting for . . . something, anything, to appear or attack.

Halfway across, she felt the warding, a dozen prickly slaps against her chest and arms, making her fingers spasm on the reins before the prickling faded and disappeared. The wards had recognized her—or, more likely, the devil's sigil she carried—and named her friend and welcome. Isobel's muscles eased slightly, but she remained alert. There was still no movement she could see, no cows lowing or the enthusiastic *he-hon* of pigs to be heard, and no one had yet come out to greet her. Was there illness here, as at Widder Creek, or had the farmstead been abandoned under threat?

Uvnee heaved herself out of the creek and up the slight bank, coming to a pause when Isobel eased the reins back, still cautious, still waiting.

Illness or violence. She had been called for nothing else yet.

The knife in the darkness. That was what the boss had called her. Maria was the Right Hand, the open hand. The Left was forever curled around a weapon.

Her right hand rested on the hilt of her knife, the butt of her blunderbuss hard against her thigh, and she calculated how quickly she could reach for the silver in her pocket if she needed it. But those musings were cut off when a woman exited one of the low houses, turning to face the newcomer, and the morning sunlight showed that the woman was native.

Isobel felt a momentary pang of uncertainty: had she given offense by riding in, uninvited? The warding had recognized her, but she had only been in a few native encampments before, and always with Gabriel at her side.

The woman called out then, saying something in a language Isobel did not know. She shook her head, lifting her right hand to her left breast and then out, ending with her palm to the sky, thumb and index finger extended, then swept her hand, fingers extended, to the right. She thought—hoped—that was the sign for not understanding, that she was doing it right, that they didn't use another gesture, that she hadn't just said something terribly rude.

Gabriel would have known.

The woman gave her another glance, then, in clear but halting Spanish, said, "Tu monta temprano, y solo."

"Lo siento si me ofender," Isobel said, sliding down from Uvnee's back, to put herself on equal ground. "Mi nombre es Isobel de Flood. La mano de Diablo."

Marie had taught them that formality and politeness could head off problems before they became problems. She had been speaking of bar fights, but Isobel saw no reason it wouldn't hold here, too. The warding had recognized the sigil, but that did not mean this woman would, did not mean that she was welcome.

She studied the woman anxiously, looking for some sign of recognition or acknowledgment. There were strands of silver in her black hair, and lines around her eyes and mouth, cutting deeply into the skin there. She was older than she appeared, far older than Isobel herself, but not elderly.

"I am Jumping-Up Duck," the woman said, still in Spanish, studying Isobel in turn. "Why have you come here now, Hand?"

That was a fair question, if awkward to answer. She fell back on a question of her own. "Is all well here?"

"Yes. Of course." The woman's face was calm, her mouth solemn, but Isobel knew a lie, no matter how well someone hid it behind a smile or a steady look.

But people lied all the time. Some did it to hide the truth, some because they weren't ready to speak the truth yet, some because they didn't *know* the truth yet. The *why* was what the boss had taught her to discern.

So. She did not think anger lay behind this lie. Isobel breathed, listened. Worry, she thought. And . . . unnerved. Something unnerved the woman, and she felt she could not, dare not speak of it. What, and why?

Isobel tried to remember everything Gabriel had told her, trying to remember the few exchanges she'd had with women in the native villages they'd visited. Few, too few; she'd relied on Gabriel too much. But still, this was no different from what she had done at the saloon, convincing people to trust her, drawing the truth out so that it could be dealt with.

"Another day, I would have nodded and left it be," she said, leaning against Uvnee and petting the mare's soft nose, making herself seem gentler, easier to speak with, one woman to another. "I would have nodded and perhaps let someone else dig into the root of your sorrow, thinking it none of my business. But the Master of the Territory sent me in his name."

She was bluffing. But Isobel had been raised in a saloon, seen the best bluff against the best and fold. She knew what she was about.

A heartbeat, then another, and the woman shook her head, although the edges of her lips turned up in what might have been a smile, if there wasn't such worry underneath. "You will join us for morning meal?"

The invitation was an admission. Isobel kept her satisfaction tight inside, and said only, "It would be my honor."

❦ ❦ ❦

No sooner had she accepted the invitation than the door of the nearest cabin opened, and another woman came out, followed by a man, and after them, a tumble of children and two skinny, rough-coated dogs, all wildly excited not by the appearance of another person but by her horse.

"They know better than to get within kicking distance," Duck said, although it wasn't clear if she was referring to the children or the dogs or both.

"Hello," the second woman said in English, pushing the children away. "I'm Elizabet." Isobel realized she was staring, and stammered out a greeting. Elizabet was pale-skinned, with hair paler blond than any Isobel had ever seen, the man with her a square, burly knot with the same pale skin and paler hair. "This is Karl," Elizabet said, and he nodded once. "Halla."

As though a signal had been given, three more people emerged from the other building, walking over to join them.

"This is Margot, my sister"—Elizabet brought the other woman over with a familial arm around her waist—"and her husband Four Wolves, and his brother, Catches in Teeth."

Isobel had caught up with her surprise enough to greet them politely. The brothers shared Duck's round face and prominent cheekbones, and wore attire similar to Karl's: long cloth pants and low boots under sleeveless tunics that showed off muscular arms. The women all wore long-sleeved shifts, the deerskin decorated with red and blue beads at the shoulder and hem, unadorned moccasins on their feet.

"This is Isobel," Duck said. "She joins us for breakfast."

As simple as that, as though it were perfectly ordinary for a stranger, a woman to ride up. Or perhaps, because it was so isolated, they welcomed any visitor without question?

After the wardings vouched for them, at least.

"I will stable your horse?" Karl asked, and Isobel offered him the reins without hesitation: they had welcomed her in hospitality, and it would give insult if she doubted it. Karl led the mare off to the stable, the pack of children and dogs following at his heels. He walked with a slight limp, she noticed, barely visible, favoring his right knee as though he had taken a blow there, hard enough to linger.

"Come," Elizabet said, and in a matter of moments, the women had set up a long plank table, with roughhewn chairs beside it, while the children settled with their plates on the ground, rough-and-tumble like puppies. Duck's husband, a silent shadow of a man Duck referred to only as "my man," joined them, bringing bowls of what smelled like maple porridge and warm meat that made Isobel's stomach rumble rudely.

He laughed at her, although he made no noise and his smile showed no teeth, and shoveled a larger portion onto her plate.

She could almost hear Gabriel's voice in the back of her ear, advising her: hospitality, and *then* the devil's business.

The food was excellent—far better than anything she or Gabriel had managed, but Isobel found herself distracted by her companions. Not the four natives—although their hair and skin were darker, they reminded her of Iktan, the old bartender in Flood. It was the whites who distracted her: Elizabet and Margot's skin was the faded white of oft-washed linens, and their eyes were the pale blue of sageflowers. Karl's were only a shade deeper blue, his eyebrows bleached nearly white by the sun.

Elizabet noticed her staring, but when Isobel blushed, ducking her head, the woman only laughed, not unkindly. "When I first saw Four Wolves," she told Isabel with a wink, "I thought he was covered in mud, and tried to scrape it off." She placed one hand on her husband's arm, a smile turned up at him. "It's a wonder he kept us."

He snorted but patted her hand with his own, still eating.

"You're curious," Elizabet went on. "How we came to be here, such an oddling group."

Isobel would not have asked but would not deny her curiosity, either.

Margot had a deeper voice than her sister, and spoke so quietly Isobel had to strain to hear her. "Our parents came to the American country, thinking to give us a better chance, but it . . . did not suit." Her shoulders lifted in a faint shrug, although there was a bitter wistfulness about her that said she did care, still, very much. "And then one day Elizabet spoke with a gospel sharp who rode through our town, and he told of us a place across the river, a wild land, god's land, where we could have purpose. To save the savages." Her laugh carried that same bitter wistfulness.

"But the gospel sharp's mission was . . . well." Elizabet shrugged as well, hers a loose movement of one shoulder, and Isobel caught a glimpse of faint red scarring along her neck, like the burn from a rope. "There was strife. Four Wolves brought us here, and here we stay."

Strife enough to drive the five of them from away from all their people, enough to bring Duck and her husband, of some unknown relation, with them. Isobel would ask no further, save one thing she needed to know. "This sharp. Does he have a name?"

Catches in Teeth answered her. "None that is spoken now."

The tribe he'd given offense to had dealt with him on their own, then. Isobel nodded and let it go.

"And here you . . . farm?" Her voice lifted, making it a question, although there were no fields to be seen, save a small garden patch between the houses.

"We hunt," Catches in Teeth said. "Enough to keep us. We welcome those who travel between the villages and the sacred lake. We keep the agreement here"—and his voice was like a rumble of thunder on a clear day, low, but sharp and clear. "Better than most."

Isobel's gaze went to his, but there was nothing in his eyes to suggest deeper meaning in his words. The Agreement had been made with long-gone tribal elders, back when the grandparents of Jumping-Up Duck's grandparents had been young, to keep balance between natives and outsiders looking to make the Territory their home as well. Did he mean to say that there were those here who did not abide?

Uncertainty fluttered within Isobel's stomach again. How was she to proceed? Were these folk settlers, to be held to the devil's management?

Or were they a tribal campment, outside of it? Was she the Hand here or visitor without authority?

In her silence, the conversation moved on, speaking of the next structure they hoped to finish before winter came around again, to house Karl and, eventually, the older boys.

Isobel let the words wash over her, hearing without listening, watching without looking too directly at anything. *Native folk won't tell you anything straight on,* the boss used to say. *At least not to us, but they'll tell you what you need to know, if you only just wait on them; be patient.* But there were winds here she could not quite catch, in who spoke of what and who did not. Native and settler, their edges overlapping, blurring. She was missing something, something important.

And so Isobel listened, watched, and waited, until the last battered tin spoon scraped the bottom of the last wooden bowl, and the children had been sorted and sent off to the creek to wash the food from their hands and faces. The women cleared the dishes away, while the men and Isobel remained at the table, Catches in Teeth taking a small, bright blade out of his pocket and resuming work on what looked to become a flute, the others simply resting after the meal. The *scratch-scratch-scratch* of Catches in Teeth's knife would be soothing under other circumstances, but she could feel his gaze on her, judging and considering, and she was aware that her weapons were with Uvnee's tack, too far away to do her any good.

When enough time had gone by to satisfy that they were all perfectly capable of going all day without speaking if they chose to, Isobel lifted her shoulders and placed her hands on the table, her left hand resting with the palm up, the sigil formed there clearly visible. And then she waited a little while more, until Duck's husband laughed, a dry cackle.

"Why are you here?" Four Wolves asked.

"You know what I am." They did not deny it. "I was woken this morning by a need for me to be here, a reason for me to be here, although I do not know what that reason or need may be yet. Something worries you. You may speak to me of it, or not. That is your choice."

Isobel let the words rest between them and waited. Patience. They would choose to trust her, or they would not, and she could do nothing more.

A child laughed down by the creek. There was the *scratch-scratch-scratch* of the knife against wood. Beyond that, beneath that, there was silence that carried its own noise within it, the weight of breathing, of thinking, of strong emotion not yet ready to speak.

Briefly, she thought of Farron, the magician who had spoken merely to fill the air with noise, who had blathered as though afraid of the silence, and then disappeared into the silence without warning without farewell. Distracted a moment, she hoped he was all right, wherever he was.

"The bones sorrow." Jumping-Up Duck's voice was thin and quiet as she rejoined them at the table. "They sorrow, and we suffer."

"Jumping-Up Duck worries too much." Four Wolves' words were dismissive, but her sense of him did not match his words; where Duck sorrowed, he was afraid. His brother remained impassive, quick, steady flicks of his blade hollowing and smoothing the tiny flute.

The two other women had also returned, reclaiming their seats without speaking. Margot's jaw was clenched, her blue eyes clouded with worry; Elizabet's were a calmer stillness.

"Jumping-Up Duck is my wife and wise." Her husband hadn't spoken before, and Isobel now understood why: like his laugh, his voice was a harsh, ugly scratch, breath forced out of a throat that did not wish to speak. She lowered her gaze and continued waiting.

"She says the devil's hand will rest upon us, shelter against what comes."

Isobel licked her lips once, and decided that yes, that had been a question. Apprehension shivered through her, cold prickles of doubt that made her bowels clench and her upper lip sweat. What was coming? The Spanish king had set loose a spellwork on the Territory months before. She and Gabriel had dealt with one creature that came of that;

Gabriel was still recovering from the wounds he had taken, and she—

No. She forced her emotions down, her thumb stroking the silver ring on her littlest finger, the surface fresh-polished, untarnished. She'd faced plague and monsters and Spanish monks who hated her, had forced a spell-creature into obedience with the Territory. If this was more illness from the spell's influence, she would recognize it. All she had to do was look.

Isobel left her hands resting on the table, feeling the roughhewn surface against her skin. She only intended to skim the surface, fingers trailing over dust, a leaf floating on water, skin held up for the breeze to brush past it. Isobel held herself back, resisting the deep call of the bones to simply breathe in the power that pooled and grew at even the faintest of crossroads, the soft-worn path between the buildings where feet trod each and every day. If anything of ill intent lingered, she would feel it.

But nothing lingered at all, no power at all beyond the wards she already sensed. Something had come through here already and swept the crossroads clean.

Isobel had been gone four days now. Not that Gabriel was counting, he told himself as he splashed water on his face, willing it to chase away the night's unease. It was only because there wasn't much else to do, short of re-sort their supplies, groom his horse and mule until they tried to nip at him in irritation, and wait for his strength to come back.

Gabriel was tired of waiting.

He reached for his boots, checking to make sure nothing had crawled into them overnight, then put them on. Their usual stop-a-night austerity had expanded over the days he'd been trapped there, clothing hung to dry over a series of mostly-flat rocks, Steady's bridle taken apart for a thorough cleaning and not yet reassembled, the area where the animals had been grazing hoof-worn, the pit a ways off where he'd been burying his refuse marked by raw earth mounded over it.

He stretched his legs out, sitting by the banked fire while waiting for the coffee to boil, and pulled off his shirt, poked gingerly at the scabbing on his ribs. Some of it crumbled off, flaking away and leaving a pale red seam on the flesh underneath, but the rest still clung firmly to his skin, the wound beneath not yet entirely healed. He'd told Isobel it looked worse than it had been, but it had looked bad enough. Thankfully, nothing had taken infection, likely due to the efforts of the Spanish monk rather than the cleanliness of the monster claws that had inflicted the wounds.

He rubbed two fingers over the thickest of the scabs, and winced. The otter-beast—the *massive* otter-beast, he corrected himself—had scored three strips across his ribs and one on his face, and despite his assurances to Isobel, he knew full well he was lucky not to be dead.

He did not feel lucky, constrained to camp while she went off, blithely promising not to find any trouble along the way.

He laughed, and if the noise was bitter, there was no one there to tell. Isobel née Lacoyo Távora of Flood. The Devil's Left Hand. The weight and the might of the devil, Master of the Territory. Finding trouble? Isobel *was* trouble. But she was also a sixteen-year-old girl who was supposed to be under his mentorship and protection, not go off riding on her own because he was too weak to ride with her.

If you don't accept it gracefully, I'll tie you to a post while you sleep. That would be difficult to explain to any riders who came by, wouldn't it?

"Brassy child," he muttered at the memory, rubbing his hands over his face, feeling the other still-healing scar, running against his cheekbone, scratch at his palm. His own fault for teaching her to tie knots, and to praise her for learning them so well. The fact that she had been right about his need to rest made it no less irritating to bear.

"Ho the campment!"

Gabriel was injured, but he could still move swiftly at need; by the time the speaker had come into sight, he'd gotten to his feet, his long knife loose in its sheath and the flintlock in clear sight and within arm's reach, if still unloaded.

The stranger was scrawny and trail-rough, his long coat stained, his hat a crushed, battered thing more crown than brim, and Gabriel would be damned if he could find a single weapon on the man, overt or hidden.

That did not mean he was unarmed, nor harmless—but he lacked the hair-prickling sense about him of a magician, either. Gabriel was thankful for small blessings. One magician in his experience had been one more than he'd ever wished for.

"Ho the Road," he called back in return, when the stranger paused a decent distance away, careful of the lines Gabriel had marked in the grass when he made camp. "What brings you to this turn?" They were on no true Road, merely a wide path leading from La Ramée to nowhere, and little cause for a rider to be passing through, much less one on foot. And he did not have the look of a man who had lost his cattle: his knees were straight, his shoulders curved, and his hands were shoved deep into the pockets of his coat rather than hanging loose and visible.

"I've nowhere else to be until my master whistles my call," the man said. "And so nowhere seemed a good place to be."

Not a magician, no, but that did not mean the man was not mad. Still, madness alone was no reason to refuse hospitality. "Enter and be welcome at our fire."

"The offer is as good as the action," he responded, ignoring the fact that the fire was barely large enough to heat the kettle over it, not much welcome at all. Keeping to tradition and ritual was safer than not, on the Road: ritual became such for a reason, and most of those reasons for a traveler's safe-keeping.

"I'm Gabriel," he said as the man stepped carefully over the soot-marked line. No cattle, no companions, just the man and his pack as battered as himself.

"Jack," the man said, and Gabriel's hand stuttered as he secured the knife in its sheath, remnants of a dream surfacing.

He stood in the middle of a creek, the water rushing over his ankles, blood-warm and filled with long, slender fish glinting silver and green in schools thick enough to look solid. He bent to scoop one out, holding it gently in cupped hands, and it looked back at him with eyes too human, set 'round with scales.

"The net comes for us all," the fish told him. "The only question is who eats you."

Not every dream was sent to tell him something; only a fool would think that, and fools died early and often in the Territory. But the morning's unease splashed over him anew nonetheless, and his thumb pushed the sheath's clasp out of the way for easier drawing, should it be necessary after all.

But he'd already invited the man in; there was no help for it but to brazen his way through.

"I've breakfast, if you're hungry."

The man shook his head. "Wouldn't say no to some coffee if you have it, though." His smile showed teeth yellowed but flat, and when he removed his hat, his gaze stayed steady on Gabriel, no flickering motion to indicate someone watching or traps—or waiting for someone coming in from the other side. But Gabriel had met men in his time who could smile and shake your hand without ever hinting at the knife aimed at your gut, and he fetched the other mug from his kit without turning his back on the newcomer, hospitality be damned.

The handful of silver half-coins weighted his pocket, but he wasn't so rude as to check them now, to see if they'd tarnished in the man's company, and the silver buckle at his boot shone the same as it had the night before. Odds were the man was just a Road loner, sheer coincidence his name triggered a memory of the night's dream.

Odds were.

Jack took the coffee, drained half the cup without care for its heat. Or, for that matter, its taste: it was yesterday's grinds, down to the dregs and gone bitter beyond any sweetener's fixing. If Isobel had been here, she would have made him toss it and start fresh. But she wasn't: four days, and a day late in returning.

The net comes for us all.

"You've his hand on you," Jack said, finishing the coffee and handing him back the empty tin cup.

"Beg pardon?" The stranger might be good at hiding his intent, but Gabriel had played cards at the devil's own table, not to mention with a handful of would-be Eastern politicians. His own face showed nothing he did not wish it to.

"Like calls to like," Jack said, and now his mouth twisted in either bitterness or humor. "I could smell it on you, like a whore's perfume."

Not a name, Jack. A title. No wonder the man had refused food and not cared for the taste of the coffee; a Jack tasted none of those things, not so long as he was under the devil's jurisdiction.

But a Jack was also no threat to him.

No threat, but possibly a warning.

"You come down the north trail," he said, turning to place the cup down and pour himself another dose. "Might you have encountered someone else along the way?"

The Jack did not linger long after that, and Gabriel did not make pretense at regret.

The effort of repacking their belongings onto the mule and throwing the saddle on the gelding left him sweaty, but his knees held and his ribs didn't hurt, so Gabriel decided he would be fine to ride.

And even if he wasn't, he would have anyway, after what little the Jack had told him.

Thankfully, Steady lived up to his name, standing patiently while he hauled back into the saddle.

"Just like falling off a log," Gabriel said to him. "But let's not rush into any gallops, all right?"

Only a fool or a cavalryman galloped at night, on unfamiliar terrain, and only a fool of a cavalryman would do so while injured. Only a fool would travel before they were ready, too, but Gabriel couldn't wait any longer.

If Isobel had found trouble, he needed to find *her*.

When he'd offered to mentor the sharp-eyed saloon girl if she'd the itch to see more of the Territory than the walls of her saloon or the borders of her small town, Gabriel hadn't known that that slip of a girl was destined to be the Devil's Hand. He hadn't known what that meant, what it would drag him into.

Truth, he regretted none of it, not the offer, nor the fact that when Isobel herself turned him down, the devil had said yes. But the irony was not lost on him: he'd made the offer for free, only to have the devil tell him to name his price. To have the devil owe you a debt was a powerful thing, but Gabriel intended to never collect on it. He couldn't *afford* to collect on it. To collect would be to accept, to accept would be to bind himself, and that was the thing he could not, would not do.

Not if he was to remain himself, avoid a fate too similar to the Jack's.

There was a deeper irony in the threads that bound him now, his dream less portent than common sense. If he concentrated, he could feel the slow trickle of water in the creek, low in the summer dryness but still enough for watering the animals, for him to wash and water without concern. As usual, it wanted to heal him, to slough off the scabs and seal the skin, and he couldn't any more than he could take the devil's payout. Couldn't let the water-sense in that deep, so close to his bones.

He'd learned the hard way that what the Territory claims, it keeps. But he would not let it own him. Isobel might yield under the forces reshaping her, yield to the devil's plans, whatever they were, but he could not. He *would* not.

And if the water's rush felt like a quiet chuckle in his ear, mocking his thoughts, Gabriel'd had years to learn how to ignore it.

He looked up at the sky: a few stretched clouds overhead, scraping around the distant peaks and fading into pale blue. The ground was soft under his boots, the grass rough-edged, and the air smelled green and dry.

Good riding weather.

The sun warm on his shoulders, he slanted his hat so the brim cast shade over his eyes, then pointed Steady north and west. The ground was a series of sloping and rising hills, the footing firm, and he rested the reins against the gelding's neck and sank deeper into the saddle, trusting the beast's common sense to keep them at a slow, easy walk. The mule kept alongside, longer ears twitching, occasionally moving faster and then looking back with an almost-human impatience.

"I know you like her more'n you do me," Gabriel told the mule. "No need to rub it in."

Steady snorted and ducked his head, likely pure coincidence, but Gabriel slapped the solid flesh once, lightly, in mock reproach. "Don't you sass me none neither. We rode for years without her or that mare; a few days apart won't break your hearts."

Now that they were moving again, the knot of tension that had gripped him eased somewhat. Isobel had common sense, a dependable sense of direction, and a solid mare who could outrun anything shy of a storm. And the skies were clear, so weather wasn't a worry. She knew how to handle a demon, and to speak polite to a native, and if she ran into a bear or a ghost cat . . . well, she had become a better shot since he'd gotten her the buccaneer's musket that fit her hands better, and this far into warmer weather, any predators would be well fed and lazy.

In all likelihood, she'd been delayed a bit dealing with the corpses, and they would cross paths soon enough.

And if not? If she had lost her way in the rising hills and narrow meadows, so unlike the wide-open plains she'd been raised on, despite having taught her how to find the Road underfoot?

Well, there was a reason he'd allowed her to ride off alone: he had a trick up his sleeve to find her.

It was difficult to relax entirely into the saddle with his ribs still sore, but he had enough trust in Steady's nature that his body eased a little more and his breathing slowed until only years of experience kept him upright in the saddle. It wasn't quite like sleeping, or even dozing, but his thoughts quieted and his eyes shut, letting other senses take over. First, feel. The sway of Steady underneath him, the feel of the reins through his fingers, leather worn smooth, and the press of his legs against the saddle, the weight of his bootheels in the stirrups.

Then sound. The syncopated clop of eight hooves on grass and dirt and occasional stone. The breath of wind against his skin, passing over the rise and fall of the folded hills. Birdsong, and the buzzing clatter of insects, and the distant *wow-ooo-wow* of a coyote pack greeting each other. Only coyote, no wolves, and his fingers eased away from the stock of his flintlock where it was strapped near his saddle. There wasn't much risk of a coyote being fool enough to attack a man on horseback, not in summer, when easier prey abounded. In winter, it would have been a different story. But in winter, he'd never have let her go out on her own.

He hushed his own thoughts, blanking them under the quiet sound of water. Smell came last: First, the ever-present, soothingly familiar smell of horse and leather and human sweat. Then the tang of sagebrush and green pine, and the faint tickle of maidenflower. And under that, once his entire self lay open and waiting, came the scent of water, from the quicksilver lightness of the creeks to the slower, stone-wet deepness below. The ability to dowse: his medicine, his curse, the thing tying him to the Territory, marking him as one of its own, finding water as easily as he could find the Road.

And then, going deeper still, finding the feel of *specific* water. The water warmed by familiar scent, the warmth of her body shaping it, the exhale of her breath scenting it.

Years and lives ago, he had spent time with a band of Hochunk, regaining his health, regaining his strength, when all he could do was listen to stories. There had been an old man once among them, one story claimed, who could find a single person lost in the Underworlds by the scent of their spit. Gabriel, who mocked no story, did not believe such a thing was possible. But this . . . this he thought he could do, after months of sharing canteens and coffee and the dampness of morning air with her. Enough to ensure he could find her like a freshwater spring in a dry plain.

"Hey, Iz," he said, pitching his voice as though to carry just a little ways away, as though she were still riding next to him. "Whatever trouble you've found, just hold tight. We're coming."

∾ ∾ ∾

Isobel was flummoxed. Everything she had been taught, all the things she had learned, told her that it was not possible for the land to be barren of power. Water flowed, wind breathed, people moved, and therefore power *was*.

Kneeling by the table without explanation, she placed her left palm down on the ground, sinking inside herself in that way she never could explain to Gabriel, opening herself to whatever the Territory wanted to tell her.

Silence.

It went beyond the cleansing she had felt: this little settlement had no connections to anything. There was no well-trod Road here, no familiar pull of the bone-deep ribbon that connected the Territory. Nothing.

Three times she tried skin to dirt, sending herself as deep as she dared, opening as far as she dared without Gabriel to watch over her, among strangers, however kind.

Nothing. Worse than silence: an emptiness where silence might be, a hollow unfilled, unfillable, driving her out and back into herself.

Fingers clenched, jaw tight enough to ache, Isobel was uncertain how much time had gone, save they all still waited, the men looking away, the women staring, near rude but so hesitantly hopeful, she could not take offense. Not for the first time, she wondered why the boss had sent her out so woefully unprepared—and how she was supposed to function once her time with Gabriel was done and he moved on.

"Something happened here," she said. "Tell me."

They all looked at Duck, who merely shook her head and lowered her gaze to her hands twined together in her lap. Isobel felt a snap of impatience: how was she to help if they would not tell her? Was this yet another test? Was she supposed to *know*?

The tension stretched, filling the air until it became hard to breathe,

Isobel's impatience becoming a thing she could feel, knocking at her bones. The older woman was their leader, they would not say anything if she would not. And Isobel could do nothing if they did not speak.

"Jumping-Up Duck. Please."

"The ground rumbled," the woman said finally, not looking up from her hands, rough-skinned knuckles clenched tight.

"A quake?" They were not common in Flood, but they happened, and the boss had said that the ground had once rocked hard enough, farther west, that those who lived there told stories of it a hundred years later, of ground crumbling and waters rising, and those who could not run, died.

"Jordskalv," Karl said. "As though waves underfoot, on a ship, in solid ground. Three times yesterday, one after another."

Isobel, trying to read him, thought his expression was less worry and more irritation at the world not behaving itself.

"The land shakes often to the west of here," Four Wolves said. "Where the ground steams and ancient spirits rest. If the dwellers-below are restless enough to stretch their hands this far . . . they are best left alone. It is nothing we need worry about. We have done nothing to offend."

There was utter certainty in his body: whatever was happening, he did not think it a threat, and he was tired of repeating himself.

Isobel remembered Ree, after the boss had told that story of the great quake, his fingers stroking the jagged ink that ran, blue against black, from wrist to elbow. "The deep bones ache," he'd said then. "They stretch and wake, then go back to sleep. Best to let them be."

"This is not the rumble of birthing," Jumping-Up Duck told Four Wolves, scowling. "It is a rumble of pain."

Four Wolves opened his mouth to argue with her, then closed his mouth and lowered his gaze, as though she had cowed him.

"Margot? Elizabet?"

The sisters glanced sideways at each other, then each shook their head.

"The earth shook," Elizabet said. "I was sleeping, the first time, but awake for the others. It was . . . disturbing. The children cried."

"They were the most upset," Margot added. "But they could not tell us why."

Isobel thought that the ground shaking needed no more reason than that to upset them, but simply nodded. "Three quakes, one after another. How long apart?"

"The first when the quarter-moon was bright," Catches in Teeth said. "The second soon after, and the third well after sunrise. We stayed in the lodge for the first. When we came out . . ." He looked distressed, his gaze flicking to the barn where Uvnee was stabled. "We had goats, not many, but enough to give milk, meat. They all fled. Only the dogs remained."

"The earth is in pain," Duck said, as though Catches in Teeth's words had opened something within her. "Pain that does not care the cause, only to find something within reach to hurt in turn." She was looking at the children as she spoke, five of them, comfortable in bare skin and clouts, their hair reddish black in the sunlight as they played with the dogs in the grass.

They should have been living with a tribe, or a village, or in a city back East, Isobel thought. Not here, isolated, alone, with parents who seemed as helpless as babes themselves. And yet there was something in her that envied them, born to nothing less than the plains and mountains, the four winds above and the bones below.

She had been born on a farmstead somewhere. Luck and her parents' foolishness brought her to Flood, to the devil's house, to become his Hand. But for that . . . what would she have become?

Isobel felt something stir at that thought, slow and deep. The sigil on her palm remained cool, but her fingers closed over it nonetheless, and her right hand crossed over to rub at the silver ring on her finger. Power, building somewhere, rising to that thought. This place might have been cleansed, but the Devil's Hand carried power within too.

Show me, she asked it, remembering the feel of the boss's hand on her shoulder, his voice in her ears, the comforting smell of his cologne and the unlit cigars he carried but never smoked. She closed her eyes to chase them, suddenly dizzy with the sensation of layer after layer like an onion under her hands, forever unpeeling until there was nothing left but tears.

Stone tears, white with heat, deep in the center of it all, and a molten whisper tracing burning scars along her skin, *under* her skin, searing her bones with words she could not understand. A story, and a warning, and something else beyond, below the silence, beyond the emptiness, seething like a pot overboiling, odorous as a blacksmith's forge.

This is not for you, it warned.

She clung to it nonetheless, searing the skin of her nonexistent hands, charring her bones into dust, ignoring the pain that rattled her like venom surging in her veins, until it snapped sharply and thrust her through the cooling mantle of dirt, back to the surface, into her own bones and skin.

Forcing her eyes open, Isobel focused on the people in front of her, their faces anxious and drawn, the dirt-streaked children stilled in the games, watching their adults watching her.

The boss had said the left hand was the quick knife, the cold eye. Gabriel had told her she was the devil's silver, cast down on the road to find danger, find it and clear it.

She only knew that if there was pain, if there was danger, she needed to find the cause and end it. But the source was not here.

The boss hadn't explained anything to her, hadn't taught her how to *do* anything. She didn't know what it was she did, only that she could do it. It wasn't enough.

It was all she had.

Isobel stood from the table, circling around the children, and came to a patch of ground where the grass had worn thin, the dirt a dry red crumble underneath. She could feel the others watching her still, although they turned their faces away now, unwilling to be rude. It made something between her shoulder blades itch, not the way that told her a demon was watching but something else, more immediate, and more disturbing. She ignored it.

If something was making the ground move, logic said it would be *in* the ground. Something that pushed her away. Ree and Molly had told stories of spirits who lived in the world below, but Isobel had only ever felt the bones, the deep-set stones the world rested upon.

Isobel looked at the sigil in her palm, thick and fine lines twisted in the doubled circle within a circle. Burnt into her mare's tack, drawn in her own skin. As Hand, she was nothing but an extension of the devil's will, and the Territory did not answer to him.

But she was also a rider, thanks to Gabriel's mentorship, and the Road that looped through the Territory could not hide from a rider once they learned to find it.

She reached, feeling the familiar rush, unlike a crossroads in that its power flowed rather than being trapped, diminishing and refilling rather than building until it burst. Southward, where she'd been, felt the strongest; the hills rising grey-brown to the east were fainter, but she could feel them, something pulsing at their heart, neither welcoming nor forbidding, simply *there*, healthy and full.

West lay the northern edge of the Mother's Knife, the farthest edge of the Territory. Northwest, Gabriel had told her, were hills and forests bordering the Wilds, trees as old as the devil, deep springs hotter than the mid-day sun.

She felt nothing to the northwest.

Isobel tilted her head, listening harder. *I'm here*, she thought, sending the thought as widely as she could, stretching herself out rather than deep, thought-fingers stroking the skin of the earth the way she would Uvnee's hide, testing for uncertainty, sending reassurance and control. . . .

Silence. No, not silence. Denial. A refusal.

this is not for you.

Isobel withdrew, found herself within her own body again, testing the limits of flesh. Her throat was sore, her back aching, and her lips were cracked and dry as though she'd been riding all day without water.

The Road had *refused* her. Isobel rubbed at her arms, feeling a chill that had nothing to do with the fact that she'd taken off her jacket, or the clouds that slipped across the mid-morning sky. She didn't understand, didn't understand anything.

She needed to talk to Gabriel.

"Drink." Margot held a wooden cup to her lips, and Isobel drank, unquestioning. Honey-water, sweet and cold.

"Slowly. A sip at a time."

Isobel knew that, her hands coming up to wrap around the cup, the sides smooth against her skin, almost too smooth to hold.

"You're shaking."

"I'm all right."

Margot's blue eyes studied her, and Isobel thought that this woman would have done well in the Saloon, would have gained the boss's approval.

"You need to rest. Come," and she tried to lead Isobel to the nearest cabin, but Isobel pulled back. "I'd rather be outside."

Margot sent one of the older children to fetch Isobel's pack, helped her make camp on a flat patch of ground distant enough that she could breathe, but still within the wards, then let her be. The others had disappeared, back inside or elsewhere. Margot was kind, they had all been kind, but they did not trust her entirely.

"Not everyone welcomes the reminder that they live at the devil's sufferance," Gabriel had said once. He had been speaking of the folk who settled in Patch Junction, but she supposed some tribes resented him too. The agreement their elders had made however many generations ago bound them as tightly as it did new-come settlers. And those caught between, like these children, given the comfort of neither tribe nor town yet bound by both.

If this place was not safe for them, where would they go?

Isobel took a deep breath, then exhaled, her hands moving in a familiar pattern as she groomed Uvnee's hide. The mare's coat was dry and clean of mud and road dust, but Isobel kept running the flat brush over her flanks, letting her other hand trail across the warm horseflesh in reassurance—although to reassure whom, she wasn't quite sure—until the long, coarse brown strands of the mare's tail were untangled and smooth. Isobel briefly considered braiding them like her own hair before admitting defeat. Hoof to ears, the mare was spotless.

"What now, Uvnee?" she asked the mare, who merely flicked one reddish-brown ear at her and shifted her weight to lean against Isobel, gentle lips and teeth nipping at the flat of her braid.

For now, she would wait. The boss met those who'd ask him a thing across the card table, took their measure with the way they played. So would she. For what, Isobel wasn't certain—another quake, she supposed; if the quiet told her nothing, then perhaps an outburst would tell her something.

Or the whispering voice might return and send her on. That thought made her palm twitch: she would happily spend her life without that sensation again. But she had given over control of her life when she made Contract with the devil, even if she hadn't understood then what it would mean.

Never bargain more than you can afford to give. All she'd had was herself to offer.

And if she did ride on . . . Gabriel had no notion of where she'd gone, what had happened to her. Gabriel also had their supplies, their extra water, the ammunition—everything. All she had were her horse and weapons, trail rations, and an extra set of unmentionables packed in her kit.

And the packet that had been addressed to him and left in the way-station. Isobel allowed herself to admit that more than curiosity weighted the desire to open the letter; she was envious of the letter itself, the connection to someone who thought of him while he was not there.

Not that she expected Marie to write to her, or any of the others at the saloon, since she had not written to any of them. She wasn't April, to compose long letters for reading out loud to everyone, after chores were done. What could she say to them; what was she *allowed* to say?

The Left Hand was the silent knife, not the garrulous one.

In the midst of what Isobel admitted was a bout of unadmirable self-pity, Uvnee suddenly snorted and bucked in alarm, nearly knocking Isobel off her feet.

"What now?" Isobel rested a hand on the mare's neck to calm her, even as her own heart raced, glanced about for what spooked the mare. There were no trees close enough to hide a threat, nothing overhead in the sky save clouds, and the wind smelled of nothing except sage and— her thoughts broke off abruptly as the ground underneath them . . .

Flexed was the only word she could think of. It flexed like a snake slithering sideways through the grass, a fish flipping through water, as though the very bones of the earth had gone soft like a pudding.

And then it stopped, leaving her feeling as though *she* were the one wobbling, not the ground below.

Her breath caught, the skin on her arms prickling in unease.

"That . . . was unpleasant," she said to Uvnee, who rolled her eyes backward, the whites showing, and flicked her ears, this time as though to agree, but she hadn't bolted. "Good girl." Isobel leaned against the mare's trembling flank, an arm over the crested neck as much for her own support as the mare's, and tried to calm her breathing. If that had been what the others had felt when they described the ground moving below them, she could not blame them in the slightest for being upset.

Isobel had lived through storms before; she knew that wind and water were unpredictable. But stone and dirt were meant to be *solid*, dependable. They did not refuse to answer; they did not suddenly *move*.

Then Uvnee snorted again, half-turning toward the road as though in anticipation. Isobel braced for another quake before realizing that the sound the mare was responding to was hoofbeats.

Jumping-Up Duck's people did not have horses, and the sound was too deep for it to be their goats returning. Panic turned to planning, and she turned, trying to gauge the distance between herself and her pack on the ground, the musket and knife still out of reach.

Then the sound came closer, and she recognized the shape of horse and rider, and the long-eared mule following close behind.

Isobel had been trained to stand back, to judge, to observe, but the moment Gabriel dismounted, she rushed at him, flinging her arms around his waist, knocking her jaw against his shoulder. There was a hesitation, his body jerking back, then his arms came over her shoulders and she was surrounded by the smell and feel of *familiar*.

He didn't say anything, just let her rest her face against the rough fabric of his coat. She was sure the others had broken off from whatever they were doing, were watching, but she couldn't bring herself to care. A warm, whiskered muzzle shoved against her leg, and she shifted one hand to dig into the mule's rough coat, feeling its side shuddering as though they'd been running for too long.

"You were late," Gabriel scolded her, finally, his voice dry as dust.

She wiggled free, indignant, then rubbed at her face, letting out a faint laugh. "You found me."

"I found you," he agreed. The skin around the scar on his face was stubbled, as though he'd had trouble shaving around it, and his dark blue eyes looked more tired than they had before, when she'd left him to rest. Guilt spiked through her, unfamiliar and unwelcome.

He pulled back a little, looking over her shoulder at something, then back at her carefully. "Something's wrong."

"I . . . No." Yes. But she couldn't explain it, couldn't add to that exhaustion with things he couldn't fix. Instead, she gripped him by the sleeve of his jacket, pulling him forward.

"Jumping-Up Duck. This is my mentor, Gabriel Kasun, known as Two Voices."

The older woman gave Gabriel a thorough once-over, then lifted her gaze to meet his own. He took his hat off and stood quietly, his hands clasped behind his back, shoulders at ease. Isobel had become so accustomed to him wearing that battered, flat-crowned hat from morning to night, it was a shock to see the sunlight catch on his hair, picking up glints of gold in the dark brown, the edges of it curling over his collar. The claw mark was more visible from the side, where the scar tissue lifted from the tanned skin of his cheek, and she found herself staring at it, then had to shake herself to look away.

"You are welcome" was all the older woman said, then turned away without introducing the others, who had hung back a few paces. Isobel was surprised, but Gabriel didn't seem offended, instead turning to her, hat still in his hand.

"Let me get the animals settled, and then you can tell me what's going on, hmmm?"

The gelding and mule were quickly unpacked and picketed to graze with Uvnee, who seemed to have forgotten entirely about the ground moving beneath her hooves. Steady, once he was assured of a picket next to the mare, settled down as well, but the mule remained uneasy, pushing its muzzle back into Isobel's hand before finally lowering it to graze.

"How did you find me?"

Gabriel hesitated, then dusted the brim of his hat against his thigh. "I had a visitor to camp," he said. "Lean, dusty fellow."

Isobel raised her gaze to the sky, seeing only pale blue overhead. "The Jack."

"He may have mentioned where he saw you last and under what conditions."

"And you raced out to rescue me?"

"I broke camp to come support you, as is my right and my obligation. So tell me, Isobel Devil's Hand, what brings us to these forsaken, shaken hills, and what mischief have you found?

Isobel opened her mouth, then shook her head and fetched a low wooden stool from her campment and settled on it, cautiously, half-expecting it to roll out from under her without warning.

Gabriel paced back and forth slowly as she spoke, beginning with the discovery of the buffalo corpses.

Gabriel held a hand to pause her. "Arrows or bullets?"

"Bullets." She hadn't thought of it then. "Settlers?"

"Mayhap, may not. Natives've been trading for guns since they first caught sight of 'em, same as horses. Stealing 'em, too. And there're fools on all sides. Did you clean the site?"

"Best I could, yes. But I made a promise to them."

"To the . . . Iz." He let the rebuke die unspoken. "Did that promise say you were going to do something right away?"

". . . No."

"The dead have time to be patient. Tell me the rest."

She did, through to the quake they'd felt just as he'd ridden up. He listened without further interruption, although his eyebrows lifted when she told him of the whisper that had woken her, and then again when she spoke of the sensation of being rejected when she tried to reach the Road.

"It's odd," he said when she finally ran out of things to say, lapsing into an exhausted silence. "After the past few months, I'd have sworn I'd never utter those words again, but that is . . . indisputably odd. Then again, the hotlands have a reputation that reaches all the way to the Mudwater."

"The whatlands?" Isobel was certain she'd never heard that name before.

"I told you that past here, the land's riddled with hot springs?"

She frowned, then nodded, remembering.

"They're not like the springs we saw down south, where you can dip a toe in, maybe even bathe. These are nasty things: you don't always know they're there, until suddenly the skin's boiled off your bones." He shoved his hand through his hair, pushing it away from his face, and grinned briefly, without humor. "Or so stories say. I never had cause to ride up there. I don't know the peoples up there, and the tribes've no need of me."

His services as an advocate, he meant. Gabriel had trained for the law back East, had been riding circuit when they met, doing small services for people as needed 'em, although she'd never quite understood *what* those things were. Here, if there was an argument that couldn't be settled, the marshals got involved, and if someone got hurt, or you needed to formalize a thing, then you went before a judge, like she did with her contract. Not so much need for an advocate, but Gabriel didn't seem to lack for folk to visit everywhere they'd gone.

"You think it's connected? The quakes, and the . . . the quietness, up that way?"

"Don't know." He sat down opposite her, wincing a little as he leaned against his pack, stretching his legs out in front of him. "Might be nothing, might be you just being tired, might be something. But if we're going up thataway, which it seems we are, we'll find out ourselves, won't we?"

She narrowed her eyes at him, the memory of the ground shaking still too near for joking. "You needn't look so pleased about it," she muttered. "The ground *moved*." The ground moved and the Road was silent, and something had scraped the power from this valley, and who knows how far beyond. And he was looking *pleased*.

"There's a story," Gabriel said, pulling his legs up so he could rest his arms on his knees, what she'd come to think of as his storytelling pose. "There's a story that comes from before we were here, before the devil claimed dominion from the Mudwater to the Knife, back when there was only the one People, with skins the color of clay and eyes like an autumn storm."

She snorted at that, and he glared at her until she cast her eyes down in apology so he'd go on.

"Back then, the story says, the land was flat, just rolling plains, and you could see from one end to another. But then one day, a child found a hollow log and started to hit it with a stick, and the sound was so pleasing to the spirits that they began to dance. And as they danced the land shook, and as the land shook, it rose, until hills formed, and then mountains. And that's why the land isn't flat anymore."

Isobel wrinkled her nose. "That's just a story."

He shrugged. "It's an old story, and old stories have truth in 'em somewhere, most of them. This might be nothing to worry about, just the spirits dancing, or the earth shrugging 'cause we're itching its back. But you were driven here by something, and you're worried about what you're reading, then yah, maybe it's something new or worrisome. So, we poke our noses in and see what bites us."

She gave his ribs a pointed look. "You haven't gotten tired of being bitten yet?"

"You volunteer this time, then," he said, cheerful enough to make her want to bite *him*.

"Don't know who we'll encounter up there," Gabriel went on, thoughtfully. "Your friends probably splintered off a Shoshone or Cheyenne tribe east of here, maybe some of their kin went farther up mountain, but if so, I don't speak much of their tongue. Never had need to learn it." He sounded regretful but resigned. "Don't suppose you could talk one of these folks into coming with us, as guide?"

Isobel shook her head, finding a thread that was beginning to pull loose on her skirt and trying to poke it back into the weave. The clothes that had been newly stiff when she'd first packed them back at the saloon were soft and faded now; sun and dirt and washing with a poor excuse for soap had left their mark. She should have bought a new skirt and underthings at the mercantile, back at La Ramée, but she'd been distracted by the ill post-rider and Gabriel's injury.

"They don't want to leave. This is their home, and I don't think they've anywhere else to go."

"They'll defend this past dying," Gabriel said. "Foolish, but understandable, I suppose."

Driven by that thought, Isobel reached out once more, bending from the stool to place her palm flat on the ground, trying to sense again what lay just beyond the small valley they were in.

Nothing. She could feel where she *was*, and where they had *been*, but the way north was still empty, like an unfinished map fading into blank parchment.

No, not blank, she thought. Scraped clean.

The feeling shuddered through her, made her want to ride for Flood without stopping, spill everything she knew, everything she had seen, everything she feared, and ask the boss to deal with it. He was the Master of the Territory; she was only his Hand, and a poor one at that. The boss might—

"Stop that."

She looked up at Gabriel, blinking. "What?"

His eyes were narrowed to slits, his face set in too-stern lines. "You were thinking that you had no idea what to do, bordering on panic, mayhap. That this was beyond your handling. That from the girl who locked horns with a *magician*, who took on Spaniards, who faced down a spell-born creature, and made them all behave?"

Gabriel was an excellent card player when he chose to be, and his body gave off little he did not want known. But at that moment, he practically shouted derision and disbelief, and Isobel felt her mouth twist into a reluctant smile.

"Not alone, I didn't," she said.

"And you're not alone now. If you're done being foolish?" he asked, and she huffed at him but nodded. "We'll need to barter in the morning, if your new friends have provisions available. If there are more quakes, odds are game will be harder to find."

She made a face. "They had goats, but they all ran off. Dried meat again?"

"I thought you liked it." He was teasing her now, trying to change the mood, and she let him.

"Not for every meal. My jaws ache"—and she opened and shut them to make the point. "We'll be able to forage, though? It's not as though plants can turn tail and run."

"All the bitterroot and lamb's-quarter you can eat," he promised, knowing full well how much she hated lamb's-quarter. "And this time of year, odds are we'll find berries, too. But better to be prepared." He glanced up across the clearing, studying the tiny garden visible from where they were with a dubious expression, as though not expecting them to have much to share.

"Lamb's-quarter and soaked beans," she said, trying to work up some enthusiasm. "Maybe trout?" Fish were limited in how far they could flee, after all. Although her previous attempts at catching trout had been less than successful, so maybe she'd make sure they packed—

"Oh." In the shock of everything, she had nearly forgotten. "There was a packet for you."

"What?"

She took an obscure pleasure in having surprised him. "At the way-station," she said, reaching over to pull at her pack, dragging it within reach so she could dig the envelope out and hand it to him. "For you."

Gabriel had taken the letter from Isobel, his fingers near numb with unhappy surprise, but there'd been no time to open it before several of the children ran up to them, wanting to see the horses, and he'd shoved it into his bag before putting the two youngest on the mule's back and leading him around in a small circle, while Isobel showed the others how to offer Steady a handful of grass in their open palm until he lowered his head and let them pet him to their heart's content. And then one of the women came to chase the children away, inviting them to join them for the afternoon meal.

Isobel's brief telling of their story, as much as she knew of it, had made him curious as to where they came from or why they'd settled here, without kin or tribe, but he pushed his curiosity as far as possible without giving offense, and they merely smiled at him, closed-mouthed, and took another bite of bread, or a drink of water, then turned to someone else and spoke in another language, closing him out until he relented. Isobel was likely correct: wherever they had been was no longer an option for them. This was all they had left, and they would not let go of it, not even to admit that something was wrong.

Foolishness, he thought, but it wasn't his call to make.

Gabriel had not exaggerated when he told Isobel he knew nothing of this region; the Territory was massive, and even he could not expect to ride all of it. But listening to them speak a dialect he did not recognize beyond a few shared trade-words was a reminder to pick up Isobel's language lessons again. English was the preferred trade language, particularly to the east and north, but she couldn't always count on that. This might not be the only time the Left Hand rode beyond the pale.

Their hosts were more forthcoming after the meal, however. He negotiated for supplies with the one called Four Wolves, who quickly separated him from a handful of half-coins left from what the devil had given him. Four Wolves drove a tight bargain, fully aware that they had no other options, but they both walked away reasonably satisfied.

With all that, it wasn't until he was curled into his bedroll, the last flickers of a wood fire warming his backside and Isobel asleep nearby, the horses and mule sleeping with their heads lowered together, that he had time to think about the letter Isobel had given him. Or, Gabriel owned, that he couldn't avoid thinking about it any longer. There were few people who would write to him, and even fewer who would be able to direct a letter so that it would reach him.

Part of him wanted to toss it onto the fire until it was nothing but crumbled ash.

Instead, he slowly reached for his pack, catching the envelope between two fingers and pulling it out. The moon wasn't quite bright enough to read by, so he pulled the coalstone out as well, pressing it down until it began to glow. Without tinder, it wouldn't spark a flame but gave off enough light that Gabriel's eyes were able to make out the lettering on the paper.

Gabriel Kasun, Esquire.

The weight of the honorific pushed at him, reminding him of the obligations he still carried, that had nothing to do with the girl—the young woman—sleeping on the other side of the fire. The obligations that made him slit open the envelope and pull the enclosed letter out to read rather than set it aflame.

> *Gabe,*
> *I hesitated sharing this with you, for it seems unlikely*
> *that you are in a position to do anything beyond fret*
> *over it, and I would not add more to the burden you*
> *already bear. And yet, the news offends every instinct*
> *I have, all sense of proper behavior. I cannot keep it to*
> *myself, else I might say something rash in circles where*
> *silence best serves.*

Abner Westbrook. Stolid, to outward appearances as plodding as a plow horse, but hiding a mind sharp as a fresh-stropped razor. One of the few true friends Gabriel had made when he went east, and the only one he could say that he had kept.

He was also a junior member of the federal judiciary, with family in much higher positions. If there was a rumor with even a single root in truth, Abner knew of it.

> *Word comes through reliable voices that our new*
> *president has determined the need to send a surveying*
> *team across the Mississippi and into the Territory you*
> *call home. He names it a 'Corps of Discovery' and*
> *claims it a simple excursion to survey this new land*
> *beyond our known borders. Congress seems set to give*
> *him as he requests, for they have dreams of expanding*
> *our limits, be it for land or metals or simply the need to*
> *plant their names into history.*
> *I know that scouts have come and gone into your*
> *Territory without complaint; Congress thinks this a*

*blanket to cover all sins. I am not so sanguine. And I fear
that Jefferson, in his hubris, plans more than he admits.*

The letter went on a few paragraphs longer, ending with a hope that
the missive found Gabriel well, etc., but he barely skimmed the rest,
down to the familiar blotch of ink that Abner claimed was a signature.

Gabriel's gut tightened, a familiar reaction to unpleasant news. It
might simply be curiosity driving Jefferson—the man was well known
to have a voracious interest in nearly everything. But the man was
president now, and that made him—Gabriel hesitated to say "dangerous," but certainly a man with far more power than before. And
power made men dangerous, no matter their intent.

But what was that power to *him*? And what did Abner think he,
Gabriel, could do about it? He was not the man he'd meant to be,
back East. That man had died somewhere mid-crossing, pulled under
and drowned.

Across the fire, Isobel rolled over, muttering in her sleep, and Gabriel
slowly folded the letter and replaced it in the envelope, then quenched
the coalstone with a touch.

Abner worried too early. It was still a matter for Congress to decide,
and while Gabriel had only spent a few years on that side of the River,
any man with sense knew that approving expenditures on such a scale
would not happen overnight. Anything could happen in that time.
America's attention might be directed back across the ocean, away
from the west. Congress might decide to withhold approval, use it to
control the president, make him dance to their tune. And even if none
of that happened, if Jefferson did push the borders, the devil still stood
between outside powers and the Territory.

And anyone, within or without the Territory, who dismissed the
devil as a threat was a fool who deserved what was handed to them.

And yet, even with that decided, Gabriel was unable to fall asleep,
watching the moon fade, until birdsong roused Isobel, and he could
pretend to wake.

PART TWO
STRANGE HILLS

Gabriel woke just after dawn, groggy and disorientated, with a rock digging into his shoulder. He reached under the bedroll and dug it out, tossing it aside with a grimace. Waking in a new place was not enough to confuse him, not after so long on the Road, and he felt no alarm, but—

It was too quiet, he realized, dragging himself into a sitting position, pushing the blanket down even as he reached for his boots. The faint clatter of metal and wood coming from the buildings, and the familiar sounds of the animals grazing nearby, the soft swish of tails and grumbles of flatulence, but there was no birdsong overhead telling him what the weather would be today.

Did quakes frighten birds the way they did other animals? Gabriel had no idea.

Isobel's blankets had already been rolled up, and her pack was missing; he assumed she was taking advantage of the creek to wash up. The thought was tempting, but he'd already slept too late. He sniffed at his wrist and amended that thought. Maybe there would be time for a quick dip, once Isobel was done.

Isobel came back into the clearing just then, dressed for riding, her face shining with pleasure and the results of cold water as she toweled the ends of her hair dry. "Either go bathe or I'm going to throw you in," she told him.

"You smell better." Duck's husband had wandered down to watch them loading the supplies, leading his observation with an ostentatious sniff of the air around Gabriel. Since it was nothing less than the truth, he signed "thank you" combined with a semi-rude gesture and continued loading the mule. The bark of laughter in response was followed by a thick-fingered clap on Gabriel's shoulder that would likely leave bruises.

To his surprise, and Isobel's pleasure, the "meager supplies" they'd acquired included not only smoke-dried meats, both deer and rabbit, but chuno—wedges of dried potato—and a packet of coarse yellow meal. Those were Nahua foods, not the sort to be found so far north, but Gabriel had seen stranger things pass through trading routes, and he wasn't about to question any additions to their menu.

But the older man hadn't come down here to comment only on his bath or the supplies. He lingered, resting a hand on the mule's neck more gently than he'd clapped Gabriel, clearly gathering his thoughts.

Gabriel finished loading the new supplies, checking over his shoulder to see that Isobel was occupied sweeping their campsite clear and dousing the remains of the fire. The other man's gaze followed his, then returned to study Gabriel's face.

"If you die there." The plural you, Gabriel noted, meaning both of them.

"We may," Gabriel admitted when the other man didn't seem inclined to go on, his harshly scarred voice obviously painful to use. Gabriel's hands kept moving, checking the straps on the mule's packs, adjusting the belly strap and making sure the halter wasn't twisted, pausing to scrape part of Flatfoot's coarse forelock out from under the strap, and scratching the base of one floppy ear.

"Will he blame us if she falls?"

"He" needed no clarification.

"If you had no part in it, no blame will fall on you." There were many things one could say about the devil, some good, more bad, but he was methodical in discovery and more just in his judgments than most Gabriel had met.

The man didn't look convinced. Gabriel could understand that: his family was alone here, for whatever reason, and seemingly had nowhere to fall back to, neither one side nor the other. The Master of the Territory's wrath would seem terrifying under those conditions.

He thought of the Jack, doomed to wander at the devil's tug, running errands the likes of which Gabriel could not imagine, even now.

"There is no safety on or off the Road," Gabriel said. "Every rider knows that." That was why they went armed with silver, salt, and bullets. "But we will do our utmost not to die."

"She will ease the earth?"

"If she can." He was not in a position to make promises for Isobel, and he would not allow her to make promises she could not be certain of. The quakes might be natural events, or the work of earth-spirits, or some other phenomena unrelated. "The devil isn't our niñera, to wipe our noses every time we sneeze."

The man's eyes narrowed at that, but Gabriel's words seemed to have eased his mind, and he turned to go without a farewell.

Gabriel watched him walk away, wondering if he'd said enough or too much.

"What was that about?" Isobel asked, approaching him as he finished with the mule. Her hair, dry now, was braided again, wisps of it already escaping to frame her face, her battered, brimmed hat hanging from a leather thong. The clear, dark eyes that looked back at him from that sun-browned face were not the eyes of the girl he had met only months before in a crowded, noisy saloon.

He studied her now, deciding how much of the conversation to share. "He was telling us not to die."

"Oh." She thought about that, her expression serious, one hand reaching out to tug one of the mule's ears in rough affection. "Good advice."

Despite himself, despite the situation, despite the pain still digging at his ribs, and the scar on his face that would likely never heal, despite days of riding ahead of them to face the devil-knew-what, despite the niggling worry Abner's letter had lodged in his brain, and the worries he carried with him day to day, there wasn't a place he'd rather be just then than to ride into trouble—*again*—at her side.

She gave him an odd look when he laughed. The devil might not take him for a fool, but he was assuredly a madman.

He slapped the mule once on the neck, letting it know it was done with humans fussing over it, and turned to Steady waiting patiently. He pulled the stirrups down and swung up into the saddle, reins comfortably settled in one hand. The gelding shifted under him, then rocked forward, ready to be gone again.

"Where's our direction, Isobel Left Hand?"

He was her guide, her mentor, but he no longer led. His job was to make sure that she learned what she needed and didn't die while she puzzled it out. So, he waited.

"West and north," she said finally, her brows drawn together, lines of tension visible around her mouth. "I can't . . . but there's something there, like . . . like a rock or root under my bedroll."

The fact that there was no clear threat should have reassured them: no emptied-out towns or monstrous creatures of foreign magic. And yet, somehow, this was worse. They were riding blind and deaf, into trouble even the Master of the Territory might not contain or control.

He had to say it. "We don't have to do this. It's not your burden to carry."

Isobel looked down at the ground, her face hidden for a moment, then swung into Uvnee's saddle with ease, tucking the fabric of her skirt between her leg and the mare's side to keep the fabric from flapping when she rode.

"Yes, it is," she said. "Because they can't, and I'm here."

And there was the Isobel the devil'd chosen.

He *tk-tk*'d at the mule to get its attention, and the three of them followed Isobel and Uvnee away from the small meadow, and up into the silent hills.

Isobel felt the lack of the Road deeply; there was a trail of sorts to follow, if she could describe the faint pattern of trampled grasses as a trail, but only if she looked hard and hoped, and there was no welcoming hum when she reached down, to reassure her. But that feeling of *wrongness* remained, and for lack of any other guidance, she followed it, Gabriel, Steady, and the mule at her back.

After a while, she noticed something. "The grass is different here."

Gabriel fell back into teacher voice without hesitation, pulling along-side her to point particular plants out. "Sagebrush, you know. Those yellow flower clumps are wild buckwheat." They rode along a bit, then he admitted, "I've no idea what the blue ones are, though. And oh, bitterroot!"

She scrunched her face up at the reminder. "But no lamb's-quarter."

He laughed and quizzed her on the trees they were passing, fewer and fewer as the gentle slope turned into a steeper climb. At every turn, Isobel expected to spot curl-horn sheep or wild goats, but the scat they passed was several days old and dried. It might be that Four Wolves and his kin had hunted this area out, or another predator had claimed it.

Or, like their goats, all the wild things had fled.

That thought made her uneasy, layering on top of the *wrongness* they'd been chasing. And not only her: when she looked back, Gabriel was checking his flintlock, the tie-down of his knife sheath visibly loosened. She did the same with her own, then asked, "Should I load?"

"Only if you're willing to hold it ready until such a time as you need to fire."

"But what if I can't load in time, if something attacks?"

He kept his face perfectly straight. "Then club it over the head with the stock until I can shoot it."

She sniffed, then turned back to stare at the ground ahead, the silence broken only by the scuffle of hooves, the trail rising farther into the hills.

Despite her unease, Isobel couldn't stop marveling at their surroundings. She had been raised with the sweeping flat sameness of grass and sky broken by the occasional tree and the distant smudge of hills. Even when they'd ridden up into the hills to De Plata and along the lower ridges of the Knife to Graciendo's cabin, she'd been so taken by the trees around her, so many and so tall, she'd not been able to imagine the idea of *mountains*.

Here, it was impossible to ignore. Bare, reddish-brown rock surrounded them, jagged patches of top-heavy green spires growing at angles, bent before the wind, and beyond that were blue-shadowed peaks taller still, their tips blunted as though they'd run into the sky and been pushed back down again.

Anything could lurk at such heights, anything could hide there, sweeping down on them like a Reaper hawk grown into a monstrosity.

"Impossible," she said out loud, willing her heart to slow its sudden patter. If there was anything larger than a Reaper, even here, rumor would have made it to the boss, hunters would try to trap it, some warning would have come down. "Stop cooking trouble you can't eat, Isobel. It's not as though your plate's not already full."

Uvnee snorted as though in agreement, and the mule, who had wandered off the trail to mouth at an unfamiliar clump of yellow-green leaves, flicked its ears at them as though to tell them both they were being foolish.

Gabriel had told her once to watch the horses if she thought there was trouble; that they would know before any person. All three were relaxed, almost playful, their ears easy and their tails swishing lazily against the occasional insect. "Listen to them," she told herself. "There's no threat here."

She remained uneasy, and Gabriel's knife remained loose in its sheath.

They splashed through a little creek running downhill and reached a point where no grasses grew, only the occasional stubborn sagebrush clinging to rocky soil. As Gabriel had predicted, they saw no game, although birds sang from invisible cover, and as they reached the top of the slope, she thought she saw the brown shadow of deer in the distance, but when she tried to find them again, they were gone.

"Better to look for bears," Gabriel said when she mentioned the deer. "They're mostly going to be down by the river"—and she didn't ask how he knew there was a river; that was a thing he would know better than she—"but if we're careless and get between mama and a cub, it could go badly."

"I've never seen a bear." She'd seen the claws of the great brown bears strung around a marshal's neck. She'd also seen the scars the man carried, scoring down his arm, too close to the marks on Gabriel's ribs for comfort. She thought maybe she could be happy without seeing a bear that close ever. Especially one that was upset with her.

They paused briefly mid-day, letting noon pass them by, then rode on slowly, allowing the horses to pick their way up the slope, the sun warm on their skin and the air thin in their lungs, filled with the scent of pine and sage. Although they saw no birds or animals, tiny butter-flies flitted around them, blue and red and orange, and when they came around a curve that looked out over a vast meadow, Gabriel pointed out a dusty wallow where buffalo had been, making Isobel feel a twinge again for the slaughtered animals she'd found and had to abandon, her promise yet unkept.

It seemed such a small thing now, and yet she had made a promise.

Isobel shifted her reins, curling her fingers into her left palm, finger-tips pressing against the sigil as though to force an answer into the air.

"Boss?" she asked quietly, although it had never done her service before. She could almost imagine that she felt his hand on her shoulder, the warm, smoky scent of his whiskey and tobacco, but she knew it was only imagination. The boss was weeks away. He had sent her here to be his eyes and his Hand, not for him to hold her hand.

She was on her own.

"Damn it, Flatfoot, get your nose off my knee; I'm not your momma."

Isobel grinned, glancing slantways to see the mule backing away from Gabriel, looking offended at having his muzzle slapped. No, not on her own. And not unprepared, not anymore.

Isobel closed her eyes and stretched her awareness out again, letting herself slide down her spine, through her legs, dropping in a way she could never quite explain out the soles of her boots and down into the ground.

She was the devil's Hand. She could not be cut off from the Territory, not so long as the Agreement held.

Show me, she asked it. *Show me what is wrong.*

The bones were there, deep and still. But where she expected the now-familiar dizzying hum of connection, the feel of power rising up to meet her, there was only a flickering awareness, something hot and heavy slipping away when she tried to touch it, shying away as though it were avoiding her.

But when she tried to grab at it, that sense of unease pushed back, powerful enough to shove her, hard enough that Uvnee hesitated, flicking an ear back to ask her rider what was wrong.

Isobel steadied herself in the saddle, weaving her fingers into the mare's rough-textured mane for reassurance, and called out to get Gabriel's attention.

"Iz?" He looked worried, reaching out to touch her shoulder. "What's wrong?"

She shook her head, settled the reins better in her hand, refusing to look at the black lines on her palm, for fear. . . . She wasn't sure for fear of what, but the unease had grown in her, real and heavy. "When I . . . when I go deep, past the bones, to see the things I see . . . what am I touching?"

Power, yes. But she'd felt power before, in the hum of the Road, the workings of wards, the swirling risk of crossroads, even the sensation of being greeted by spirit-animals, of standing in the presence of magicians and demon. Standing before the boss, their blood drying together on a Contract. This had been different.

Gabriel hesitated before answering, but she thought it was the hesitation of someone thinking about their answer, not because he was avoiding it. "Truth, Iz, I don't know. What you do, the way you can look, what you can see . . . that's the devil's own skill, not something I'm given to understand."

People had small skills, small medicine. To ease pain or find water, like Gabriel, find the Road, cajole beasts, read dreams, or make things grow. A greater medicine was to walk the winds the way magicians did, and it came with a greater price.

The Hand bore the mark of the Master of the Territory, carried his medicine. And he had sent her out not understanding what that *meant*.

She trusted the boss with her life, but for the first time ever, she wanted to shake him, too.

"It won't let me in," she said. "How'm I to be useful if I can't reach it?"

"It's not only you, Isobel. I can feel the water here. I know there's a river down a ways to our left, that there's a stream running underfoot . . . only, it's like listening to the rain through a roof, or voices through a wall. Faint, muffled. And I can't feel the Road at all. Not even behind us, where I know it runs."

"That makes you nervous." She rubbed a hand against the back of her neck, squeezing tense muscles to force them to ease.

"That, plus what you're telling me, makes me tremble in my boots," he said without any hint of shame, pulling his canteen out and taking a long drink. "There should be something, Isobel. There's no portion of the Territory that hasn't been walked by someone. Some hunter's trail or journey-path, a cut between two villages, or trapper's route. My reach isn't as far as yours, but I've experience to offset that. There's always *something*. And here, it's . . . gone."

He replaced the canteen on his saddle and pulled his hat down farther over his forehead, which she'd learned meant he didn't want to talk any longer.

She studied his profile, then turned her attention back to the mountains above them, trying to listen, trying to hear something deeper than her own breath, or hoofbeats against grass and stone.

The lack frustrated her, made her feel a failure, failing the boss, failing her Contract.

Shhhhhhhh.

Slowly, the frustration was replaced by the memory of having a fever as a child, wrapped in heat, cooling cloths over her skin, the murmur of soothing voices rolling over her, warm comfort telling her to rest, to not worry, to sleep and all would be taken care of. But when she pushed further, underneath that murmur was the roiling stink of illness and fear, the fever-burn and sweat-chill, something queasy-making in her gut, pushing to escape. . . .

no! Something flared in her chest, like a chicken trying to escape the hammer, wings beating furiously.

A massive cloud of butterflies erupted from the grass ahead of them, swirling in a mass before disappearing into the sky. Gabriel swore in surprise even as Uvnee danced a little, shying away from the dozens of wings. Then there was silence, too quiet, the greenish hush of the sky before a tornado, and Flatfoot's sudden loud bray nearly sent Isobel out of her skin.

"God have mercy," she heard Gabriel say, before the ground disappeared under Uvnee's hooves, sending the mare scrambling for footing, Isobel nearly falling out of the saddle, her fingers digging into the mare's mane, her legs wrapping around the mare's body even as she tried to adjust to help the mare stay upright, trying not to do anything foolish, knowing that something was terribly wrong but too busy to figure out *what*.

And then it was over, the ground stilling again, the world righting itself. Isobel knew it was over, could feel it was over, but unlike the quake the day before, this one echoed in her own body, a sharp and sudden pain that only slowly faded to a dull ache.

closer too close

"The blazes was that?" Gabriel, his voice far away, faded.

Isobel couldn't answer, tucked in on herself, Uvnee at a full stop below, confused by why her rider had pulled the reins in so tightly, now that the earth had stilled again.

Show me, Isobel demanded.

"Isobel? Iz?" Gabriel's voice faded in and out, the dull hot ache pushing at her, pushing her away, out of this meadow, off this hill, pushing her away. . . .

Then there was pressure on her skin to match the ache inside, hard warm hands pulling her down, and she cried out when her boots touched the earth, the pain tearing through her again until she was scooped up, cradled like a child, and a familiar, soothing voice in her ear.

Eventually the fog cleared from her eyes, and she could think again, without the ache or pain.

"I'm all right. Put—" Her voice cracked, and she tried again. "Put me down."

Gabriel hesitated, and she managed to unclench her fingers enough to pat his arm, the fabric of his jacket rough against her skin. "I'm all right."

Her voice cracked a second time, but he eased her to her feet, keeping one arm wrapped around her shoulders in case she crumpled again.

Isobel winced as her legs straightened and her foot touched the soil again, but the earth lay quiet below her, the only pain a faint lingering echo in her flesh.

"Isobel?"

For the first time, she thought she heard fear in Gabriel's voice.

Isobel thought fear might be better than the numbness she felt, the odd hollow emptiness. She shook her head a little, unsure. "Did you . . . did you feel anything?"

"Other than the ground trying to kick us back onto the plains? That wasn't enough?" He took off his hat and ran a hand through his hair, leaving tufts of it sticking up, like the feathers of an upset crow. She didn't feel even the faintest urge to smile at the sight.

Uvnee, her reins dropped, had started grazing peacefully as though nothing had ever disturbed them. Isobel stared at the animals, wishing she could forget things so easily.

"Mayhap," Gabriel said finally. "Like an itch, the worst itch I've ever felt, somewhere I couldn't reach. It started just before the quake hit, and ended . . . I'm not sure when. But you felt something more. Worse."

It had felt like every bone in her body was breaking, cracking under some sudden shock, and she wasn't not sure, entirely, that nothing *had* been broken.

"Duck said . . ." Isobel let the words trail off. The native woman had said that the earth was sorrowing. But that had not felt like sorrow to her. It had felt like *rage*. Rage so tightly controlled, she wasn't surprised the earth itself shook. But what caused it? What *felt* it, to cause that?

"It has to be part of the Spaniards' spell," she said. "Splintered off, landing here. It was meant to unnerve and disturb, to make people doubt . . . to doubt that the boss can protect them."

She was convinced that the Territory had somehow altered the spell as it came over the Mother's Knife that spring, changed it from bad medicine to . . . not good, but less harmful. That was why she had allowed the creature in the hot spring to live, even after it attacked him, because the Territory had claimed it. But Isobel had no idea what else the spell might do, what sort of creatures it might sow, or how they might act.

"Wonderful. And us without a magician this time." Gabriel's voice sounded . . . amused? She swung around to look at him, leaning against Steady's bulk for support. His face was turned up at the sky, his brimmed hat back on his head and his eyes closed against the sunlight, but his mouth was curved in a tight-lipped smile.

"What?" she demanded, suddenly angry at him.

"People ask me if I'm not bored, riding the Territory day in and out," he said without opening his eyes, still smiling. "Every day, exactly the same . . ."

Isobel remembered the pain wracking her body, the look in

Jumping-Up Duck's eyes, the rage shaking the ground below her feet. Nothing about any of this was amusing. And yet, she sank to her knees on the dirt, surprised to hear hiccuppy laughter matching his own.

"Too much," Gabriel said finally, when they'd both calmed down. He handed her a square of cloth, the red fabric sun-faded but clean, and she blew her nose, then tucked the square into her own pocket rather than handing it back filled with snot.

"Ow." He shifted, placing a hand over his ribs, shaking his head at Isobel when she would have scolded him. "Scabbing held, just aches a bit. Laughing hurts, but it helps, too."

He was right. Isobel didn't understand why, but some of the pressure she'd been feeling had lifted off her, some of the echoing emptiness filled.

More than just today, just then, she thought. Weeks she'd felt that pressure, maybe longer. Since she'd felt the Spaniard's spell break against the Territory, seen it cause illness, death, where it landed? Since she discovered what carrying the devil's sigil would require of her, would *make* her?

Maybe longer. Maybe since the morning of her sixteenth birthday, when she'd told the boss she wanted to stay . . . only to have him shove her out of the house like a second-hand tool loaned to someone else.

Isobel knew every bargain had a price. She'd read her Contract, she'd seen the words, but she hadn't understood what it would feel like to pay it. Maybe nobody ever really did.

She took her own hat off, wiped the line of sweat away from her hairline. Molly would be horrified at how tangled her hair was, how cracked and ragged her nails were. Neat and presentable, Izzy, she'd say. Always be neat and presentable, no matter what you were doing.

Isobel felt a giggle trying to rise up again, imagining doing what they did wearing a saloon dress and slippers. Then she imagined Gabriel in a saloon dress and slippers, and the horror of that sobered her faster than running water in winter.

She thought about what Gabriel had said. "Would having a magician here be better or worse?" Bound to the winds and craving power they stole from others, a magician had been no soothing thing to travel with, but Farron had been useful, and Isobel thought that perhaps, in his own way, he had been fond of her as well.

"Worse," Gabriel said promptly. "He may not have been our enemy, in that time and place," he added, as though reading her thoughts. "But he wasn't our friend, either. Never forget that, Iz."

"I know." She did. Even the boss gave magicians a walk-around when he could. Dream-walkers and medicine folk, people with skills, they remained themselves, no matter how skilled they became. Magicians did not. The winds rode them, filling them with power, and that made them changeable as the winds and twice as mad. They were not to be trusted.

She still missed him.

"If this is another spell-creature . . ." Isobel put her hat back on her head, the weight against her hair like an embrace, the shadow it cast over her eyes a welcome relief. She looked down at her hands, curling her fingers over the black sigil on her left palm, the circle and *infinitas* that told anyone with sense that the thing so marked belonged to the devil.

"If it is another spell-creature, you will track it down and deal with it," Gabriel said, so matter-of-fact that she had no choice but to believe him.

It didn't matter that she hadn't understood, not entirely. *Maleh mish-pat*, the boss had said, and even if she hadn't understood them, she had felt the words in her own bones, in the marrow and blood like a thunderclap. She would become the cold eye and quick knife, the final decision-maker in the isolated expanses of the Territory when the devil himself could not be.

Gabriel's responsibility was merely to keep her safe, to teach her what she needed to know to survive. This . . . whatever waited in the hills above them was *her* responsibility, not his.

"Back in the saddle," Gabriel said before she could marshal an argument to that point, checking to make sure Steady's saddle was still cinched tight, and then swinging himself onto the gelding's back.

His look told her clearly that they were in this together and she was to stop being foolish about it, and she wondered if she should worry that he could read her that well. "If the quakes are worse as we ride to the north, then that's where the source is, most likely. Into the hotlands. Another day's ride at least, assuming the ground stays still for us."

A day's ride without the guidance or safety of the Road, into hills that refused to let her see them, where the ground underfoot could hide boiling pools, to find a creature, possibly spell-born, that was in such pain and rage that it wanted to do nothing but destroy. It was nothing to laugh about—none of this was anything to laugh about—but as Isobel remounted, she felt a bubble of that laughter lingering nonetheless.

She'd been so proud of herself before. She had traveled with a magician, conversed with a dream-walker, outwitted Spaniards, defeated a creature of power, and she had thought that she'd conquered a mountain—only to discover that she was standing on the plateau of foothills, the larger range still to come.

Isobel was thinking something. He could tell from the way her shoulders flexed every so often, as though shaking off one idea only to have another settle. He watched but did not interrupt, keeping alert to their surroundings and letting her work her way through.

The ground beneath them remained stable, but there was a sense of tension in the air that Gabriel did not like, reminding him far too much of the queasy stillness before a demon-wind blew through. He studied the ground to either side, constantly looking for potential shelter, and when they paused at another stream to refill their canteens, he looked for the glimmer of fish in the shallows but saw nothing but stones and mud.

Still, that proved nothing. The fish might have been spooked by the quake, taking to deeper levels or shadowed alcoves. That would explain why they'd seen no deer grazing, no rabbits in the grass. He thought of the supplies they'd taken on, and mentally recalculated how long they would last, if they could not find any fresh meat at all, and the gentle warmth of the day, the clear blue skies and soft air suddenly felt more ominous than any gathering clouds. Even the mule seemed to feel something, not straying to investigate anything that looked tasty but staying close by, until Isobel lifted her head to sniff at the air, then took a deeper sniff and let out an exclamation of disgust. "What's that smell?"

He tested the air and recoiled as he caught what she had.

"It's worse than the buffalo," she said. "Like . . ."

"Like it was ill when it died and the carrion-birds won't touch it." He looked up and noted that there were, in fact, several carrion-birds circling overhead. He squinted and wished for a spyglass: one of those birds seemed too large to be a buzzard.

A Reaper hawk here would not be unusual—in fact, this was the sort of ground they preferred: high cliffs for their nests and scattered meadows where prey could be flushed and caught. But buzzards normally cleared the sky when a Reaper appeared, since they could become prey as easily as anything on the ground.

He scanned the ground again for whatever was causing the smell but saw nothing. The smell was faint enough that it might have been hidden in the tree line, though he hadn't thought the breeze strong enough to carry corpse-stink that far.

Or maybe, he thought, whatever it was wasn't dead yet.

Isobel moved her mare closer, the two animals matching steps near perfectly, the mule close behind. "Something's watching us." She took the pocket square he'd given her earlier and held it over her mouth and nose, attempting to keep the smell away. Her voice was muffled behind the cloth. "Again."

"Another demon?" They'd attracted the attention of one before, when trailing the Spaniards. But that demon had been sent packing, and they'd heard or seen nothing since then. And demon didn't smell like this, didn't smell at all that he'd noticed; it would be easier to find—and avoid—them if they did.

"No? No." She sounded more certain the second time. She looked up then, too, and seemed to notice the Reaper overhead. "I think we should find cover, get out of sight."

Gabriel didn't think she was aware of the timbre that crept into her tone, the dark echo that lingered around her words, but when she spoke in that voice, Gabriel listened. He knew what she was.

And even if he hadn't, he was not a fool.

"Trees?" To their left, there was a cluster of narrow pines with enough room for a horse to pass between. Gabriel had grown up in the deep woods, spent much of his early life following his uncles and cousins as they gathered their lines, but he didn't like taking them under tree cover; his line of sight was too limited, and things could be lurking overhead as well as behind every trunk, hiding in every shadow. But if Isobel's instincts said to hide, they would hide, and this was the only cover available.

She nodded, and turned her mare toward them, kicking the horse into a fast trot. The mule followed her, and he picked up the rear, shifting the reins into his left hand so that his right was free to reach for the knife in his boot or the one tied to his saddle equally. The carbine strapped to his saddle would be of no use except as the club he'd teased her about before, but he loosed the strap around it nonetheless.

Once they were through the first line of trees, Isobel slid down from the mare's back, picking up the reins and leading her deeper into the gloom. The mule looked as though it might balk, and Gabriel had a moment's rare sympathy with the beast.

"She knows what she's doing," he told the mule as he dismounted as well and followed them into the shaded cover, hoping he sounded more confident than he felt. At least, he noted, the trees were old enough that their lower branches had died off, removing one potential source of ambush.

"Here." She stopped, although that patch of ground seemed no different to him from any of the others they'd walked over. "This is good?"

She'd chosen a natural clearing where an older tree had died, the fallen trunk slowly crumbling back into the soil. The clearing was blocked at one end by a massive chunk of reddish-brown rock sticking out of the ground, a little higher than Steady's shoulder, two trees bent to grow around it. The space between the remaining trees was reasonably flat, open enough for all three animals to move freely without stepping on one another or their riders, but not much more than that. He wasn't sure he'd be willing to risk a fire, but the stone outcrop was wide enough to block the wind, and it wasn't likely to become too cold, or to rain, since the sky had been clear. . . .

He took a deep breath and exhaled slowly, reaching for the ever-familiar pull of flowing water. For a moment, he couldn't find it, his pulse racing in near-panic, then he felt the steady trickle of an underground spring, muffled and distant, as though he were hearing it through a heavy fog.

"No fresh water nearby," he told her, sparing her how difficult it had been to discover even that. "Good thing we refilled the canteens."

"I thought springs were common here?" She was untacking the mare already, setting the saddle carefully to one side of the fallen trunk, then pulling out a brush to clean sweat-matted hide and hocks.

"Further west," he said, doing the same for the mule, who had come to stand next to him. "But from what I've heard, even the ones that aren't burning hot aren't ones you'd want to drink from. Ask me before you drink from anything, unless I've already checked it." He wasn't willing to risk a bad case of flux, or worse, when simple caution could avoid it. He finished untacking the mule, placing the packs on the ground, and turned back to start working on Steady. "Are you sure—"

He never got the chance to finish the sentence. Something hit him in the side, a heavy blunt blow that he was able to identify from past experience as hooves, and the world went dark red, and then black.

"Gabriel. Gabriel Kasun. Open your eyes."

The voice was familiar, strained with panic, tied to a sense that he needed to be up, needed to . . . do something.

Open his eyes. He could do that.

The knife clutched in his hand was bloody, but so were his arm and chest, either from the old wounds reopening or new ones he couldn't tell, and from the way Isobel's wide brown eyes kept flicking back and forth, he suspected there was blood on his face as well.

"What happened?"

Isobel shifted back on her heels, and behind her, sprawled on its back, was the largest ghost cat he'd ever imagined—no, larger than that, nearly as long as a horse, its tawny pelt marked with black at head and tail.

But even from that distance he could see its ribs through the pelt, and when he took a deep breath, the same smell they'd both picked up earlier: something dying.

"Waters of Jordan," Gabriel said, and collapsed onto his backside, wincing as the scarring on his ribs joined the new welts in a chorus of argument. "Waters of Jordan, the size of that thing." Then the last seconds before the attack came to him, and he twisted, trying to see the rest of their camp. "Flatfoot?"

Isobel paled, and shifted on her knees, both of them seeing the mule down on its hocks and struggling to get up, its own hide striped with claw marks and blood. "Oh!"

"He took it down, not me," Gabriel was saying even as he crawled toward the mule. Steady was already there, muzzle down against the mule's neck as though to give comfort, Uvnee whickering her own concern but unable to move closer, unwilling to step over the cat's corpse. "Flatfoot became Flying Foot." He reached the mule and spoke softly to it, running a hand over the heaving flanks. "Get the mare before she bolts," he snapped. Isobel started, then jumped up, stepping cautiously over the corpse, draping a cloth over the mare's eyes to lead her to where Steady waited. Gabriel turned back to the mule, looking him over again before doing anything.

"Will he be all right?" Isobel crouched to the side, her gaze switching between him and the mule, her face ashen, her eyes too wide and wild.

"If we can get him up, I think so." Gabriel tried to infuse certainty into his voice, knowing he failed when she flinched. "Need to see how deep those claw marks are. They're not too bad, I don't think." He ran his hand gently over one, and the mule shuddered, but new blood didn't gush from it.

"Just scoring," Gabriel said. "No worse than mine. We're a matched set now, you little idiot." He coaxed him up gently, hands under thick-furred belly. "Come on, up, there you go, old man. Iz, water and the coneflower salve now!"

She scrambled to her feet again, racing to dig the items out of their packs. She came back with the salve and a canteen, and a pale blue cloth clutched in her hand.

"Good. Clean the wounds," he told her, taking the packet of salve from her other hand.

"But your—"

"Iz. Now."

He waited to watch her uncork the canteen and splash a little water over Flatfoot's side, using the old shirt to wipe away the blood. He'd been right; the claw marks were ugly but shallow, and the bleeding had mostly stopped already. There were deeper wounds by his tail where the beast had tried to bite down that looked ugly but weren't bleeding. She cleaned those out too, keeping up a steady stream of nonsense words while she worked, her left hand stroking the mule's flank as she worked, reminding him that it was her touching him there, not another predator.

The mule shuddered under her touch, its eyes rolling nervously, but it allowed her to work. Gabriel added a little of the water to the salve and let it soften, then stepped away to check on the horses, running quick hands over their sides, murmuring nonsense into their ears. He didn't have time to picket them, but when the salve had reached the proper consistency, he dabbed a pinch of it on their muzzles, near the soft skin of flaring nostrils. The bitter smell would not mask the dead cat, not entirely, but it should be enough to distract and calm them.

"Just a bit," he told them, letting them lip at his palms, hoping for a treat. "Just a bit longer, can you do that, hmmm?"

Steady leaned against him, Uvnee looking over the gelding's neck, and he decided the risk of them bolting was likely over, assuming nothing else crashed down at them. Returning to Isobel's side, he checked the job she'd done, then nudged her aside, showing her how to apply the rest of the salve over the wounds, the pale blue paste drying quickly on the skin.

"It will keep flies out, too, while they scab over," he told her, then frowned at her hands. "Is that my shirt?"

"Hush, it's the one you tore last week and never got around to repairing. Now sit down and take off your jacket and let me see."

Gabriel eased himself out of her grasp. "After we get—"

"Now"—and Gabriel found himself sitting on the ground and letting her check his bandages. Fortunately, nothing seemed to be bleeding again, the remaining scabs white and firm, the scarring pale red and fading.

"You'll live," she said, relief making her voice crack.

The mule had wandered a few steps closer to the horses, the three of them calm, although they kept a distance between themselves and the corpse, pressing against the outer ring of trees as far from the rock as they could get.

"It must have had its den there," Gabriel said, following her gaze to the rock. "That's what we smelled when we came into the clearing."

Isobel had recovered the loose feather, twining it back into her braid, smoothing the strands down with nervous hands. "I led us right to it."

"No way you could have known," he said. "Cats are sneaky bastards, quiet and smart. You don't know they're hunting you until they've decided to attack—but mostly, they won't, any more than a bear or Reaper. We're not their preferred meal. This one was too ill, too hungry to be cautious."

She wanted to believe him, he could see it in her eyes, but something held her back. He cursed the devil's face for making her so responsible for things outside her control, but merely reached up to tug at her braid, drawing her with him as he went to inspect the corpse.

"I'll own I've never seen one this big." Gabriel bent carefully and lifted one massive paw up to examine it. "Male, doesn't look like he lost too many fights before this one. If the quakes were scaring off smaller animals, no wonder he was desperate enough to try us. Good thing they're solitary; would hate to think there was another around."

"Just the thought makes me close to wetting myself," Isobel admitted. "How are you so calm?"

Gabriel gave a choked laugh and held up his free hand, showing her the gentle tremor rocking it. "After, you're allowed to panic. The trick is in remaining calm during an attack."

"How do you learn to do that?"

"You don't," he said, letting the paw fall back to the ground. "Help me move this somewhere not here. I don't want to move the mule tonight, if we can avoid it, and I'd rather not have a scavenger find its way in here while we're sleeping."

Assuming either of them slept at all that night.

Dragging the corpse out into the meadow took longer than expected, and smell lingered on their hands and clothing. Isobel had paused on their way back, plucking something from the ground and then handing him a handful of roots that, when crushed, gave off a light, greenish foam that, rubbed into his skin, made the smell fade.

"Catie used to break out in a rash from lye," she said, wiping her own hands down. "She used to do this instead. Called it soaproot. I don't know that this is the same plant, but it looks close enough."

Isobel was talkative, fussy, but there was something she wasn't telling him, her thoughts bound tight inside her head, those sharp eyes clouded in a way they hadn't been just that morning. Gabriel was too tired to dig at it tonight, though. Isobel was a sensible girl: she would come to him in her own time, when she was ready.

They didn't build a fire, but Isobel sketched out a circle with a charred stick and followed it with grains of salt to create a temporary boundary around their campsite, while he checked the mule's wounds again and made sure they had enough water and grass within reach, then sorted through their supplies for a cold dinner.

"Cheese," he said with triumph, then peeled back the cheesecloth. "Soft rind; it won't keep long. Here, cut this into thin slices, fold it with the venison. Better if you can melt it, but still good cold."

She looked dubiously at the combination, but her expression after the first bite was nearly blissful, and they worked their way through the meal without speaking, then settled their kits for the night, the horses and mule darker shadows against the trees.

"I'll take first watch," he said as she came back from performing her private acts on the far side of the horses—neither of them comfortable going farther than that, despite being reasonably certain there was no more threat nearby. "Get some sleep, Isobel."

She removed her boots and wrapped herself in her blanket, laying her head on her pack. But he could tell that her eyes were still open.

"Gabriel?"

"Mmm?"

"If another quake hits, will the trees fall on us?"

He looked straight up, the tops of the trees lost in shadows, the only illumination coming from the coalstone dully glinting between them. "They've stood tall for a very long time," he said. "Go to sleep, Isobel. We'll be all right."

He waited, but she only turned over, pulling her blanket over her shoulders, and soon enough he heard the quiet huffs that told him she'd fallen asleep.

He should close his eyes and try to rest, too. The mule had saved his life, but he'd still taken a blow, and everything from his collarbone to his knees ached in sympathy. And now that Isobel had raised the thought of another quake, he was reasonably certain he wouldn't be sleeping well that night, no matter how exhausted he felt.

What he wanted was to be able to talk with someone else, someone wiser or at least more experienced. What was the point of knowing medicine folk if he couldn't use their wisdom?

Graciendo, the old bear of the mountain, would tell him to go to sleep. Old Woman . . . Old Woman Who Never Dies would tell him to do the things he was avoiding before it soured in his heart.

Old Woman had always been the wisest, anyway.

The envelope was creased in half from where he'd shoved it into his pack, a corner now dog-eared with use and travel. He held it in his hand but didn't remove the letter from within. There was no need: the words lingered in his thoughts, like flies on a carcass.

He might have left the States, but he hadn't forgotten them, and he never made the mistake of thinking the States had forgotten the Territory. He tried to keep an eye on the political machinations, more out of wariness than actual interest, but he hadn't seen a broadsheet since Patch Junction, and even that had been weeks old.

But it seemed that Jefferson had taken his election to the presidency as justification to run every harebrained scheme he'd ever thought of— or stolen from someone else with even less sense. And Congress . . . Gabriel didn't have the familiarity that Abner did, obviously, but he knew the type well enough from his time at William and Mary: arrogant with education and privilege, certain that a thing must be right because they determined that it was right.

And they all thought that they had a right to the land to the west of the Mississippi River, the Espiritu Santo, where the devil had first stopped the would-be conqueror de Soto, the first time the devil had stopped an armed force but not the last.

Unlike the Knife's snow-coated peaks, the Mississippi could be crossed easily in force if one had enough boats, enough guns. An expedition, funded with the coffers of a solvent nation?

The devil did not block anyone from crossing his borders in peace. Settlers, trappers, scouts—even the Spanish monks had been, if not welcomed, tolerated.

Gabriel smoothed one finger across the envelope, hearing the faint crinkle of paper like a guilty secret. Would this letter prove intent of threat? Would the Master of the Territory—or his Hand—consider it such? And if so, what would they consider *him*? Gabriel Two Voices, split between two lands and settled in neither.

He slid the letter back into his pack and picked up the loaded flintlock, resting it across his knees until it was time to wake Isobel for her turn.

Hand

Not a voice, not a whisper. A noise, that filled the spaces between heartbeats.

Hand

It wanted something. Wanted her to . . . what? She tried to form the question, but she had no mouth to speak, no arms to sign, no eyes to see, only the sense of something pressing and pulling her, needing her, rough and hot under her skin—

Isobel's eyes opened, lashes stuck together, a taste like ash in her mouth. Her vision focused enough to tell that sunlight was only beginning to filter through the trees, and most of that was blocked by something large, warm, and bristle-haired.

She scrunched her face up in disgust at the too-warm breath on her cheek and shoved the mule's head away, but it refused to move, reaching down again to lip delicately at her hair and then, when she didn't move, to take a larger chunk and pull.

"All right. All right." She slapped at the side of its face until it let go, then reached up and scratched one floppy ear to show there were no hard feelings. It was still the hero, after all, and those strong blunt teeth could as easily have taken a chunk of flesh, but it had been gentle—as gentle as a mule knew, anyhow.

She shoved its head away again before it could decide she wasn't moving quickly enough, and crawled out of her bedroll, shivering as the cold air hit her bare skin. The light was oddly green, filtering through the trees overhead, but she thought it just past dawn, if that. Gabriel was a lump nearby, his blanket pulled over his head, only the faint snoring proof that he was alive. In the dim light, the blanket's colored stripes looked faded and grey. She had fallen asleep on watch, she realized. The thought shoved her into full wakefulness, searching the surroundings for any sign of disruption or danger. The air was still, the horses with their heads down, dozing as well, only the mule awake, staring at her with liquid brown eyes as though expecting her to produce carrots for his breakfast.

"If we had carrots, I'd be eating them myself," she told the mule. "And maybe I'd share. But we don't, sorry."

The mule snorted as though it understood, and ambled back to where the horses slept, cropping unhappily at the grass as it went. She dressed as quietly as she could, fastening the buttons of her blouse and skirt, drawing fresh stockings up over her legs, and shaking her boots out to make sure nothing had crawled in overnight before lacing them onto her feet.

She ran a hand down the fabric of the skirt, frowning. Gabriel had warned her to pack light when they left Flood, but simply airing out her clothing whenever opportunity arose was not the same as a good laundering, and she'd pay all the coin in her purse for a new skirt, one without darns or stains.

"And carrots," she said, compiling a list. "And fresh bread and butter, and a pillow and linens, too."

None of those things were likely to appear, not here, and likely no time soon. Unless she felt the urge to tan her own hides and make a deerskin shift, like a native, what she carried would be what she wore.

She thought wistfully of the dresses she'd left behind in her room in Flood, the soft slippers and pretty shawls, and then sternly put those memories aside. Turning to wake Gabriel, she heard a *thwick-thwick* from behind her, the noise enough like the familiar scratch of cards on table felt to make her pause, thinking her memories were playing tricks on her ears.

Then it came again, real and true, and a breath or two of searching found the source perched on the stub of a tree branch just above her head.

The owl was massive enough to make the branch creak underneath it, brown and white feathers fluffed against the morning cold, golden eyes in a flat face staring down at her, unblinking.

"I'm not a mouse," she told it, frowning fiercely. She was not a mouse, and odds were, this was nothing more than an ordinary bird, its pre-dawn hunt disturbed by intruders sleeping where they should not be.

The beak opened as though it were going to respond, then its wings lifted and it swooped off the branch, coming close enough to her head that Isobel ducked instinctively. By the time she straightened again, her hands lowering from her head, it was gone.

"Well, then," she said softly, unsure if she was relieved or not. She wouldn't deny that advice would have been appreciated, but spirit-animals, in her experience, delighted in speaking things that were utterly useless unless you already knew what you needed to know. Her previous encounter with a spirit-snake had left her more confused, not less.

And an owl . . . No. She had no wish for an owl to speak to her, now or ever.

A firm cough and a clod of dirt tossed at Gabriel's shoulder was enough to rouse him, pulling the blanket off his head and sitting up slowly, aware, since she had not shouted, that there was no danger requiring immediate action. She waited until he ran a hand through sleep-tousled hair and nodded at her, before going to check on the animals.

The salve on the mule's side had flaked off overnight—he'd likely rolled on the ground at some point to scratch an itch—but underneath the dust, the cuts looked to be healing, without any heat or pus. She washed them out again with water anyway, paying special attention to the punctures. She didn't think more salve would be needed, but if Gabriel thought otherwise, there was enough left to cover it and still have some left.

Some, but not much.

"No one else get so much as a bruise," she told the horses, gathering up Uvnee's lead and trusting the other two to follow her through the trees, back to the meadow, checking carefully first to see if there was any sign of another predator lurking. The carrion-eaters had gone from the pale blue sky, and the only things she could smell were the sharp tang of the trees and a thin, cold scent she was coming to identify as "mountain."

The sick, musky smell of the ghost cat was gone, buried along with it.

She staked the horses' leads to pegs in the dirt and walked a perimeter around them, breathing quietly and listening to the simple sounds of breeze and insects, watching deep blue and pale green butterflies lift and descend, the horses quietly, contentedly cropping at the grasses, moving shoulder to shoulder without alarm. Finally certain that there was no immediate threat, Isobel left them there to graze and went back to their small camp. Before she could see it, she heard noises: quiet, familiar grumbles and thumps that made her smile despite her worry. Like the thump of slippers on hardwood floors and the *flickerthwack* of playing cards, those were the sounds of comfort, of home, and she had missed them.

Gabriel had gotten a small fire going while she was gone, and started breakfast.

He looked up as she approached. "Horses grazing?"

"Mmmhmmm. Staked their leads, left 'em unhobbled." If spooked, horses could run enough to lose their way back, and they couldn't afford to take time to hunt them down or go ahead on foot, but if another cat were around, or a bear, three sets of hooves could mount a fierce defense, time enough for their riders to arrive with loaded guns.

And hopefully, nothing more fierce than butterflies would appear. Isobel wasn't sure she believed in luck—she'd grown up in a gambling house, where luck had very little play—but she thought for certain they were due some, if it did exist.

"Flatfoot looked good," she said, taking the offered mug when it was ready, and letting the sharp aroma tickle her nose. "Skin wasn't warm; there was no sign of pus. I washed the cut but didn't put more salve on."

"I'll check it before we saddle up, but if he's healing on his own, no need to do more," Gabriel agreed. "No upsets during the night?" She paused, a bite of corncake halfway to her mouth. "No. Nothing." No need to admit she'd fallen asleep: the horses had not been disturbed, she'd seen no sign of danger. She simply would not make that mistake again.

"Good. Soon's you're done, we should pack and go. Full day's ride ahead, and we've no idea what to expect."

A flash of annoyance—she *knew* that—was tamped down. He wasn't scolding her, only telling her what the day would be like, seeing if she had anything to add. He'd done such before, often enough; why did she react now?

"Sky looked clear," she said instead. "If the ground stays still . . ."

Her mood was uncertain, some tingling sense of unease she'd learned to heed, not a push or a pull, but a sense of something *wrong*. Gabriel frowned into his mug, and she wondered if he felt the same, the sense of *needing* to look and at the same time needing to turn away, to ignore everything to the north, pretend that the ground had not shaken, that Jumping-Up Duck had never spoken, that she had never felt the push to . . .

Something didn't want her there, was pushing her away. Why?

"Douse the fire," she said abruptly, and as though he'd been waiting for those words, he dumped what remained of his coffee on the ground by his feet. "I'll fetch the horses."

Rearranging the packs to keep weight off Flatfoot's wounds took a little time, but soon enough, the camp was cleared and they were ready to go. Isobel shifted a little, trying to find her balance with the additional pack slung over Uvnee's rump.

"Clear to ride?" Gabriel asked, as relaxed into his saddle as he'd been the day they left Flood, although his long coat was now rolled and stowed on the back of his saddle, and the look he gave her was less judging than expectant.

She listened the way he'd taught her, taking in the feel of her surroundings as well as the sounds and smells, expecting that sense of being watched to return, for the smell of something wrong to touch her nose. It didn't. "I think so," she said, but didn't move. She remembered how she'd known something was wrong the day before and then how she'd frozen just before the attack, remembered the size of the ghost cat, the weight of each paw and the curve of its claws, and the starveling look of its ribs.

"Iz?"

"Yes," she decided. The cat had been ill, and hungry, its prey fled. With the cat dead, the threat was gone. "Clear to ride."

Despite her continuing unease, Isobel found herself enjoying the morning ride. Although the trail still climbed through chalky red hills, it occasionally led them through long, narrow valleys filled with summer grasses and the dusty green of sagebrush, dotted with short-trunked pines and white-barked firestarter. There was the occasional waft of something unpleasant on the breeze, similar to the cat's musk but less sickly-sweet, but it was offset by the smells of green growing things, and the warm spicy scent of horseflesh and sweat that Isobel had come to know as well as the scent of fresh linens and liquor from the saloon.

Home. Isobel took off her hat and wiped her forehead where sweat had gathered. Home had always been the saloon, the town of Flood, the farmlands and riverbank that bordered it: her entire world within the safe-wards, the familiar pulse that surrounded her, fitted itself to her, and she to it. She had thought it all there was, all that was important.

Did they miss her, Iktan, Molly, and Ree, Catie and the others back in Flood? Did they wonder what she was doing, or had she faded from their lives already, only mentioned in stories of things that happened a long time ago, maybe told to the new girl who slept in her bed, did her chores?

When the boss had sent her out with Gabriel, she had thought it punishment. Had thought being sent away the price for what she had bargained for. Respect. Power. The ability to shape and change things, the way she'd seen the boss and Marie shape and change things.

She hadn't understood what power felt like then. Hadn't felt the sickening dizziness, the way it stretched her thin, burned and broke inside her. The understanding that it wasn't hers, none of it: that she was only a tool, a barranca for waters to run through.

Her right hand, still holding the reins, reached for her left, the thumb pressing into the palm where the lines of the sigil had appeared so many weeks ago. They had been faint at first, thin raised lines she could feel to the touch. But now it was as much a part of her hand as the lifelines crossing it, the marks dark and clear, the double-ended loop enclosed within an open circle. An *infinitas*, Gabriel had called it.

Infinite. Endless.

Then Isobel paused. Marie had no such mark on her hand. Surely she would have noticed it: Marie's hands were always visible, resting on a shoulder or directing where things should go, carrying a tray or wrapped around a glass. . . . Did the mark fade? Or was she the only one identified that way, like a saddle or some other object, claimed so that it couldn't be stolen. . . .

"Iz." Gabriel's voice cut into her increasingly uncomfortable musings, and she looked up with a sense of relief, to see what had caught his attention.

They'd come to another valley, this one with a creek cutting across it, and on one side of the creek she saw now what he had seen: bare skeletons of wood, curved and bent into the ground, and piles of black ash. It took looking-for, but once she did, Isobel could identify the structures that had been there, imagine the hide stretched over the wood, the placement of campfires and the food cache, now dismantled and taken away.

"A hunting camp?" It did not have the feel of a settled camp, the grasses not worn enough to show well-trod trails or refuse piles.

"Likely," Gabriel agreed. He had pushed his hat back in a gesture that meant he was thinking about what might have happened, his gaze moving over the scene in front of them carefully, taking in all detail, even the things that she would miss, the things that didn't seem important, and putting them together to mean something.

Isobel was getting better, but he had years of experience and training. So, she settled herself deeper into the saddle, patted Uvnee's neck, and waited.

"Not a hunting camp," he said finally. "Summer camp, maybe. They were here for a while, a few months, and then they left. And they left quick."

Camps weren't abandoned; she knew that much. They were chosen carefully, returned to every year. "Like something scared them away?"

"If I were to place a bet . . . yes."

"The quake." She said it with certainty, although she knew nothing for a fact.

He shifted in his saddle to look at her. His face was scruffed again, the lack of fresh water meaning he didn't bother to shave, and the shadows under his eyes were darker, making his face look sallow. She suspected his wounds were giving him pain but knew he would not admit it if she asked.

"Mayhap." Something about his tone was odd. "Probably," he went on. "But this is their land, Isobel. They know it like . . . like you knew your saloon. There's nothing here that they should be that afraid of, to run rather than face it. Not even the ground shaking."

"Duck said—"

"Duck wasn't born here." His words were sharp, stopping her objection mid-throat. "There's something you know when you're born a place. You feel it, different from anywhere else. You know when the wind's wrong, or the water's running slow, if the birds are flying too low or too high. . . .

"I've never been up this way before," he said, "but stories say the ground's always been unsteady. There are places out there where the land cracks open on a regular basis and steam rises into the sky." He sounded almost wistful, as though he'd enjoy seeing that. "Duck and her people, they came here from elsewhere east. Hearing stories isn't the same as understanding. But the people who hunt here . . ."

"The people who hunt here?" she prompted when his voice trailed off.

He looked up into the sky then, and she followed his gaze to where a single raptor was now circling, far overhead. Not a Reaper, something smaller. She had a sudden thought it might be an owl, even the one she'd seen, but it was daylight: owls were creatures of dusk and dawn.

"This is their home," Gabriel said. "Even if they thought they'd offended a spirit, angered enough to shake the ground, they'd try to appease it, not run. This"—and he indicated the abandoned camp in front of him with a jut of his jaw—"doesn't make sense."

"Neither does a cat that can check its prey before leaping," Isobel said without thinking, and then stopped when his attention skewed directly, fiercely, on her.

"What?"

Gabriel had been born to the Territory. He'd seen and heard more oddities than most would believe, walked in true-dreams, and broken bread with creatures of legend. Isobel's tale should not have made his hair curl—and yet it did.

"Tell me again," he said, after Isobel finished explaining her reaction to the cat's attack the night before.

They had dismounted, walking the horses as they moved through the deserted camp, and he could see when she took a deep breath and then exhaled before she responded.

"It will not change no matter how many times I tell you," she said, her voice terse. "I knew we were being followed in the valley. And when we were untacking the horses, I knew there was something behind me, and I wanted to turn around, but I couldn't. It was like . . ." Her voice trailed off, and she shivered once. "Like dreaming, when you know you have to move but you can't; your limbs won't respond."

"And you're sure it wasn't simply fear? There's no shame in that," he added quickly. "A ghost cat, up close, can turn even the hottest blood into ice."

Her eyes narrowed in a glare, and she looked like she would have liked to've taken a swipe at him, had she claws. "I wasn't scared," she said with asperity. "I didn't even know the cat was there, not until it was already on us. I was uneasy, I knew something was wrong, and then I couldn't move."

She was aware of things he was not. It was possible, Gabriel supposed . . .

"And I wasn't afraid," she repeated. "I know what fear feels like now. This was . . . I just couldn't move. My body wouldn't listen to me."

He sucked at the inside of his cheek, thinking.

"Gabriel?" Her voice had lost that edge; no longer defensive, she was asking her mentor for reassurance.

"These are strange hills to begin with," he said finally. "And becoming stranger. If you feel . . . odd again, Isobel, tell me."

"If I can speak, I will."

"Brat." He glanced sideways at her, relieved to see some of the tension gone from her face, although he was not fool enough to believe that she had let the worry go. Fair enough; neither had he.

Nor was the deserted camp easing his fears. There were no indications of illness or attack, nothing to suggest an outside cause for this to have been abandoned in such haste.

They'd seen abandoned settlements before, in Clear Rock, where the Spaniards' magic had touched and eaten all that was flesh. But this ruin lacked the uncanny echo of that place, the sense of something having passed through. Those living here had gone of their own will. He couldn't say why he was so certain of that, but he was. And yet.

The horses seemed calm, but the mule stayed close to the horses, its ears and tail twitching more nervously than its wont. That might be a reaction to its wounding—or it might be sensing something none of them could.

"Spaniards," Isobel said, and her voice made it a curse.

"Are you certain, or is that a guess?" He would defer to her call, but he needed to hear her evidence before he would agree.

"A guess," she admitted reluctantly. "It doesn't . . . feel like what happened before, but . . ."

"But you don't want to think about there being something else that could do this," he suggested. "It may be purely natural. The ground shaking . . . I told you, it's not so unusual, not up here." He dragged through his memory, trying to find something else to tell her to ease her fears. "You didn't like the story of drumming the mountains; another story says the He Sapa, the Black Hills, were born when the spirits underneath were so angered by the pride of those who dwelled on the surface, they thrust upward, killing all who made such prideful noise, and left the Hills behind as a reminder that we are not so powerful as we like to think." He'd seen those mountains himself, felt the palpable sense of presence that lay on them like a mantle; he would not be the one to say the stories were untrue, however improbable. "So in the memory of the elders, it's happened."

Isobel was listening, but he wasn't sure if that attentive pose was for him or something he couldn't hear. "The boss said the same, only far west of here, that the land shook so terribly . . ." Her words trailed off, and she tilted her head and knelt down, her fingers plucking something from the ground. She twisted slightly to show it to him. Three long, narrow barbs lay flat across her palm, glinting a dull red in the sunlight.

"Quills," he said, picking them up and rolling them between his fingers. "Dyed, flattened . . . That's Apsáalooke, maybe Nakoda work? I didn't think they were this far south." He looked around, reevaluating the deserted campsite, still rolling the quills between his fingers. "Or we're further north than I thought."

"You don't know?"

She was right; he should know. He carried a map of the Territory in his memory in addition to the ones he had rolled in his packs. But more than that, even without a Road here, an experienced rider should know where they were, have some sense of location.

But when he tried, there was nothing there for him to touch.

Something blocked him the way Isobel had described earlier. Gabriel swallowed, his throat suddenly tight. Ground that shook, ghost cats that could freeze a human as easily as a hare, and something keeping him from reaching any sense of the Road itself . . . The Territory was an uncanny place on the best of days, but he was a betting man, and the odds kept shifting in a way that made him want to quit the game.

"The devil runs an honest game," he said, almost to himself. "But that doesn't mean someone else can't cheat."

"Gabriel?"

"Strange hills," he repeated, twisting his mouth up in a smile for Isobel's benefit. "Spell or natural, monster or man, you've been drawn to look, and so look we will."

She didn't seem reassured.

"Whatever's hiding itself here, Isobel, it's not able to block everything. I can still sense water; you still know when there's danger. It can't stop us." He looked at the quills in his hand, then tucked them into a pocket of his jacket. "Mount up. Whatever happened here, they didn't leave stories behind. We need to find someone who can talk to us."

Assuming there was anyone left to speak.

The abandoned campsite was soon out of sight but not out of Isobel's thoughts, keeping them shadowed and sharp. But the land around her tugged her back as the trail wound its way higher. The air felt thinner, drier, but the scent of things warm and growing filled it, butterflies clustering around them whenever they paused, flitting through the air as they rode past, and Isobel thought that, under other circumstances, she might have enjoyed this ride.

Had she not been woken out of sleep and driven to a place where the land shook, the animals fled, and the bones went silent under her touch. If not for the fact that butterflies and insects were the only other life they now saw. If not for the fact that she felt the prickling against the back of her neck again.

"We're being followed."

"I'd be more surprised if someone wasn't following," Gabriel said, his gaze sweeping the surrounding hills without an outward show of concern. "We're strangers, whites, and whoever lives here was spooked enough to abandon a hunting camp mid-summer." There was a bite of something in his tone at odds with his outward calm. "If anyone's remained in these hills, they'd be fools not to keep an eye on us."

"Natives, you mean."

"Likely, although I wouldn't rule out a trapper or two, maybe done with civilization and looking to be left alone. If so, they'll likely just watch us and not interfere. If we're on tribe lands, though, they may take a greater interest."

"Why don't they ever just come out and say what they have to say, instead of stalking us like . . . like rabbits?" Her voice rose as she spoke, until the last words were more a challenge, thrown out into the land-scape.

"Because they don't." Gabriel's voice was still terse, but she could hear the faint tinge of amusement underneath, and it infuriated her. The need to *do* something pressed from the inside, struggling to reach into the bones below her, even knowing that it would push back, that she was somehow unwelcome, unwanted, despite being a rider, despite the sigil in her palm.

And yet Gabriel rode as if nothing had ever bothered him, shoulders loose, his entire body practically melting in the saddle, like the ground might not shake under them at any moment, nor some beast or native leap out.

Isobel reined herself in, Marie's voice in her memory schooling her. If Gabriel was calm, there was a reason. If he was amused by her worry, then there was a reason. It might not be one she liked, but there was much that she did not like, and that did not change the fact of it.

She exhaled through her mouth, reaching out to stroke Uvnee's neck, tangling her fingers in the mane briefly for comfort. Learn, she told herself. That is why you are riding with him.

"Fine. Why *don't* they?"

His shoulder raised in a shrug. "Because they don't. If you're aiming to ask me the whys and wherefores of how a native behaves, Isobel, I'm going to think you haven't learned a thing in all this time. They do as they will, and each tribe does it different, and none of them do it as we might."

He laughed a little, a faint chuckle. "If it makes it sting less, I've observed we confuse and confound them equally as much."

"The boss understands them." She knew she sounded like a sulking child, but it seemed unfair, that this was the way it was.

"Wiser men than I have failed to understand what the devil knows or why *he* does as he does. No one even knows why he *came* here, Isobel, nor why he cares what happens to us. Let it be enough that he chose and trusted you to act in his stead. Trust that; it's carried you through so far." He paused. "Well, that and me."

"You have a high opinion of yourself, even for a rider," she said, and had the pleasure of seeing a flicker of amusement on his face, fading into an expression that reminded her of the man she'd met that first night, wryly amused, his attention split between the cards in his hand and the girl bringing him drinks.

Isobel still did not understand why he'd noted her, or what had driven a passing stranger to offer mentoring, or why the boss had decided to intervene after she had turned his original offer down, but she could not imagine taking the Road with anyone else—or worse, alone.

That gratitude did not ease her unhappy sense of misuse. "But why won't they speak to us? They know we're here to help."

Gabriel slowed Steady down a pace so that the horses were side by side. His profile was the same as it ever was, dark blue eyes and dark-stubbled cheek, deep lines around his eyes, the narrow white scar from the spell-beast's claws clearly visible in the sunlight. She still thought him a handsome man, card-slick when he chose to be, but he was *Gabriel* now.

"Are we?" he finally said.

"What?" She thought at first she had misheard him or he had misunderstood her.

"Are we here to help?" He looked at her then and then looked away. "I'm here to help you, and you're here because the devil sent you to ride, and we're here because you've a feeling, but does that help them?"

Isobel felt like she'd been slapped. "Jumping-Up Duck said . . ."

"She said something shook the land from sorrow. Did she ask us to find the source?"

"I . . . No." Isobel forced herself to consider the words and motions of the adults at the table. They had refused to leave, had said Duck trusted the devil to protect them, but at the same time . . . they had never asked her to discover *what* it was. Almost as though they knew and were resigned to their fate.

A growl echoed in her thoughts, that anyone should be so resigned. "We need to know what's happening."

"Yes." His voice was stripped of argument. "We do. But you need to consider why you need to know."

"Now you sound like the boss," she said, petulant, and that got another chuckle out of him.

"Then maybe you should listen."

When the boss said something like that, he didn't mean for her to spout back with a sharp-tongued reply. So, Isobel shut her mouth carefully and paid full attention to the ground in front of Uvnee, the smell of the summer-warm air around her, the feel of the saddle pressing back against her seat, the feel of sweat slicking down her spine, and the weight of her hat on her head, the brim shading her eyes but not her chin. The feeling against the back of her neck, of being watched. And then she set it all aside and paid attention to what remained.

This wasn't like the kind of test Gabriel used to set, for her to identify a bird on wing, or the trail of an animal, or a plant by a single leaf. This was like what she used to do for the boss, to look at someone and tell what they wanted, what they were thinking. What they needed.

Only, she thought she had. She'd studied Duck and the others. She'd seen their worry, their fear. And, a faint voice inside her said, she'd added that to what *she* was feeling, the push that had driven her there. The *wrongness* of the land there having been scraped clean, when they'd been there long enough for some power to have gathered.

"It wasn't wrong," she said out loud. "Something *is* wrong."

"Yes." Gabriel was solid in his agreement on that.

But nobody had asked her to look. They'd given her supplies, hadn't stopped her, but they hadn't *asked*.

A whisper of need had driven her there . . . but she hadn't heard it since then. Hadn't heard anything. What had changed?

It started with the buffalo. The buffalo were none of the devil's concern, outside the Agreement, and had no claim on her. But she had been drawn there, as had the Jack.

The Jack had walked away. Isobel had not.

What had drawn them there?

The sigil told her when something needed caring for, when a Hand's touch was called for. But the sigil had itched when the whisper was silent, and the whisper had called her when the sigil was still, and then both had gone silent when she rode into these hills.

There was something about these hills.

She only realized she was holding the reins so tightly when Uvnee stopped, turning her head slightly as though to ask her rider what was wrong. "I'm obligated to look, to make sure nothing's wrong. To deal with anything gone wrong." That had been the terms of her bargain. To be his Hand where he couldn't reach, to protect those who abided by the Agreement.

And Duck's people abided. They'd said so. They had children who were of both bloods, who belonged to the Territory. Isobel had felt that, and the feeling had not set her wrong yet. Yet . . .

Doubt wriggled in her gut, like being water-sick.

"Is there a difference between being asked to do something and knowing it has to be done even if nobody asks you to do it?"

Gabriel blew out a breath. "There are some who'd say that's the burden of leadership."

She closed her eyes, concentrating on the feel of the mare's bulk underneath her, the dryness of the air, the familiar, steadying smells of leather and horseflesh, of dirt and greenery, the sound of hooves and the creak of saddle leather and the soft whuffling breathing of the mule, keeping pace at her heel. "What do you say?"

"I think—"

Both horses pulled up short, jolting their riders in the saddle and causing the mule to let out an indignant protest as he smacked his head against Uvnee's side. Gabriel slapped his hand down on the stock of his carbine before realizing that there was no threat.

Or rather, the threat was standing still in front of them, body turned so that it blocked their way, neck lowered so that it seemed to be staring directly at them from under the many-pronged antlers spreading like a crown over its head.

"Wapiti," Gabriel said, a hushed tone, as though afraid to spook the creature. Isobel took in the bulk of it, easily a match for broad-chested Steady, and the wicked-looking tines of its antlers, and swallowed hard, trying to make herself as small and still as possible. It was after rutting season, but you could never tell what might set a bull off. Underneath her, Uvnee let out a soft huff that sounded terribly loud, and the creature—wapiti, Gabriel called it—snorted at her in return, a louder, wetter noise.

Then it shifted, the neck lifting until its head was level with theirs, and Isobel was caught by the intensity of its eyes: the head might look like a deer's, but there was no dumb beast staring back at her but an intelligence, sharp as an arrowhead and just as deadly.

Next to her she could hear the creak and rustle of Gabriel shifting in his saddle, the clink of a hoof against a stone, the soft breathing of the horses, but everything else was held silent, even the air around them.

Then the great deer snorted again, louder, and shook its head, the rack of bone coming terrifyingly close to them, before it wheeled and bounded off, faster than she would have thought it could move.

"That . . ." Her voice caught in her throat, stuck between fear and awe. "That wasn't just an elk."

"Not just," Gabriel said, his voice as hushed as hers and just a little shaky. "Isobel, in all my years, I've encountered a total of four spirit-animals, and three of them have been since riding with you. I can't say it's a change I welcome."

Four, Isobel thought, remembering the owl who had not spoken, then frowned, counting back. "Three? Two. The snake, and this . . ."

"And a second snake, when . . . It doesn't matter," he said, cutting off whatever he was going to say. "Just that next time you ask if something's watching us? Assume that the answer is *yes*."

He flicked Steady's reins, and the gelding moved forward again, Uvnee following without her having to give a command. She glanced over her shoulder and saw the mule still standing there, its ears pulled back as though it weren't convinced the elk wasn't going to return.

"Flatfoot, come," she called to it as though it were a dog, and the mule shook its head briskly but followed, blowing hard through its nose in protest.

"There's something strange, though," Gabriel said once they'd caught up with him.

Isobel felt a giggle bubble up, deep in her chest. "Stranger than that?"

"Look around you, Isobel. Your people back in the village, they said their animals had run off, yeah?"

She nodded. "Not the dogs but their goats, yes."

"There's grazing enough here for an entire herd of elk, and that should mean predators as well. But there's no sign of elk or wolves, not for days, not even a curlhorn, and the last cat we've seen sign of was the one that attacked. We haven't seen so much as a rabbit in days."

Isobel looked around as though something would appear to prove him wrong, but all she saw was the same steep meadow, scattered with occasional scrub brush, with trees along the slopes, and beyond that, the flat-topped mountains. He was not wrong; even close to towns, there was more life than this—birds overhead, skittish rabbits and gophers underneath. . . . All they were seeing were butterflies; all they were hearing were the occasional bird and insects.

"You said yourself they ran off when the ground shook. That would explain why the cat was so starved, if all its prey ran off and it was too sick to follow. And maybe why the hunting camp was abandoned."

"Likely." Gabriel took his hat off and swiped his hand through his hair, then replaced the hat again, tugging it down over his forehead. "That's why I had us take on extra supplies. But when people and animals both abandon an area, and there's a wapiti guarding it . . . that's never good news. Not ever."

If there had been good news, they wouldn't be here, she thought but saw no point in saying. He knew that too. "You think we should turn back?"

"I think a wise man would have turned back days ago. But the wapiti let us pass. If the spirits are upset, they're not upset with *us*."

Isobel's palm itched, and she glanced down at it as though there might be an answer there. But skin, grimed with sweat, told her nothing. No summons, no guidance, only the lingering memory of that echoing silence, of being pushed *away* rather than drawn in.

Something in the hills didn't want her there. And she might be a fool, but that only made her more determined to go.

Gabriel took second watch, neither of them comfortable enough to trust circle or wards alone. As the night previous, it had been quiet— too quiet without the calling of coyotes or wolves, the snuffling of night-squirrels or foxes, the crackling branches of night-grazers passing wide around the fire. He felt himself begin to doze, eyelids slipping shut even as he fought against it, tension and exhaustion weighting them down. He would have traded his best knife for a cold rushing stream to dunk his head in, if only to wake himself up again.

Half-awake, he became aware of something murmuring in the

distance, as though someone spoke softly in another room. He held himself still, feeling the press of a rock into his thigh, the dampness of the morning air, the scratch of his blanket over exposed skin, and the press of his bladder where he needed desperately to relieve himself, and waited.

The sun pulled itself over the horizon, but the sound did not come closer, nor did it resolve itself into distinct words, merely a susurration of sound replacing the liquid chirping of birds. He breathed deeply into his chest, eyes closed, and waited. He'd been dreaming in that half-awake state, he thought. A twilight dream was not to be ignored, but the details skittered out of reach, crumbling like old wood at his touch.

Old Woman had been there, cross-legged on a rock. She had been ageless eleven years back when he'd stumbled blindly into a campement de nomades of the Hochunk, on his ignominious return to the Territory, and she had not changed since.

"Be wary," he thought she had said, looking down at the long pipe between her hands, unlit, unsmoking. "Be wary and step lightly."

Old Woman Who Never Dies had been the one to show him how to dream true, to not fear what the voices had to say but to listen. Not all dreams were true dreams, but there were threads that wove through them all recently, red like the quills in his pocket, catching his eye and drawing him back to them each time.

"Be wary and beware," the snake said months before. *"Your enemies are not who you think. But then, neither are your friends. The land twists."*

He had thought it referred to the magician, Farron—no friend, but no enemy either, at that time and in that place. Or Graciendo, the ancient bear, who might turn on him as easily as he aided. Or even the snake itself, wise but with its own purpose, its own concerns.

Now, half-asleep and his brain filled with that susurration, he thought of the one he had not considered: Isobel.

Gabriel rejected the thought even as it crept in, yet it lingered on the threshold, refusing to fade. Not that Isobel might be an enemy; he knew the girl, even if he did not always understand her, and she was faithful and true. But every soul in the Territory knew what the devil was, even if they never spoke it out loud, and she was bound to him, his Left Hand.

The title alone should have chilled him. He thought of the woman who held the title of Right Hand: slender and dark, soft to the eye but with a voice of corded iron; when she suggested something, others made it happen. A woman to respect but never to fear.

But the Left? Like any rider worth their salt, he knew his stories. The Left Hand dispensed justice, not favors. The Left held a fire that burned rather than warmed. He rode with the most terrifying thing in the Territory and called it a girl.

"Gabriel?"

Isobel's voice cut through the near-constant murmur, silencing it.

"Yeah." His voice was sleep-rough, as shaken as his thoughts.

"Did you hear it? The whisper?"

He would not have called it that, but . . . "Yes."

He waited for her to say something else, but she was silent again. The noise did not resume.

He lifted his hands to his face, feeling the scratch of bristle, the crust of sleep in his eyes. His hair was sweat-matted, and he ran his fingers through it, thinking his mother would sigh to see it at such a length. She would sigh to see him anyway. How long had it been?

He forced himself into movement, throwing back the cover and reaching for his trousers, pulling them up over his flannels. Shaking his boots out, he could hear the sounds of Isobel doing the same across the fire pit. When he turned to face her, his lips already forming the suggestion that they not linger here, the sight of another body warming their hands on the remains of their small fire stole his words away.

The man was ancient. Long hair hung loose over a round, wrinkled face, down to bony shoulders, the white strands thick but dry. The skin of his arms and chest was wrinkled with age and sun, patched with scars and burns. Well-worn moccasins rose to mid-calf, blue and yellow quills stitched into the hide. Gabriel did not recognize the pattern nor the paint design that ran up the man's bare leg, a pale red arrowstick marked with irregular black slashes.

The elk had been a guardian, but it might also have been a warning. There were haints in these hills. Old ones, ancient ones, bound by equally ancient wards. Harmless in the day, to those alert, but under moonlight, while mortals slept . . .

Gabriel eased his breathing, opening his hands in a welcoming gesture. "Old father, welcome to our fire," he said, first in French and then English, not wanting to risk using the wrong tribal language and possibly offending their visitor if he spoke in an enemy's tongue. "We have not yet made coffee, but we will pour you some when it is ready, if you wish it."

"Ha," the old man said, which reassured Gabriel that he was in fact alive, and not a haint come to pester. "Coffee, oui. Ces vieux os aime- raient ça."

French, then. Gabriel flicked a glance at Isobel, who had stepped back from the fire, not in retreat, he thought, but to better study the newcomer. Her hair was unbraided, falling down over her shoulder in locks almost as long as the old man's, and Gabriel had a moment to think that she could be the man's granddaughter, with her sun-dark skin and her wide-boned face.

The thought knocked against his earlier ones, and he pushed them all aside; he needed to navigate this carefully and not be distracted. Was this man another guardian? An ally? Or an enemy?

"I am known as Two Voices," he said. He waited to see if the old man would acknowledge it or look at Isobel expecting a name for her as well. He did not.

Gabriel repeated his words in French, and the old man nodded acknowledgment then but still did not look toward Isobel, nor indi- cate any awareness that she stood there, barely a length from his knee.

It was that way, then. Gabriel caught Isobel's attention, then tilted his head toward the horses. She scowled at him but turned and walked off in that direction, leaving them to each other.

Once she was gone, Gabriel sat down cross-legged next to the fire, the ground uncomfortably damp under his seat, placed his hands on his knees, and waited.

Isobel felt rage quiver in her bones, anger born out of hurt and insult. To be sent away like a child, when she was the one who had brought them here, she was the one who could fix what was wrong? She bit the inside of her lower lip and stalked toward the horses, motionless shadows, their heads down as they dozed. Gabriel hadn't even introduced her, hadn't even acknowledged that she was there, and the old man . . .

Putting her hands on Steady's neck, the gelding lifted its head and whickered at her, hairy nostrils flaring wide as though to make sure she was who she smelled like.

"Stop that," she said, pushing the blunt head away, running her hand along his flank to move him to the side so she could get to their supplies. The gelding let her pass, only to have the mule come up and lip her hair, pulling hard enough for her to notice.

"Stop it," she told him, then glared at Uvnee, as though daring the mare to try something too. The mare waited placidly, brown eyes watching, waiting for Isobel to get over her temper and offer a treat.

"All right," Isobel grumbled, digging one of the last mushy apples out of a pack and cutting it in three. They moved toward it like children offered sugar candy, and Isobel felt some of her anger and frustration fade as she watched them, their tails switching peacefully, the soft sounds of teeth crunching louder than the voices of the men by the fire behind them.

She yawned and stretched, feeling her back crack, rolling her shoulders. She'd slipped into her skirt and boots the moment she realized they had a visitor, but the boots were unlaced, and the strings of her chemise were untied, too tempting a target for the mule; she laced them quickly, then bent to deal with her boots. The sky brightened even as her fingers worked, and when she looked up again, the stars were already fading, the moon gone before the sun.

"It's not like I could have understood what they were saying, anyway," she told herself, pushing the mule so she could check the scars on its side. It had only been three days, but the claw marks had closed neatly with no sign of infection, and he merely twitched once under her touch and twisted his neck to nose at her hands, searching for more apple, while the horses moved back to their casual grazing.

"That's it, mule; no more." She cast a look over her own shoulder to where the men sat around the fire—one grey head and one dark bent toward each other, Gabriel's arms moving in sign language—and sighed. Gabriel had sent her away for a reason. She might not like it, but she had to trust him.

The mule snorted at her, then turned away, shifting its stance and dropping its head to go back to sleep.

"You do that," she told it, feeling a twinge of envy. The past few nights, she had not slept well, startling awake in the night, then unable to drop back off, half-waiting for the ground below them to shake again. That it hadn't almost made the waiting worse. And the whisper this morning . . . Why had it returned? Isobel might have accepted stumbling into things to learn them, but she resented it no less now than she had at the first.

Feeling strands of her hair cling to her neck and chin like fingers, she began braiding them out of the way, although without the leather tie she'd been using, the end of the braid began to come apart almost immediately, adding to her frustration. The feathers she usually tied into the braid were tucked under her bedroll where she'd placed them the night before. Surely, Gabriel would not object to her returning for those?

Before she could convince herself that it wouldn't be eavesdropping on their conversation to do so if she couldn't understand the language, Gabriel's voice rose, calling her name.

The old man was still there, his hands clasped around one of their tin mugs. Gabriel was refilling the second one, handing it to her. She took it, settling herself on the ground next to him, her skirt folded under her legs.

"His tribe is the one whose camp we saw," Gabriel told her. "The others left when the ground trembled; he stayed. More from stubbornness than bravery, I think. He saw us arrive last night, watched until a sign came to him that we were to be trusted."

"A sign?" She thought immediately of the great deer, but if Gabriel had been told, he was not sharing. She bit her tongue and nodded at her mentor to continue.

"Near as I might determine"—Gabriel looked at her rather than the old man, who ignored them both—"we were right; something has scared the game away. But it started before the ground began to quake."

He glanced at the old man then and made a hand gesture, a sharp move of his right hand and elbow. The old man nodded once, although it didn't seem to Isobel that he was agreeing. She tried to study him without being rude, to read him the way she'd been trained, but it was like trying to watch a sunbeam; no matter how intently she watched, she could never see it move.

"Jumping-Up Duck said that the land sorrowed, yes? He says that the land is frightened."

Isobel's gaze flicked away from the old man, down to the ground at her knee. The grass was sparse but green, dotted with tiny blue flowers she didn't recognize, six-petaled, with a white center. She touched the fingers of her left hand against the ground and felt only silence in response. She pushed deeper, pressing her palm down to the ground and waiting for warmth to tingle through her, spreading her awareness into the earth, along the bones of stone underneath the soil, the connection to the Territory that the sigil—her Bargain—gave her. Power hummed quietly, a spider's web stretching forever, delicate and thick, and she felt the now-familiar dizziness as her own awareness melted into something far greater. Isobel stretched a bit further, reassured, before a sharp snap hit the center of her hand, the pain racing up to her elbow and making her entire arm twitch away, her body folding in on itself, cutting the connection like a cauterization.

No

All self-certainty Isobel'd had since that first flush of power in her palm shriveled like a leaf in the fire, and her fingers dug into the ground, shoving dirt under her nails, as though to deny what had happened. A pain twisted in her chest, like a sob, a scream, trapped under her ribs. Was she doing something wrong? Had she forsaken her Bargain, somehow broken it unaware? Had the boss . . .

No. She couldn't bear to think of it, and so she would not. The whisper. She clung to that: something had driven her to that tiny village, something had called to her again that night. *Something* wanted her here, wanted her to help.

Gabriel was still speaking. She forced herself to put aside pointless worry, to make sense of the words.

"He says he can take us to where it started."

Isobel was too quiet. Gabriel tried not to watch her as they packed up the camp, saddled the horses, tried not to let his concern show, not for her sake but because he was not certain of their new companion, not yet, and concern could be taken for weakness.

Once they were ready, the old man whistled, and a pony nearly as old as he, black-and-white and tough as old roots, came to his side. He rode it without saddle or bridle, legs wrapped around its sides and a hand on the simple halter, and for the first time since he was a boy, Gabriel felt awkward in the saddle.

They rode all day without speaking, their guide ahead, Isobel and Uvnee to Gabriel's left, the mule behind, up steep, backtracking trails and through narrow valleys that, just as the old man had said, were devoid of life. Overhead the occasional bird circled, but it never swooped, and the grass underfoot never rustled with the passing of small game. Once, up against the sheer rock face, Gabriel was certain he saw movement that might have been goats, but they were too far away to be certain; they might simply have been rocks, shaped and colored to confuse the eye.

No wonder the ghost cat had attacked them. No game underfoot, and too ill to flee from the hills, they must have seemed like a gift, delivered into its lair.

"Forgive us, little cousin," he said under his breath. "But I had a greater wish to live."

And if they couldn't find game for themselves at some point, well, there were still supplies in their packs, although with three of them, it wouldn't last for long. He'd survived on grubs and roots once. He'd rather eat the mule.

The trail took a turn up again, and he leaned forward slightly, trying to take some of the press off his ribs. Sleeping rough and riding up mountains might not have been the best way to heal, but once Isobel went chasing after whatever this was, he'd had no choice but to follow.

Isobel turned to look at him, obviously wondering what he found amusing. Her hat—brand-new not so long ago—was now sun-bleached and worn at the brim, and there was a dip over one side that made her look oddly rakish. But the stubborn line of her jaw and the set of her mouth were familiar. It wasn't puzzlement or annoyance—she was upset.

He kneed Steady closer and spoke softly. "Tell me."

Her gaze flicked ahead to where the old man and his pony rode, seemingly unaware he had companions, then back to him. "How do you know . . . How do you know if a Contract's been broken?"

He almost laughed again, then realized that she was serious. "Isobel. You *can't* break a Contract. That's what *makes* it a Contract. What's bitten you, to even wonder that?"

"I can't . . . I can't touch anything. I've been trying. Ever since . . . I've been trying," she repeated. "I can only get so far, and then it stops me. And I thought . . . I was afraid that meant . . ." Her voice dropped almost too low to hear. "That the boss'd decided he didn't want me anymore."

He was about to tell her, again, that she was being foolish, when her choice of words stopped him. "It?"

She frowned at him, clearly not having realized what she'd said.

"You said 'it.' Not 'something': 'it.'"

Her shoulders lifted in a shrug, a one-sided flip he recognized from his own movements. "It," she agreed. "Does it matter?"

He had been trained as a litigator; word choice mattered. But he let it go for now. "To calm your fears, if the devil were to cast you aside, you would be in no doubt of it. But he did not. He never throws away a thing of value."

She gave him a wan smile at that, but it was better than she'd looked before.

"That settled . . . are you all right?"

"Gabriel." Now she sounded exasperated, which suited her better. "No, I'm not all right. Something dragged me—us—all the way up here, I can't *feel*, and I don't know what to do, and now we're following some old native who won't even give us a name, to somewhere we don't know, to find we don't-know-what that's doing we're-not-sure-what, on the chance that maybe I'll be able to stop it from doing whatever it's doing, and I can't even . . ."

She ran out of breath, or words, and heaved to a stop, her jaw tightening again. She stared over Uvnee's ears, reins tight in her fingers, and shook her head, a tic jumping in the side of her face. "No. I'm not all right. But it doesn't matter, does it?"

No. It didn't. That was the other thing about being of value to the devil, he supposed, and thought again of the exhaustion in the eyes of the Jack, unable to stop save at his master's order.

"What does it tell you?" He glanced at her left hand, and her gaze followed suit without prompting.

"It's quiet. I don't think it knows either."

Gabriel didn't like that. The sigil was more than a sign of who she belonged to; it was her connection, the conduit of whatever power she wielded. More, it had warned her of danger before. For it to be silent, when she needed it . . . The devil's hold only extended the length and breadth of the Territory, be it by his own decision or another's. Maybe they were too close to the borders . . .

No. Her mark had flared when they were in the Mother's Knife itself, in places once ruled by the Spanish. Here, he should be able to reach her.

"I can't feel," she had said.

Unless whatever blocked them from touching the Road blocked the devil as well.

The idea that something could stop the Master of the Territory within his own borders was not one Gabriel wanted to consider. The devil had sent Isobel to be his eye and his ear as well as his hand. If something were able to circumscribe his reach . . .

. . . what else was happening that the devil might not know about?

Gabriel thought of the letter in his pack, of the forces pressing against the Territory, and remembered the half-dream and Old Woman's words. *Be wary. Be wary, and step lightly.*

It might have meant nothing, might be nothing. He should have told her of the letter. It was too late now.

"Ici."

Isobel recognized that word when the old man finally spoke, so she reined her mare in and looked around.

It didn't seem all that different from any other valley they'd ridden through. The sunlight was beginning to fade, but there was enough light to see that the grass appeared undisturbed, the rocks unshattered, none of the devastation that the boss had said would happen where the earth shook so violently. She looked at Gabriel for a lead, but he was swinging out of his saddle, briefly out of view on the other side of the gelding.

She made a face and followed suit, letting her boots land lightly on the dirt, not aware that she was braced for something to happen until nothing did. Her feet pressed against the ground, and nothing pressed back. It was as still and silent as it had ever been before she took Contract with the devil. No, even *more* silent. In Flood, she had felt the town itself, the protective boundary-wards that encircled it, the constant flow of power through the very floorboards of the saloon, though she'd not realized then what it was. She had grown up in proximity to the devil; power had been as present in the air she breathed as the sulphured smoke from the blacksmith's forge.

Here, there was only the sharp, bitter smell of the trees covering the slopes around them, a perfume of flowers she couldn't identify, and under it all, the faint acrid bite that had met them when they entered the hills that they'd ascribed to the ghost cat.

Then, it had been unpleasant, the smell of illness. Here, it reminded her somehow of home, of the morning stink of Gregor's smithy, and the smell of dough rising—except unpleasant, unnerving.

She hadn't realized she was walking toward something until she felt the others gather behind her, Gabriel at her shoulder, the old man a few paces behind. She paused, the toes of her boots neatly lined up as though a ward lay in front of her, telling her to stop. The grass and flowers past her toes looked the same as every other part of the meadow, nothing jarring or out of place.

"Careful"—and Gabriel's hand was on her elbow, fingers curling around the fabric of her jacket, digging through the cloth. "There's something . . ."

"I feel it," she agreed. She turned, her face lifted to the sky, pushing her hat back, watching a single bird winging across the broad blue expanse. It was massive, the sun glinting off dark feathers, and she knew she should feel fear: that was a Reaper close overhead.

Instead of fear, awe overwhelmed her, awe and trepidation; the sense that every beat of its wings was echoed in the thud of her heart, the catch of her breath. Reapers, like buffalo, were creatures of the Territory; they carried some of its medicine within them. Watching it, her head tilting back, the sun glinting at the corner of her vision, Isobel was able to forget, briefly, that she had been cut off, was able to forget anything existed beyond that beat pressing through her flesh, down deep into the bones of the Territory itself.

Then awareness returned. Reaper hawks were hunters, not scavengers: Gabriel had warned her to be careful, that it would not hesitate to attack a slightly built human if it were hungry enough.

"What is it looking for?" she asked. If it lingered here when there was no hunting to be found, there was a reason. Might it also be ill? She remembered the ghost cat, remembered the feel of the plague-ridden settlement of Widder Creek, the stink of the camp burning in their wake, then sniffed the air again, as though something that far away, that high above, could be scented. The air smelled as it had before: tainted, but not ill.

Her feet carried her to the left, the two men following her, until she came back to where the horses and mule waited, clustered together and watchful, well aware of the threat overhead. Only then did Isobel realize she had paced off a circle, large enough for a decent-sized camp, room for people and a fire and horses to move comfortably—but she would no sooner set up camp within that circle than she would walk into a fire. Nothing within the confines seemed any different from outside: the same grasses and flowers, the same ground underneath, the same . . .

She blinked, half-expecting that her eyes were playing tricks on her. Something had moved within that circle. Something unseen, and yet she could see it, indirectly, out of the corner of her gaze, the turn of her head. Directly, it was not there.

Underneath the surface of that circle. Something . . . seethed.

The old man grunted once, a satisfied noise. "Ici, came," he said, the first word he'd spoken in English, and then he used a word she didn't understand. From Gabriel's expression, neither did he. The old man said it again, then made a complicated gesture with both hands, ending with a move as though tossing his hands away in disgust.

"Strangers," Gabriel said. "Strangers with . . . Strangers coming with harm. He says that this is where men came, with intent to do harm. I think."

"Strangers . . . Who?"

Gabriel slapped his hands against his thighs, and turned to the old man again. "Qui, grandpapa? Qui ai venu? Absáalooke? Sutaio? Des blancs?"

He got a grunting assent then, and another hand gesture, this one looping like a bird's flight.

"Des blancs . . . Avec les couleurs de qui? Ont-ils portent des bannières?"

Another series of hand movements, and then the old man fell still again, his dark eyes intent on Gabriel's face. He had yet to acknowledge Isobel's existence at all.

"Many men," Gabriel said. "I think that's what he says. White men, but not together, not one band . . . not one tribe. Many white men gathered here. Meaning harm."

"A fight?" That was all she could think of, to have that many men in one place, not coming together. A fight or a gathering to avoid a fight, the way men came to talk to the boss, some years, late nights with whiskey and Marie bringing trays of food into the boss's office, low voices talking and then leaving, and the boss looking tired the rest of the day, as though they'd taken something out of him.

She'd thought that's what she'd be doing when she'd gone to the boss: bringing in trays and helping soothe tempers, not . . . not standing on a mountain with a Reaper hawk circling overhead, without any idea what she was supposed to be doing.

"Does it look like a fight took place here?" Gabriel asked, and she bristled before she realized that he wasn't making fun of her; he was *asking* her.

Isobel stilled her temper, forced her heart to slow. It was not Gabriel's fault she was upset, not Gabriel's fault the bones had rebuffed her, that the sigil was silent, that her doubts tried to strangle her. He was her mentor; he was here to help.

When she felt calm enough, she turned to look at the circle again.

It was only grass, undisturbed, unbroken. Browning in places from lack of rain, likely, but nothing that should catch the eye. What had she sensed? She could not bring herself to touch it, would not cross the line of the circle she had walked, but moved along the outside, her feet knowing where to step, as they had before.

Nothing above, where men would stand. Something below the surface, but something above as well, some movement in the air, unseen yet present. Lingering.

Some haint, not yet bound to a boneyard? Some mountain version of a dust-dancer, driven by instinct to move, destroy? No. It didn't feel right to her in the marrow and gut, where she'd known other things, and she had to trust herself, especially now, when other strengths were kept from her.

The devil had chosen *her*, Gabriel'd said. She needed to trust that.

Their guide had said white men. Coming down from the north? Trappers and hunters came down often enough but rarely meaning harm, unless one were a wolf or beaver. And she could think of nothing a trapper might do to cause the earth sorrow or anger. She thought again of the buffalo she had seen, and shook her head. The coureurs des bois were not so foolish, nor would their métis cousins be so wasteful, and even if they were, that had happened days from here, where the earth did not quake, days before Duck's people said the first quake had struck. She could not see how it was related.

And yet. She could feel a cord running through them all, a thread stitching the fabric, connecting them . . . and she had been stitched into the cloth as well, drawing her to this place.

Were these more men of Spain come across the border, from the northernmost of their lands? She had allowed the surviving monks to depart the territory unscathed; had that been a mistake? Or had the strangers come from the east? It was not unknown for scouts to venture in from the States—she and Gabriel had seen a rider wearing American colors, not so long ago—but to ride so far from their shared borders? Unlikely, but not impossible, and if it was possible . . .

Isobel felt something curl inside her, and she recognized it for anger, hot lashings needing expression, a target.

"Many men, not together," she said out loud. "A meeting." The thought of others coming from outside, gathering here where the devil's hand could not see, sent a shiver down her spine. Nothing good could come of that.

"But how could a meeting of anyone cause the ground to shake and the animals to flee?"

"Animals are your first warning that something's amiss," Gabriel said, and she hadn't realized he was standing so close to her, his voice quiet near her ear. "If the birds go silent, if the hare freezes, or deer stampede, you'd best look to your horse and knife."

She knew that; he'd taught her that.

"The animals fleeing, the ground shaking, they're the wound, not the weapon?"

"Or a symptom of a disease," he agreed. "Like swelling of the pox, or fever. Ignore them now, Isobel. They've told you everything they can."

Gabriel fell silent, and she stepped forward, hesitated, then took another step, past the unseen line in the grass, into the circle. The smell intensified, the impression of something bubbling under the surface growing stronger. She remembered what Gabriel had said, about the hot springs lurking under the crust, boiling hot enough to scald flesh from bone, and paused, fighting the urge to move backward, cross back over the line, to safety.

Except that safety was an illusion. She needed to know what rested below the surface.

"Isobel?" Gabriel, paces behind her. He called to her, not to call her back but remind her he was there.

She was afraid to reach, afraid to feel the stillness again or, worse yet, rejection. But she hadn't been given a choice. Isobel took hold of the anger that thought brought, stoked it, and then fed her fear to it until it snapped and crisped into ash.

Nothing remained. Not fear, not anger. She risked exhaling, then took a deeper breath in, tilted her head and let her eyes go hazy, waiting.

Nothing. The air remained still, silent, not even the sound of the breeze around them entering the circle. She looked down, and where the grass was lush and green outside the circle, here at her feet it was sere and cracked, a crusted grey froth seeping through the dirt. She thought if she bent to touch this earth, it would sear her skin, melt her bones.

The air smelled the same. But the longer it wrapped around her, stroking its way into her nostrils, the less it reminded her of home, the acrid tinge tickling the back of her throat and making her want to sneeze.

Something burning, but not the smell of the kitchen or the forge, not quite the same. What did it remind her of?

Isobel looked up, away from the ground, letting her vision haze as she stared at some point halfway between there and the nearest mountain as her right hand reached for her left, fingers curling, thumb stroking gently across her palm. The sigil hummed to her; she could almost feel it as a separate thing within her, sliding like a fish under water.

The thought should have bothered her, but in that moment it simply *was*. Everything dropped away, her center spinning so slowly she felt motionless. Isobel took her right hand away, knelt down, and despite her earlier fears, pressed her palm against the ground.

Her lips formed two silent words: *maleh mishpat*.

The next thing Isobel was aware, she was on her back, blinking up at the wide expanse of sky and noting that the moon was visible already, a pale white ghost overhead. Two sets of eyes were blinking down at her, the blue ones concerned, the brown unreadable.

"Iz? What happened?"

She blinked back up at them. Her head hurt. Her back hurt. So did her ribs, she realized when she tried to take a breath and coughed instead.

The last time she'd ended up like this, she'd gotten thrown off the back of the pony Marie used to pull her little cart. The pony hadn't liked being ridden. The pony hadn't liked much except Marie, actually.

"Isobel!"

Gabriel's shout made her blink again. He was closer now, kneeling beside her, while the old man had backed off, his arms crossed over his chest, staring away from her, as though he'd suddenly realized he'd acknowledged her presence.

"Why doesn't he like me?" The words came out unbidden, childlike.

Clearly, Gabriel hadn't been expecting that. He ran a hand through his hair, then ran it down the side of his face, glanced at the old man, then back at Isobel. "I think he's trying to show you respect," he said. "And you confuse him. Are you all right? What happened?"

"What happened?" she asked him in return. Thankfully, he understood.

"You stepped forward and went still, and then you bent down, and then you were flying through the air like Flatfoot had kicked you in the . . . in the gut."

She nodded and closed her eyes, opening them a second later to Gabriel's voice.

"Isobel. Come on, Iz, open your eyes, wake up, there's my girl. Can you sit up?"

She nodded and let him lift her up enough that she could sit on her own. She'd been right: everything hurt.

"What happened?" he asked again.

She was about to say that she didn't know when she realized that she did.

"Something happened here." She licked her lips, feeling where she'd bitten herself, a strip of skin tender underneath. They knew that already. *What* had happened? "They took from here, drained it dry."

"Like a crossroads?"

She nodded, touching the silver ring on her little finger as though to reassure herself that it was still there. She looked down and noted—too late—that it had gone from brightly polished to nearly black with tarnish. The power had been drained from here, but before that . . . Their silver had not reacted to the village, had not discolored during their ride. Only here.

Crossroads gathered power simply by existing, feeding off those who traveled them, until either someone came along to draw the power out or something bad happened. Which rarely occurred, because if a magician didn't find it first, a road marshal would. Or, now, she would. She was the silver the devil cast into the road, Gabriel said.

But there was no crossroads here, no Road at all, no power gathered. Why had her ring tarnished? What had thrown her out of the circle when she tried to touch it?

"My buckle didn't tarnish," Gabriel said, twisting to show her his boot. She reached out to touch it, the metal cool under her fingertips, even as he drew his knife to check the silver inlaid in the hilt.

"So . . . only in there?"

He slid the knife back into its sheath but left the strap open. "Yah."

Something had been drained within the circle. Was it the same something that had scraped the little village clean, that kept them from feeling the Road, kept her from reaching the bones? She could feel the answer fluttering at her fingertips, but there was a soft buzzing in her ears, and chasing those thoughts was like trying to catch a fish with one hand.

Her knees wobbled as she tried to stand, and Gabriel helped her to her feet, holding her steady until she shook him off gently. Now that she knew what to look for, how to see it, Isobel wondered that she'd ever missed it: steam rose from the ground, a low-lying mist swirling and sinking and rising again.

Had it been that obvious before?

"Can you see it?" she asked Gabriel.

"See what?"

"That's an answer of a sort, then," she said, not bothering to explain. Had it been there before she stepped inside, and she couldn't see it, or had her stepping over the line been the cause? Had she . . .

"See what, Isobel?"

"Shhh." Their earlier concern, that this was another ribbon splintered off from the Spanish spell-storm, faded as she felt around the edges of what lay in front of her. Whatever this was, whatever this had been, it had not come from outside but within.

Territory medicine.

If a medicine-worker had done this, there would be no need for the Devil's Hand. That left two possible answers, one more palatable than the other.

"When was the last time a marshal came through?"

Gabriel turned and asked the old man her question, or at least she assumed that was what he was saying. He listened to the response, then shook his head and turned back to her. "They don't."

Marshals were supposed to ride the entire Territory; that was part of their oath.

"There's no Road here, Isobel," Gabriel said. "They can't exactly cover a Road that isn't here."

She lifted her gaze again to the circle in front of her and shrugged in resignation. "Magicians, then."

Gabriel's response wasn't in a language she knew, but the tone was clear enough.

PART THREE
VOICES

Magicians. Gabriel shaped the word in his thoughts carefully, as though the word alone could do damage. Like spirit-animals, he'd spent his entire life having no contact with them, and now . . .

A fly buzzed at his face, and he wiped the sweat with his sleeve and pulled his hat back over his eyes although the sun was behind him and low enough now not to be a bother. "You could have settled down, been a farmer. Married well, raised a packet of kids, never had a surprise a day in your life that didn't involve storms or locusts."

He looked over his shoulder, up from the narrow, nearly overgrown creek he'd found, to where Isobel was still pacing the meadow, careful to stay clear of the area she'd now marked off with rope and pegs, as though she thought it might break open and swallow her whole if she went too close.

"Not that I'm asking for locusts," he said quickly, in case some Power might be listening. With the way their luck had been breaking recently, and this close to the Wilds . . . "Or storms. Let's not make this more exciting than it has to be, mmm?"

He might have asked the old man to put in a good word with whatever his tribe worshipped, but the old man was nowhere to be seen. The three horses and mule, saddles and packs removed, were doing a slow graze nearby, picketed to keep them out of Isobel's way—the mule especially, who'd kept trying to stick his muzzle into whatever she was doing.

Given his druthers, Gabriel would have marched them all out of the meadow entirely. The idea that magicians—one was bad enough, but more than one?—had gathered here made his gut clench and his fingers twitch to curve around his knife's hilt. Even when they claimed to be allies, magicians were trouble, dangerous trouble. More? Gathered for a purpose unknown?

Not that magicians needed reason for their actions. They were mad as March hares, each and every one of them. And he included Farron Easterly in that, despite whatever aid he had given them previously.

"All else, I can bear," he told the slow-moving waters of the creek, watching silver-sided fish twist and turn away from his shadow. "Winter storms and dust-dancers, mysterious illnesses, monstrous beasts trying to chew my face off"—and he shifted and winced at the reminder that he was not as healed as he claimed—"and even being dragged off-Road to ride into unsteady ground like a sunstruck fool. But magicians? It's too much."

His hand flashed out, the glint of metal in his hand, and he pulled back with a long, fat fish impaled on the blade, still wiggling in a desperate attempt to get back to the safety of the water.

"Thank you," he told the fish, knocking it against a nearby stone to end its struggles. "But we need your strength."

It took time to land another; the streams were nearly barren as the meadows, although fish lacked the ability to flee entirely. The sun had dipped even lower on the horizon, he noted as he rose to his feet, wincing a little. Two would have to be enough for dinner tonight. He cut off their heads and gutted them both, letting the offal float away in the water, reminding himself to refill the canteens from upstream, and turned to see Isobel watching him—or staring at something he couldn't see; he would not hazard a guess at this point.

He moved to her side and dropped the fish into her hands. She caught them instinctively, shocked out of whatever she was thinking, then gave him a dirty look.

"I catch, you cook." She didn't have the patience yet to wait until the fish came to hand; the last time he'd let her try, she'd ended up stabbing herself with the blade, not the fish.

"What about him?" She jerked her head indirectly at the old man, who had reappeared and was now sitting by the fire. He was working a strap of leather between his hands, winding it back and forth to soften the fiber.

"Woman's work," Gabriel said, just to see her eyes narrow at him.

A dry, coughing laugh interrupted whatever she was about to say, the old man obviously able to read their body language, even if he didn't understand their words.

"You're wearing yourself to a nub, trying to find something you can't see yet," Gabriel told her, two fingers on her shoulder to head off any comment she might make. "The fish will give you something to do with your hands instead."

She made a face at him but didn't argue further, taking the fish to the fire and sitting—markedly—across the fire from the old man.

Gabriel wiped his hands on the grass, then pulled the frying pan from the mule's packs and passed it over to her along with a chunk of dried fat.

"Onions," she muttered. "We need onions. And fireweed or bitter-root. Would it be rude to ask him to go pick leaves?"

It would. But when Gabriel made the hand sign for foraging and jerked a thumb away from the fire, the old man put aside the strap of leather he'd been working on and followed him.

Isobel finished filleting the fish, dropping them into the pan that was sizzling on the fire. There was enough wood nearby, cracking-dry, that they didn't have to worry about kindling. She had become accustomed to simply pressing a coalstone to create a small blaze, but Gabriel wanted her to remain proficient with flint and steel, too, just as he insisted she learn to forage and not depend on the supplies they carried.

She couldn't argue with that: she might have become accustomed to dried meats and soaked beans, but that didn't mean she cared to eat them two meals a day, and certainly, her gut was quieter when they'd greens and fresh meat to eat.

The men came back just as the fish began to crisp, bearing a double handful of the plants she'd asked for. Or at least Gabriel did. The old man's hands were empty.

She glared at him, and for the first time he stared back at her, dark eyes under a hooded brow, steady as a hawk until she felt uneasy enough to look away. He wouldn't speak to her, and when he did look at her, it was like that—Isobel glared at the fish instead, which could not stare back.

It was because he hadn't given them a name, she decided. People needed names. Even the mule had a name. If she knew what to call him, he wouldn't make her feel so uneasy.

"Broken Tongue," she decided finally. "I will call you Broken Tongue. And you will not respond, because you won't know I am talking to you."

She glanced up at him from under her lashes, but he didn't react. She said it again in Spanish, and he tilted his head but gave no indication of understanding or showing any desire to look her way again. Gabriel needed to teach her more sign language, because "friend," "food," and "danger" were useless here.

Gabriel shook his head, handing her the leaves she'd asked for, then set to scraping the dirt off the wild onions he'd dug up. "He'll know. If he'll respond or not, that's another thing entire." He used his smaller knife to slice the onions against a nearby rock, while Isobel shredded the leaves, lifting them to her nose to make sure they smelled right, then scattered the bits into the pan with the fish. They made a satisfying hiss against the heated metal.

Ree used to say, when you didn't know what to do, clean dishes. Dirtying dishes worked almost as well. She studied the browning flesh, using a finger to test doneness.

"Just a bit more," she said. "We've only the two plates, though."

"The old man can use my plate," Gabriel said. "I've eaten off worse than bark before."

Isobel was going to say that the old man had likely eaten off worse as well, when she froze, her fingers lifting from the fish, still close enough to the flame that she could feel the heat against her skin.

"Iz?" Gabriel's voice was hushed, not worried but questioning, while the old man set aside the strap of leather he had picked up again and waited, his hands resting on his knees. She swallowed, her tongue suddenly too large and her throat too dry.

The sigil in her palm flared once, prickly heat, matching the prickling on the back of her neck, and she knew without looking that the ring on her finger blackened further. Power gathered around them.

She didn't want to look, not with her eyes, not with the awareness the sigil in her palm gave her. She wanted to pull the ground over her head and hide, but the ground wasn't allowing her in, so she had no choice save to flee or look. And the burn of her palm wouldn't accept flight, demanded she turn, stand, greet the presence that had joined them.

We dance to the devil's tune, a whisper of memory reminded her, Marie's eyes wise and sad. *We don't get to choose it.*

Isobel stood, turned. There was still enough sunlight to see the shadow as it moved, although Isobel had a thought it might be visible under moonlight as well, or better. It would not be seen if she looked for it; lingering at the corner of her gaze, present more when it moved than when it remained still, the fluid tumble of water, the drifting swirl of steam. She knew it for the same thing she had sensed within the circle, the broken remnant of whatever had happened there.

And yet that thing had been drained, broken. This stirred with power, prickling the hair on Isobel's arms and scalp; stripped of its substance but none of its danger. The fact that it had left the circle, was not constrained by it, left Isobel uneasy; she did not know what had been done there, did not know what the magicians had called into the circle or why they had left it here, if they had left it at all. . . .

LAURA ANNE GILMAN

She had been trained to read people, to tell what they needed, what they wanted, but there was nothing to read here. Nothing save the prickling sensation of power gathered, wound like husks around corn. Was this shadow the bait of the trap, or the one who had set it?

Isobel forced her panic down, lifting her left hand palm-up so that the sigil was visible, if their visitor could see it. "Here I am," she said. "Did you call me?"

She heard the old man saying something and Gabriel's hushed response, but it was as though they existed elsewhere, heard from a distance. She breathed in through her nose, then out through her mouth, feeling her weight shift in her boots, heels sinking against the ground. This time, she did not try to go deeper, did not risk rejection, but rather spread herself out, the roots of a cottonwood running just below the surface, knotted and strong.

The non-shape in front of her shifted, as though trying to avoid her touch, but never so far that it disappeared. Like a cat, she thought. Wanting food, fearing a kick.

"If you need aid, and it is in my power to aid you, tell me how," Isobel said, her left arm steady as she held it out. "The Devil's Hand is offered to you."

Every child in the Territory knew the touch of a boneyard warding, the cool press of go-away-do-not-disturb that wrapped itself around the dead and kept them safe. It was a dry, smooth warning, without malice or fear. The thing that pressed against her now was none of those things, like nothing she had ever felt before. It sparked like tinder, hot and rough, and forced itself inside her, under her skin, and reached for her bones, scrabbling with a thousand tiny claws to take hold, to pull her inside out and consume her.

And yet she knew it for what it was: a haint, a ghost who had not been honored, not laid to proper rest.

For an instant, she was terrified. Her stomach contracted, pressing itself against her spine, even as her bowels threatened to loosen, fear and sorrow flooding her thoughts until there was nothing else.

Then the lines in her palm flared, red-hot, and she yelped, pain racing through the bones of her arm, shaking everything else out of its way, and she could breathe again, her thoughts and emotions her own. She panted, chest heaving, and tasted something hot and bitter on her tongue.

The presence off to her side flickered once, limned in darkness. For a heartbeat, it was massive, flaring over her, blocking the sky, and then moved so swiftly she could barely follow it, plowing into her with the force of a rockslide. She felt the blow this time, felt her knees buckle and her ribs crack, and she froze, so cold, unable to breathe.

Old. So old, so very old and so powerful and so *angry* and so *hungry*, and it writhed and seethed, the whirling center of a storm, *grit and stone and bitter heat.*

Then there were hands on her, hard and rough, and she was being dragged away, thrown away, and the sound of another voice in words she couldn't identify, a rising chant that sank down into her skin, into her bones, warming them until she could feel herself again, feel the air moving in and out of her chest.

She opened her eyes, then closed them again. There was a snort of warm, fetid air on her face, and she opened her eyes to confirm that yes, there was a thick, pale brown muzzle a handspan from her nose, too narrow to belong to horse or mule, even without the multiple points of bone equally close and three times as terrifying. But between nose and prongs, wide-set brown eyes studied her, then closed once in what she suspected was meant to be a wink.

"Isobel." Gabriel's voice, farther away than the elk's head but still close by. The glow around them had to be coming from the coalstone, because past that pale light, night surrounded them. How long had she been insensible?

"Yes." Her voice was raw, as though she'd been screaming.

Gabriel's wasn't much better. "What happened?"

She managed to shake her head, as the elk shifted slightly, until it towered dizzyingly over her. "It didn't want my help?"

It took a little while before the elk backed off enough to allow Isobel to sit up, and even then, Gabriel was hesitant to approach her, as each time he moved in her direction, the prongs would lower again and a deep, wet snort would be issued, warning him off. It wasn't until the moon had risen overhead, its waxing white light making the spray of stars seem somehow dimmer, that the beast faded out of the firelight.

It did not go away; she could hear and smell it, just out of sight, but it was allowing them room to tend to her now.

She couldn't sense the haint at all; it was gone, but she didn't think it had gone far. She suspected that it *couldn't* go far. It might not be bound within the circle, but something here held it fast, against its will.

Broken Tongue touched her forehead, his fingers dry as twigs. "Vous êtes—" and he used words that Isobel didn't recognize, followed by a hand sign that she thought meant strangers, and then . . .

"Euh . . . des étrangers avec les mains ouvertes?" Gabriel hazarded, frowning. He clearly didn't know the hand signs either. The old man considered, then gave a shrug.

"Ils peuvent être des amis, peut-être."

"What?" Isobel asked, trying not to move her head, for fear of more dizziness.

"I think we have moved from useless to possibly not entirely useless," Gabriel told her. "He's, I think, calling us 'friends-not-yet-made.'"

"Pas pire," he told the old man, nodding. "Good enough."

The old man scowled, his lips thinning. "Mais elle est pas assez forte."

"What did he say now?"

"He's worried about you." But the look that Gabriel gave the old man told another story. Did her mentor still somehow think that she couldn't read him? She knew that his ribs still ached, that he was concerned about something he wasn't telling her, and that he was lying to her now.

"Do you remember what happened?" he asked again, even as his hands were moving gently against her skull, her braid undone so he could check for injuries to her head. She knew she wasn't hurt, but she also knew that telling him that wouldn't stop him from making certain.

"What did you see?" she asked in return.

"Nothing. You stood up and looked around like you'd heard something, then you reached out your hand"—and he tapped her left hand with a forefinger—and told whatever you were looking at that you wanted to help. And then a breeze came up."

"Warm or cold?"

His hands paused a moment. "Cold." He pulled back and poked one finger at her jacket, helping her ease it off her shoulders. The skin under her blouse prickled without its warmth, even as his hands braced against her ribs, and he had her inhale and exhale. "And then you . . . I'm not sure, but you seemed to be arguing with something. And then your hoofed friend over there showed up and knocked you flat on your back."

Isobel turned her head, wincing as her muscles protested, to where she was reasonably sure the elk waited, draped in the shadows.

"Thank you," she said.

"It was our quiet friend who dragged you out of the way," Gabriel said, misunderstanding her words. "I think whatever you were doing is what changed his opinion of us."

She risked turning her head again to look at Broken Tongue. He was sitting by the fire again, legs crossed in front of him, the firelight casting him half in and half out of shadows. "Merci," she called, not expecting him to acknowledge her.

He didn't.

"Do you feel up to eating something?" Gabriel asked, moving away slightly. "We saved you some of the fish." He grimaced. "What didn't burn, anyway. But there's some left, and bread, if you can stomach it. Then I want you to move around a little before you sleep."

She thought about arguing, then thought about the elk keeping guard in the shadows, the way it had, she was certain, *winked* at her, and she nodded, allowing Gabriel to wrap a blanket around her shoulders and fetch a plate. Nothing else would happen tonight, she thought. Not while the guardian stood watch.

She looked up and saw the old man observing her. His face fell in shadows, but there was something that made her tense again, then glance to where she thought the elk stood. If she'd learned anything from traveling with Farron Easterly, it was that someone could be an ally and not be trustworthy. And "friends not yet made" did not promise friendship would occur.

She lifted her chin and stared back at the old man, black gaze steady against brown, until Gabriel came back with her dinner and they both looked away.

There was no birdsong. Gabriel noted that before he was fully awake: more proof that something was wrong, that there was danger lurking, even if he couldn't see it.

Caution prickling his skin, he slipped out from under his blanket, leaving the other two sleeping by the remains of the fire, and went down to the creek to wash his face. There was no sound to alert him, but when he looked up, the elk stood on the other bank, its antlers silhouetted by the pale dawn light rising behind them. He paused, half-bent to the creek, and watched the animal as it moved, placidly chewing at the grass, occasionally lifting its head to scent the air and then returning to the grass again.

The fact that it lingered was curious; that it had appeared not once but twice was both reassuring and worrisome. He had named it wapiti, but it had not spoken, had not offered unasked-for advice, and spirit-animals excelled at unwanted advice. And yet it was clearly more than an ordinary creature, no matter how it behaved now: it had acted with intelligence when it had let them pass, it had acted with intent the day before when it knocked Isobel away from whatever had been threatening her.

The thought drove him to pick up a stone and flip it, violently, down the creek, making two skips before sinking into the current. After knocking Isobel away, the wapiti had wheeled to face whatever had attacked her, placing itself as a barrier while grandfather darted forward to pull her to safety. An elk and an old man had been of more use than he'd managed, aware something was happening but blind to whatever it was. Useless.

And why is that, a voice asked him. *Why was grandfather able to see, and you were blind? Hnnn?*

The voice—mocking, but not unkind—was familiar. Old Woman had been the one to take a bedraggled, half-mad man out of the mud and teach him to breathe the Territory's air again. Not that he'd wanted to at the time.

You are what you are and this is the place where you are that, the Hochunk woman had told him, sucking thoughtfully on the pipe she carried with her at all times. It smelled like aged skunk to him, but he was never fool enough to say so. *The harder you ran from it, the harder it chased you. But it cannot catch you without you willing it so.*

Gabriel's back teeth ground against each other. He did not will it. He would not. He would not be *owned.*

The elk raised its head and looked at him, as though it had heard his thoughts. "Don't you lecture me either, elder cousin," he told it, and leant down to splash water on his face. When he looked up again, skin tingling from the cold, the elk was still staring at him.

"Do you want to be turned into pemmican?" he asked it, and it snorted once—laughter, Gabriel was certain of it—and departed, its hooves kicking in a graceful, thudding lope that covered ground faster than anything that large should move, leaving the grass upright and uncrushed in its wake.

Gabriel reached down again to touch one hand to the surface of the water, letting its chill cool his own skin, the *awareness* of water filling him. This was real, physical. He could sense where this narrow creek led, could trace back to its source higher in the mountains, the thick packed snow that fed it, the tiny rivulets and deep-down springs that connected to it. Like the Road, it was all one. All connected.

It was also seductive, that feeling, coaxing him in until he would drown of it. Gabriel jerked his hand back as though the water had suddenly become steam-hot, wiping it against his pant leg.

"No." He looked out where the elk had disappeared to, then up into the sky, wispy white clouds moving east to west, echoes of his dreams carried in their shapes. "No."

He refilled the canteens he'd brought with him, carefully, not allowing his hands to linger in the water, and went back to rejoin the others.

Isobel was sitting next to the rebuilt fire, combing out her hair. In profile, the strong bones that had first drawn his eye were even more apparent now, the softness of saloon life worn to finer lines. She would never have been pretty, but something drew the eye and left it there to linger. Her hair was brighter than the old man's, reddish highlights glinting in the black, and her flesh wasn't the same copper, but with the two of them sitting together by the fire, for a moment he was all too aware of his paler skin and blue eyes. Never mind that he'd been born to the Territory same as she, that his father and grandfather had been hunters in the Wilds; in that instant, he was an outsider.

And who holds blame for that? Old Woman asked again in his thoughts before he shoved her out.

"You have water?" Isobel's question broke the moment, and he nodded, handing her one of the canteens. She placed her comb down on her knee and poured the water into the battered tin pot, placing it on the tripod to bring the chicory-and-coffee mixture to a boil. Then she sifted her fingers into her hair, swiftly plaiting the long strands into a single braid.

He sat down and watched her face, how her lips pursed, bright eyes hooded as she concentrated on what she could feel between her fingers rather than what she could see. There was an intensity to her that he'd admired since the first he saw her, a determination to do, to *be* something, with an intensity that would accept no obstacles.

It was a quality he'd admired, even knowing it attracted trouble the way a carcass attracted buzzards.

"How are you feeling?"

"Better." Her hands didn't pause until she reached the end of the braid, tying it off with the loop of leather cord he'd cut for her. She then reached into her pack and pulled out the two small feathers Calls Thunder had given her, back in De Plata, one greyish-blue, one banded white-and-black, both slightly ruffled along the edges now, each barely the size of his thumb. She wove them into the braid with that same nimble surety and seemed oblivious to the fact that her actions had attracted the old man's attentions.

"Tsigili," he said. "Et jasur."

Isobel looked at the old man, then at Gabriel, clearly expecting a translation.

"Je m'excuse, qu'est-ce que vous avez dit?"

The old man gestured at Isobel with two fingers held upright. "Des plumes."

It was, Gabriel thought, a question more than a statement. "Étant données à elle par la parleur-des-rêves dans De Plata." If the feathers did have some medicine-meaning, better the old man know Isobel had been gifted them by someone with the authority to do so, rather than claiming them for herself.

The old man pursed his lips, dropped his fingers, and that seemed to be the extent of his interest.

Gabriel pushed, delicately. "Vous savez ce que signifient-ils, grand-papa?"

He grunted. "Le devin et le potin, le messager." More pursed lips, then, almost grudgingly: "Elle comporte de nombreux symboles forts."

Isobel was watching them, her gaze flicking alertly between them. "What did he say?"

"Your feathers. I told you someone would know what they meant."

Her expression livened at that. He had told her that feathers meant something, but he hadn't known what, specifically, and Calls Thunder, who had given them to her, hadn't explained.

"And?"

"The birds they come from, one is far-seeing, the other carries messages." Gossip, the old man'd said, but Gabriel wasn't going to tell her that. "He says that they're strong medicine."

"But what do they mean?"

Gabriel was suddenly immensely tired. "I don't know. Calls Thunder gave them to you, so I'll assume that it's for you to learn, not me."

Her face fell, and she cast her gaze down toward her lap. "I only gave them a hairpin," she said, soft-voiced, reaching up to touch the feathers gently. "It didn't *mean* anything."

He hadn't expected her thoughts to turn in that direction. He forgot, at times, that she was barely past sixteen; for all that the devil had laid on her, for all the power she held, she was still in many ways so very young.

"Was it something you treasured?" He knew it was; the hairpin had been made from bone polished smooth from care and use. "That was all Calls Thunder would consider, if you gave them something you valued in return."

Gabriel had long suspected that the dream-talker had given Isobel not a gift but a marker. Isobel of Flood, Isobel Devil's Hand, could claim no special standing among natives. By giving her those feathers, he thought, Calls Thunder had marked her as someone of worth, of power. They might be enough to keep her safe in awkward situations, if she stepped wrong or the Agreement was in doubt.

Might. He would not rely on them, nor allow her to, either.

"The thing that attacked me, in the circle." She changed the subject as she took the coffee pot, now boiled, off the tripod and poured it into mugs, giving the first one to the old man. "I thought at first it might be a haint, that someone had died here and not been properly warded. But the feel of it . . . was wrong." She paused, then handed him the second cup. "Haints sorrow, and sometimes they're fierce-mad. But this didn't . . . this didn't feel right."

Gabriel blew on his coffee to cool it, then took a sip and winced. She'd over-boiled it again. "Well, it wasn't a fetch, or we'd be trying to sew our faces back on."

"I don't know what it was." Her voice was tight, too high, and he waited while she stirred what was left in the coffee pot, frowning at the grounds as though they could tell her something but wouldn't.

"You think whatever it is"—he made a vague gesture with his cup—"is causing the quakes?" It would follow: this was where the old man said the quakes began. "And the magicians . . . were they trying to contain it, or did they create it?" His bet would be on the latter.

"I don't know. Yes. Whatever happened there, it's tied in somehow. I just . . . Magicians. Plural. That's worrying."

Her matter-of-fact tone surprised a laugh out of him. "Just a bit, yes."

"Corbeau, pas de buse," the old man said, and lifted his mug to indicate the area behind them. "Ils ne sont pas . . . ici juste pour manger la vieille viande." His hands lifted and spread, one following the other to the right, then down. "Ils sont venus pleins de connaissances, et les bêtes sont parties, et le ciel est devenu vide, et la terre a tremblé." And then he stopped, as though he had run out of words.

"They . . . came full of knowledge? And the beasts left, the skies emptied, and the ground trembled," Gabriel translated, although he wasn't quite sure he'd gotten it entirely correct. It made no sense to him, and from Isobel's expression, she fared no better.

"Ground trembled" was reasonably clear, though.

Isobel jerked her head as though dislodging an unhappy thought, then reached over and took the mug out of his hands, drinking half the contents in one long pull before handing it back. "And the magicians? Did they flee too when the ground shook?"

When Gabriel asked him, the old man lifted his shoulders in a gesture that needed no translation. He did not know.

Isobel had just refilled the mug with the last of the coffee, Gabriel scraping the last bit of corn mash and honey from his plate, when the old man stood up without a word, walking away from the fire. They watched as he clucked to his pony, sliding the woven halter over its head and draping his pack over its back like a blanket.

"He's leaving?" Isobel glanced at her mug, then at the camp's morning disarray. "Are we supposed to follow?"

Gabriel made no move to get up. "I don't think so. He's satisfied his curiosity and led us to where we needed to be. He's done."

"But . . ." Isobel stopped herself from complaining like a child, biting her upper lip. She didn't like the old man, and he clearly didn't have much use for her or her boss, but he had helped them when he'd no obligation to do so. Isobel had no right to ask more of him. She stood up, stepping in front of the old man and his pony before they could leave.

"Merci," she said, and made one of the few gestures she knew for certain, hands up and palm down, fingertips pointed at the old man and sweeping in until her thumbs pointed at her own chest, almost a reverse of the boss's gesture when he spoke of the Territory. "Thank you."

He looked at her then, and his right hand clenched and rested over his heart, then he brought a single finger up and touched his forehead, opened his hand and placed it palm down at his heart again, sliding it out to the right. Then he smiled, a narrow squint of his eyes more than his mouth, and reached forward, his finger pausing just shy of touching her, before his hand clenched again and dropped to hip high.

"He says you are wise," Gabriel said behind her. "A child still, but wise."

She felt her eyebrows go up but kept her voice civil. "I suppose that's his way of saying 'well done'?"

"More or less." She could hear the laughter in her mentor's voice, and her own mouth quirked up in response, even through her frustration. The old man nodded once at Gabriel, then got on his pony and left.

We don't say goodbye on the Road, Gabriel had taught her. *The Road curves around on itself, and you just assume you'll meet again.* She didn't know that she ever particularly wanted to see the old man again, but it was an odd comfort, nonetheless, to think that she might.

"So, what now?" Gabriel asked once the pony had ambled out of sight. "Do we go? Stay?"

Something cold stirred in Isobel's gut at the question. The presence had left them alone during the night, but it still lingered, trapped in its own pain. Something terrible had been done to it here, something that reached out beyond this place, as far down as Jumping-Up Duck's people, and maybe farther than that.

"I need to find out what happened here," she said, turning to face him, half-expecting argument or outright refusal. Instead, Gabriel simply sighed and poured the dregs of the coffee over their fire, listening to the flames hiss down into embers.

"Of course you do. Which means we'll be chasing after magicians."

Isobel ducked her head at the expression on his face, an odd, determined distaste. "Not yet. First, I need to settle the haint."

"No. Absolutely not." He spoke even before she'd finished, his words trying to drown out her own. He'd stood up too, his arms crossed against his chest. She was tall for a woman, but he could still tilt his head and look down, making her feel like a little girl scolded for doing a poor job sweeping the floor.

She opened her mouth to continue, to explain, and he cut her off. "Last time, it was only the wapiti and the old man who saved you, Isobel. And neither of them are here now."

Of all the objections he might have raised, that she hadn't expected. "You're here."

"I'm useless." He spat the words out, then stopped, drawing a quick breath as though he hadn't meant to say them, was trying to pull them back. Isobel blinked at him in shock, then crossed arms across her own chest, refusing to retreat further.

"I can't do what you do," he said, softer this time. "Even the old man could see it, could see you were in trouble, and I just . . . stood there." His jaw clenched, and he rubbed at his face as though exhausted. "I can teach you how to behave around marshals and unfriendly miners, I can talk my way past bandits and natives, but Isobel, when you throw yourself into the crossroads, I can't help you."

"That's not . . . I'm not asking you to." Her voice wobbled a little, and she fixed it, irritated. "You said it yourself: I'm the silver. I need to find what's wrong and fix it."

Devil's silver, he'd called her. Throw her at something that felt wrong and draw the power out, make it safe again. She rubbed the fresh-polished ring on her little finger, watching it glint in the sunlight.

"I have to do this, Gabriel." She didn't look at him as she spoke, her gaze trained on the ring and the black lines in her palm. "It might stop the quakes, might . . ."

"Might. Fine word. Or it might—"

Destroy her. He needn't say it out loud. Silver, in the presence of power, tarnished. Too much tarnish and it became useless.

"It's not a choice I'm making. I *have* to."

"I know." Anger and frustration laced his voice, but it wasn't loud anymore, and she risked looking up at him then. He had turned away, looking east, the morning sun warm on his face, highlighting the lines at his eyes, the faint strands of grey in his scruff, features as familiar and dear now as any she'd known since birth. "I don't like it, but I know."

"I'm sorry." She wasn't quite sure what she was apologizing for, but there was something under his words, dark and swift, that made her ache.

And then she was engulfed, his arms around her shoulders, the familiar, comforting smell of him wrapped around her, and she let her cheek rest against the rough cloth of his shirt, feeling his breath rise and fall.

"Ah, half the time we're chasing into or after things pell-mell, we haven't the chance to set things to order first. This'll make for a nice change," Gabriel said, his voice the rough drawl she hadn't heard since the saloon, the one that made him sound charming, harmless, made a person think he wasn't smart or dangerous.

But he was—smart and dangerous. And he trusted her to be the same.

"It's just a cleansing," she told him, intentionally flippant, to match his tone. "Nothing different than draining a crossroads or calming a spell-beast with blood in its mouth."

"Oh, yes," and the drawl was definitely on full display. "Nothing to worry about there at all."

She twisted slightly, and he let her go, stepping back a pace. "How do we do this, then?"

She had no idea. "Take the horses a bit farther off. In case—" She looked at the roped-off ground where the grass had died, where she could still see faint traces of steam rising from the ground, even if Gabriel couldn't. "In case something happens."

He nodded, neither of them discussing what that "something" might be. Her relief at not having to explain was measured by a desire that he would stop her, refuse to let her do this.

She knew he wouldn't, that wish only the remnant of her fear, burnt to ash but still clinging to her skin. Something here had scraped power from the Territory. Scraped it, taken it . . . and kept it here. By what, or for what purpose, she could not tell, but even if the haint had not lingered, that much power threw things off-balance, perhaps enough to shake the ground, scare away those who lived near it. A magician might claim it, or a marshal might drain it, but neither of those were here now.

And the haint . . .

She felt again the aching, sorrowful rage, and shuddered.

"Salt."

Gabriel, in the middle of moving the horses and their packs to the requested distance, reached into her pack and tossed her the cloth-wrapped bundle that contained what was left of her salt stick. She held it in her hand, weighing it against how much she might need, then walked to where she'd felt the presence most strongly before, at the edge of the browned, dying grass.

The last time she'd done anything like this, she'd been driven by something other than her own will, the knowing of what to do rising up from within her when she needed it. She felt none of that now, as though she were still cut off from the bones, the deep stone, leaving her bare and alone.

"Boss? A little help, please?"

She waited, a breath caught in her chest. No whisper filled her ears, no sense of what to do slipped into her thoughts, only her palm, itching, and the weighted awareness of *something* lurking, tied to this meadow, this ground. Not the haint: something deeper, warmer. A whisper of resignation, then a tentative touch of strength, protection, *belonging*, followed by the tingling prickle of the wind over bare skin.

Isobel exhaled. Something had changed. She didn't, couldn't stop to question it; whatever had responded wasn't the boss, but it was enough to know that she had allies here, somehow.

She crumbled some of the salt into her hand and started walking out a circle, then stopped. "No." She licked the salt off her palm, then took a few steps back and handed the stick to Gabriel, who, finished with the horses, had been waiting, watching. "Draw it around me."

His gaze flickered from the salt to her, then he picked up where she had left off, leaving a faint, glistening line of salt in a circle just outside where she'd roped off, white against the grass where the dead turned to green again.

While he did that, Isobel walked inside the circle, letting an awareness of the protection he was laying down flutter against her skin. She was within, contained but not constrained, the warding silent until something came to rouse it.

"Be at ease," she whispered to whatever watched them. "Be at ease; I bring no harm."

Dead grass above, something seething below. Isobel worried her lower lip between her teeth, not-thinking, not-feeling, simply walking, careful of where she placed her steps, watching where the steam rose in narrow tendrils, then faded into the clear. Walking an inner circle until she felt the sense of whatever had attacked her ease: not gone, but no longer quite so vigilant, so tense.

Salt around them and silver within. For cleansing, every child learned. For protection. The buckles on Gabriel's belt, the ring on her finger, the coins they carried in their pockets. Polished bright. Crumbled salt and polished silver, rising from the waters and the deep bones. But they were tools, only tools. Were they the right tools?

What else dealt with power?

Isobel reversed her steps, tracing the circle widdershins.

The lands they'd ridden through had been scraped dry. A crossroads gathered power, became dangerous, and needed to be cleansed on a regular basis. Every child knew that. But a crossroads drained would seek to refill itself. A land that had been scraped dry . . . what would it do?

There was something she was missing, some detail she hadn't been able to glean. The quakes, the missing animals, the slaughtered buffalo, the haint lurking . . . She could feel the thread connecting them slide across her fingers, and she realized she'd veered from the circle she'd been walking, creating a new pattern within: the double-ended loop of the Devil's *infinitas*.

Let it happen, came the thought scented with amber whiskey and the taste of warm, sweet smoke.

Step and drag, the toe of her boots leaving no visible sign in the crackling brown grass, then step and drag with her other foot, alternating carefully, completing one loop, then a diagonal crossing in the middle, slanted crossroads that sent a spark up her heel, ricocheting along her spine as she crossed it, then another loop, slow and careful, at the other end.

She knew that Gabriel had finished the outer circle, could feel the moment it was completed, an almost audible snap under her own voice, and it was only then that she realized she was humming, a nonsense lullaby one of the girls used to sing to their baby.

"Sweet drop of water, from lake you flow
   sweet drop of water, into river you go.
   Silver your cup, and medicine your bone."

Another pass of the loop, another spark up her spine, tingling along her scalp when she crossed the midpoint, and then a third time, until something told her she was done.

Isobel paused at the center point, planting her heels one on either side, and wiped sweaty hands against her skirt. The ground hadn't cracked open below her; the steam hadn't burned through her soles or tangled around her ankles. The distant echo of *flickerthwack* sounded somewhere in her memory, the devil's hands turning the cards, and she could feel the odds flip slightly in her favor.

Maybe.

The sun had risen enough to be in her eyes while she worked, and even with her hat shading her face, she had to squint, turning to find Gabriel standing on the other side of the circle, watching her, his back to the east so it seemed almost as though the sunlight haloed him.

"Whatever you're going to do," he said, his voice low but carrying, "best do it now, before the sun's too high."

Dawn and dusk and the high point of noon: that was when a magician's power was greatest, at the times of winds and transition, a good time for wise folk to be still and not draw attention to themselves.

Isobel grinned back at him. She was about to draw attention to herself in a most significant fashion.

She gathered her skirt in both hands and settled on the grass, letting her fingertips rest on the ground. She could feel something—not the shadowy presence, something deeper, hotter—moving below, pressing against her, but she ignored it, instead focusing on the sigil on her palm, the black lines echoed in the soil around her. The authority of the Master of the Territory, carried within her.

Power was power, Gabriel'd said once. The trick wasn't what you were given—or how—but how you used it.

The sigil itched, then burned, pale blue flame engulfing her palm for an instant before racing up her arm, down her spine, her muscles twitching and her eyes watering, sparks scraping from the inside out, making her laugh with relief: the bones might refuse her, the boss might not be able to find her, but she still could do this.

Reassured, she pressed her palms into the ground and whistled for the winds.

And they came. Eight winds, four by four, pushing each other like restless colts, hungry cats. They came not because she summoned them but because they chose to, simply because they could.

Magicians whistled for the winds and let them blow through, emptying out what had been and replacing it with . . . She felt the touch of the winds on her and knew, understood, dimly, distantly, the sweeping hunger that could never be appeased, only redirected.

Power fed on power.

The boss and Marie had taught her how to treat power; Gabriel had shown her how to speak to elders; Farron had warned her of the temptations of madness. Isobel held those doors closed, contained herself, allowed the winds to probe and push without giving them domain over her, without allowing them *within* her. *I belong to another.*

Amusement returned, tumbling, sly laughter, but they did not provoke her claim. There was no malice in the winds, nor kindness, nor humor, only power, relentless and rising.

Isobel thought of figures gathered together in this space, figures of wind and flesh, then imbued the image with curiosity, a question. *Will you share with me knowledge of a thing, free ones?*

The breeze cooled, swirled. Power had risen here, given flesh and form, but they cared nothing for the how or why. Nothing of flesh interested them for long.

Thank you for—

She felt the air swirl once more and then fall still before she could complete her thanks. She was flesh and boring.

But something lingered outside the second circle, behind where Gabriel sat with his hat pulled down over his eyes, his body propped against the bulk of his kit, the horses and mule behind him, stirring restlessly. The remains of their fire, the warm smell of chicory dumped over coals still lingering in the air. And the smell of something else, sulphur and yeast and warm, sweet smoke.

Isobel reached for it, then hesitated. Nothing died as quickly as a fool in the Territory. Another one of the boss's sayings when he was feeling particularly acerbic. Isobel could see him leaning back in his chair, unlit cigar tucked between his fingers, a glass of whiskey at his elbow, watching the people watching him out of the corner of their eyes, that half-smile on his face as though she were listening to him tell stories while she swept the floor, a child of ten again.

If this were the haint that lingered, it was no friend to her. And if it were the presence that she had felt lingering around it . . .

She had no proof it was a friend to her, either.

But stopping here accomplished nothing.

She closed her eyes, feeling the snap and spark of the sigil within her, molten under her touch, filling the lines of the *infinitas* drawn in the ground, filling the black lines on her palm, filling the shape of it within her. Then her eyesight blurred and her head spun, something more than herself taking over her body.

Isobel resisted, scrabbling for control, until she felt a faint familiar brush across her ear, not words but sensation, impulse. Command. *Come.*

She knew it, knew it as her own blood, as the sound of sunlight and the weight of rain, trusted it as she had not trusted the winds. She let go, let it wrap around her, let it show her what it would.

Dizziness rocked her, then her sight sharpened again, painfully bright. The grass covering the meadow was still green and healthy, tiny flowers scattered throughout, but where insects should have chirped and birds hopped after them, there was nothing. Where animals should have burrowed and hunted, there was emptiness.

No, not emptiness. Not the void she had thought it before. The animals and insects had not fled but been pushed, the space left behind filled by such rage and sorrow it became impossible to remain, impossible to exist in its presence.

This was what she had touched before. The emptiness that had rejected her—had pushed her away rather than allow her to be consumed.

She did not attempt to speak to it this time, did not engage, but let the wards Gabriel had drawn sustain her, let herself breathe against the awareness of them, then past them, sinking into the sigil drawn around her, the hot breath of what commanded her.

And then she let herself sink into that space.

Wind. Fire. Restless, scorched heat, enough to darken the soil, set an entire mountain aflame. Not lightning, nothing so mindless, but more powerful, alive, drawn by force from the skies and driven into the stone. Nothing human, nothing even once-human. Something angry, something lost.

Something *old*.

Gabriel Kasun hadn't survived a childhood in the Territory, nor studying law back in the States, without learning how to deal with situations he did not like. The first rule was to take as much control as he could and let go of everything he couldn't.

After completing the circle of salt, he paused until the warding clicked into place, then pulled his pack over to make a seat and settled himself to wait. Often things happened fast, sometimes they happened slow, and there was no force of his making that could decide which it would be.

He looked for the wapiti, but if Isobel's guardian was still around, it was not showing itself. That was either reassuring or worrisome.

He checked Isobel next; she had seated herself on the ground, her right hand now resting on her knee, her left hand on the ground beside her. Her face was calm, eyes open but seeing something he could only imagine, wisps of hair floating loose from her braid and framing her face. He turned and looked over the rest of the meadow. Nothing soared in the sky, nothing rustled in the grass, and he had the sudden disturbing sensation of being the only living thing between the mountains he could see and the river he could sense.

Then the mule brayed and Uvnee called back, a scuffle indicating that someone had bitten someone else, and the sensation broke.

"The worms are still here, at least," he told himself. "If we die, they will have a suitable feast."

It was a thought he'd had before; it still didn't help.

Restless, he took out his boot knife and checked the blade, noting that the silver inlay had tarnished again already. He pulled out a strip of linen and cleaned the discoloration away, then tested the knife's edge and, satisfied, slid it back into its sheath. As he bent forward, something caught his eye, glinting in the sunlight.

Caution warred with curiosity. Anything here and now would be suspect; something that called to him now, when Isobel was vulnerable . . .

And yet she was protected within the circle he had made, as safe as anything might be—safer than he was, most likely. And that glint might be something that would lead them to answers to what had been done here and by whom . . .

He rose to his feet, moving carefully toward where the glint had appeared. Tracking a thing that did not move was more difficult than one that did, but it was not impossible, and the angle of the sun aided him, reflecting light when he moved his head just so, revealing its location.

Gabriel crouched but hesitated before reaching for it. Was it a trap? Would this lead him into the claws of whatever had attacked Isobel?

If it did, the distraction might give Isobel more time to do whatever it was she was doing.

With that thought, he turned his head to check on her one more time; she hadn't moved, far as he could tell, save both her hands were now resting palm down on the ground, her head bowed, the brim of her hat hiding her face entirely. The grass under her seemed tipped with a greenish light, the strands moving as though brushed by a breeze, but the air was unpleasantly still where he stood, sweat forming under his arms and under his hat in a way that couldn't be blamed solely on the sun. His mouth was dry, and he rubbed the back of one hand against his lips, feeling the chapped skin catch and pull. The air was dryer here than he was accustomed to; it burned the inside of his nose and throat unpleasantly.

Irritated by his own hesitation, Gabriel leaned forward, keeping his weight on his heels, and closed his fingers around the source of the reflected light. His brain told him it was small, and metal, and cool, even as he was standing up, moving backward, away from the dubious patch of grass, back toward Isobel—and the stick of salt still resting on top of his pack.

Only then did he open his hand and examine what he'd found.

"Hail and high water," he swore, closing his fingers over it as though that might make the object disappear or change into something else. But when he took a deep breath and opened them again, it was still there, a simple bronze circle with three words stamped into it: JUSTICE. INTEGRITY. SERVICE.

The badge of a US Marshal.

Gabriel had encountered more than a few of that breed in his time, and for the most part they'd been straightforward, solid men. Not the sort to be found so far from their domain, and assuredly not without orders.

"What were you doing here, Marshal?" he asked the badge. "And what did you stumble into?"

. . . *Our new president has determined the need to send a surveying team across the Mississippi and into the Territory you call home. He names it a 'Corps of Discovery' and claims it a simple excursion to survey this new land beyond our known borders.*

"You wouldn't . . . ," he breathed to a man sitting in a faraway city, who could never hear his words. "Oh, you couldn't."

No. If Jefferson wished to send men into the Territory, he would use the scouts that already had clear passage by the devil's mercy. Not a marshal. Not someone with official standing, consequences.

Mayhap the badge had been stolen? They were not particularly valuable, conferred no particular authority without a letter of warrant. One of those gathered here might have picked it up: who knew what a magician might take; they were all mad, and as prone to mischief as a crow.

He tried to imagine a marshal coming west, turning magician, and failed utterly. Impossible. Or improbable enough to be impossible.

Gabriel turned the badge over in his hand, as though studying it might give him some better answer. It was a simple hammered circle, the star embossed on one side, words on the other, similar if not identical to the ones he'd seen back in Philadelphia.

It had been years since he'd been in the States, but he remembered it well—the energy, the vigor . . . and the sense that they were already pushing at their limits, the eagerness among politicians, farmers, and merchants alike to expand their hold.

Exhausted, worried, uncertain, Gabriel admitted to himself that Jefferson's initiative was not merely academic curiosity, nor that it would end with a simple survey. The reports the scouts carried back would speak of expanses of open land, and in those distant rooms, someone with more greed than sense would think the tales of the devil myth and superstition, that the land waited only for a steady hand to take it.

He thought of Isobel's friend April, who looked to the east, who hungered for the things modern civilization could bring. Her friend, and others who thought that way, were fools. Gabriel had lived in the civilized world, if only for a few years. Had spent time in the web that its politics and laws wove, binding them to each other, constantly compromising. He knew what came with civilization and the cost those things demanded.

He closed his fingers around the badge once again and slipped it into his pocket. Marshal or no, surveyors or no, it didn't matter. The devil had held the Territory safe against Spanish and French incursions for hundreds of years. If the States thought they would have a different result, they would learn otherwise.

And with that thought, Gabriel turned back to Isobel and forgot everything else.

With a dizzying jolt, Isobel dropped back into the cage of her own flesh. One shuddering breath, then another, and she settled within herself again, the keening memory fading to something more bearable. But she could see it now: sinew and hide stitched with power, dry channels of bone without blood or sweat to soften it, a raging spirit caught within it.

Trapped.

Isobel stood, her knees still uncertain under her weight. Her toes were cold within her boots, her fingers numb, as though it were winter and not nearly mid-summer, and she was hollow as though she'd not eaten for weeks, a dry scraping hunger that made her thoughts muddled and her limbs weak.

It had tried to consume her and nearly succeeded. Nearly. But she had its measure now: immense pain and rage, bound by sorrow. It could not rise into the winds; it could not dive into the earth. Trapped, not within the circle the magicians had carved, but in the narrow band of the living, trapped between stone and air. What had the magicians attempted, what had they thought to capture, and how had it gone so horribly wrong?

The horses shifted and shied as though they too felt it, the mule kicking fitfully. Isobel suspected that, like the dogs, only their loyalty kept them here when all other animals had fled.

How had the magicians caged such a thing, and why?

"Because they were fools," she said, her words sounding hollow and flat within the circles. "And because they were mad." Magicians dared where most would cower, because there was only one goal they reached for: to become more powerful simply for the sake of power. Farron had admitted it without shame. He would have consumed her, too, if she had faltered.

The spirit had been ancient and powerful. . . . Having been touched by the winds, she could near imagine how a magician might salivate over such a thing.

But Farron had also told them that magicians did not gather together, that when two met, they would destroy each other. Had he lied? Possibly: she had liked Farron but she would not trust him. Or perhaps something had made his words into a lie. Whatever had been intended, only one question mattered: should she continue? If she cleansed the bindings and released it—if she *could* release it—would that fix what they had done or worsen it?

This was no mortal thing to be read and understood, to be influenced, however skillfully. It was more, and greater, and Isobel felt the scratch of fear as she realized that the moment she pushed through the protection of her circle-and-loops, the moment she touched that presence again, despite her protections, it could easily destroy her.

That fear scratched deeper, cracking her confidence. Something had tried to keep her from this, had known she wasn't enough to face it. Had shown her what was bound here, what would destroy her.

"You weren't trying to stop me," she murmured to it, as though talking to one of the cats that crowded the alley behind the saloon, half-wild but crowding for kitchen scraps. "I think you were trying to protect me, weren't you? But I'm here now. Let me help."

Kneeling again, placing her hand down against the grass, Isobel breathed in deeply once and then exhaled, sinking as deeply into the ground as it would allow her.

Something waited, just beyond the void, shimmering and alive. Isobel did not reach for it but waited. If she had eyes, she would avert her gaze; had she hands, she would fold them at her sides; had she form, she would stand tall, not proud but strong.

"I am Isobel née Lacoyo Távora, Isobel of Flood, the Left Hand. My blood is on the devil's Contract, his sigil on my palm."

Forever in waiting, encased in the void, fear scrabbling at her, the memory of those claws tearing at her, the sensation of nothingness, of being forever trapped until she lost all sense of self and name . . .

"I am Isobel née Lacoyo Távora, Daughter of Flood, Devil's Hand, the cold eye and the quick knife, and this is my responsibility."

Something moved within the shimmer, heavy and slow. If the earth could sigh, it would sound thus.

Come. Not a command this time, not an invitation, simply direction. It led her along the surface fissures, dipping deep into the earth, stroking along the roots that grew there, and she sensed the bindings that held the presence to the valley, deep bone and soil wrapped around it, smothering its flames, air pressing down over it, flattening its wings, and how they shivered desperately for release, revenge.

And each time it shivered, the earth did as well. She could feel it, her fingers curled around its tendrils, a quiver in the flesh of her leg, a tremor in the bone of her elbow, impotent rage finding the only outlet it could reach. The sky pressed on her, the bones reached for her, and she allowed it, felt herself flatten and fade.

we fight for power, she understood.

The haint had no voice save to howl. The shivering didn't slow, the furious and frustrated anger sharp and clear as icicles, loud as hail against a wooden roof. It bit at them, battered them, trying to find a lie in their words, a weakness in their defenses it could lash out against. If the magicians had been mad, so too was their victim. Mad, and filled with the power it had scraped from earth and wind before it was caged. There would be no reasoning with it, no freeing it. It was ancient, and mad, and desired only to destroy.

Hold, the whisper asked of her, pressing her down further. *Wait. Hold.* It would hold forever, but Isobel could not. The haint sensed her weakness, claws scrabbling, tearing her inside out the better to feast on what was within, jealous and resentful; she had come to it and it would keep her, all that she was, for the price of what had been done to it.

Isobel felt it within her, howled her own rage, and as though summoned, the void flowed, molten and hot, pumping around and into and through her, forcing the haint back enough that Isobel could pull at that flow, drawing one swirl then another in pure instinct, looping in her thoughts; *You will not consume me.*

A desperate, flailing *thudthudthud* of hollow-boned wings battered at her, then there was a cold flare where her palm would be, and Isobel screamed, her eyes—*she had eyes again and hands and form*—opening to find herself covered in sweat, gritty with dust, still sitting in the middle of the *infinitas* warding, in the middle of Gabriel's circle.

Beneath her, the presence raged, still trapped, still lost, but it could not touch her.

When she looked up, Gabriel was on his knees just outside the circle, his hat off and his face visible in the light . . . the fading light—how long had she . . . It didn't matter, save that now she could feel the hunger rumbling inside her ribs, the ache that came from sitting too long without movement, the slow fade of the molten silver from her blood, until she was only flesh and bone again.

She lifted a hand to her face, and her fingertips came away grimy and wet, her eyes sticky and sore. "I am Isobel née Lacoyo Távora," she said, barely able to speak, her throat thick and swollen. "I am the Devil's Hand, the strength of the Territory, and you will not have me."

Gabriel made a motion as though to reach for her, then checked it. "What happened?" His voice was cracked, as though he'd been yelling.

"It . . ." Pity and despair and grief chewed on her, understanding what she had seen burned into her bones like a brand. "They trapped a spirit, something old and powerful." *Something beautiful.* "They pulled it from the air and trapped it, *reshaped* it the way we carve wood to make a boat that they would ride. . . ." Great, choking sobs wracked her, pulling the dust from within to scatter on the trampled-down grass in front of her. Gabriel reached across his wardings then, breaking them without ceremony, and pulled her into his arms, his body sheltering her as she wept, the *infinitas* under their knees glowing with a faint green light.

Gabriel felt as though someone had dragged him through a berry bramble—the price for breaking his ward-line so roughly—but that was the least of his concerns. Once Isobel cried herself out, he'd reached back for his canteen and rinsed her mouth, her spittle laced with a greyish-blue foam that he didn't want to think about. After her first flood of words, she'd gone silent, shaking and shivering, her skin cold to the touch, then flaring too warm before going cold again.

He had no idea what to do, so he left her there, within what remained of the wards and the fading green glow, and fetched blankets and another canteen of water, and came back to her, draping her in the blankets and letting her rest against his shoulder until the worst seemed to pass and her shivering calmed.

This was Isobel, he told himself. Izzy.

The sun dropped lower in the sky, turning it a pale red along the ragged edge of the horizon. The horses shuffled closer to the circle, the mule going so far as to push his black-and-brown muzzle over the salt line where he had broken it, to sniff at the humans within before drawing back. But there were no other sounds: no howl of a coyote or wolf pack, no chittering of insects, no cry of birds overhead, not even the slough of wind down from the hills to rustle the grass. It was uncanny, as the girl next to him was uncanny, and the urge to saddle up and ride away, alone, shivered through his own body, even as he held her to him.

There were things simply accepted in the Territory. Spirit-talkers and dust-walkers, the danger of crossroads and the power contained within the bones. The power of the Devil to make his end of a bargain come through. Medicine that filled this land, even as those beyond its borders had forgotten it, or burned it to the ground. But an ancient spirit was something else entire. Near every tribe had a story of things that had hunted before man was shaped from dust and water; Gabriel could retell half a dozen himself, and he was certain there were more he hadn't heard, ranging from the all-powerful to merely dangerous. . . .

Stories. Legend. Myth.

How many magicians had it taken to bind it? And why? And what had happened to them after? He wasn't sure he wanted to know the answers to those questions, save to the most important one: how did they—how did Isobel—release it without it killing them, too?

"I can't."

Isobel's response was so soft, her face turned against his shoulder, he barely heard it. He hadn't realized he'd asked the question out loud, then wondered if he, in fact, had.

"What they did, they *changed* it. It can't go back, can't . . ." She hiccupped again and stopped speaking. He wrapped his arm around her shoulders and pulled her closer, willing his own body heat to calm her again.

"It killed them," she said finally. "The ones who did this. Not all, I don't think. But some. Most. They're . . . they're trapped too."

He didn't want to know more. He suspected they would both be having night terrors for months to come, even now.

"So, what can we do?" He rested his chin on the top of her head, reassured when she shrugged him off, glaring up at him. Her eyes were still red-rimmed and glassy, but the spark that had first drawn his attention had returned.

"Find them," she said. "The ones that escaped. Find those bastards and—"

Anything she was going to suggest was cut off when her jaw snapped shut and her eyes went wide. He followed her gaze and felt his own jaw unhinge partially in shock. Not a pace away, just outside the trail of salt, a massive bird folded its wings and cocked its head at them.

A Reaper.

Gabriel had only ever seen them from below, soaring far overhead. The thing was as monstrous on the ground as it seemed in the air, even with its wings folded back, the talons long as fingers and covered with scales, digging restlessly into the ground below, flexing and releasing in a way that was near mesmerizing. Its breast was dun-colored, the wings banded brown and cream, and the massive, bald head boasted a dark, heavily hooked beak, and a ruff of brown feathers folded back over wide-set eyes that held a distressing intelligence.

Gabriel forced his gaze away, then flicked back to it, refusing to be cowed or intimidated.

That hooked beak opened and a shrill cry emerged, making his bowels vibrate in sympathy, and a shiver of fear broke his bravado like kindling.

"Little sister."

It took Gabriel a heartbeat to realize that the sound had come from the bird, carried under a second harsh cry. Beneath his arm, Isobel shuddered as though ice had touched her skin or someone had told her bad news. But when she responded, her voice sounded as composed as though the bird had just asked her if she wanted another cup of tea.

"I am honored, elder brother."

Uncanny, Gabriel thought again, cold sweat prickling his brow. Always call a spirit-animal cousin; do not presume on the relationship; do not—but the Reaper hawk had called her little sister first.

"You are not honored; you are terrified." The bird shrieked again, raw laughter shuddering underneath it; there was no humor in that laughter but the cruel pleasure of a predator sensing prey. Gabriel forced himself to take a slow, quiet breath through his mouth, then out through his nose, calming his heartbeat and trusting Isobel's instincts, despite every instinct of his own.

"I am honored that you have chosen not to eat us," she responded, a hint of sass in her tone, despite the tremble Gabriel could feel in her body, and suddenly she was familiar again, his Isobel. "And I assume that you have reason for that, and for bringing yourself to ground to speak to me."

The Reaper hawk tilted its head, the heavy, curved beak opening and closing with a clack. "Is that how you speak to your master, little sister?"

There was just a hitch, a hesitation, as Isobel considered and then chose to ignore whatever insult the bird had intended. "Yes, actually. It amuses him."

It likely did. Gabriel had spent only two days in Flood, but the devil had never shown a preference for truckling, and his sense of humor had been as dark as his coffee.

"Does it amuse you, knowing that he sent you here to die?" The beady golden eyes fixed on her, the head tilting to the other side, its neck stretching out, feathers ruffling as the sharp black beak came too close—but still remained on the other side of the salt line. Gabriel thought that something held it back. His warding-skills were good but they were not that good, not with the salt line broken. Something else protected them.

"He didn't . . ." But Isobel's certainty faltered.

"He sent you out into the world without a hint of what you would need, what you would see, what you would be called upon to do. With a stubborn half-born as guide?" The bird shook out its feathers and its wings unfurled, displaying a span easily the length of a grown man. It was beautiful in a terrifying way, and if it was not intended as a threat, Gabriel would eat his hat and Isobel's both.

"We have allowed your master his time, trusted the strength of his oath, watched him, waited. But there are those who do not abide, who will not listen."

The bird did not look at him, did not so much as acknowledge his existence, but Gabriel felt the words as though they'd been delivered with talon and beak.

"Choose your sides now, little sister," the Reaper told her, "and be prepared for the consequences."

"Do not threaten her on this ground."

There was no way a creature that size could have appeared without them noting it, even with the massive distraction in front of them. The Reaper lifted its wings, a full threat display, but the elk merely lowered its head until the points of its antlers were angled directly at the bird. Even covered in summer felt, they were capable of as much damage as the Reaper's talons.

Isobel's squeak was the only indication that she was still aware, that and the way her heart was beating too rapidly, so that he could feel it slamming against her rib cage, as though it were trying to escape both her hold and his grasp.

The two creatures stared at each other, then the Reaper launched itself into the air, talons outstretched as those massive wings flapped once, twice, and lifted the bird away from them before landing again, refusing to give ground.

"What?" Gabriel's mouth was dry, and he couldn't form the words without coughing. He took a sip of the canteen he'd brought to Isobel, and tried again. "What the—"

Isobel's hand on his knee stopped him, her grip too tight, her fingers trembling, but the message clear: *Do not speak.*

"I thank you for your help, before and now, elder cousin." She reverted back to a cautious formality when speaking to the wapiti, as though aware that it had not given her permission for familiarity, aware that those antlers were close to their faces as well, sharp enough to gouge and tear the same as a Reaper's claws.

"It does not aid you," the Reaper said, its words a low screech. "It uses you, as your master uses you. As a toy would be used and then thrown away when it is broken."

"They are not toys," the massive elk responded, shifting its weight in clear threat, the antlers moving closer until the Reaper was forced to take an ungainly backward hop. "Weapons, perhaps."

"And as easily discarded. I would counsel you better, little sister."

"You would counsel selfishness and destruction," the elk spat, its head lowering again to display its antlers to best effect, and that they were aimed at the Reaper, not them, was small comfort.

"I would counsel survival." The great head tilted again, showing what Gabriel thought was either great bravery or abject stupidity in ignoring the rack of bone directed at it, to look at Isobel. "Walk away, little sister. Let the stones fall as the ground moves them. Let the power go where it will."

"You speak as though she retains choice. What has been done cannot be undone." The elk backed up, lifting its head, and Gabriel thought it less a retreat than it no longer deeming the hawk an immediate danger. "You bear the mark, and the weight of that obligation." The elk wasn't looking at Isobel now, but its words were plainly for her. "The Territory must be protected."

"The quick knife," Isobel said, her voice muted, as though echoing something else said long ago. "The cold eye and the final word. But—"

"The final word is yours," the Reaper told her. "That will forever give you choice."

Gabriel's patience broke. Pulling Isobel up with him, he shifted enough to draw their attention from each other, the dramatic flourishes he'd learned to use in front of a judge rushing back with his ire. "Enough!

You are wiser than we, none gainsay that, but if you will insist on only back-clatter and manipulations rather than useful advice, you can both be gone and be damned!"

The Reaper hissed and lofted its massive wings at him, their shadow rising taller than he stood, but not even that could pause Gabriel once he started. "Whatever her Bargain with the devil, it is her Bargain. That is the Law. Whatever your purpose in counseling her, you would be best served to come outright and state your intent so that she may judge your advice fairly."

Even as he spoke, Gabriel wanted to laugh at his presumption: spirits, demons, magicians—those with power said very little plainly and took direction not at all. But his anger seemed to have taken them aback, as though they'd forgotten that he—or she—might have an opinion at all.

And then they were gone, only the harsh sound as the raptor took flight as indication that they had not simply faded into the air like morning mist.

A hissing laugh broke the stunned silence that followed. Gabriel kept Isobel behind him as he turned to find the source, having to look down into the grass to locate it.

This snake was the length of his arm, flecked in yellow-brown scales, with the tail poised but still as it considered them, its head raised up out of the grass. The long pale tongue flickered out, and it slid closer, skirting the edge of the salt circle much the same way the others had, though Gabriel got the feeling that if the snake wished, it would simply slide over the warding without hesitation.

"What *now?*" He was out of patience with the medicine world.

Isobel slipped from behind him, casting him a sideways look that was part exasperation and part amusement, then went down on her knees again, to be on more even ground with the snake, trusting that it had no intention of lunging at her to strike.

To be fair, none of them had offered violence at any point. Not toward her, at least.

"Have you come to offer conflicting advice as well?" she asked, her voice light but shaking with exhaustion. "Or merely to watch for your own amusement?"

"Issssss there a differerenssssse?"

"The boss took lessons from you, didn't he?" Isobel muttered.

"He hassssss known ussss well," the snake admitted. "Little coussssssins. You have come a long way." The rattler shifted, its scales brushing through the grass. "How far yet will you go?"

Isobel lifted her hands as though asking the winds for answers. "Gabriel was right. You all talk around the problem, make it sound like you're being helpful, but you're not."

More hissed laughter. "No. We are not. We tell you only what you already know but will not let yoursssssssself hear."

She lowered her arms. "I'm listening now."

"Then I do not need to ssssssssay anything," the snake told her, and its tail rattled once before it dropped into the grass and slid away.

Gabriel licked too-dry lips and ran a hand over the scarred side of his face, casting a glance up into the clear blue sky and the hills rising around them, as though expecting yet another form to appear. Nothing did. He summoned all of his irritation, his frustration, and his exhaustion into one word. "Sssssnakes."

Isobel clamped a hand across her mouth and bent forward, her shoulders shaking with what could have been either tears or laughter.

He wouldn't judge her for either.

Isobel's limbs felt loose, her skin too cold, her bones too hot. Gabriel had gotten her out of the circle, had broken what remained of the warding and scattered it properly, then seated her by the fire, which he'd built back up, and put a kettle of beans and dried venison to boil. But she'd been aware of all that vaguely, as though through a fog, until the smell of the broth reached her nose, and the thought of warm food woke her stomach, suddenly aware that she was deeply, painfully hungry.

The sky was darkening, the air cooler. How long had she been sitting here? How much time had she lost?

Isobel could still feel the press of the ancient spirit, like a bruise on her skin. If she touched it, if she looked at it, she thought it would overwhelm her. So, she looked at anything but. She looked at the fire crackling around the coalstone, eating the kindling and grasses she had gathered the night before. She listened to the horses shuffling and breathing, the crunch of their teeth and the swish of their tails. She smelled the scent rising from the jacket draped over her lap for warmth, deep and smoky and sharp, with an unrecognizable flavor that she could only identify as being Gabriel himself.

Gabriel. Panic hit her, until she was able to identify the noise of him settling the horses for the night, his voice speaking softly to them, calming them. They might not know what was happening, but horses were prey, not predators, and they knew when something dangerous was nearby.

The haint-presence lingered but at a distance, and underneath, Isobel could taste something else, taste or smell or touch, she wasn't certain, and she had no desire to chase it, the hot sweet sulphur smell that she'd not been able to shake since they came north.

Or before, she thought. Since she saw the slaughtered buffalo. Since the whisper first tangled in her dreams. It lured her, drove her, protected her. . . . It burned like the sigil but it felt no part of it, harsh and liquid in her bones, burning her like a coalstone, heat without ash.

She lifted her head and looked out into the valley, but the shadows were too dark to tell if there was a massive elk lurking at the edges still, a Reaper perched in the trees, or snake curled in the dirt. She was afraid to think about any of it, her fingers curling into her palms, her skin cold without its touch, afraid to poke at that for fear the whisper might come back, demand that she *do* something, and a greater fear that it might not.

"Better?" Gabriel was closer now, standing behind her.

She didn't understand the question, didn't understand how to answer it. She stroked the jacket over her legs, focused everything on the feel of the canvas under her fingertips, rough and warm and real.

"Isobel." His voice was a rope, settling around her wrists, pulling her in.

"What would you do?" Her voice was too high, too thin; she didn't recognize it.

"Doesn't matter what I'd do or not do." He sat down next to her, mimicking her pose, legs crossed, boots tucked under him. The firelight turned him into shadows, and she wondered what she looked like to him; did he see her truly, or was she, too, shadows and smoke? "Matters what you think's best."

Once upon a time, she'd thought the boss knew everything, *was* everything. Then she'd thought she knew something, understood how the Territory worked, could bend magicians to her will, defend against intruders, make newcomers part of the whole.

But the Reaper's words had shaken her, the anguished madness of the ancient spirit had broken her, not because they existed but because she could not fix them, could not make them make sense.

The world was meant to make sense.

Doubt settled in her lap. She hadn't been able to keep her promise to the slaughtered buffalo, hadn't been able to track those killers. What had made her think she could do anything here?

"You should take the animals, go away," she told Gabriel. "The ancient spirit ignored you, ignored them. You could go, be safe."

"Probably should," he agreed. "Not going to. The which you already knew, so let's be done with that foolishness, all right?"

She felt the scold like a slap, her cheeks coloring as though his hand had in fact made impact. He had made a Bargain with the boss; of course he wasn't going to leave her.

"All right." The feathers brushed against her neck as she moved, but for once, they gave no reassurance. She bit down on her lower lip, her hands knotting in the worn canvas of Gabriel's jacket still draped over her knees, and once again, the texture of it cleared her thoughts.

"Three spirit-animals. The—what did you call it? The wapiti, to remind me of my duty. The Reaper, to tell me to save myself. And the snake, to say . . . nothing useful." She considered those words, then changed them. "Nothing obviously useful. But it follows us—for amusement, or is there something below its words that I'm not hearing?"

"'Our friends are not always friends, our enemies not always a danger.' That's what it said before."

"You thought it meant Farron."

Gabriel chuckled. "I did. But reading anything too narrowly runs the risk of missing the evidence."

She didn't quite understand what he meant, but the way he said it reminded her of something else. "The boss always said advice was only worth the intent of the person giving it. And every person who bothered to give advice had something they intended by it."

"He's had a long time to study human nature." Gabriel's voice was dry, but she could hear the humor underneath and clung to it. So long as Gabriel could joke, she could believe there was hope.

"I want to leave," she admitted quietly, not looking at him, not looking at anything in particular. The fire crackled and snapped, and one of the horses groaned quietly. "I want to throw my pack on Uvnee and ride out of here and never look back. Go . . . anywhere. Go north. Leave the Territory."

Abandon her Bargain. Just the thought chilled her, made the lines on her palm feel like they were carved of ice, like she'd never be warm again.

"Will you?"

She swallowed, her mouth and throat too dry to work properly. "No."

Saying the word eased something inside her, and only then did Isobel acknowledge that she might have, that she had been that close. But even if she had, the Contract could not be broken.

Next to her, Gabriel sighed, and there was something in that exhale that was more than relief, more than satisfaction or regret.

"Gabriel?" She had to stop and take a sip from the canteen, to moisten her throat enough to speak again. "Would . . . Would I have been able to leave the Territory?"

She had never considered it, never had cause to once she'd chosen to make Bargain, to stay. But now the question pinched at her.

"I don't know," he said. "But . . ." There was a hesitation. "Even if you left, I don't think you'd be able to stay away. Not for long. Not and remain sane."

There was pain there, and a story. She rubbed at the flesh of her palm with her thumb; the gesture that had been comforting, before, now felt like the tug of reins at her neck, a bit in her mouth.

Some folk left the Territory, gave up whatever they'd hoped to find and left. Her own parents had come and then gone again, leaving her behind.

"You should leave," she said again. "Not the Territory, I mean . . . here." She made a vague motion with one hand, meaning the meadow they were in, and the valley they'd traveled through to get there, all the way back to Duck's village, and maybe even before. "At least until I . . . do what I need to do."

He said something in a language she didn't know, pungent in tone, then, "You said it ignored me. And the horses. We're not at risk."

"For now. The haint . . . Something wards it here, contains it. But it's not . . ."

"It's not a friend," Gabriel finished for her, and she nodded. Sky and bone, they had pressed against her when she tried to reach the haint, had done something to her when she was within it, changed her . . . but the memories were mist-swept, foggy, and she was afraid to look closer.

"And you won't leave." It wasn't a question, but she shrugged help-lessly, then looked up at him. "The sorrow and the pain. If I don't ease that, this meadow, this entire valley . . . nothing will come back. Nothing will live here." She paused, wondering how she knew that but knowing it all the same.

"You're not going to try and reach it again."

She would have argued with him, save that he was right. If she tried again and whatever had protected her before failed, the haint would consume her easily as the Reaper hawk ate a rabbit. "There's one thing I can do, I can try to do. But I'll need to summon the magicians."

Gabriel sat down next to her, his hands resting on his knees, and she had a moment's irritation that he could do that so easily, without having to worry about skirts tangling. "You said the remaining ones had fled; even if you did track them down, they owe no allegiance to your boss; you have no hold over them." Unspoken: that if they'd scattered, each looking out only for themselves, it would take them a lifetime, or more, to find them.

"Not them," she said, pressing her thumb deeper into the sigil until it hurt. "The ones who died."

Gabriel made her promise to wait, to rest, but neither made even a token effort to sleep that night. Their bedrolls untouched, they sat by the fire and listened to the horses grumble and snore, the mule's occasional flatulence loud in the too-quiet night air as the moon rose overhead and passed through the sky, the stars faded, and the first hint of pale red appeared in the east, heralding the return of day.

Isobel's eyes were still sore and crackly, her nose was running, her legs ached, and her back felt as though she'd been riding hard for a week, not sitting on soft grass next to a warm fire. She had taken her boots off at some point, and her toes were cold, and her scalp itched, reminding her that it had been days since she'd been able to wash her hair, and the cleaning powder she'd been given was long gone.

"Devorah was right," she said. "I'd kill for a bath right now."

It was the first either of them had spoken in hours, and the sound of her voice made Gabriel jump.

"I could find water for you if you needed," he said finally. "The stream isn't enough, but . . ."

"When we're done," she said. "When we're done, we'll ride down out of here and find a town with a proper bathhouse. With *soap*."

Her words had the feel of an oath, the weight of inevitability, and she took some comfort in that. She would get her hot bath. And soap. And everything that came with that.

When they were done. If they were still alive.

"Best get to it, then," Gabriel said, although he didn't move.

Isobel groaned and reached for her boots.

What she planned to do wasn't forbidden, either by Territory Law or the devil's Agreement. It was simply . . . wrong. The dead were to be respected, protected. Boneyards were warded to ensure that, the rituals performed to allow spirits to be at rest, not linger in the pains of the living.

But magicians . . . could they ever truly rest? They gave themselves over to the winds in exchange for power, let madness fill them like a fever, and she had seen how they did not die easily, if at all.

Except they had died here. Died and been trapped with the creature they'd sought to summon, unable to break free, unable to pass on. Had it been their own working that trapped them mid-death? Or something else?

And the haint . . . its bones were likely so ancient, they not been warded at all, the rituals unperformed. Whatever she did could affect it as well, and to what end she could not imagine.

"I should be accustomed to uncertainty by now," she said, torn between resigned bitterness and dark amusement.

"The surest way to get killed is to stop to think about what you've already decided to do," Gabriel said, not looking up from his task. "You've been given the tools for the job, Isobel. Trust that."

She looked at him, carefully scraping grains of salt from the stick, gathering them onto a scrap of cloth, and then looked up at the sky, thinking about what he had said. About trust, and tools, and if the boss had truly sent her out unprepared. If *Marie*, who had likely packed her things, would have sent her out unprepared, without whatever she might need.

Opening the pack she'd just taken off the mule, she dug her hands deep along the sides, trusting instinct, sliding questing fingers past her journal and pencil, past the seemingly essential odds and ends she'd taken with her from her bedroom and never unwrapped, until her fingertips found a bundle wedged into a corner of the pack, slick and hard and unfamiliar, and curved her fingers around to pull it free.

The object inside the wrappings was not more salt, or silver, or anything she recognized, merely a stone a little longer than her hand and wide as three fingers, worn flat on either side, the ends blunted. It felt smooth to her fingertips, but there were figures etched into one side, the lines stained a deep red. If she looked too long at them, she felt dizzy—the same sort of dizziness she felt when she reached too far into the bones, went too far from herself.

Isobel was certain it hadn't been among the things she'd packed, and equally certain, although she hadn't asked, that Gabriel hadn't brought it with him or picked it up along the way.

She rubbed the pad of her thumb across the wrapping, feeling it slick and cool, and thought, not without some unease, that it might have been a parting gift from Farron.

She closed the cloth back around it, wrapped it again in an old stocking that needed darning, and shoved it deep into the pack. They were not in such need yet that she would test a magician's gift, however it was meant. But neither would she toss it away.

"Here," Gabriel said, closing the bundle of salt grains to make sure none spilled before he was ready. "Not that I'm certain salt is enough to keep magicians from more mischief. I'd be more pleased if we'd enough silver coin to ring them in as well."

They'd been over this already, the coins they had, polished and replaced in Gabriel's pocket, already beginning to tarnish.

Silver warned and silver cleansed, but it could not compel.

"They summoned a force of wind and fire," she said. "Summoned it, trapped it, tried to force it against its will to submit to theirs." Insult thrice over. "And it in turn tore them to shreds. Releasing them from that would be a kindness. I only need make them understand that."

She moved past him, picking up a charred stick where it lay in the smoldering remains of their fire, letting it drag against the ground as she moved with a measured pace, steering well clear of the dead grass and the swirling steam rising through the dirt.

"I'm not certain they'll see it that way." Gabriel dropped the remains of the salt stick onto her pack and studied the bundle in his hand, then looked up at the sky dotted with pale strands of clouds drifting southeast. "They're mad to begin with, magicians, and I doubt being dead has soothed them in any way. Do you truly think, even within a warding, you will be able to control what comes to your call?"

"No." She saw no point in lying. "I might have been able to stop Farron one on one. But he was as curious as he was mad, and seemed fond of me—that would have worked in my favor. More than one . . . only if they were distracted. If they turn on each other, I might . . . but if I waited to challenge the survivor, they would be so glutted with stolen medicine, I would fail and die."

Gabriel put his head down into his hands as she spoke. Isobel ignored him.

The only way to stop another magician was to steal their power. Only another magician was mad enough to try that; the eight winds did not respect flesh or blood and wore down even earth's bone. Having brushed against the winds, Isobel wanted no part of it. But power could be *emptied* from a thing. That was how crossroads were kept safe; part of a road marshal's obligation was to test and drain them as they rode through. A magician was a container for power; all she had to do was empty them.

Marshals were trained, Gabriel said. If a marshal had ridden here, would they have sensed something was wrong, *known* what was wrong?

Isobel glanced at the sigil in her palm, then down to the sigil she was tracing in the grass. The circle-and-tree badge of a road marshal tied them to the Road; they were bound to the Territory by their oath. Her sigil obligated her to the devil directly. But Gabriel's comment, that even if she left the Territory, she would not be able to stay away, had felt too true to ignore. Something within her echoed with it, the rolling plains and jagged mountains, the woods and the creeks, the pulse that she'd felt the first time she touched the bones, felt the Road, saw a buffalo herd, heard the cry of an owl in the dawn.

"You bear the mark, and the weight of that obligation," the wapiti had said, in this same place, not a day before. *"The Territory must be protected."*

Because she was the Hand? Because she was the nearest it could find? Because she was fool enough to listen?

Even as she drew the wards in the grass, prepared herself for what was to be done, the Reaper hawk's warning lingered. The doings of magicians were none of the devil's concern, and the welfare of natives was none of the devil's agreement; they had their own medicine folk for such things. What had the Broken Tongue's people done when the ground shook? They had run.

Isobel very badly wanted to run.

Instead, she completed her circuit, the boneyard markings unfinished to allow the dead to enter, then waited while Gabriel echoed the external circle with salt twice.

"If anything breaks through one line, do you think a second will stop it?"

The look he gave her could have stopped a hungry bear in its tracks.

"If I had the salt for a dozen lines, I would draw them," he said, his words tightly bitten off. "And shift a stream alongside to boot. This is a fool's idea, you're a fool for doing it, and I'm a fool for allowing it."

He wasn't angry, though he sounded it; he was worried. Fools die. It was a joke, a curse, a warning. A reminder.

"Ward yourself and the animals, too," she said. "Just to be safe."

He nodded, holding up the flap of cloth to show that he'd crumbled enough salt for that, too.

She waited until he had hobbled the animals and warded the circle around them, before she settled herself at the center of her own warding, her legs tucked under her, skirt wrapped around her legs to keep them warm, her spine as relaxed as she could make it, shoulders rounded and soft, head bowed until the line from the back of her neck to her hips was a soft arc. Her hands rested palms-down on her knees as she breathed in and out, in and out, feeling her heart ease and her pulse steady and slow, feeling her blood rise and fall with the movement of her chest, her thoughts thickening and clearing, leaving her soft and strong.

She thought Gabriel was wrong, but he had a point about being careful. Too often they'd been unready, unprepared when she needed to act. This time, she would be settled, as secure in herself as she would be in the saddle before a gallop.

Her hands slipped from her knees to the grass in front of her, fingertips curling into the ground below. Her body followed, leaning forward until she was bent over her knees, her head bowed, her breath barely moving the grasses in front of her.

The boss's voice rolled in the back of her memories, the lessons she hadn't realized were lessons, listening to him speak while they did their chores, at night after the saloon had closed. Power—medicine, magic—lingered where it had been used, like ash after a fire. Anyone with a patch of silver and some sense could tell if power lingered and avoid it. Avoid anything that used it. Like magicians.

Like her. The thought was bitter in her mouth.

But magicians took from more than crossroads. They took from one another—no loss to the rest of the Territory, so long as they kept their battles somewhere isolated. But they were greedy, hungry. They'd take from anything they could. Farron had been ready to consume the spell-beast they'd found if Isobel hadn't warned him off. He'd threatened to consume *her* if she faltered.

She might have been able to fend him off. One magician. Maybe.

Isobel let that thought go, feeling it ease out of her, sliding down her spine and fading away, leaving her thoughts thick and clear again. She wasn't trying to defeat magicians nor steal from them. She wanted to help them.

Even they, even crazed, would not be so foolish as to try to steal from the devil once they recognized the source. But the power within her would draw them close enough.

Her palms made contact with the grass, then the dirt below. There was a sting against her, like a sharp blade slicing down to bone, a queasy shock, and she had learned not to push too deep, half-anticipating that void, that refusal again.

I don't want you, she told it. *I will not interfere with your captive. Let me pass.*

There was a timeless hesitation, suspended, and then she slipped through the barrier, careful not to touch it and risk rousing the spirit. Safely inside, Isobel set the lure of her own spark, inviting the restless dead to come to her.

They swarmed.

push shove grab hold tug push. the sharpness of insubstantial fingers digging into her clawing at her, nails scraping claiming pressing. A flash of heat warned them off, the devil's sigil flaring in the nowhere-place they were, a waft of tobacco and sulphur, soap and spice, the *flickerthwack* of cards turned on felt, the clink of fine glassware and the soft murmur of voices speaking needs wants secrets, the feel of blood welling on her fingertip, pressed against fine parchment, the touch of the Devil's hand on her own, *and the grabbing, grasping sensation retreats, not to disappear but to wait, impatient, overeager, for another chance.*

Five, she counted. Five sets of hands-that-weren't, five greedy, hungry mouths wanting to suck the marrow and the power from her bones.

Five magicians, dead and trapped under the grass, trapped under the soil.

Do you know who you are? she asked them. *Do you know who you were?*

Anger responded, anger and frustration wrapped around a pulsing core of need, without conscious thought or function, and it lunged at her, no longer five but a single entity, only aware that they needed and she *had*.

These things had been human once; she knew how to deal with them. The sense-of-Isobel skimmed just out of reach, resting within the dry bones of the cage, and then raised the ante.

She waited, waited waited an infinity of waiting, tracing the loops of the devil's sigil in her mind, dark green flame flaring along the curves and lines, the loops and lines tarnishing and silvering in its path, turning and turning until they were all dizzy with the turning, dizzy with greed. They took the bait, then she turned and slipped into them—

Sensations filled her, overwhelmed her, and she forced them into some kind of sense, some frame of comprehension. Hunger, the ever-driving hunger for more, for more knowledge, more strength, more understanding. The sensation of being driven by the winds, hither and yon, chasing the scent of power, the lure of understanding. The crooked finger of invitation, suggestion. An Other, speaking of secrets unknown, power unclaimed. A sensation more than a knowing, an awareness rather than a vision; not trusted, never trusted, warily they gathered, driven/lured/prodded to this place, this valley, gathered to circle, bearing ritual and power, to reach up and pull, beyond their capabilities but together, together, with ritual and power. . . .

It stirred, and they pulled; it flew, and they chased; it dove, and they pounced.

Power. Immense, impossible, overwhelming. A chorus of voices singing alleluia, screaming alleluia, binding and rending, binding and rending, over and again, clawing at their own flesh, tearing out their own thoughts to find space to gorge themselves. . . .

—slipped past them, coming out the other side, shaking as though she'd run the full distance of the Territory, sick and wheezing.

Too much. Too much for her, too much for still-mortal blood and bone; she could contain power, but she was not power, not yet, only the sigil keeping her intact, only the sigil keeping her whole. She touched her skin and felt it crackle and slip off, black scale flakes shedding off her bone.

The world shook underneath her, around her. Rage. Fear. Sorrow. Betrayal.

Gabriel had never minded waiting. As a boy, he'd learned to wait his turn; as an advocate, he'd earned to wait for witnesses to say the important thing, the accused to say the wrong thing, the judge to make a decision. As a rider, he'd learned to let the miles wash over him, settling in each moment without demanding the next.

Waiting on Isobel tested that, the need to do something, to act, gnawing at him. Instead, he reached for the water, bypassing the smaller rivulets, the tiny pools, to touch the river he'd sensed before. Running water, not the panacea that silver was, but anyone born to the Territory knew that there were things that did not, could not cross running water intact.

If he could have diverted a stream, as he had suggested, he would have. It wouldn't have been enough. The river itself, summer-low, wouldn't have been enough.

"I knew you were trouble the minute I saw you. But such interesting trouble." He pulled his water-sense back, shoved his hands into his jacket pockets, the just-polished quarter- and half-coins tucked there, smooth and cool to the touch. He suspected that they were now black with tarnish but felt no need to check.

"Stand pat," he told Flatfoot, the mule's head upright, watching the shadows, while the horses grazed. "If I need you, I'll call."

He walked circuit of the salt circles, making sure that the horses hadn't disturbed the delicate white lines, and the skin on his arms prickled half a heartbeat before the mule let out an unhappy moan. Two heartbeats later, the ground under them undulated, reminding Gabriel of the times he'd ever been on a boat, the sickening, swaying sensation that had unnerved him so much, he'd sworn never to leave solid ground again.

Quake. Stronger than the one he'd felt before, by a magnitude.

The horses, hobbled, were unable to run away, but he forced himself to move between them, a hand on each neck, calming and soothing. The mule's eyes were rolling, and its skin shuddered as though a swarm of flies had landed on it, but it stayed put, as though its stillness would calm the ground below.

Within her own warding, Isobel had slumped forward, her upper body bent over, her legs tucked underneath her, and she wasn't moving. He didn't know what was happening, had no way to check what was happening, not unless he broke his own warding and hers.

As though warning against that, the ground trembled again, hard enough to rock him sideways. Had there been two tremors before, close together? Fool that he was, he hadn't *asked*.

Steady let out an unhappy whinny, and Uvnee snorted and pressed closer against him, nearly pushing him over. "Easy, girl. Easy. It'll be over soon."

He hoped it would. Before, the trembling had faded nearly as soon as it began; this had gone on far longer than that. He thought it had, anyway. The swaying sensation made it difficult for him to judge time passing; he couldn't quite focus on anything, but eventually, the unnerving shivering of the world ceased and the animals calmed. He waited a while longer until he was reasonably certain that the quakes had ceased, then broke his wards and ran to where Isobel was still slumped, unmoving.

The urge to reach through, to pick her up the way he had before, was like a physical pain, but he dropped to his own knees just outside her circle instead. Unlike before, she had created this warding: even if he were able, his breaking it would lead to nothing good.

He waited, aware of an ache in his foot where he thought one of the horses had stepped on him in their distress, the discomfort of sweat drying on his skin, and the warm ache of his ribs where he'd likely torn open a scab, but did not move, as though afraid movement might cause some new trouble, afraid to miss even the slightest change in Isobel's position.

When she did shift, the faintest exhale and a sideways slump of her body, he risked calling to her. "Iz? Izzy." He had not called her that in weeks, months. Isobel was the cool, collected girl he'd met in the saloon. Isobel was the Devil's Hand. But this girl, slumped sideways, her hands and face dirty, he could only see as Izzy.

"Izzy, let me in."

He felt the wards fade, and risked moving across, knee-walking to her side, careful hands lifting her, brushing hair out of her sweat-streaked face.

"Welcome back," he said, placing two fingers under her chin and lifting her face enough that he could check her eyes. They were clear, if a little dazed-looking. "You had me worried."

"So . . . So much . . ." Her voice was faint, and he could see the instant she wandered away from him again.

"Iz, no. Look at me, Iz. Isobel."

Her eyes were too dark, the pupils blown wide, but she was there, trying to focus.

"Look at me, Isobel. Listen to my voice. Can you do that? Come on, come back."

He had her cradled in his arms now, draped over his lap, and kept his voice steady and calm, despite the panic trying to shove its way through. Once had been foolish enough. Allowing her to do this a second time . . . But only she could have. When he touched the Road or used his water-sense, he went so far and no further. He could go no further.

You choose to go no further, a voice reminded him, and he brushed it away irritably.

Isobel . . . Each time, he saw her sink deeper, reach further. Each time, it changed her. She saw things, felt things, was connected to things in a way she could not explain and he didn't want to think of.

Uncanny. The magician, Farron, had tried to warn him. Had told him not to think of her as a girl, or woman, but as a tool. A weapon. A Hand. The Reaper hawk and the wapiti had said the same thing, differently.

He couldn't. She was the Hand. He knew that. Watched her discover that fact herself, over and again, each time coming away different, the weight of what she was becoming not obvious to her yet, not entirely, but clear enough to those around her.

But she was also Isobel. And he had promised to stand by her. To train her. To keep her alive.

To not leave.

"Can you sit up?"

She looked puzzled, as though not even aware that she was lying down, then nodded. Her eyes were still glassy, flitting back and forth as though she didn't quite have control of where they looked yet. She hadn't taken a blow to the head that he'd seen, hadn't moved except to slump forward, but he would take no chances.

"All right. Slowly . . ." He eased her up, keeping his hands on her shoulders until she was settled on the grass again, looking around her as though not quite certain where she was still. He wanted to ask what had happened, if she'd learned what she'd wanted to know—but held his tongue, waiting.

It didn't take long.

"I was wrong." Her voice was flat, scraped and thin. "I didn't understand."

He had grabbed a canteen when he went to her side, he realized only as he was pulling the cork with his teeth, gently tipping it to her mouth, allowing her only a scant swallow before taking it away again.

"The spirit they called was hungry, so hungry. So *old*. They thought to bind it to them, to consume its power, to . . . split it among them? Or duel until only one remained. But they failed, and it consumed them. Burnt them to char, burned them from the inside out, even as they forced it to take form, warped it into something it was never meant to be. The ones who fled . . ." She shuddered, her entire body trembling in his arms. "They did not escape. They are unmanned, unminded."

Mad dogs, loose in the Territory. Magicians were bad enough but single-minded in their pursuits: only rarely did mortals get tangled with them. Unminded . . . they might lash out at anything that crossed their path. Lash out and destroy—a single rider, or an entire town, it would make no difference to them. They needed to be back on the

Road, find a badgehouse, let the marshals know. They carried their own medicine, marshals did, for the protection of the Road.

For now, Gabriel could only worry about what was in front of him.

"And the dead?" Had she been able to free them, to bind them, to send them to wherever resting souls went? Or would they now come back mad but whole, the way Farron had?

She shook her head, a hand reaching up to pluck at her braid, tapping the feathers still tied there, a nervous tic. "Shards of what had been, all the madness, and none of the control. There's no one being there but the tangled mess of what was, seeking power to replace what was lost." Her hand left off her braid, reached up to touch his fingers where they curled over her shoulder. Her skin was cold, the calluses on her fingers rough as cording.

Her eyes cleared, but she wasn't seeing him. "There's illness here, Gabriel. Worse than any pox or fever. I only touched part of it before."

"How bad?" Could she cure it, he meant, or control it, the way she'd cleansed the land before, against the Spanish curse.

"It's caged for now. Held. But the quakes . . . There's a thread tying them all together now, woven of power and blood. The spirit's trying to break free. Scraping what it can find, fighting. . . ." She took a deep breath through her nose. "And if it does, if it breaks free, it will take them with it."

"And that's bad."

"The story you told me, about the Hills That Danced?" She shook her head, eyes now wide and wild. "It will be much, much worse."

He didn't want to ask it of her, but he had to. "Is there anything you can do?"

It was as though she didn't hear him at first, her head tilted, listening to something he could not hear, had no wish to hear.

"No. The Reaper had the right of it there, at least. The spirits will do as they must, the air will press down and the ground push up, and they will contain as they can. . . . They will not allow the madness to spread. But it pains them to do this, and that pain is a real thing. This will become a barren place. The animals will not return, the grass will die, the creek run dry. It will become. . . ." She struggled for words, and he realized, as a chill touched his skin, that he was not hearing her words but another's, pushed through her throat.

"Poisoned," she finished finally. "Envenenado."

"Forever?"

"For many lifetimes. Maybe all the lifetimes."

Half a day passed, the sun warm overhead, and Isobel could not shake the chill from her skin. She could feel the blanket over her shoulders, the heat of Gabriel near her, the flickering of the fire he'd built up, making her a tisane he said would warm her blood. None of it mattered. The cold ran deep inside, pushing everything else away. Her gaze dropped down to her hands, and she spread her fingers out in front of her, palms down, looking at them as though they were not her own.

She had done what was needed, had done only what was needed. That made it no better, that she had done it at all. The dead were to be protected, not abused, and yet she had. She had gone among the dead and forced them to her will. Without hesitation, without compassion. She had pushed herself into the sodden mess of what remained and forced them to speak to her, to tell her what she needed to know; had shoved herself into their most pained places and taken what she needed. The fact that she had disturbed no wardings, had uncovered no bones, did not change that fact.

And she knew that she would do it again if it were asked of her.

The elk—wapiti, Gabriel called it—had been right: she had duty, obligation. A sworn contract, turning her into the devil's tool. Whatever power she contained, it was nothing more than that. She was no more a person than Gabriel's knife or gun.

She looked at her hands and remembered something else.

"It was an easterner." Her voice was too steady, too calm. It should shake under the weight of what she had done, what she had learned.

"Who was?"

Gabriel moved away from the fire, took her hands in his, turning them, wrapping the fingers around the handle of her mug, the battered tin almost too warm to hold. Still, all she felt was cold.

"The one who brought them here, convinced them to do this. I saw it in their . . . in them. He came across the Mudwater, American colors on his saddle." Their awareness of the man was muddled by death, by pain, by the pressure they were held under, mangled by their own madness, but that much she knew: the creak of the leather of his saddle, the smell of him, the flash of the colors marking him as an outsider, giving him passage across the borders, a single man without troops.

But a single man could be as dangerous as an army.

Gabriel sat down opposite her, pushing her hands up, reminding her to drink the tisane. She took a sip, merely to oblige him. It was green, and sharp, and warm, but she did not feel warmed. "He spun them a story of . . . of the power they could gain if they did this. Of power elsewhere if they were strong enough to take it. That he would show them if they did this one thing. . . ." She shook her head, less in disbelief than amazement.

"He made promises." Scraps of smudged ink, half-mumbled words, the soft flutter of dust in sunlight. "Rewards . . . power if they aided his government?"

"They were fools to believe him," Gabriel said, his voice hard. "There's nothing for them out there. Whatever medicine remains east of the Mudwater, it's been locked down, harder to find. A magician outside the Territory would be like a wolf in a vegetable plot, surrounded by food and yet starving."

"They wanted to believe." Isobel understood that much. "They wanted what he promised, enough to work together."

Only, there was no "together" for magicians. Farron had told her true. Each and every one had turned on the other the moment the spell was cast, driven by fear and greed, each determined to claim the ancient spirit's medicine for themselves. Had they managed to not . . .

She tried to imagine Farron multiplied, even more powerful, but the smudged, bloody, hungry madness was all she could feel, even splintered into death.

"Did . . . did they tell you anything else? About the American."

Gabriel's voice sounded strange, strained. He had said he had spent time across the River, that he had studied the law there. He had told her about the city he had lived in, the press of people, and the ways they lived . . . but he had never said if he was happy there, if he'd been sorry to leave.

Doubt scraped its claws at her, and she closed her eyes, refusing it. "I only saw him as they saw him," she said. "As they remembered him, and what's left of their thoughts . . ."

"It's important, Isobel."

She couldn't refuse him, not with his voice scraped that raw.

"He was tall and cast a dark shadow." It made no sense to her, that one man might cast more of a shadow than another, but that was what they remembered. "His face was dark, like a crow's"—a crow, yes, tattered wings and bright eyes—"but there was a brightness to him"—and her free hand raised up to touch her chest, settling on the left side, just under her shoulder—"here."

Gabriel said something that sounded rude and pained in that language she didn't know. She opened her eyes to look at him. "Gabriel?"

He shook his head, then reached into the pocket of his jacket, pulling out something that glittered faintly in the slant of sunlight. "A brightness . . . like this?"

The metal, when dropped into her hand, was heavy as a stone and burned like a coal, although she knew it was neither. The edges were smooth, well-worn, and the engraving on both sides was almost too faint to see.

"What is it?" It felt familiar, but she did not recognize it.

"A marshal's badge."

Her brow wrinkled in confusion—the marshal's sigil was the Tree within the Circle, not this.

Gabriel gestured to the badge. "The name's the same, but they're . . . more prescribed, and at the same time, with a wider—" He broke off as though suddenly realizing that he was lecturing her. "Sorry." His smile was weak but rueful, and real. "The marshals in the States are more than peacekeepers. They're answerable to the federal government rather than the states themselves."

Isobel shook her head, not understanding half of what he was saying, save that the owner of this badge, the man who had somehow convinced magicians to destroy themselves, had come from the East. On orders of their leaders.

Bitterness and bile rose in her, and she flung the badge away, hearing it land in the fire with a sick satisfaction, although she knew the flames were not enough to destroy it.

"Pushing, always pushing, if not Spain, then them. Can't they leave us alone?"

Gabriel laughed then, and the sound was so clear, so pure, and so lacking in humor, it reached through her rage.

"No," he said. "They can't. They never have and they never will. Borders are uneasy things even at the best of times, Isobel. And to them, the Territory . . . It's a fruit they want nothing more than to bite into and consume.

"But this . . ." He reached for a stick, using it to fish the badge out of the fire, then left it on the ground to cool off. She stared at it, half-resentful that he had rescued it, half-fascinated by it. "He's dead, isn't he?"

She found it difficult to care. "He led them to their death." A horrible, unending death she would not wish on any, not even the already-mad.

"Magicians can't be led to anything, Isobel. You know that every bit as well as I. They can't be controlled; they can't even be properly aimed. Whatever they did, they chose to do. And they all paid the price."

"Why are you defending him?" There was something in his voice, something that wasn't grief, wasn't anger. Isobel knew she could dig it from him, could study him and read it off his face, his body, but she couldn't find the energy to turn and look at him.

"Everything's paid the price," she said instead, letting it drop. "The ancient one is trapped, the dead are trapped . . . this meadow, the entire valley, maybe all the way down to Duck's settlement, who knows how far north . . . ruined." Poisoned. The scraped lands would never recover, not while the haint—the haints, trapped together—remained. And they were too powerful to bind and ease into rest.

"The tremors?" Gabriel spoke her thought before she could.

She licked her lips, surprised to feel skin peeling from them, as though she'd bitten them raw and not realized. "If the cage holds. I do not think they will worsen." She reached for certainty, but every certainty Isobel had held now felt like salt between her fingers, sliding out of her grasp.

And tangled in all of that, the memory of claws digging into her, trying to consume her. Claws—and the burning heat of silver, the spirit that lived here scraping out her marrow, curling inside the hollowed-out bones.

"There's nothing more I can do here." Admitting it hurt, an unaccustomed failure. "If I try again—I would make things worse."

The presence, the trapped shape of the ancient spirit and the remnants of the dead magicians: they were aware of her now. She was a reminder of what they could never be again. To remain would be a taunt; it would be dangerous and cruel.

She should have heeded the warnings and never come here at all.

PART FOUR

FALSE CROSSROADS

It took Isobel longer to find the strength to stand than it did for Gabriel to pack up the remains of their camp. She watched him, uncertain in her own skin, shifting uneasily, curling her arms over her knees, her spine crackling when she moved, toes too thick for her boots, elbows and fingers awkward, as though they belonged to someone else, stuck onto her body as an afterthought.

She should get up, help Gabriel. His own wounds were still causing him pain; he paused after saddling Uvnee, placing his hand against his side with a wince. But she saw that the ache did not stop him from bending again to pick up the now-cooled bit of metal from the ashes, sliding it back into his pocket, and something within Isobel sparked with bitterness that he would touch it, claim it, the last remnant of the man who had caused all this.

Her hands slid down the fabric of her skirt, the cloth rough under her palms, as though to wipe something from her skin. She did not know if it were some remnants of the magicians, or the ancient spirit, or the deep bone whisper that lingered within her, or some stirring of all three, or if it would remain once she had left the valley or fade over time, only that she could still feel claws scrabbling at her, the wet, smudged smears of something left within, ground into her, impossible to shake or wipe loose.

She thought of her journal, the leather cover worn, the pages nearly half filled in, the basis of her reports for the devil, part and parcel of her contract. She should write this down, too. But she didn't move, even though it was in her pack, within reach. It felt unpleasant, all this, and she would rather not touch on it, not even in her thoughts: too raw to put into words, too *close* to write down yet.

And she wasn't sure what to write about her anger at Gabriel.

"We're set." Gabriel stood over her, blocking the sky, casting a cool shadow over her skin. He offered her his hand, and she took it, letting him help her to her feet, his hold lingering while she tested her balance. Her head no longer swam, and her knees held, so she nodded once at him and he let go, stepping away.

"All right?"

A weight of things asked in those two words, but she could only answer one. "I can stand."

"Can you ride?"

She nodded and went to Uvnee, who for once held still as Isobel fitted her boot into the stirrup, as though aware her rider was not entirely steady yet. When she had the reins in her hands again, her legs wrapped around the rounded sides of her horse, the weight of the saddle against her backside, Isobel felt something give a little, the brittle crackling softening back to flesh and muscle.

Gabriel had waited while she mounted Uvnee, not offering help, and then swung into his own saddle with only a hint of stiffness.

"We're a pair, we two," she said without thinking, not meaning to admit her own aches nor comment on his own. Thankfully, he merely grinned at her, teeth showing briefly before he tugged his hat lower over his forehead and told Steady to get a move on.

It would be all right once they left this place. She hoped.

The sky had clouded over since dawn, low-hanging white streamers now obscuring the mountains, turning the sun's light into a warm, hazy glow. It felt peaceful, restful, save the silence made it ominous. The world was not meant to be so quiet, reminding her that every living thing save them had fled, that the ground below them was neither solid nor safe, that the furious, rage- and sorrow-mad presence still lingered, trapped not by any warding but something far greater, far crueler.

Part of her ached to go back, the sensation of a chore left undone. The other part longed to flee, to never look back.

At that thought, Isobel looked into the clouds, almost expecting to see the Reaper hawk soaring overhead, but the sky was empty. Behind them, the great deer was nowhere in sight. She resisted the urge to look down; no snake would be lurking under Uvnee's hooves, no trail visible in the low grass. Once spirit-animals had their say, they did not linger.

Alone save for each other, they picked their way across the meadow, Gabriel leading them not south the way they'd come but east, where the hills rose up in jagged, reddish-dun slopes, the green patchwork against bare stone, sharp arrows of white-barked pine stretching into the sky. It looked inhospitable, as though to set a single hoof or boot would cause the slope to crumble, but when they came to the edge of the meadow, she saw a narrow trail leading up and out.

"How did you know it was here?"

Gabriel rubbed the back of his neck with one hand, gave her a half-shoulder shrug as his only answer. There were still things her mentor knew that she didn't.

Isobel reined Uvnee in and stared at the head of the trail as though it would apologize. Instead, all she felt was the scrabble of hard claws prickling in her skin, the restless flutter of something attempting to plant itself within her. . . .

Gabriel paused as well, watching quietly as she slipped out of Uvnee's saddle and drew the salt stick from her pack. There was barely a palm's length remaining, cool and moist against her skin.

Isobel bit her lip, rubbing one thumb along the stick, feeling grains of salt scrape loose, sticking to her skin. Whatever lingered within her, she could contain. But she carried only a memory, a shade. The greater threat remained.

There was no warding she could add, no way to hide this meadow the way she had done for Widder Creek. It was too vast, too much power contained within. One unwary traveler, one foolhardy magician drawn by the scent of power, curious about the rumbling of the earth . . .

Isobel did not know what might happen but thought it would not be pleasant.

With that in mind, she slipped the knife from its sheath at her side and used it to cut across her palm, sliding the edge across the sigil marked there. The blood welled up without any pain, and she closed her palm around the stick of salt, letting it stain the white.

"Iz." Gabriel's voice, nearby. Not a question, merely telling her he was there, if she needed him.

She nodded, then used the bloodied salt to draw the devil's sigil once, twice, three times on largish rocks several paces apart. Salt, for protection. Blood, the blood that had been sealed to contract with the Master of the Territory, to bind it to the stone and hold it there.

Bad hunting, the sigil would tell hunters, thinking to find game here. *Angry spirits*, the sigil would tell wanderers unwarned. *Danger*, the sigil would tell the unwary. *Stay out*.

When she was finished, she placed the remaining stick back into her pack and looked at her palm. The cut had healed, the sigil quiet in her hand. Isobel felt nothing but cold.

"I should mark the other entrance," she said faintly. "Someone might come. . . ."

"The wapiti guards that entrance," Gabriel reminded her. "If the spirits are so concerned, let them do a share of the work."

"But . . ."

"Isobel." His voice had gone hard, shoulders tense, the battered brim of his hat pushed back so she could see his face. "Back on your damned horse before I throw you on and tie you there."

Her eyes wide, she remounted and followed him onto the trail, the mule grumbling behind them.

The path Gabriel had found led up into the ridges, hardscrabble trail and bare rock covered by low brush. The footing was unsteady, dirt barely covering fist-sized rocks, occasionally winding along steep cliffs, and Gabriel couldn't stop his thoughts from contemplating what might happen if another quake hit while they were here, imagining the way the ground might ripple and fold, shaking them off the way a horse might flies, and with as little concern.

Telling himself that the cause of the quakes was contained, that they were fewer and further between, did not ease him, not when Isobel kept glancing around her as though expecting something to rise up or fall down on them, how careful she was to not look back the way they'd come, as though the haint she'd riled might be coming after them.

It would not. He was mostly certain of that, as he was mostly certain the ground would not shake under them now.

Steady picked his way along the trail, living up to his name, and Gabriel distracted himself by studying the ground itself, the way the peaks stuttered to jagged stops, the runnels where water had flowed. He wondered if the local people had a story to tell of that, about why the peaks were flattened like tabletops, why the water deep within the bones tended to explode upwards with heat rather than flowing calmly into springs or pools. He wondered who might live here, with the dry air and the poor soil where nothing could grow, and the only thing to hunt would be sure-hooved sheep that would laugh at a stumble-footed mortal on two legs.

Catching a glimpse of a rabbit or squirrel would calm his nerves, he thought, but there still wasn't a songbird to be heard, much less anything land-bound. He glanced again at Isobel, her own hat pulled forward, her shoulders rounded until she might almost be asleep in the saddle, save for the look-arounds and occasional pat along her mare's neck, stroking encouragement.

The sun rose higher, and the trail led them through a thick, sudden mist and then above it. When the trail broadened out enough, they paused to stretch their legs, allowing the horses to rest. There was nothing to be seen but more jagged-edged peaks of dun rock and green pine to every side, the sky wide open above them, the sun filling the pale expanse with glare intense enough to slide even under the brims of his hat, making his eyes squint and water.

They also discovered at that point that the insects, at least, had returned; they managed to surprise a flock of butterflies rising out of a scrabbly patch of flowers, and when they paused for lunch just before the sun reached apex, Isobel was itching madly where something had bitten her.

"You can see forever from here," Isobel said, shading her eyes to look out over the peaks. The angular shapes of trees dotted the slopes below them, broken by blotches of grey rock and red cliff and the occasional sparkle of sunlight off water, where a creek or lake hid in the folds. "What's that up there?" She pointed to a more-distant peak, where the reddish-brown faded to white.

"Snow," Gabriel said after a moment to follow where she was looking. "It's still cold enough there for snow to linger."

Isobel stared at it, then shook her head, not disputing him but likely not believing him either.

"Snow, in mid-summer." For a heartbeat, she was young and wide-eyed, then she shook her head again with a quiet laugh, as though that were the most marvelous thing she'd ever heard and she didn't believe it for a moment.

He made a note to take her north into Metís territory during spring, when the trails were passable again but snow still blanketed the ground, and wondered if they would still be traveling together then.

The meal finished and the horses rested, they remounted and picked up the trail again, finally heading down. The path now was nothing more than a deer track, overgrown at both sides and more rock than dirt underfoot, occasionally falling away on one side to a deep ravine.

They'd just come off one such turn, the sun directly overhead, when he heard Isobel's voice behind him soft but urgent. "Gabriel. Hold up."

He half-turned in the saddle, calculating how long it would take him to load and be ready, his hand settling on his knife instead. Mounted, the blade didn't give him enough reach, but if there were another ghost cat looking for desperation prey . . . And if it were another magician, at high sun, neither gun nor knife would do him any good.

But the look on Isobel's face when he glanced at her wasn't worry or concern but amusement. She might have felt him looking, lifting her chin to draw his gaze to a narrow rock overhang just ahead of them. "We have company."

It took him a moment to see what she meant, then he couldn't believe he'd missed it: dun-colored and elongated, clinging to the side of the rock like a lizard, its head cocked at an angle that was more curiosity than threat: demon.

Back east, the gimcrack novels wailed of the terrible cruelty and malice of demons, that they existed for nothing more than to lure humans to their death and damnation, that they were tools of the devil himself, with eyes of fire and teeth like a tiger. The truth was that demon were creatures of stone and dust more than fire, and while fierce—he would not wish to fight one—they were more mischief than damnation. To a rider alone or a homestead in the wrong place at the wrong time, that might spell disaster. But he rode with the Devil's Hand and had less concern.

"Good day," he said, tipping his hat as he would if they'd met a matron mid-town. "Are you collecting toll for this passage or merely passing the time of day?"

It had been a long while since he'd had cause to be flippant, and nearly as long since he'd heard his companion giggle.

The demon merely stared at them, alert but seemingly unconcerned, its head swiveling uncannily on its neck as they rode by.

"You think there are others?" Isobel asked.

"In these hills? Likely. But they're not liable to challenge us"—she knew that, having encountered demon before, trailing after the Spaniards—"and we should be coming down out of the rocks soon enough and be past them."

"You can tell?" She sounded surprised, then there was a long silence, followed by a relieved-sounding noise. He thought that in her place, he would not have been eager to reach for the Road either.

He waited until they had left the demon a dozen paces behind, the trail widening enough that they could ride side by side, before asking, "Can you still feel . . . it? The valley, I mean."

The haint, he meant.

He couldn't read people the way she could, not natural like breathing, but tension practically shimmered in the way she held the reins, turned her face away from him. "A little. Faintly. Like . . . like thunder in the distance, at night. And there's a . . ." She hesitated. "A sense that I'm not done?"

"Something you've forgotten?" His own hands tightened on the reins, and he felt something in his jaw pop. He would tie her to her saddle and lead the damn mare on a rope all the way back to Flood if she even hinted at wanting to go back there.

"No. Not forgotten." Her voice dropped, darkened. "Just . . . undone. Waiting."

He looked at her again, but her head was down, and all he could see was the top of her hat and the edge of her chin before it sank into the collar of her jacket. He was reminded of a turtle he had seen once, half-buried in mud, contemplating the riverbank before him, thinking deep and mournful turtle thoughts.

"We should be through this pass well before dusk," he said, not looking away. "Plenty of time to find a decent-sized stream for bathing, maybe even one deep enough for swimming. You need another lesson or three before I'm satisfied you won't sink like a stone."

That lifted her head up sharply, and the glare he got at the reminder of her single attempt to swim made him urge Steady on to a faster pace, just in case she decided to chuck something at him.

But even that little easing of the tension disappeared when they crested that last bony ridge and saw the warriors waiting for them in the valley below.

Gabriel had been born in the Territory, his father the son of Eastern settlers, his mother the daughter of a Métis woman. Their farm had been successful enough that he'd been sent off to school when it was clear he had no skill for growing things, with his siblings content to stay behind. He had grown up seeing Métis cousins and the occasional Anishinabeg or Dakota come through, either hunting or trading. He had grown up learning hand language, picking up words here and there, had learned what certain markings and attire meant, and when it was a time to speak, and when he should remain silent, and his time with the Hochunk had taught him how to admit that he did not understand a thing.

He had no idea what it meant, that these five men stood in front of them, their chests bare of decoration or design, bows behind them, knives sheathed. Their faces were round and stern, two bareheaded with narrow braids at either side of their heads, three with their heads covered by long fur caps that, when one of them shifted, Gabriel identified as wolf skin.

Warriors, for all that they showed no weapons in their hands. Behind them, dogs shifted—not bulky travois-dogs but lean creatures who might have shared a grandparent with the wolves these men had killed. They were held on no lead but awaited a command either to stand down or attack.

Apsáalooke, mayhap. Or not. He tried to find some connection to the old man who had traveled with them, but their moccasins were of a different pattern, and the old man's face had been so ancient, so lined, that he could see no familial resemblance here.

"Gabriel?" Isobel had fallen a pace behind him, shifting Uvnee so that they were half-hidden behind Steady's bulk, back with the mule.

The girl he'd first met would have lingered, curiosity overcoming common sense; after their encounter with the Spaniards, the Hand might have pushed forward, demanded their respect. Her behavior now was that of a seasoned rider—wary but polite, aware that they would see her only as a white female, without age or status. That she was the Devil's Hand had no meaning here.

He didn't look back at her, playing the part as he swung out of the saddle and walked forward to meet warriors on their own terms.

Pausing a few paces away, he waited, watching them without meeting their eyes, then focusing on the man to the left standing half a step ahead of the others. The wolf skin on his head draped over his bare shoulders, and Gabriel guessed that he was in his early twenties, perhaps slightly older, and the others with him were a similar age or slightly younger.

Old enough to be experienced, young enough to still be firebrands. That made them dangerous, no matter what their intent. And without knowing for certain what tribe they were, without knowing the politics of this region, making any assumptions could be deadly.

The Road promised adventure, not certainty. Thrice so, traveling with Isobel.

Gabriel lifted his right hand, palm out and fingers spread, to his shoulder and twisted his wrist back and forth several times, then made the sign for trouble, making it a question. They studied him, and as ever, there was a moment of fear, that he had made the wrong sign, that his innocent question—what trouble exists?—had in fact given offense, unintended.

One of the younger men, one without a wolf's mantle, stepped forward, an almost violent movement, and was held back by another, his hand on their arm.

The leader flicked his gaze from Gabriel to behind him, then back to Gabriel again, sizing them up. "You have been to the shaken valley."

His English was rough, with an accent Gabriel could not place, but he spoke it well enough to be understood, which was a relief. If something were to go wrong, he'd rather Isobel be aware of it at that moment, not after he'd had time to translate.

Shaken Valley. As good a name as any, he supposed.

"We have." Were they going to blame them for what was happening? He did not allow his muscles to ready for attack or his hand to reach for his knife, however much he craved the reassurance of it in his hand just then. He cursed that he had left the carbine latched to Steady's saddle; not that it would gave been much use against five opponents, but if nothing else, the wooden butt made an effective club.

"The valley shook while you were there. You angered the spirits."

"Ah . . ." Gabriel wasn't sure trying to explain that it had been a pack of magicians would go over well. Magicians might claim some of the Territory's medicine in their madness, but they were still whites, still outsiders. Gabriel's skin was pale, and he had been in the valley where spirits had been angered enough to send the game away and shake the ground for days in all directions. He was reasonably certain they didn't need any other correlation to assign blame.

He didn't want to fight them, but he had no desire to die, either.

"Iz, be ready to ride forward." He hoped that his voice conveyed what he couldn't say: that she was not to get off her damn horse, that she was not to hesitate, that whatever happened to him, she was to get the blazes out of there as fast as she could, trampling them if need be.

The men could not catch Uvnee once she took flight, but those dogs would certainly be able to inflict damage if they were given a chance. Four dogs, five men. Steady, given cause, could take one, possibly two of the dogs out, plus one of the men. The mule would be able to protect itself, even with the ghost cat's scarring on its hide. He could take two of the men out, maybe three, before they dragged him off Steady's back.

All those thoughts flashed like heat lightning and were gone, leaving him loose for whatever was to come. He gave a quiet command, and Steady's square head lowered, thick neck curved in a way that would warn anyone accustomed to horses to steer clear of his teeth and hooves.

If they could not pass in peace, he would at least buy time for Isobel to reach safety.

Gabriel grinned crookedly; when the devil had promised him peace in exchange for this duty, he should have assumed it would be this way.

His expression must have been fierce; one of the other men wearing a wolf's mantle drew back, eying him consideringly. Gabriel dropped Steady's reins entirely and lifted his hands in a gesture that asked, "What are you waiting for?" in any language, and let his grin widen. They might wear a wolf's skin, but he could *be* one.

Since leaving the valley, Isobel had focused her attention on how Uvnee placed her hooves, the narrowness of the trail, the blueness of the sky, and the intense irritation of the insect bites on her hands and neck, as a way to—not to forget; there was no way she would forget—put aside what had happened behind them. Even the demon, normally cause for concern, had been merely a distraction, all the more so when it did nothing but watch them as they rode past.

It was like kneading bread: you let your body do one thing, pay so much attention to it, there was no room for anything else. Empty mind and full hands, Ree had said, over and over, when a loaf turned out badly. If you worried about the baking, you would ruin the dough. And so, she'd focused on the trail and the placement of her hands on the reins and the way she leaned in the saddle to keep Uvnee balanced, until the feel of claws and wet smudges faded.

But when she followed Gabriel down that last rise and saw the men waiting for them, Isobel felt her stomach clench and tighten, hot fingers sliding up her spine and spreading along her scalp. Not anger, not fear, but something beyond that, something fierce and inevitable and closer to, if she had to name it, intense *annoyance*.

She reined Uvnee back, allowing Gabriel to take the lead as she studied the five the way the boss had trained her to read people—taking in their stance, their expressions, the way they grouped themselves—to see what it was they wanted that they would not allow themselves to name.

They were angry, she decided, and they were afraid, and they were very brave to come this close to where they knew an angry sprit lived. The fact that the ancient spirit was not angry at them did not matter; they had come to see what *had* angered it, to do what the spirit wished them to do to end its anger.

And they had done it on their own, she thought, watching their faces. If they claimed a victory, it would be theirs alone, but if they came to ruin, the spirit's anger would not find its way back to their people as well.

She felt a twinge of sympathy for them that faded the moment they made a move toward Gabriel. Her mentor's hissed warning was heard and ignored. She would not leave him here.

Her blunderbuss was strapped to her pack; even if she could lay hands on it without them noticing, she couldn't ram shot and powder fast enough to be useful. Her knives, both the one at her waist and the larger one strapped to Uvnee's saddle, were within reach, but she would not stand a chance against even one of the warriors facing them.

The sigil in her palm remained cool, without an itch of power. The Agreement the boss had with the tribes required only that they maintain the peace so long as no insult was given—and gave them the right to determine insult. Even against the Hand herself, if she were foolish enough.

She had not been responsible for what had happened in the valley; magicians were not under the devil's authority—the tribes could not hold the boss responsible for what one might do any more than they could blame him for the wind or the rains.

But if a white man had led them here, had meddled in such a way to injure the Territory itself, using magicians as his tools . . . the tribes would be within rights to hold the boss to account.

Isobel wished she'd thought to pack one of Polly's headache powders as well as her cramping remedy.

The Right Hand might have soothed tempers into something calmer.

But Marie was not here, and Isobel saw one of the warriors reach for his bow, while another's knife cleared its sheath, and Gabriel was just *standing* there.

Isobel felt her larger knife come to her hand, and then it was no longer in her hand but blade first in the grasses, inches from the toes of the one with the drawn bow.

"Hold!"

She might have shouted the word; she might have cried it. Neither the blade nor the word would have been enough, but she heard their heartbeats pulse in the air and caught at them, stilling them, slowing them to where they could not move at all.

Six heartbeats fluttered in her palm, the *pulsepulsepulse* a softer sound than her own breathing, so delicate, so easy to close her fingers, tighten and squeeze . . .

The Hand opened her palm and kneed Uvnee forward, the mule close at her heels. One heartbeat stuttered and fell, and behind her she knew Gabriel was swinging into Steady's saddle, leaning forward, his body still not quite his own, tied to her own will, her *irritation*.

Five pairs of eyes followed her as she rode past, a darkness seething in them. Isobel could feel the hatred surging like a living thing, pressing to break free, to lunge, pull her from Uvnee's back and rend and tear her into shreds. She had never been hated before, not with this hot, focused intensity, and the urge to strike back against it, to clench her fingers and still their heartbeats utterly, washed through her, a flame to kindling.

Instead, as they left the five behind, she forced her fingers to ease, uncurling, letting the heartbeats flutter away one by one.

She waited, listening for the sound of pursuit, for cries of rage or anger. Instead, there was silence, stunned and, she thought with no small satisfaction, respectful.

"Izzy."

She wasn't Izzy anymore. She hadn't been Izzy in a long time.

"Isobel, what did you do?" His voice was hoarse, framing a hundred questions in the one.

"I don't know." She couldn't explain it, couldn't shape the knowledge into words. There was the feel of something moving within her, molten and slow, and it was both strange and familiar, and deeply uncomfortable. "If they had attacked, you would have been hurt, maybe killed, and it would have done nothing. If they had tried to attack me, I . . ."

Her voice faltered. What would she have done? She kept her eyes steadily on the grassy slope in front of Uvnee, did not allow her thumb to press into the center of the sigil, the way she had learned to seek reassurance. She had acted as the Hand, but the sigil had remained cool, the slow burn inside her coming from . . . from where?

She thought of the molten whisper sliding within her, holding the ancient spirit caged, holding the poison within itself, and her throat closed up and her eyes cast down, and she had nothing more to say in answer to Gabriel's question.

Thankfully, he did not ask again.

Gabriel hadn't realized he was trembling until the warriors—and their dogs—were distant behind them. He recognized the reaction; it was the same sensation he'd get after making an argument to the court, when expected opposition hadn't been raised, when it was all over and in the judge's hand to decide.

He'd never thought to feel that again in the Territory.

He looked over at Isobel, who had pushed her hat back and lifted her face to the sky, where the blue had disappeared again behind clouds, pale white broken by darker, more ominous ones. It didn't feel like a storm was brewing; they'd likely not have to worry about more than a passing shower, and there was far less risk of a sudden windstorm here, surrounded by sloping hills, than the plains. But he scanned the horizon anyway, looking for potential structures or outcrops where they could take shelter if needed.

There was nothing as far as the eye could see save the dip and rise of sagebrush-dotted hills, and occasional clumps of rock, broken by a tree here and there, solitary against the sky.

"They knew we'd be there. They knew where we'd been."

"Yah." There was what looked like an abandoned farmstead to the northeast. He hadn't thought to head that way, but then he hadn't thought to head this way at all, so it was never-no-mind what he chose, he supposed.

He angled Steady in that direction, Uvnee keeping pace next to him. The mule wandered off, chomped a few clumps of grass, then wandered back. Gabriel saw something spook under its hooves, furred and fast, and felt one knot of worry ease.

It also reminded him how very hungry he was. When had they last eaten something more than coffee and cornmeal or dried meats? Too long. He reached into the nearest saddlebag and pulled out a chunk of dried apple, eying it with resignation. It wasn't a warm meal and a comfortable chair, but he'd had worse.

"Eat something," he told Isobel.

"Not hungry."

"Didn't ask if you were. Eat something."

She said something uncomplimentary about high-handed riders, but when he turned to look, she was rummaging through her own saddle-bag, pulling out a mushcake and biting into it without any enthusiasm whatsoever.

"It could be worse," he said. "You could be stuck eating grass."

She contemplated the remaining cake in her hand and gave a shrug. "Without honeycomb on it, I'm not sure there's much difference."

Her argument was solid.

She took another bite of the cake, then fed the rest to the mule. "How did they know?"

"Remember what I said about not knowing why a native does something, Isobel? Goes for how they know, too. Some mutter about tricks and medicine; I think they just gossip better than we do."

She didn't smile at that, the way he'd hoped.

"Those magicians, the ones who didn't die . . ." She took a deep breath. "They're bound to cause trouble. They won't be able to help themselves. They've been broken, their madness no longer controlled. Lacking the power they'd hoped to gain, they'll scrabble for any they can find, and damn the cost. Not only crossroads, Gabriel. Anything with power. Any*one*."

A tic in her cheek jumped once, twice, and she reached up to touch the two feathers in her braid, fingertips ghosting along their surface.

"You, you mean?"

"Or you." She turned her head to look at him. "Any rider who can feel the road, any dowser, anyone with planting skills . . . Any dream-walker. White or native. They won't care; they'll just take."

Gabriel drew a breath, considering the ramifications of a magician attacking a native encampment, trying to take the power of one of their elders, one of their medicine folk.

"Magicians are not bound by the Agreement," he said, but they both knew that wouldn't matter, not if a tribe were driven to anger by such an insult. Not if the magician were white-born. And hundreds of years of careful, cautious coexistence . . . shattered.

Where the Spanish spell had failed to undermine the devil's hold on the Territory, that could succeed. The anger Gabriel felt didn't surprise him, but the guilt did.

"We have no way to find them, save we hear of disaster after the fact. The Territory's too large to go chasing after rumor, Isobel."

The look she turned on him, full of a savage, quiet frustration, should not have made him want to laugh so badly.

"I *should* be able to find them. What use am I if I can't?"

Something leapt out in front of the horses, causing Uvnee to shy—a brace of rabbits, startled by their approach. Then something swooped overhead, and Gabriel looked up, expecting to see a hawk or eagle looking to catch an easy dinner.

Instead, brown-and-white wings spread over them at an angle, an owl turning slow circles, two beats and soar, two beats and soar, and the faint, sharp sound of *oooo-aw ooo-aw* in the breeze.

"The poor bastard must be starving to be out during the day."

Isobel heard Gabriel's comment, but all of her attention was on the owl swooping overhead. It could not have been the same owl she saw in the trees that morning; there was no way it could have flown this far, no reason for it to have flown this far. Owls did not wander, particularly in daylight, and the likelihood of it following this track in search of prey seemed slim at best.

And yet.

Isobel reined Uvnee to follow the owl's lead, angling away from the path they'd chosen. Every story she'd ever heard claimed that owls were bringers of bad news, of death, of sorrow. But that was what they'd been following all along, hadn't it? And all those things . . . the boss always said they were what taught wisdom, too.

Wisdom isn't knowledge. Knowledge teaches you it's not wise to risk. Wisdom tells you why you should.

They'd been playing faro after hours. Molly and Jack and the boss, and . . . Suzette, it had been. Isobel had been freshening their drinks, listening to the conversation. They had been talking about death, and loss, something that had happened outside of Flood that Isobel hadn't been privy to. And the boss had said that about knowledge and wisdom, and the conversation had paused, then moved on to something else.

She'd remembered that, even though she hadn't understood it. She still wasn't sure she did. But maybe . . . a Hand needed wisdom even more than knowledge.

"Isobel?" Gabriel's voice was a question, but she knew he was already following her, the mule snorting its displeasure like an old man told to change chairs just as he got comfortable, as they picked up a slow trot, the horses showing pleasure at the chance to run, even for a bit.

The owl stayed just ahead of them, then dipped and with a fold of its wings, disappeared into a hollow, beyond which a stand of tall narrow pines rose. If it went into the trees, she would lose it. . . . Isobel felt her breath catch, something drawing her on with more urgency, and she dug her heels into Uvnee's sides, startling the mare into a jouncing lope, Steady and the mule quickly left behind.

"Isobel, damn it!"

Gabriel's shout was exasperated, and the drumming of hooves told her he'd kicked Steady into a gallop to catch up. But Uvnee was faster and Isobel was lighter, and they stayed in the lead until she suddenly pulled the mare up, hauling on the reins like the greenest rider afraid of falling off.

The mare kicked her hooves and bucked lightly in protest but seemed no more inclined to go forward than Isobel.

Her breath harsh and rattling in her chest, Isobel looked the way Gabriel had taught her, her gaze sweeping from left to right, never resting too long on any one thing, taking in the details without trying to understand them, finding everything that didn't belong, anything that might be a potential threat.

The pale trunks of firestarter mixed with spindly pine along the far edge, hemming two sides of the meadow with green shadows. The third side, to their left, ended in pale, jagged-faced rock rising well over her head, sheer enough that not even the most ambitious goat or demon would try it.

But none of these were threats, none of those things held her attention past noting, because of what waited directly in front of her.

Tucked into the hollow was a wide, flat expanse of grass growing blue-green, a dream-perfect place to turn the horses loose and let them romp and graze for days, an entire herd of horses, lacking only a stream to make it perfect. But something other than horses had gotten there first.

Closer to the rock wall, the grass had been charred in two thick lines, maybe twenty paces each, black and sooty, not quite in the center of the meadow, and where the lines crossed, two figures paced around each other, snarling and snapping, their arms moving, shoulders shifting, legs stalking, until they seemed less human form than dust-dancer, swirling towers of dun-colored wind.

Magicians. Isobel recognized it with a gut blow, their power rising and swirling within them like too-strong perfume, making her gag. And within that swirl she tasted a now familiar scent lingering in the heart, the hot burnt smell of sorrow, and madness.

She had found two of the surviving magicians from the valley.

Her skin prickled, nausea rising into her throat, but they did not look up, did not look away from each other, didn't notice she had come thundering over the ridge. They were trapped, she realized, watching them circle each other like wolves over an elk carcass, caught somehow within a makeshift crossroads, the power within both bait and trap.

But how? Isobel rested her palms on the mare's neck, reins forgotten, and breathed steadily, trying to calm both the animal and herself. Magicians were drawn to crossroads like bears to berries, but only for the power within them, and a crossroads gained that power slowly, over time. Something so new-drawn would have nothing within it to pull; even Isobel, at this distance, could tell that the only power there was what the magicians had brought themselves.

But that power . . .

Isobel stiffened even as she urged the reluctant mare closer, and her mouth went dry. Magicians . . . they were not mortal any longer, but they were born so, born human. Even when they gave themselves over to the winds, they were still human. But what swirled within these two figures was not.

A sliver of understanding fell into her hands, fitted into the space that had been empty. They had escaped with their lives, these two— but they had taken the ancient one's medicine with them. And more— the pounding of her pulse echoed the thundering of hooves within them, their coats the shadow of ancient wings; the sacred blood of the Territory poured over their hands and splattered their faces. She could see it on them, fresh as the moment of slaughter.

Her palm burned and her eyes itched, and Isobel realized she had urged the mare even closer, until Uvnee balked, planting hooves and tossing her head, white-rimmed eyes and trembling sides telling Isobel in no uncertain terms that she would move no farther.

Isobel slipped from the saddle and took another few steps forward, drawn by her rage, only to feel herself yanked backward, a hard hand on her shoulder. The hours of training Gabriel had forced her through kicked in, and she broke free of the hold, throwing herself backward— away from the crossroads—and reaching for the blade in her boot.

"Hold," a voice commanded, and only then did Isobel realize that she was not the only one outside the crossroads trap. A figure glared at her, a wide-brimmed hat pulled low, a long leather coat over shirt and trousers much like Gabriel's, down to the worn leather riding boots, but the shape . . .

The woman seemed to realize Isobel was female at the same moment, but other than pushing her hat back to better study the newcomer, she did not react, her attention only a quarter on Isobel, the rest returning to the scene within the crossroads.

Silvering hair glinted under the sunlight, a high forehead and sharp bones below, and Isobel realized that she knew that face, although she couldn't place it. Had this been someone who had come through the saloon, someone she had read for the boss? That didn't seem right, but she couldn't figure it closer until the woman reached up and tugged at the lapel of her coat, revealing something that also glinted silver in the light.

"Stay where you are," the road marshal told her calmly, her attention still on the crossroads. "Don't be a fool; you don't want to get any closer to this."

Isobel's memory for faces placed her then. The dining hall in Patch Junction. The woman had been seated at a table with another woman, the only table without a man at it, and Isobel had noted that. It had also been the first time Isobel had ever seen a woman in trousers. Months later, Isobel understood the appeal when most of your day was spent in the saddle.

"We've been tracking the same prey," she said to the woman, careful to keep her body still; this woman had the look of someone who slept with both eyes open and a hand on her weapons, and only a fool would give her cause to violence.

"Then you're a fool, girl, and like to be a dead one soon enough."

Isobel didn't react to the insult, digging her fingertips into the flesh of the sigil to remind herself of what mattered, keeping her gaze on the marshal, with only a flicker of her eyes sideways to where the magicians still circled each other. "No fool, and not dead yet. Unlike you. How long do you think you can hold them there?"

Isobel knew the answer already; she could feel where the makeshift crossroads was already beginning to fray under their assault. It might have been enough to hold one, but two, driven to an even deeper madness than usual? The marshal was fortunate it had not broken already.

The owl had done them all a good turn, directing her here, and she thanked it silently, hoping it would hear.

"That's none of your concern," the marshal replied, "and nothing a posse should be poking at."

Isobel almost laughed, even as she heard Gabriel ride up behind her, the creak of leather telling her he'd swung down out of the saddle. She lifted a hand to tell him to stop but didn't look away from the marshal, willing the woman to listen to her.

"We are no posse, following no bounty," she said, and then turned her hand so that the palm faced the marshal. It was perhaps too far for her to see the mark etched into her palm, but as the woman had shown her sigil, so too would Isobel.

"My name is Isobel. And your trap is fading. Will you allow me to aid you?"

The marshal glared at her suspiciously, and Isobel suddenly understood the expression she'd seen more than once on the boss's face, when someone took heavy losses at the table but refused to come out and ask what they'd come for, and end the game.

"They are not fugitives under the Law," Isobel said, and there was more ice in her voice now, irritation surging again. "You have no right to hold them, even if you could." The Law gave road marshals the right to bring those accused of crimes before a judge, to intervene in arguments between settlers, to negotiate quarrels between natives and settlers if requested to do so, but the Law, like the devil, held no sway over magicians. Only the winds themselves held that, and the winds did not care.

"Complaint has been made against them," the marshal responded, and Isobel realized—belatedly, annoyed at herself for the failure—that the marshal was not alone. Two men stood behind the woman, far enough away that Isobel had not noticed them, faint shadows compared to the flame of the figures in the crossroads.

She narrowed her eyes at them, frowning. "What complaint have they made?"

"What right is it of yours to know?"

"You'll dance all day if you keep this up," Gabriel growled, and before she could stop him, he was striding past Isobel, the edge of his coat flapping behind him as he walked, hat in his hand, indignant, heedless of the magicians still pressing their will against the trap that held them.

The marshal did not back down but stared back, left hand dropping to the butt of the pistol at her waist, right hand reaching up to touch the space where her sigil rested.

Isobel had never considered that a marshal's sigil might be more than identification, and called herself a fool even as her attention was drawn again by the crossroads, the impossible-to-ignore flickers of madness and sorrow growing fiercer as the trap lost power. Whatever Road medicine the marshal had used to construct it, the magicians were perilously close to erasing it—and when they did, they would consume each other. And, without thought, caught in that madness, anyone within reach.

Gabriel must have sensed her desperation, because he wasted no more time.

"Marshal, this is Isobel née Lacoyo Távora, the Devil's Hand, and she ranks you in this regard. Stand down and let her aid you."

∽ ∽ ∽

Gabriel's interruption was one of desperation, inserting himself where he had no right being, but the marshal had sense enough of her kind to not be a fool, for which Gabriel would ever be thankful. He could *feel* Isobel tense and then relax behind him as the marshal eased her hands away from her weapon and stepped back just enough to no longer be an immediate threat.

"Been a while since a Hand rode out of Flood," she said, not taking her gaze off either one of them. Not a fool, but not fool enough to accept them at only their word, either.

Isobel stepped forward then, her left hand outstretched, palm up, so the marshal could see it better. She glanced once, then nodded, and Gabriel had cause to wonder if she'd seen the sigil in flesh before, the way she took it in stride once Isobel'd identified herself.

"So, what would you have done, Hand?" The marshal crossed her arms over her chest and eyed Isobel. "Unless you've some way to bind not one but two magicians and force them to answer questions . . . a honey pot seemed my only recourse."

Gabriel should not have found her description of the trap amusing, but the visual—of the magicians as bear cubs with their paws caught in the sticky bait—forced him to press his lips together so he didn't smile.

Isobel only scowled at the false crossroads, tugging at her braid with one hand. "How did you do it?"

The marshal—who had not yet given her name—smirked a little at that. "Not all tricks are in the devil's cards," she said.

Isobel accepted that with a shrug of her own, circling—at what he hoped was a safe distance—the two figures still stalking each other around the center of the crossroads. She paced them, then turned and walked the other way, going counter-wise.

That seemed to draw their attention away from each other, and Gabriel tensed, but other than one of them hissing at her when she drew close, neither made any move beyond that, and it seemed to Gabriel's eye, at least, that they drew back into the crossroads, their movements slowing to an almost resigned pace.

He had no idea what she'd done and no desire to ask. Let them all keep their secrets; he wanted no part. He moved to gather Uvnee's reins with Steady's, rope-penning them with the mule. If they were truly panicked, it would be easy enough for them to pull up and run, but anything shy of that and the ropes would remind them to stay put.

Isobel circled around crossroads once more, then stepped away. Her hat hung from its cord down her back now, strands of hair escaped from her braid to curl around her face, and Gabriel thought that she looked very young if you didn't know better.

"It will hold, for a while longer," she said, and her voice was quiet, tired. "Enough time for us to talk, at least." She turned and looked at Gabriel, the plea clear in her gaze; he nodded once and walked over to join them.

"Those two," he said, tilting his head at the figures who had kept their distance. "You say they claimed insult?"

The marshal glanced at her companions, then turned back to them. Her arms were still crossed against her chest, but the rest of her pose had eased, and Gabriel was reminded suddenly of a professor back at William and Mary who would stand like that for the entire lecture. He'd been militia when he was younger, rumor said, and had forgotten how to sit down.

"These men have claimed insult given to them." The marshal studied Isobel, ignoring Gabriel. Her eyes were light-colored, her skin tight against her bones the way some folk aged, sun-spotted, and he thought she'd been a handful and a half when she was younger and with more to prove.

"Insult, against magicians?" Isobel's voice skirted scorn and amusement, but only just, and he thought that was a thing she'd sucked from the devil's teat, for it to be that perfect.

The marshal extended one arm and flicked her fingers inward, telling the two figures to come closer. They did so, though reluctantly.

"Magicians are still men. You say they have no right to that claim?"

The younger man opened his mouth as though to protest the marshal's question, but his companion—an older man, dark hair trimmed close to his scalp and greying at the temples—placed one hand on his shoulder, silencing him. Like Gabriel, he knew enough to stay out of this.

The younger man shook off the hand, and on closer inspection, Gabriel decided he was not young after all, but merely carried that air of youthful arrogance. His hair was long, pulled into a queue that fell halfway down his back, and his worn cloth jacket and boots told Gabriel he was Eastern-born, likely a military man turned scout. His kind—restless, quarrelsome—were fleas on the back of respectable folk, but like fleas, there was no escaping them.

The other man's clothing was of better quality, if equally worn, and his boots said he, too, was a riding man, not accustomed to long miles of walking. There was a look about the man's eyes, though, a steadiness where his companion shifted, and Gabriel thought of the badge tucked into his pocket, and thought for certain there'd be a matching pinprick in the man's lapel where the sigil should go.

But he didn't offer it back to the man. Not yet.

"I say, first, that claiming insult against a magician is a fool's walk." Isobel's tone was tart, her hands fisted at her hips, shoulders back and chin up, all signs that she was bracing for a brangle. "And second, that they drew the insult on themselves by meddling where they had neither right nor reach."

Her gaze shifted from the marshal then to the men behind her, and Gabriel couldn't say for certain, but if he'd been the recipient of that stare, he might have apologized for anything he even thought he might have done. These men were either made of sterner stuff, or they were in fact fools, because the older man tried to rebut her charges.

"If I understand your use of the term, I gave no insult, none that any sane man would take." Sharp tones, clearly bitten off, eyes narrowed.

"I merely offered these men an opportunity to better themselves, to bring under harness forces that—"

"Your first mistake was thinking that they were sane," Isobel snapped at him, cutting his words mid-shaping. "And your second was approaching them at all. Are you yourself mad? Or did you have some deeper intent in your actions?"

Gabriel stilled, the letter from Abner suddenly a burning-hot coal against his skin, despite the fact that it was safe in the pack draped over Steady's saddle, his earlier fears confirmed. If this man had been sent by the president, if Jefferson thought somehow to utilize the medicine of the Territory for his own use . . .

Only a madman would do so. A madman or a fool . . . or someone who did not believe the stories that came out of the Territory. Someone who thought with a logical mind, searching for explanations that could be turned and controlled.

Someone who thought the Territory merely another parcel of land to be owned and used.

Isobel, unaware of his thoughts, had turned on the older woman. "Are you aware of what you protect? What they have done?" She didn't wait for a response but plowed on, her body practically shaking with rage, hands clenched at her sides. "These fools, for some reason I cannot scry, thought to make use of magicians—not one but many."

The marshal scoffed at that. "No one can convince a magician to do anything it does not chose to do. And there is no insult in bad ideas, else we'd all be up before judgment on a regular basis."

"If you offer them something they want badly enough, magicians are manipulated easy as any," Isobel said. "Enough to come together, enough to perform abominations without honor, to entrap an ancient and force it back to flesh, to strip away its medicine for their own use."

The marshal's eyes widened and she drew a breath in as Isobel's words sank home. "Impossible."

"I would have agreed," Gabriel said before Isobel could lose her temper, "except it seems to have been more improbable than impossible."

The woman's gaze flickered between them, then to the two Americans, staring at them as though seeing them truly for the first time.

"They failed."

"They succeeded," Isobel corrected her, her voice the edge of a blade. "Well enough that those magicians slaughtered buffalo for their medicine, well enough that those magicians were then powerful enough to use that to pull an ancient spirit into their grasp—but not well enough that they could hold that grasp. Well enough that the Territory itself had to intervene."

Gabriel's attention flickered to Isobel at the mention of the buffalo, his fingers tightening in reaction to what she had described. The primal heart of the Territory, slaughtered . . .

No marshal who lived past their first year carrying the sigil was slow on the uptake. "Blood and stone . . . The quakes. That was their doing?"

Isobel's tone eased in the face of the woman's clear shock and fury. "These two were the instigators. The two you have trapped here . . ." She didn't look at the magicians within the crossroads, but Gabriel could tell from the set of her shoulders that it was an effort to resist. "They were among those who lived."

"You have no proof." The older man stepped forward, ready to argue his case, and the marshal turned on them, her disagreement with Isobel of far less import than her new-kindled anger with the two of them.

"You, do not speak," she warned him. "Nor you, either." She stabbed a finger at the younger man's chest. "The word of the Devil's Hand carries far more weight than anything you might say in these lands. If you'd half the intelligence you think you own, you'd know that much at least."

Under perhaps any other circumstances, Gabriel would have been amused, but Isobel's eyes kept flicking sideways, the urge to look at the makeshift crossroads clearly held back by a thread, and he was imagining every scrap of silver he owned coated with thick black tarnish. . . . There was nothing amusing about this at all.

"The devil's what?" The older man was shaking his head, looking at the marshal, then Isobel again, and then to Gabriel, as though another man could explain it all in ways that made sense. The younger man, at least, looked distinctly uncomfortable, like a man who'd woken in a jail cell and only slowly remembered the events of the night before.

"Oh, you poor, foolish bastard," Gabriel said. "They told you nothing, did they? They sent you here to treat with magicians and told you nothing of what you dared, what you risked."

Despite himself, Gabriel felt relief: the things he had told Abner had gone no further, or at least not into the hands of the men who'd sent these two their orders.

"Tell me, did those orders come from Jefferson himself or some even greater fool?"

Whatever bluster the American would have attempted to hide behind, the marshal cut him off before he could do more than open his mouth.

"Enough." She turned to Isobel, lifting her hands in a gesture of appeasement. "Whoever they are, whatever they have done, the false claim will be judged and proper restitution determined. There's a judiciary a few days from here—"

"This is not a matter for a judge." Isobel's voice was sharp, and Gabriel felt his spine straighten in response, alert to violence even though he knew she would not, was reasonably certain the marshal would not, let it go that far.

"A false claim of insult is a matter of Law."

Gabriel licked his lips and damned himself for a fool. "The Law is set for the affairs of those within the Territory. These men are outsiders, two for where they come from and two for what they are. Surely it would make more sense to have the Master of the Territory consider their actions and determine their punishment?" He cast a glance at the makeshift crossroads and the two figures now standing still, watching them. A shiver ran down his spine, remembering what Isobel had said. These were not quick-witted Farron, not allies even for a moment. If they broke loose while these two argued jurisdiction . . .

"How would you even transport them?" he went on. "You with

one horse, them with none? You'd walk them two days to stand before the bench?"

"That is exactly what I aim to do," she said. "My duty." Her hand had shifted to her waist, where the pistol snugged into a leather harness. Gabriel didn't know too much about handguns, but he'd seen the like before, back East. If it came to bullets, they had already lost.

"The Tree is equal to the *Infinitas.*" Isobel's voice, Isobel's words, but with an undercurrent, an echo he'd not heard in her recently. They had invoked the Master of the Territory, and he had come.

The Tree was *not* equal to the *Infinitas.* That awareness simmered in Isobel, resentful. But in this instance, it took precedence. It *must* take precedence. The Devil was Master of the Territory, but he did not own it, nor did he wish to. And the Left Hand was the *hidden* force, not the overt. The rebuke was gentle but clear, and Isobel bowed before it, objections tromped underfoot before they could rise.

Patience, maleh mishpat. It wasn't his voice but the memory of it, and below that the whisper again, pouring molten into her ear, both of them counseling her: *Abide. There is a greater plan at play.*

She did not understand, but she was not required to understand, only obey.

"You may take these two to stand in front of the bench," Isobel said. "And your Judge will pronounce judgment on them for claiming false insult." The Americans, she suspected, would likely be stripped of everything save boots and saddle and sent across the Mudwater, warned never to return. "But the magicians are . . ."

The marshal went toe to toe with Isobel, a handspan taller but more slender, age giving her a brittleness Isobel could sense more than see, but a wicked cunning as well. "They must be taken to tell their portion of the story. Then the judge will decide."

Isobel narrowed her eyes, the heated prickle of power seething behind them enough to make her want to shake the marshal, to scream in frustration at the woman's blindness. Because she had trapped them, she thought them controllable. Thought herself *in* control, as though anything flesh could control these winds. "Then we will travel with you."

A heartbeat, stretched and tense, and the marshal dipped her chin, dark eyes intent on Isobel's face. "Agreed."

Gabriel broke the awkward silence that followed. "If we're to travel together then, might we know your name?"

The marshal looked surprised, as though only now realizing that she had never identified herself. "LaFlesche. Marshal Abigail LaFlesche."

Gabriel took her offered hand first, shaking it firmly. "You've Umonhon work on your jacket," he said. "You've kin there?"

"My mother's sister's husband." Her hand brushed the design on the arm of her jacket, as though to reassure herself it was there, then she offered her hand to Isobel, who took it. The marshal's fingers were narrow and hard, and Isobel thought that she would not fumble with either knife or gun if the need arose. But not all threats answered to blade or bullet.

Then again, she had crafted a false crossroads that caught not one but two magicians, however distracted. Isobel would not underestimate the marshal either.

"So, these two, we can bind and walk." Gabriel gestured to the Americans. "But how now do we deal with the remaining two?"

LaFlesche smiled then, the long bones of her face at odds with the sudden gleam of intelligent mischief in her eyes. "Well, it's a fine thing you came along when you did, then, isn't it?"

The magicians had stilled once Isobel had added her own warding to the trap, but they were aware of her now; their eyes followed her as she came closer, tracking her movement the way she thought a ghost cat might, waiting for the ripe moment to leap, to rend and tear. . . .

She reminded herself that the massive ghost cat had died when it tried to attack them, and that these two were already bound by the marshal's work, and weakened by their struggle against each other. But she would not underestimate them, even so.

"You should have kept to your ways," she told them, although she was not certain if they could hear her through the bindings, or if they were still able to comprehend human speech. Magicians went mad enough, but what she had touched in the valley had traveled past that madness into something far worse, a windstorm of thorns, thunder, and lightning. Simply because these two retained human shape, she should not assume anything human remained within.

The only way to tell would be to push at them, push herself *through* them, and that was the very thing she had no intention of doing; if the whisper came back to suggest it, she would cut it from her head with a dull knife before listening.

One of the magicians, slender-built with eyes the color of a coalstone, hissed at her again when she drew close. His face was hatch-marked with scars, raised white lines that looked too regular to have been accidental, and he had only four fingers on the hand he raised to her, as though to scratch at her eyes through the binding, only to draw back his arm with a yelp.

The wards held. But for how long? The false crossroads had drawn them with the promise of power without there being anything in truth for them to draw on—and she was still vastly curious as to how the marshal had managed that—and they had near-drained each other in trying to escape, but . . .

Magicians. A wise soul ran from them; they did not draw closer.

"Odds are no one ever claimed a Hand was wise," she said to herself, and then raised her voice so that the two inside the warding could hear her but the others behind her could not.

"If it were left to me, I would crack you open and scatter your ashes back to the winds. But false claim of insult has been brought against you, and the Law says that you must stand by while they answer for it." She didn't think they understood what she was saying, but the second figure, bulkier, his face hidden by thick chunks of dust-black hair, turned slightly when she spoke, as though he were listening. "You will come with us, without struggle, to stand before Law."

And once there, well. The Tree might carry the Law, but its roots were deep into the Territory itself. What they had done, to the ancient one they'd abused, to the buffalo-spirits they'd slaughtered, to those harmed by the quakes that followed . . . that would not go unanswered.

"Do you understand?"

Isobel waited for a response but expected none, and none came. Accepting their silence as consent, she dropped to one knee and placed her palm not against the ground itself but on the joint lines of the warding.

It hissed and hummed against her, identifying her as not-to-be-contained but not yet willing to yield to her.

She spread her fingers, feeling delicately along the tangled lines. Some push of the winds from within, driven by the magicians' madness, tangling with the warm, earthy feel of the Tree, a sense of the marshal's own self that matched that hard, capable hand and the intelligence in her face. And there, the tang of sulphur and bone where her own warding took hold. One overlaying the other, tangling where they met, neither giving way.

Another time and place, Isobel would have been tempted to sink down, unpick the threads of the Tree, reweave them into her own understanding, learn how the marshal had crafted a crossroads where none should exist. But now was not the time, and this was never the place.

Instead, she followed the scent of sulphur and bone, catching and pulling at her own work, reweaving the barrier into a net to cast over the two figures rather than the crossroads entire. But the lines were too tangled, the living thrum of the marshal's sigil and the hollow echo of the crossroads beneath it knotting them up, barely able to contain the cold-fire fury of the souls trapped within.

The magicians, sensing what she meant to do, fought her, pushing her away and tugging her off-balance, bleeding wind and shrieking in silent thunder, searching for a weakness they could seep into and crack her open like a nut.

She flailed under that push and tug, grabbing for the power shimmering and sparking, fingers scratching at the sigil in her palm, demanding the help she had been sworn, that had been sworn to the strength of the Territory.

But rather than the now-familiar dizziness, memories of mornings in the saloon came to her; the softness of how the sun rose, light touching rooftops and sliding into windows where drapes had been drawn aside, the first cry of a cockerel and the stamp-clang of the blacksmith's hammer, the first slam of a door and the copper rattle of pans in the kitchen, the chiming of the winding clock as the day began. She missed it all with a sudden shocking intensity, her first true understanding of homesickness, and—trusting instinct—she grabbed hold of it, grabbed hold of the stillness before dawn, the hush before the first waking breath, the stillness of a beloved voice before it spoke and the echo after a farewell, and shoved it all into the warding, binding it with molten threads of silver, even as she gripped the earth and bone with both hands and pulled it tight.

The magicians screamed, the howling of a winter wind crashing over a rooftop, the roar of a spring storm taking down any tree that dared stand in its path. Isobel's knees buckled, cold sweat coating her skin, but the Tree withstood, and the bones withstood, and slowly, slowly, the wind died down, sulky and sullen. The sigil in her palm flared, cold itch and a burning light, and the figures within the binding went to their knees, then onto their sides, inert, harmless, asleep.

Isobel felt the false crossroads crumble, the original warding dissolve, both the marshal's and her own, leaving only the new-shaped binding wrapped around two figures, sodden and silent on the grass. Only then did her gaze fall on the objects tied to their belts.

She knew she should stand up, back away, say something to someone, but she couldn't remember what or who, or how to move at all. Her fingers were clenched tight, her knuckles gone white, but she couldn't bring herself to undo them until hands covered hers, warmer and familiar, easing the fingers apart, smoothing them straight, thumbs pressing into her palms until something gave, and she collapsed against Gabriel's chest, his voice a soothing rumble of nonsense, his breath warm against her hair.

He was speaking a language she didn't know, and she could not tell the words, but they soothed and calmed anyway, until she pushed away, his hands no longer touching her but close, close by in case they were needed.

She took a breath, then another one when that didn't hurt.

"Get them off them," she told Gabriel. "Get them *off.*"

He looked at her, puzzled, and when she gestured weakly with one hand at the bodies, looked again, more closely. Then he was moving, bending by the bodies, cautious, removing the scraps of buffalo hide from their belts, returning to Isobel's side with them held gently in his hands.

She touched one of the scraps with the edge of her thumb. Her eyes and throat burned as though she'd been standing too close to a black-smith's fire. "Burn them and bury them," she told Gabriel. "Please."

"I will," he promised. "Isobel, I will."

She nodded, witnessing his vow, and he sat back a little, giving her room to breathe.

"Are they—?" The marshal, standing off to the side, the two men grouped behind her. The long-haired one was scowling, looking down at the ground, then off at the trees, at the horses, at anything that wasn't on two legs, while his companion merely . . . stood there, his hands clasped behind his back. He put more weight on his right side than his left, she noted.

"Alive," Isobel told the marshal. "They're . . ." They weren't asleep, not exactly, but Isobel didn't have words for what she had done. "They will remain still," she said. "But that won't hold for long." She was already feeling the tug of power that, even sleeping, the magicians contained, pushing against her, looking for a crack to push through.

Like holding your breath underwater, trying to resist the stream's current, only the other way around, air trying to find its way into her lungs.

A few days' walk, the marshal had said. It would have to be enough. It would have to hold.

She managed to ignore the push of power long enough to stare at the two men behind the marshal, narrowing her eyes. "Should I do the same to them?"

"Hey!" That got the younger man's attention, his gaze going to her finally, outrage in every patch of his body.

There was a rumble in Gabriel's chest that sounded like amusement, then he said, "We only have three horses and the mule. Best keep them awake and walking."

They might have looked relieved; Isobel couldn't tell and didn't care. Closing her eyes again, she flexed her fingers, feeling the bindings around the magicians the way she would feel Uvnee's reins against her skin. Three days. She could hold them for three days.

After that . . .

After that, she would worry about that.

They'd waited only long enough for Gabriel to build a fire and burn the scraps of hide until they were charred, the thick, putrid stench finding its way through the kerchief held to his nose, then he dug a hole and buried the kerchief-wrapped remains with a silver quarter-coin and a splash of the marshal's whiskey as an appeasement to the spirits.

"She satisfies her promise," he told them, casting a glance over his shoulder to where Isobel sat, still exhausted from whatever she had done. "Be at rest."

He wasn't sure if anything was listening, or if he *wanted* it to be listening to him. But it seemed to ease some of Isobel's nerves.

"Rider." The road marshal crooked a finger at him. "Come be useful."

Wisely enough, she didn't want her companions-turned-prisoners helping her tie the insensate magicians into the saddles. While Isobel held each animal's halter, murmuring soothing words when they shifted or skittered, they slung each body facedown across a saddle, looping rope over their thighs and chests to keep them in place.

He studied the knots under his hand thoughtfully. "How long did you say it was to the judge?"

"Two, three days, at a steady walk," LaFlesche said. "We switch out the horses, between yours and mine, and so long as everyone can keep up"—she shot a glare at her awake prisoners—"we should do fine."

"You've done this often? Slinging people across saddles like sacks of meal?"

"Usually they're awake enough to walk. Or I drag 'em."

Isobel's expression, overhearing that, was somewhere between horrified and thoughtful, and he gave her a stern look and a firm headshake until she rolled her eyes at him. He gave Steady a final pat, thanking him for putting up with the body slung across his saddle, and went to fetch his hat and pack.

"Boots up!" LaFlesche called. "Time to move."

Gabriel did not enjoy walking. The moment they switched the body off Steady, he had to fight the urge to mount and ride on ahead of the rest of the party. He cast another sideways glance at Isobel walking alongside him, leading Uvnee, who was now carrying one of the magicians. The Hand was sweating, even though the day had been cool and overcast since they hit lower ground, her skin too ashen for comfort. He worried but said nothing. What was there to say? The magicians needed to remain insensible until such a time as they could contain them somewhere, ideally in a lockhouse. If there was a sitting judge in this town, it seemed likely that they would have one there.

Then he'd force Isobel to rest. Until then, she had no choice. So, he did the best he could: he gave her something else to bite at.

"Notice anything?"

She lifted her head at that, her nostrils flaring as though testing the air. "We're being watched."

"Of course we are."

Isobel glared at his nonchalant tone, as though offended that he had noticed it before she had.

He felt his lips twitch. "Isobel. Two riders, a marshal, and two easterners, with two magicians slung over horseback like sacks of potatoes? The only wonder is that the entire Territory hasn't lined up to watch us go past, complete with games and feasts."

He wondered what stories would come of this, told to the children of those who'd been there to see it, if he'd live to hear any of them. He'd come back someday if he could, to listen.

Assuming he had the chance. His off hand touched his ribs; he couldn't feel the scarring through his jacket and shirt, and the ache was absent save when he bent forward, but he knew they were there, a constant reminder that riding with the Devil's Hand was not an easy—or safe—road. And that was without lugging two wind-mad magicians three days to an unknown destination.

Or the risk of being tried for the crime of killing an unarmed man. Because after one day of their company, he was close to taking the carbine's stock to the side of the younger American's head simply to shut him up. Because apparently even the sulkiest of prisoners felt the need to speak after a while.

By the time evening came, he learned that he'd been right: the younger man was a scout, name of Anderson, and he had been hired to escort US Marshal Paul Tousey safely across the Territory and back again. Like every ex-Army scout Gabriel had ever met, Anderson was bitter, cranky, and not prone to taking orders from anyone graciously, much less a female. He grumbled about having to walk, he grumbled about being dragged off to "some jump-up," and he particularly grumbled about being dragged off by, in his words, "two wimmin." Gabriel's laughter at that hadn't helped his mood at all; he had clearly expected more sympathy.

LaFlesche solved the problem by shoving a rag into his mouth and affixing it with a cord so he couldn't spit it out.

Tousey, on the other hand, seemed quietly resigned to the situation. He had offered nothing more than his name and occupation, but on the morning of the second day, Gabriel had handed him the badge he'd found. The marshal held it in his hand briefly, then pinned it to the inside of his lapel, his hands shaking only slightly.

"Thank you" was all he'd said, but there had been a wealth of meaning there. Gabriel didn't hold with letting a thing define who he was, but he knew Isobel took comfort in her sigil, figured marshals would too, no matter what side of the river they were sworn to. Too, Tousey placed his feet with the careful consideration of a man who'd been surprised by snakes or gopher holes at least once, but without taking his attention off either the land around him or his companions. He slept that way as well, Gabriel had noted: quiet but alert. Without Jefferson's intervention, the marshal might have found himself in the Territory anyway. Or not.

Their horses had fled when the magicians began their circle, Tousey admitted midway through the second day; they hadn't thought to hobble the beasts. "I'd ridden that beast all the way from the Mississippi," he said. "Territory-bred, they told me. Went the entire journey without spooking or startling. But the moment those two and their kind . . . did whatever it was they did, the fool beast lost what little mind it had."

"Magicians are something else entire," LaFlesche said, and Tousey had only shaken his head, as though he still was not entirely certain he believed anything they were telling him.

Isobel had merely snorted, walking with a hand on Uvnee's neck as the mare plodded along with one of the magicians weighing her down, still less than pleased with the burden, from the way her ears kept twitching.

"We were warned . . ."

We, Gabriel noted. He didn't think Tousey referred to the scout with him, which likely meant that other marshals had been sent into the Territory. Had they all been sent to search for magicians? If Jefferson were as canny as was claimed, he'd have more than one spoon to the pot.

"Warned of what? Clearly, not to not meddle." Isobel had been ignoring the Americans as best she could in such proximity, but that seemed to push her too far. "What did they warn you of, then? Because from here it was nothing useful."

But that was all Tousey was willing to share. LaFlesche gave Isobel a hard stare, as though to remind her whose prisoners they were, and Isobel snorted again, then walked more swiftly, striding ahead of their group.

"She's young," Gabriel said to LaFlesche, watching her go. "And still green as grass, for all that she's learned since we set out." And bitter, he thought. That was something new, and unwelcome. Finding the source of the buffalo's death seemed to have deepened her anger, not lessened it, as though despite fulfilling her promise, something still spurred her on.

"She needs to learn faster" was all LaFlesche said.

Isobel could hear them talking behind her, although the words themselves were too low to be overheard. She knew it was petty, knew that she had snapped when she should have been calm, but neither Gabriel nor the marshal seemed to understand the pressure of warding like this, around two different objects, constantly moving.

And telling them, trying to explain, would make it sound as though she were weak or complaining—and she wouldn't do that, not in front of the marshal, and of a certainty not in front of outsiders.

She did regret irritating the marshal, for purely selfish reasons. LaFlesche had been on the Road long enough that her stories must be fascinating. Isobel slid a hand under her hat and scratched at her scalp, wondering if the older woman knew a source of the dry washing powder Devorah had given her, if that was a thing women on the road shared, and if she'd annoyed the woman into keeping that secret from her.

But all these, regrets and distractions, were mere irritations compared to the stress of traveling with magicians.

Warded and unconscious, they were currently carried by Uvnee and LaFlesche's tough little pony, whose Umonhon name Isobel couldn't pronounce but suspected meant "pain to live with." The mule had taken one whiff of the bodies and put up such a fuss that they'd decided to leave it with the packs. Flatfoot trailed them now, staying within sight—and within protection range were it needed—but at whatever distance the mule thought was safe from the threat traveling within their party.

Isobel felt much sympathy for the mule, but she wasn't allowed to join it. She couldn't go far at all: while Gabriel and LaFlesche took turns riding ahead to scout the path they were on, Isobel needed to stay close to the bodies, fully aware that if they woke, she might not be able to do anything to stop them again, but she would be the only chance their little party had.

And they were still being watched. If that made her uneasy, the scout seemed ready to jump, twitching like a rabbit, forever looking over his shoulder and muttering under his breath. That, more than Gabriel's reassuring words, made the unease bearable—anything that worried him that much couldn't help but please her.

Still, she watched her mentor finally give in to his obvious impatience with their slow walk, swinging up into Steady's saddle and trotting ahead, and wished that she were with him, leaving these strangers behind. And if part of that craving to feel Uvnee under her, the wind in her face, was the desire to ride away and never come back, abandon this entire mess . . . surely there was no shame in thinking dark thoughts, so long as you kept control over them.

But with Gabriel gone, she had to drop back and join the others, out of respect to the road marshal if nothing else. Thankfully, the older woman didn't seem to take offense at her silence, nor did she seem perturbed, but merely strode along, her trousered legs covering the ground more easily than Isobel in her skirts.

"What's it like to ride in them? Trousers, I mean?" Isobel finally asked, as much to silence the noise in her head as any real curiosity.

LaFlesche seemed surprised by the question, glancing down at her legs as though she'd only just noticed the fitted material. "I honestly don't recall anything different. Been a while since I wore skirts for anything other than fancy dress for a party, and that was . . ." She laughed at herself. "Well, a while ago." She sobered then, looking sideways at Isobel, then back ahead to the trail. "When I was younger, there were some as thought I was trying to be a man, and figured they'd remind me otherwise, but most folk, they see the sigil, and they mind their manners well enough. And those who don't, well, they learn quick the Road doesn't suffer the weak, not for long."

"You ever . . . regret?"

"What, taking up the sigil or taking on the Road?"

"Either. Both."

LaFlesche chewed over her answer a bit. "My gram, she came all the way from the old world, didn't stop until she landed in Junction and kitted an even dozen; she used to say that we don't choose our way, the way chooses us. Not sure I believe that entirely—everyone's spent time on the wrong trail at some point—but there are some things . . . I don't believe the sigil chooses us, but I'm not entirely certain we choose it, either. Maybe it's a meet-in-the-middle sort of thing? Like falling in love."

"Wouldn't know about that," Isobel said with a shrug.

"Never fell nose over knees for a shy smile or a sideways look?"

"Not yet." There'd been some good-looking boys back in Flood, but she'd thought them just distractions, and she knew better than to fall for a charmer at the card tables.

"Ah, well, there's time. Just remember love's a lovely thing but it's not all that's in the world, and you'll be fine."

Isobel thought about Peggy, whose husband had died of illness, and how that seemed to have set her free, and Iktan, whose wife was a tiny, quiet thing who never lifted her eyes to anyone but was always smiling like she had a secret, and Marie, who like the boss had a stream of lovers but none who stayed, and thought she'd have no trouble remembering that.

They fell silent for a while again after that until they came down a slope and to a small but strong-running stream, Steady's hoofprints clear on the sandy mud on its shore. Isobel placed her hand out, halting the marshal when she would have waded into the shallows.

"If there were a danger, your mentor would have left sign," LaFlesche said, a little irritated at being halted.

"Safe or no, it's running water. You really wish to take them across without thinking this through?" Isobel stared at the road marshal in disbelief. Running water could break bindings; that was why most folk claimed land near creeks but didn't try claiming the creeks themselves, no matter how much their crops or flocks might need it. Crossing a stream was the first thing you did if you managed to offend a magician, assuming you lived that long.

"You're the Devil's Hand," LaFlesche said, squinting down at Isobel in what, in another woman, might be called confusion. "Surely a creek like this could not break his bindings?"

Isobel felt the faint urge to scream. She had done it, not the boss. His power but *her* action. And since she wasn't entirely sure what it was that she had done, she had no idea if it could be broken by running water.

There was no way she could tell the marshal that. Not in front of the two Americans, not . . . not ever. The Devil's Hand. She spoke for him— in their eyes, she *was* him.

Isobel had been raised to keep a clean mouth, but at that moment, she could have cursed Gabriel for riding off and leaving her alone with this.

The marshal took her silence for assent. "So, we simply stand here until—"

"No, hush." Isobel was trying not to think, trying not to be distracted by the quiet singing of the water against stone, letting the sense of *how* rise up in her.

Help me, she asked the sigil, the whispering noise. *Help me do this.*

Once again, she was in the saloon, folding linens, sweeping floors, kneading bread, watching the boss deal out cards. *Flickerthwack* against the green felt. *Flickerthwack* the water against stones.

Magicians were wind, the binding was earth's bone, the risk was water.

Water wore against stone same as wind, but not quickly. Water could move stone, but not easily.

She ducked under the reins and stepped between the horses. The magicians were laid out so their heads were to the outside, their feet—one set booted, one bare and bloodied—were to the inside. Part of her quailed from touching them, protested even being this close to the push and lure of the power trying to escape, but she forced herself to place her palms on their ankles, feeling the unpleasantly papery touch of skin even through cloth and leather, sinking deep the way she did to bone, finding the pulse within the rush of blood and the give of flesh, slowing it until it was slower than water, slower than the wind, slow as stone and bone, and she nodded once, her voice saying, "Now go."

The water was winter-cold even through her boots, the thrumming of power trying to escape softened but not silenced entirely, and Isobel pressed forward, pressed deeper, keeping the binding intact despite the water washing over it, until they were on the other bank, some-one bringing the horses forward, leaving her standing, stock-still and unutterably dizzy, only to fall to her knees.

"Isobel? Hand!"

She opened her eyes to see one of the men—Tousey, she remembered—kneeling in front of her, his hand outstretched, LaFlesche's hand round his wrist, keeping him from touching her. The other man, Anderson, was nowhere to be seen, and she'd've worried more about that if she could stop the bells from ringing inside her head.

"It's all right," she said, and both hands retreated. "I just . . . Water?"

Rather than a canteen, as she'd expected, LaFlesche disappeared and returned with a tin cup filled with creek water. She took it with a nod of thanks, then sipped, the water burning a path down her throat, then splashed what was left into her hands, pressing them to her face, the cold shocking her to full alertness.

"Do you need to rest?"

"No." Yes, but not until Gabriel returned or they caught up with him.

"We have company." Anderson's voice, a low, unhappy growl, and

Isobel twisted without standing up to see what he was talking of.

Three paint ponies, bare-backed and bare-headed, and three riders standing beside them, their hair long and loose, their bodies marked by colors in patterns too distant to determine.

"Scouts, likely," LaFlesche said, matter-of-fact.

Tousey was less calm. "They were following us? Why?"

Isobel had spent most of her strength getting to her feet but was pleased to feel her knees remain steady. She made the clicking noise that got the mule's attention, and while it was still reluctant to approach the horses too closely, it came to her side, allowing her to lean on it. "Like we were here for their entertainment," she responded finally, recalling Gabriel's words. "Though you were likely watched since you crossed the River, came into the Territory proper. By one tribe or another. Just because they allow us here doesn't mean they trust us. Particularly not you. But they wouldn't do anything unless you did something first. That's the Agreement."

"They knew better than to attack us," Anderson spat, and LaFlesche didn't quite roll her eyes skyward for patience, but Isobel could tell the marshal wanted to.

Isobel felt no such restraint. "You're fair game now, if they want. Only thing that's keeping them back is you're with us."

She nodded to LaFlesche, who got the horses moving again. Anderson, his arms crossed over his chest, his hat pulled low over his face, stomped after her, every line of his back showing what he thought of her, of their watchers, of the entire situation, while Tousey seemed to be considering her words, studying the silent figures next to their ponies.

"Like I said, you were of no interest to them," she said to Tousey, gesturing for him to walk with her, ignoring the scout. "Not until you gave insult."

He tilted his head sideways, looking at her through half-squinted eyes. "You keep saying that. I take it, it means something more here than back home."

Isobel blinked and looked ahead at the other woman, who had

turned to listen but simply raised eyebrows back at her. This was on her, then. Isobel sighed. "What do you understand about the Territory?"

"You are an autonomous territory comprising the lands from the Mississippi River, what you call the Mudwater, to where the Spanish claim their lands." He jerked his head back, indicating the mountains rising in the distance behind them. "No known form of government or military, and yet you manage to keep peace with the Indian tribes. . . ."

LaFlesche laughed at that, a harsh bark of amusement.

"We don't keep the peace," Isobel said sharply. "We obey it. That's what you don't understand."

"Explain it to me." It was part command, part request, and Isobel would have bristled if it hadn't been the same tone of voice Gabriel would use when he was testing her.

"The boss—the devil, you call him. He made an agreement with the tribes, long time ago. The Agreement. Boiled down, so long as settlers do right by the land, don't go where they're not allowed, and don't give insult, we can make a home here. You—everyone who comes across the borders—you have to prove yourself."

"To natives?"

"To the Territory."

He didn't understand, she could tell. "And what does the devil do in return?"

Isobel intentionally mimicked the boss's thin-lipped smirk. "Keeps your military folk out, for one. Every soul here knows if it weren't for the boss, you or the Spanish or maybe even the English would've marched in years ago. You're afraid of him."

"Not the French?"

She kept that smile on her face and shrugged. "The French, they like the Wilds better. They just send trappers and traders, then go home."

"Or stay and make babies," LaFlesche added, gesturing at herself.

"And you're saying we . . . gave insult." She could practically see his thoughts working behind that stern facade.

Anderson snorted again, now sullenly bringing up the rear of their group, but said nothing. Isobel ignored him. "You came into their lands without permission, you encouraged magicians—all mad as a bag of cats—to do things they should have known better than to do"—she shot a glare at the oblivious bodies being carried next to them—"and in doing so, you not only ran off all the game but set the ground to shake hard enough to unnerve even the elders." *What* the magicians had done was Territory business, not for outsiders. "You think that doesn't give insult?"

"I . . ."

"What did you *think* you were doing?" The marshal asked the question, and she seemed genuinely interested in the answer.

"It was . . . I was under orders . . ." He suddenly seemed to remember that he was in fact a prisoner, being carted off for judging, and slammed his jaw shut with a hard click.

Isobel pushed down the urge to shake him until understanding dropped in, and let him fall back to walk with Anderson. She watched them through narrowed eyes, but neither gave any indication of planning to bolt; she suspected they knew there was no point, there was nowhere they could run that would help them any.

She could have explained it to him until they died of old age, Isobel thought, and it wouldn't have made a difference. Understanding wasn't being born here; the saloon had its share of folk who'd come to the Territory full-grown, and they understood. The old trapper couple she and Gabriel had stayed with, they'd come late to the Territory, and it had accepted them. But her parents hadn't, at all, not from the story the boss told.

Were there natives like that? Broken Tongue, he'd said his people ran when the ground shook, but he hadn't. Why had he been different?

"The creek didn't stop our watchdogs," the marshal said, as dry as if they were discussing the weather, breaking into her increasingly troubled thinking. "One group's been with us since I caught up with the boys; the other joined in after you came along. They're ignoring each other, near as I can tell, but keeping us under observation."

Isobel brought her attention back to the problem at hand. Was that second group the warriors who had been waiting for them when they came down the mountain, or someone else? "Do you know who?"

The marshal stretched her arms over her head, fingers laced, and arched her back until something cracked. Isobel envied the other woman her loose-tailored shirt and trou once again for the way they allowed her to move with less restriction. Next mercantile they came to, she was buying a pair with whatever coin they had left.

"No clue," LaFlesche said. "Suspect one's Sutaio, but they've not let me see them except to tell me they were there, never close enough for useful detail. Other might be . . . well, could be anyone, up here. These hills are where you settle if you don't agree with how the elders are doing things back home."

Isobel thought of Jumping-Up Duck and her village, hiding where no one might follow them, afraid to leave even when the ground shook, of the great deer and the Reaper hawk, the way the magicians had traveled to that particular place to do what they did. . . .

"Do you know any stories about the hills behind us, other than that?"

La Flesche cocked her head, thinking. "I'm not from these parts, so I'm not the best to ask. If you mean the tribal stories, I mean."

"There are other kinds?"

The road marshal laughed. "I'm nearly sixty, Isobel. I've heard all sorts of stories, from all sorts of folk. Some truer'n others. But mostly, around here? There's not much said. Which is odd, come to think of it."

"Odd, yes," Isobel said. But she thought she knew why. The great deer—what Gabriel called a wapiti—and the Reaper hawk had not come to her: they had already *been* there. For the land, not her. Or, not the land but what the land held.

Some places were more powerful than others. Flood was one of those places, either because of the boss or why he picked it. De Plata had been another; she'd felt it when she walked past the silver mines, something deep and strong in the mountains.

She had felt the power in these hills, too. And she had allowed that power to touch her, slip inside her, bind itself to her.

What had happened to her up there?

She reached for her canteen and took a swallow, having to force the water down a suddenly tight throat. "Do you think the magicians knew those hills were sacred? That that's why they went there to do what they did?"

The marshal tilted her head, giving Isobel a sideways look. "I try not to think about the whys of what a magician does," she said. "And I'd advise you don't either. Good way to chase the moon, that."

"But . . ." She bit her tongue and let the other woman think that she'd agreed. Magicians were none of their concern . . . and none of the boss's either, he'd said. But they kept being tangled in *her* concerns, and that meant she needed to think about such things.

She'd trusted the whisper when it sent her into the hills, had led her deeper; she'd first assumed it came from the sigil, from the boss. But it wasn't. What *was* it?

"Whatever you're thinking, Hand, stow it." The marshal's voice was hard but not unkind, and Isobel nodded. There were more immediate worries to deal with. First, to deliver the marshal's prisoners, preferably without anyone else dying.

"Our watchers. Do you think they'll interfere before we reach your judge?"

"No." LaFlesche sounded certain of that. "White men, army men, makes it our problem, just as you said. With luck, we remove the problem, maybe things will go back to as they should be."

Things as they should be. Isobel thought of the destruction she'd seen already, the abandoned homes, the slaughtered buffalo, the empty skies. The way the ground shuddered underfoot, so deeply disturbed by the sorrow and madness it was forced to contain. "That's a fool's dream, Marshal."

That was enough to kill the conversation, and the four of them walked on, occasionally pausing to shift one of the sleeping bodies to keep them from falling, until Gabriel rode back with the news that the town was just up ahead.

PART FIVE

A COLD EYE

Under ordinary circumstances, Gabriel would never have ridden off, leaving only two to guard four, even if two of the four were unable to move, much less attempt escape. Under ordinary circumstances, Gabriel would have been useful if the prisoners attempted to escape. Here, the road marshal was more than competent to shoot Anderson in the knees, should that be required, and Tousey . . .

The American would honor his parole. At least for now.

And that left Gabriel feeling itchy and useless until LaFlesche had flat-out told him to scout ahead, ensure that the way was clear. She was humoring him, but it put him back in the saddle, where a rider belonged. And he felt only a little guilt at the look Isobel gave him as he picked up Steady's reins.

In truth, he had hoped that his not being there would give Isobel and LaFlesche a chance to talk openly, about . . . things.

He wasn't sure what sort of things he meant, but there had to be things. There were questions Isobel was bound to have that he couldn't answer—and would likely make a disaster of if he tried. Devorah had made a start at it when they'd shared a fire for the night, but the other rider was a dubious influence on anyone, much less a green rider. LaFlesche might not have been his first choice—he knew nothing about her, and Isobel'd had rough brushes with marshals before—but she was older in years and steadier, responsible. That had to count for something.

He hoped.

But when he rode back, having sighted what he presumed was their destination, his first thought was that he'd made a terrible mistake. On the surface, all looked calm: Isobel and the marshal were walking together, looking little different from when he had left, but Tousey had either gone back or been sent back to walk with Anderson, just far enough behind the women to make it clear that he was not part of their conversation, while not so far back that the marshal might consider it an attempt to escape.

By the time Gabriel'd reined Steady in, his assessment was that one of the women had said something that had irritated Tousey but not so much that he was fool enough to argue with them. Anderson, on the other hand, seemed much as how he'd been all along: bitterly unhappy and biting his tongue with it.

Scouts weren't much for others' company on their best days anyway; that was what made them good at their work. He'd heard of a few who occasionally came to the Territory, but they didn't settle around the towns, instead disappearing into the hills, as far from people as they could get. Gabriel had no objections to that—there had been days he'd been tempted to do the same—but they weren't exactly quality company. Particularly when they felt they'd been hard done by.

Whatever had happened, he'd likely hear about it soon enough.

"Town's up ahead," he told Isobel as he swung down out of the saddle, feeling his boots hit ground with relief. He could spend days in the saddle if need be—and preferred it that way—but after their experience riding blind, every time he connected with the ground again and felt the reassuring surge connecting him to the Road, it was as though someone'd lifted a weight off his shoulders. And if he felt that way, he could only imagine Isobel's reaction.

Speaking of which . . . "All quiet here?" He glanced at the bodies slung over saddles but couldn't tell if they'd moved at all.

"Marshal Tousey received a brief lesson in Territorial history," Isobel said, "and Marshal LaFlesche is reasonably certain that not one but two different bands are following us at a polite distance, but other than that, it's been peaceable."

"Three," Gabriel said. "There's one that's been ahead of us, a single rider. They know where we're going and want to make sure we get there, I suppose?"

LaFlesche chewed over that news and his implicit question. Her face might be sharp with age, but he wasn't fool enough to think that greying hair meant the mind was any less. Most marshals took to the road around the start of their third decade, so that meant she'd been riding for nearly as long as he'd been breathing. He might disagree with her, but he wasn't going to underestimate anything she said.

"It's not for me to pass judgment," she said. "That's not my call. But three times is trouble in anything. Your words earlier—you think these two were sent by someone else to cause trouble?"

Isobel flicked her gaze at Gabriel, then went back to studying the ground as they walked, leaving no doubt that she, too, was waiting on his answer. He grimaced, the flicker of guilt he'd felt earlier slashing back harder, twisting deeper.

Isobel should know about the letter. If Jefferson were planning a push into the Territory, however he couched it, it was relevant to her responsibilities. Likely relevant to the situation they were in now.

Her responsibilities, not his. He had been told a thing in confidence. Abner trusted him with things that should not have been said, particularly not to someone living in the Territories with the ear, however indirectly and unwanted, of the devil himself. And he didn't *know* for a fact that the two were related.

Now you're being a willful fool, a voice said, and it sounded too much like Old Woman for his comfort. And still his companions waited for him to speak.

"I think that the United States government looks over the Mudwater and sees only open space," he said finally. "Open space and resources that they believe could be put to better use than ragtag settlers and savages. And the new President, Jefferson, is a man of . . ." He hesitated, thinking of what he knew and what he had heard. "Curiosity."

He looked up and then looked away from Isobel's expression, a thoughtful, wondering face that means she was hearing more than he'd said.

"Curiosity is always trouble," LaFlesche grumbled, kicking at a rock in her way and watching as it landed in the dirt several paces ahead of them, dislodging a faint puff of dust. "Bad enough having folk stirring up the muck because it amuses them, but you get people with ideas handing them sticks, and it never ends well."

She spoke as though from experience, and he noted for the first time that the butt of her pistol was braced low, barely a flick from her grasp at all times. She didn't seem like the sort to hit first and ask questions later, but she was a road marshal, tasked to violence when it was needed, and he'd best not forget that.

As though she'd just remembered it too, she made a graceful turn-around as she walked, the edges of her coat flaring out as she overtly rested her gun hand on her belt, and called out, "Gentlemen. As we're about to enter what passes for civilized ground in these parts, and as you are, technically, in my custody, I'm going to have to ask you to submit your wrists to cuffs for a brief time."

Cuffing someone meant if there was trouble, they couldn't take care of themselves. Marshals and posses alike found it better to trust in parole, that they wouldn't do anything foolish otherwise. Anyone born to the Territory would know being bound for an insult, a presumption they would not honor their word. Here, now, with what Gabriel had just told her . . . well, if Gabriel was wrong, he was wrong. And if he was even a sliver of right . . .

Better thought overcautious than proven a fool. And the distraction from his own words was welcome just then.

The scout scowled when she dangled the silver straps in one hand, his face scrunched like a porcupine in daylight, and Gabriel braced to take him down if there was trouble, but the American marshal sighed and stepped forward, his arms offered up in front of him.

"Be gentle; I bruise easily," he said, and LaFlesche let out a huff that could have been a laugh as she clapped one of the straps over his wrists in a twisted loop, tapping them once to wake the binding. He tilted his head, studying the seamless clasp, then strained a little, but Gabriel thought it more to see how the binding would react than any real attempt to break his wrists free.

"Comfortable enough?"

"Comfortable enough," he agreed. "Lighter than the ones we carry, too. I don't suppose that little trick'd work outside the Territory?"

"No idea," LaFlesche said. "Hand?"

Isobel seem startled to be addressed. "I . . ." She paused, then reached out to touch the bands where they crossed Tousey's wrists. "No. I'm not even sure it would continue to work if you were to get too far from Marshal LaFlesche—" Her cheeks flushed as she realized that might not have been the wisest thing to say.

"Too late," Gabriel said cheerfully as LaFlesche stepped past them to cuff the scout as well, ignoring his quiet mutters. "And if you ran," he said loud enough for the scout to hear, "I'm reasonably handy with a rope, been known to haul in a running calf at twenty paces."

He was lying through his teeth, but it was worth it for the glare he got from Anderson and the chin-down smirk Isobel tried to hide, knowing full well that he was lying.

He suspected, with what waited for them ahead, that might be the last bit of amusement any of them had for a while.

When Gabriel said they were within striking distance of their destination, Isobel had felt the brief urge to burst into tears like a child, restraining herself only because she was aware both their prisoners and the marshal were watching, alert to any sign of weakness.

What she felt, most of all, was exhaustion. The magicians . . . To the outer eye, they did not seem to have moved, facedown over horseback like sacks of flour, but Isobel had felt an increased push on the wards that morning, and it was only growing worse. The shorter, square-shouldered magician was trying to wake, wind swirling within him like a dust storm gaining power, and her the single tree standing in its path.

She held, but just barely, and at the cost of sleep. Another day, or if the other magician also began to push, the bindings would fray and fail.

Had it been only them, her and Gabriel, and perhaps only one magician, she might have risked allowing it. She was curious what might remain of them, away from the rage of the ancient spirit; if there might be a way to reclaim them, the way a stream filtered clear again after a storm, or at least learn what they had done, what they had woken. But she could not risk it. The road marshal might have accepted her position and authority, but the other two, the Americans, had no reason to believe she was anything more than what she appeared: a young female, with a horse they could use to escape. If they thought for an instant that she was distracted . . .

After two days, she was reasonably certain that Marshal Tousey would not be so foolish, but she hadn't needed Gabriel's side-glance cautions to know the sort of man the scout was. Not everyone who came into the saloon back in Flood had been gentle, or kind; folk made deals with the devil for revenge as often as for survival. If he saw opportunity, Anderson would slit their throats and steal their horses, the mule, and their boots. She would not give him the chance.

And Gabriel was hiding something from her. It was likely nothing, and Isobel suspected she was being foolish, but it wore on her nonetheless. And there never seemed a private time to bring it up, traveling with so large a group.

They came to the creek Gabriel had said was just before their destination, this one low enough that the water barely brushed the horses' hooves. The marshal glanced at Isobel, who gave the other woman a go-ahead sign, the water too sluggish to pose much risk, although she took up position between the horses nonetheless as they moved down the slope and into the sun-warmed current.

"Gentlemen, bound hands does not make your legs suddenly shorter or slower. Lively, now!" LaFlesche called out, having noted a distinct slag to their pace as they slogged, wet-footed, to the top of the bank on the other side. "And there we are," she said in satisfaction, coming to the rise of the bank and looking out.

Isobel brought the horses up and checked to make sure their burdens hadn't shifted, then went to stand by LaFlesche. A wide dirt road elbowed toward them, then cut across a squared-off plain backed by low-sloping hills. Squinting, she saw the road led to the tall brown shape of a palisade wall.

"Our destination," LaFlesche said with no small relief.

But despite chivvying the prisoners, it took them most of the available daylight to reach the gates. It hadn't rained recently, and dust from the road flew up into their faces and into their mouths and noses, forcing them to cover their faces with kerchiefs to breathe cleanly, and slowing their pace.

"I'd near forgotten why they call 'em the dust roads," LaFlesche grumbled after she'd had to wet down her kerchief a third time, wringing it out with a moue of distaste at the dirty water dripping from the cloth. "Worse than cottonwood. Worse than mud, worse than anything."

"From dust ye came and covered in dust ye shall remain," Gabriel said. LaFlesche glared at him from behind the reaffixed cloth over her mouth and chin, while Isobel pulled her hat down further in a vain attempt to keep the dust out of her eyes and hair as well.

When they'd come within a dozen paces of the tall wooden gate, they saw an odd dozen long-barreled muskets aimed at them over the top.

LaFlesche paused, putting out a hand to stop anyone from taking a step closer. "Marshal Abigail LaFlesche, bringing prisoners for judging," she called out. "And honored guests" was almost an afterthought, and Isobel felt something inside her growl at the insult.

"Hush," Gabriel said quietly, and she felt herself flush again at evidence it hadn't been as inside as she'd thought.

Half the muskets were pulled back when they heard her voice, the remaining seven remaining tilted down at them.

"So much for them not havin' military," Anderson sneered, looking at Tousey, but loud enough for the others to hear. "Lyin' savages, even the whites."

"I will gag you," LaFlesche said almost conversationally. "Unless you'd rather me simply cut your tongue out?"

The scout glared at her but clenched his jaw shut without another sound.

There were male voices on the other side, and the gate slid open, revealing a small forecourt and a cluster of buildings beyond.

The moment they crossed the threshold, Isobel felt something shiver up her legs; the town's warding, noting the arrival of strangers. Her throat closed in a panic, realizing that she hadn't considered that the warding might object to the magicians or to the binding laid on them, but the wooden gates of the town closed behind them without alarm or outcry.

A judge lived here, LaFlesche claimed. Perhaps the warding had been crafted to allow for prisoners coming in and leaving? Isobel took a deep breath and felt the bump of a hand against hers; Gabriel had shifted Steady's lead to his other hand and now stood next to her, his hat tipped forward against the afternoon sun that angled over the low rooftops of the buildings, reflecting almost too brightly against . . . She squinted, then tilted her head. Yes, there were bits of metal on the roofs, angled against the edge.

"Snow-breakers," LaFlesche said, seeing where her attention had gone. "Winter here, the snow piles up, gets heavy enough to break a roof if you're not careful. Ice, too. So you want it to come down . . . but not all at once."

"The snow slides off the roof . . . The bits are sharp, breaks it up so it doesn't all come off at once?"

"Mmmhmmm. You ever been knocked on the head by a month's worth of snow, you appreciate that."

While Isobel was considering the idea of that much snow, wondering if the woman was making sport of her, the marshal turned to welcome the man who was coming forward to greet them, a gaggle of others just behind him, staring as though they'd never seen strangers before.

Isobel had to admit that maybe they hadn't, at least not like this.

A single figure pushed through the crowd, elbowing the others aside with casual disdain. "Marshal LaFlesche, isn't it? I'd say it's good to see you, but marshals never bring anything but work, and you likely remember how much I hate that sort of thing."

The man was old, not ancient, but what hair he had left was sparse and white, curled tight against a balding pate, and his face drooped like an old dog at the jowls. He wore a fitted black cloth coat, the shirt underneath it fastened up to the neck, and trousers with a neat darn in the knee, but his boots were polished clean, despite the dust that seemed to settle over all else.

"Good to see you still up and kicking, Judge," the marshal said in return, shaking his hand. "And yes, I'm afraid I'll need you to drape the bench one more time."

The judge pulled his head back, examining the newcomers with an expression that reminded Isobel of nothing so much as a turtle suddenly startled from his log. "All of them?"

"Ah, no, my apologies. Judge Pike, this is Gabriel Kasun, and Isobel . . ." The marshal hesitated, as though uncertain how to introduce her.

"Isobel née Lacoyo Távora," she said, stepping forward. "Most recently of Flood."

"Ah." The old man's narrowed eyes studied her, giving nothing away. "Come from the Old Man's lair, eh? Well, you're welcome to Andreas, despite what you bring, though there's little to recommend it these days. We're mostly emptied out for planting and grazing, just us oldsters left behind. And what of these others—are those two dead, or do they sleep as such?"

"Ah. Well, and there's a story to be told," the marshal said, rubbing her jaw, a rueful tone to her voice. "These two"—the marshal indicated the Americans, their hands bound in front of them—"are accused of having made false claim of insult."

"Against you two?" the judge asked, turning back to Isobel and Gabriel.

"Against them," the marshal said, gesturing to the two bodies slung across the saddles.

"Ah." His narrow-eyed gaze went to them, noting the faded clothing and worn boots visible from that side. "And they are . . ."

There was a silence: Isobel felt no need to be the one to inform the judge that they'd brought two magicians, however unconscious, into his town, and apparently neither did Gabriel. LaFlesche coughed once, then took up her burden.

"Magicians. Bound and warded," she added quickly. "But we couldn't simply leave 'em there."

"Yes, you could have," the judge said, and for the first time, Isobel felt like she might have an ally here. "What the blasted night am I supposed to do with *magicians?*"

Run, don't walk. Isobel hadn't realized quite how much traveling with Farron Easterly had changed her—and Gabriel—until she saw the panic in the judge's eyes.

"Drape the bench and pronounce judgment, of course," LaFlesche said, almost cheerful, and Isobel wondered if maybe the magicians weren't the only mad ones in their party. From the way Gabriel wiped a hand down the front of his face, leaving two fingers across his lips as though to keep himself from saying anything, she wasn't the only one having those sudden misgivings.

"I'm too old for this nonsense," the judge told her, then waved irritably at the people still lingering behind him. Most of them, Isobel noted, were not much younger than he was, mostly male but with a few women among them, silver-haired and deep-creased skin. "Stop hovering like a flock of hens and be useful," he barked at them now. "Put the walking ones in the holding pen." And he turned back to LaFlesche to ask,

"I'm presuming you have their parole they're not going to run?"

"They're not bound to the Territory," Gabriel answered for her. "If they break parole, nothing will chase after them."

"There was no need to tell them that," LaFlesche said, tight and quiet.

"I waited until we were inside walls, didn't I?"

The judge turned to stare at Gabriel as though seeing him properly for the first time. "Hrmph. Well, Andreas's walls are good at keeping things out; we'll see how well it keeps 'em in. And those two . . ." Isobel hadn't thought it possible for his eyes to squint further, but they did. "You, girl, you the one keeping 'em down?"

Isobel nodded.

"Then you stay with 'em. Lucky you. Lou, take 'em to Possum's; let him earn his keep for a change."

Lou was one of the few women in the group, her hair silver-brown and her ash-dark skin lined with age, but she walked with a firm step and flesh on her bones. "We supposed to haul the horses in as well?" she asked tartly, eying the animals up and down.

"Would serve Possum right if you did," the judge said. "But no. We still got that sledge around here somewhere?"

It seemed that they did.

After sending two men off to fetch the sledge, Marshal LaFlesche and the judge escorted her prisoners down the street as though they were honored guests. Most of the gaggle followed them at a safe distance, leaving Gabriel, Isobel, and the woman named Lou. And two unconscious magicians, three horses, and a mule, the latter having wandered off to pull at the weeds growing along the edge of the gate.

"The boys'll be here with the sledge in a minute. You want to untie 'em and get 'em on the ground, or will that be a problem?" Lou's words were blurred soft around the edges, and Isobel had to work to understand her, but when the question came clear, she shook her head. "We lay them flat at night, and it didn't seem to affect the binding."

"Well, then, get 'em down."

Gabriel pushed his hat back and gave Lou a mocking salute, then turned to untie the heavier of the two magicians from Uvnee's back, while Isobel unknotted the ropes on the marshal's pony, who turned its head and gave her what seemed, to Isobel's thinking, a grateful look.

"Didn't like carrying dead weight, did you, huh? Can't say as I blame you." The magician wasn't much taller than she and seemed barely skin and bones under her hands, but pulling him down from the saddle still staggered her backward, forcing Lou to catch her with a hand flat between her shoulder blades.

"Help me," Isobel started to say, but the woman had already stepped back, pulling her hand away as though Isobel's body had burned her.

"They're . . ." Lou blinked at them, then slid her glance sideways to where the mule seemed to be looking back at her with a "don't ask me" expression. "They're safe?" she asked, with her hands trying to emphasize what she meant by safe, but Isobel thought she understood.

"For now, yes." Three days, she'd had them down; she could feel them both struggling below the surface now, lashings of power and anger mixed with frustration, and worse, a dawning awareness of *her* as the source of their binding. She was not confident that, in their madness, they'd be able to remember that it had been the ancient spirit that burned them, not her, nor would they care even if they did remember. But for now . . . "Their bindings hold."

"I only ask, not to offend, but the wards on our walls are for keeping things out, not once they're already in," the woman said hastily, as though hearing an edge in Isobel's voice. "And if they wake as mad as they're made out to be . . ."

Isobel declined to tell the woman that these two were even madder than most. It would help no one. "There's no worry until sunrise, at the least," although it was as much a guess as a gamble. "Your ward-maker should be able to reinforce their work, specific to where you keep 'em, at least long enough for the judge to hear the tellings."

She coiled the rope and hooked it over the pommel of the pony's saddle, and slapped its hindquarter gently to tell it she was done. The pony simply snorted once, then ambled off to join the mule in search of edible grass.

"I'm assuming your ward-worker didn't go off to help with the planting," Gabriel said when the local woman made no response, pulling the taller magician off the saddle and laying him next to the first without any particular care. "If they did, you'd best send a message now and a fast pony, too."

Uvnee, not as sanguine as the pony, shuddered as the weight left her back, ears twitching and eyes rolling nervously now that she could see what she had been carrying. Isobel stepped over the bodies to soothe the mare, stroking her nose and speaking reassuringly about what a good girl Uvnee had been, while Steady sidled closer and rested his head over the mare's neck as though to add his own reassurances.

Lou shook her head. Her hair curled like early ferns, bobbing over her eyes when she moved, shoved out of the way with a gesture Isobel recognized from seeing Gabriel do it—the move of someone more accustomed to wearing a hat, who never thought to tie back hair that would be sweat-tamed soon enough. Not a rider, but someone who worked outside, with her hands.

"No ward-maker to speak of 'cept Possum, that old fool, and young Georgie, who's yah, gone for planting. Never had much need for one. Andreas's been here longer than we have; when the first traders came down from the north, they asked to build their cache here. That was more'n fifty back; they're long gone, and we just use what was set. Every now and again, it needs reminding, but—" She made a gesture with her hands that seemed equal parts resignation and apology.

"You—" Gabriel stopped whatever he'd meant to say, then started again. "And there's none of the tribe remaining nearby?"

Lou shook her head again. "They were a small tribe even then, story says. Most of 'em married out into other tribes or just . . . wandered off."

Gabriel didn't often sigh, but when he did, it spoke measures. "Most of what I know's from east of here; I'd be more likely to foul it than fix if I poke around. You might take a look-see, check if anything needs remaking."

Isobel started to protest that she wouldn't know the first thing about a town boundary that old, one that someone else set, that she hadn't ever studied wards, and what she'd done to bind the magicians wasn't anything like, but Gabriel's look held her cold.

He was telling her she was the only maker they had, never mind she was no maker at all.

She bit her lip and nodded, telling him she understood. More bluffing, and hope no one called them on it.

If she weren't feeling so queasy and worn, Isobel thought, it might be funny. Wasn't so long ago she'd thought just being the Hand meant folk would respect her, thought bearing the devil's sigil meant she could do whatever was needed—she'd known how to close off the infected homestead, hadn't she? Had been able to find the spell-beast, to stop the Spanish monks from making things worse, to feel not just the Road underfoot but the whole of the territory rolling like thunder in her bones. She might not be a maker, but she had *power*.

But the truth of it was that none of that knowing had come from her, and the moment she'd been cut off . . . she'd been useless. Helpless. An old man'd had to save her from the spirit's anger. A road marshal had been the one to capture the magicians, bring the Easterners in for judgment.

A whisper had to come tell her where the problems lay.

"You're a ward-maker?" The words were dubious that anyone of Isobel's youth could be useful, the question digging into Isobel's own doubts like a spade to dirt, but making Gabriel's silent warning more urgent as well.

When Isobel didn't object to the title or deny it, Lou pursed her lips but said only, "Well, don't go fussing with ours too much unless'n you must; we've got to be able to raise it again come winter."

"I . . . what?" Isobel wasn't sure she'd heard Lou's words correctly, but the two men returned with the sledge before she had a chance to ask the woman to repeat herself.

The sledge was nothing more than a heavy wooden slab set on runners that curled up in front. Isobel took a closer look: there were narrow sheets of iron hammered along the edges of the runners, gripping the wood tightly on either side.

"To cut through the snow," Gabriel explained, then gestured to one of the men who brought it out to help him lift the first magician onto it. The wood was old, polished smooth with use, with leather straps that buckled over it to keep the load in place. "You'll be able to pull this?" he asked the other man. "Fully loaded, I mean."

"Can haul a full hunt's worth back through mud if need be." The man Gabriel spoke to was barely Isobel's height but twice her width, and she thought, glancing at his shoulders and back, he might be able to pull the entire Territory, given enough rope.

While the men were fussing with the bodies, Isobel touched Lou's shoulder lightly, pulling her attention away. "In winter?" Isobel asked, then off the woman's puzzled glance, clarified, "You said you have to raise the wards again, come winter?" The thought of easing a town's wards at all seemed mad to Isobel, but surely there must be a reason.

"Well, yes. Andreas's here year round, but most of the folk in it . . . We go out to the fields in the day, spring through autumn, or out on hunt for a while at a time." Lou's tone made it clear that she thought explaining this was akin to explaining the sun rising, but Isobel tried not to take offense. "Once winter comes, though, neither beast nor man's got cause to go beyond the walls. We get wolf packs up here; by midwinter, sometimes they're hungry enough to do foolish things. And that's only the ones on four legs. So, yah, come the first snow, we raise 'em up and settle in."

Wards were not curtains, to be taken down and rehung. They were . . . part of the town, woven into every structure, every soul. . . . Surely, Lou was mistaken somehow.

"You stay inside all winter?" Gabriel's voice was politely incredulous, and Isobel could tell from the set of his hip and shoulders that the very idea was near making him shudder. Isobel looked around the town— it was pleasant enough, if quiet, but the flat-log walls they'd passed through suddenly seemed to loom overhead, blocking out the sky. She thought she understood a bit of his revulsion at the idea, though she'd never ventured far from Flood either when the weather turned cold. But then, she'd never ventured much farther than the creek when the weather had been fine, either.

"We're lively enough, come snow-months," Lou said as the two men pulled the ropes over their shoulders and began to haul the sledge away, Gabriel walking alongside to ensure the bodies didn't fall off. "Once everyone's tucked back inside. And there's always work to be done. You want a hide or fur, Andreas's the place to find it. No quality better." She seemed to suddenly recollect herself and gave an apologetic smile.

"Now your man's sorting the prisoners, let's get your animals stabled, and then I can show you the ward posts, yah?"

The stable was more of an open shed, the roof low and the walls slanted, with a coarse rope net in place of a door, but the roof and walls seemed sturdy enough, and it was dry and cool within, with two shaggy brown dogs curled up in the corner who came out, tails wagging, when they led the animals in, showing no alarm at these strangers invading their space.

And, Isobel acknowledged, even though the rope gate wouldn't hold any of them, least of all the mule, if they wanted out, the entire town was enclosed; there wasn't far they could get to.

"Just turn 'em loose," Lou said, making a wide gesture with her arm. "We've only a few animals here right now, so they've roam of the place."

Isobel made short work of untacking the animals, stacking their gear on a low wooden platform, then making sure they had fresh feed and water. "Someone'll come by and haul your gear to wherever you'll be staying for the night," Lou said, watching Isobel work. "Come on, then."

Isobel gave Uvnee a final scratch under her ear and a promise of fresh carrots if she could find any, before following the other woman back outside.

"Nearest one's this way," Lou said, and started walking, not looking back to see if Isobel was following. "So, you're from Flood, hey? What's it like?"

Isobel shrugged, not sure what the woman expected. "Same as any, seems like. People, buildings, problems."

"More problems than most, being that close to the Master of the Territory."

"I suppose?" Nobody had ever asked her that before. "It's not . . . People tend to be quiet about their problems," she said. "They come and they go, but you don't exactly know why they came or what they leave with. That's their business. And when you live there . . ." She tilted her head, then shrugged. "He's just the boss, is all." She'd never known anything else, to compare.

"Ahuh." Lou didn't seem convinced, but Isobel pushed the question back to the other woman. "And Andreas? You've lived here long?"

"Born here. Left for a bit, did some trapping along the north side of the border, stayed with my father's people for a bit too, but then I came back. The Territory doesn't like to let go for long, yah?"

"So I've been told," Isobel agreed, most of her attention turning to the houses they were approaching. They were low to the ground, hewn wood above stone, with a stone chimney rising from the middle of each building, more solid-looking than anything she'd seen before, as though they intended to squat there until the mountains fell down. The chimney reminded her of the homesteading they'd stopped in months ago, where a thick hide covered a hole in the roof where the cooking smoke escaped. If the winters were as harsh as the marshal'd said, she imagined being able to circle around a stove, rather than having it at the other side of the room, would be useful in keeping warm.

The buildings were otherwise unremarkable, although Isobel couldn't exactly say that Flood had been any prettier; there was no reason to paint or prettify if the wind and rain would take you back down to grey again. In all the places she'd seen, Patch Junction had been the exception, with its paint and flowers and trying to be something it wasn't.

That thought made her frown. She had liked Patch Junction. It was busy and bright, and full of bustle, built on an old crossroads, Gabriel'd said; the original settlers had cleared the crossroads and built a trading post into a real town, with farms circling around it. So why now did simply thinking of it fill her with unease?

She shook the feeling off with an effort. Too long on the road, too long not seeing anything other than trees and rocks and the back of Gabriel's head. That was all.

"Back here," Lou said, leading her between two of the houses. "Here's the first post."

The houses were not built up against the enclosing town wall after all, Isobel discovered. There was a narrow alley that ran behind the houses, the space between them and the much taller wall barely wide enough for two people to walk along abreast. There were no windows on this side of the houses, just rough planking, the chinks between them filled with plaster. She took a closer look, curious. The plaster was rough to the touch, like petting a newborn calf.

"Rock dust and the hairs we scrape off hides; stiffens the plaster," Lou told her. "Not so much for insulation, though. Inside, you line the back walls with as much hide as you've got. But over here, this is what you wanted to see?"

When Lou had mentioned a ward-post, Isobel expected something like she'd seen outside Clear Rock, a medicine-sigil burnt into a marker or maybe a boulder, holding the power in place. Instead, Lou showed her a collection of bones hung against the inner wall, some held there by thick black nails gone red-rusted, others seemingly wedged into the wood as though they'd grown there. Most of the bones were the size of her hand, others longer, some bleached white and the rest crackling-brown with age and weather, and Isobel reached out her own hand to touch one, only to pull her fingers back as though she'd been slapped.

"What is this?"

Lou's brows drew together in confusion, her head tilting as she looked first at Isobel, then at the bones, then back at Isobel. "The ward-post," she said, as though a child should have known that.

Isobel rubbed her fingertips together, reassuring herself that she could still feel them. The wardings of Flood's boundary were sunk deep in the earth, circling the town from river to farms' edge. You could feel them when you stepped over, and they felt you, knew if you belonged or were a stranger, if it should alert the boss or let you pass. The wards she'd encountered elsewhere, at campsites and farmsteads, had been weaker but similar: woven into the ground the way a stream cut through stone. Even the makeshift hollow crossroads the marshal had created, the warding there had been passive, waiting for something to push against it before reacting.

This . . . was *awake*. She thought of the sensation she'd felt when they crossed the gateway, and wondered if she'd caused this, or if it had been that way before.

Lou was still staring at her, waiting on her to say something.

"How old is this?"

"Told you. Since before the town *was*. Folk who were here started it, we just"—Lou shrugged—"built around 'em."

Isobel stared at the bones, her eyes itching as though road dust lingered in them. The folk who were here, Lou'd said. The folks who were here.

"And you alter them. Weaken the bindings in good weather, raise them for cold." Isobel shifted to look more closely at the bones without getting any closer. "The older ones are mixed with the new—they're moved?"

"I don't know. I'm not . . . I don't handle them. Told ya, Possum or young George does that." For the first time, Lou seemed to realize that there might be something wrong. "They're all right, aren't they? The wards? They're . . . they're still working?"

Isobel would have sworn nothing could drag her attention from the shimmering, seductive hum of the bones, but those words pricked her into movement, her jaw dropping even as she turned to stare at her companion instead.

"You can't feel them? At all?"

Lou shook her head once, her brow pinched with worry. "Not . . . not the way Possum can." She bit her upper lip, then licked at it nervously. "I mean, we know they're there, we see 'em keep out the storms and the beasts, so they must be there, right? And Possum would say something if they weren't?"

Lou assumed they were working, but she didn't *know*, the way Isobel had always taken for granted, had felt wards shift under her like a horse under saddle, or a dog pushing close to be petted.

The realization was a blow to her gut, only from the inside out, leaving more questions behind. Could the woman not feel them when she went in or out of town? Although she was older, her gait was steady and she seemed strong, but maybe she didn't leave town often anymore, didn't have reason for the wards to touch her.

"Maître?" Lou had taken a step back, as though Isobel were more unnerving than the bones.

"They're fine," Isobel said. "The wards, they're . . . they're fine."

"Ah." She nodded, swallowed, her throat clenching around the movement, and looked away from Isobel and then back, as though afraid she might be accused of rudeness. "Well, there's a relief. We don't get many riders up here 'cept the occasional marshal, and truth is, not many of us have the touch so's noticeable 'cept Possum, and he's, well, he's Possum." The older woman spoke too quickly, her hands pressing against each other as though for comfort, but Isobel had none to offer.

"The touch?"

"Yah know—" Lou gestured, blunt, calloused fingers and bitten-down nails, spreading them out as though she were smoothing a cloth in front of her. "Territory's touch. Makes you likely to do things, like scrying or growing."

April, back in Patch Junction, was a grower; she could make flowers bloom and crops flourish by her touch. Isobel had never thought much of it; that's just who April *was*, the way Gabriel could find water and Grace, the blacksmith's daughter, sang birds into the pot.

"Anyhows, that's how it touches some. And some other of us"—Lou indicated herself—"it passes right by."

Isobel shook her head, not to say no to whatever Lou was saying but to try and rid her head of the buzzing, like someone'd let a hive of bees in between her ears.

Gabriel had said that everyone could feel the Road if they just listened the right way. She'd just assumed wards were like that, that all you had to do was listen.

The buzzing slipped down into her chest, making it difficult to breathe. All the things she'd done since taking the Road, since signing her Contract, she'd tacked up to the sigil on her palm, her doing the devil's will the way she'd bargained to, but she'd been able to feel the wardings long before then, long as she could remember. And not just feel them but *hear* them humming in her.

The way the whisper had, when it urged her up onto the hills, when it coaxed her into reaching for the haint, up in the valley.

When it had called to her, outside the mine, up in De Plata.

Something inside her.

Molten strength pushing through her, wrapping itself around her. Pushing up into her, hot metal into cold water filling the forge filling her with steam and stink.

Dizzy, she tried to walk away, thinking if she moved aside she could think again, breathe again. Instead, she stumbled, although her feet would have sworn the ground was smooth, her arms coming up in reaction, hand outstretched, fingers and then palm coming into contact not with dry wood or warm flesh but dry, crumbling, burning bone.

Isobel screamed, the sound torn from her throat with Reaper's talons, and the air around her went black.

The men pulling the sledge seemed disinclined to talk, which Gabriel supposed he understood; saving your breath for breathing was wiser. Still, he had a rider's natural curiosity, and if they had no interest in answering his questions, there was nothing to say he couldn't learn by other means. It was hard to stop a man from looking, so long as he kept half an eye on the bodies, too, to make sure they didn't slide or, Devil forbid, start to wake.

The circle-and-sigil he sketched at that thought was a childhood reflex, making him flush and turn his attention more firmly to his surroundings.

The trail they were walking on had been packed down hard with use; there were occasional puffs of dust but nothing like they'd encountered outside. Wide enough for the sledge or three people walking abreast, but not a wagon; if they hauled anything here, it was by sledge or wheelbarrow, or something equally narrow. Looking up, he noted the stockade walls curved slightly, not quite a circle but shaped more like an egg, and he tracked how the trail they were on curved around as well. The center of the town was a decent-sized green that had the worn look of grass cut not by scythe but teeth—a community graze, most likely, where they'd keep their livestock in the winter.

After the green, the trail split in two again, both forks lined with low cabins, most of them with their doors open. None of them looked new-built, but they were all in solid repair, able to withstand near anything the Territory might throw at them.

So: A well-established town whose founders had been allowed to build on a site that had been in use by the tribe that had lived here first. That spoke well of the first settlers but gave him a quavering sense of worry, too. Why had the tribe abandoned this place? It was well situated, with fertile land close enough for them to farm . . . Had the hunting suddenly gone off? Surely, the settlers did not lie—the town had been here long enough to have drawn ire if it were not wanted, and not even the tallest palisade would protect them from warriors determined to take back their lands. Had it been freely abandoned? What had the settlers bartered that was valuable enough to earn them that?

Or, more worrying, had something gone wrong here, that the tribe refused to stay, handing it over instead to foolish whites to suffer the consequences?

He felt his fingers twitch again and forced them still. If there had been something wrong, surely someone would have felt it by now. Two generations they had here, at least. Not the oldest settlement in the Territory, but for as far out as it was, old enough, and isolated.

More likely that was the answer, Gabriel decided, looking at the simple sturdiness of the buildings. The local tribe had been small, the woman had said. They'd likely welcomed the newcomers as potential allies against winter and nearby tribes, and then over time lost their children to those tribes or even the town itself. His mother could tell the same story of her family, trade alliances leading to marriages and children. Even two generations could be enough for a small tribe to disappear, if that were so.

Thus mostly reassured, he followed the men and the sledge down the second trailway, past open, empty doorways, and then a patch of open space, until they came to a halt in front of a wood-and-stone hut. It was small, barely tall enough for a man to stand upright, and unlike the other structures, this door was firmly closed.

"This is your lockhouse?" Looking up, Gabriel saw the marshals' sigil not only painted on the door but carved into the wood, at least a fingertip deep. The paint filled the gouges, a darker red than he was used to seeing elsewhere in the Territory but reassuringly familiar.

"Locked up close and safe as certainty," a voice said in his ear as one of the sledge-pullers pushed open the door and started unloading the bodies with ginger caution.

"You must be Possum." It wasn't a guess: narrow face, a shock of greying hair, and red-rimmed eyes over a disturbingly pointed, pink-skinned nose, and if the man in front of him had been called anything else, it would have been a crime.

"And you must be one of the road rats the marshal drug in. Welcome to Andreas." Possum crossed long, bony arms over his chest and stared through the open double doors as the men laid the bodies out on the dirt floor. "Mind you don't smudge any of my sigils," he warned. "Or I'll repaint 'em with your bodily fluids; see if I don't."

The two men took about as much notice of his threats as a horse did a fly.

Given the opportunity with someone who seemed to like to talk, Gabriel took it. "Solid, maybe, but a bit smallish. Your judge not throw many people into lockup?"

Possum shrugged, still glaring. "Bandits get what's coming to 'em, they try Andreas's walls. But winters are long, people get cussed, specially when they ain't seen sunlight in a week. Easier to lock 'em in here than have to deal with sorting out the bloodshed after."

Gabriel felt his eyebrows rise, then pursed his mouth and nodded. No lie there.

"Most a' them sigils in there just make a fellow feel too lazy to cause trouble," Possum went on. "Kinda like giving 'em whiskey without the mean part."

Gabriel nodded appreciatively. "I don't suppose you'd teach me those?"

Possum snorted, a wet, deeply unpleasant noise. "Nope."

Gabriel was surprised both by the answer and the matter-of-fact way it'd been said. Bindings were the sort of thing that were shared freely, for the most part. To refuse a polite request?

Isolated, he reminded himself. Likely more than a bit wind-touched, some of them. He ought not take offense. They were guests here, however official the marshal's presence might be, and Isobel hadn't given her title. Even if she had, nobody save the marshal and the judge need answer to her if they didn't wish to.

And perhaps more to the point, the lockhouse was now home to two magicians: it was not all that surprising that the man might not want anyone poking about the wards just then. Isobel had said they wouldn't wake anytime soon, but he knew her, and he knew she hadn't been certain on that. So, any sane man'd prefer to be on *this* side of the walls, if she was wrong, and keep the man responsible for those walls in his good graces, not annoy him with pushing.

Still. The refusal was odd. Gabriel frowned, hands jammed into the pockets of his jacket, watching as the two men finished their work and came back out into the sunlight, closing the door behind them. The sigil flared once, a barely-there line of flame, before it returned to simply being paint.

The two men picked up the lines of the sledge and hauled it off without a word of farewell. Possum grunted after them, then turned to stare at Gabriel. "You plan on standing there all day?"

"No." He decided, good graces or no, that he didn't like Possum much, and from the way the two men had disappeared with the now-empty sledge, he didn't think they did much either. "If you could direct me to the judge's cabin, I'd be most appreciative."

Despite his politeness, Gabriel made certain his tone couldn't be mistaken for a request.

"Can't miss it," Possum said. "Just keep walking down the way until there ain't no more to walk."

There was a thump from inside the hut, something solid hitting ground, and Gabriel jumped, giving the now-closed door a suspicious look, doubled when something inside let out a muttered curse that lifted the hair on the back of his neck, even through the door.

"Don't you worry none about them," Possum said, looking like he hadn't twitched since his feet first planted. "Short of them calling down Mother Breeze herself, them walls aren't going nowhere and neither is they."

"You're certain?"

"Said so, didn't I?"

He could stay and risk whatever Possum might do if annoyed enough, or he could go find the judge—and, by proximity, hopefully also Isobel and the marshal—and tell them that at least one of the magicians had woken.

Gabriel briefly considered a third choice: getting his horse from wherever they'd stashed him, loading the mule up again, and riding back out through the stockade walls. He'd signed on to mentor Isobel, to make sure she knew how to survive on the Road, how to deal with marshals and handle posses and bandits, how to handle herself in bad weather, and how to feed herself when supplies ran low. He'd done all that.

In particular—and bargains were all about particulars—he had discharged the terms of his agreement with the devil. Isobel Devil's Hand could fairly be called competent, with competence, res judicata.

He clapped a hand onto Possum's thin shoulder, causing the man to startle where sudden noises did not. "I'll be off, then."

"You do that," Possum grumbled, and then pretended he was no longer there.

Following Possum's directions, Gabriel strode down the roadway, touching the brim of his hat in greeting when he encountered locals, all of them older, most of them male, all of them looking askant at the stranger, though none stopped or spoke to him. The lack of curiosity might be pushed off on their age, but Gabriel compared it to the hunger for news he encountered elsewhere throughout the Territory, and felt a return of his earlier uncertainty.

The roadway continued its curve, and to distract himself, he mapped it out in his thoughts, the hard-packed dirt and the low buildings and the stockade walls that rose twice as high overhead, curving like the cup of hands around the town itself. A single entrance at front, anyone entering forced to pause just inside the gate, then splitting around the common area to rejoin in the back . . .

He smiled, satisfied to see his assumption was correct: he came to the end of the roadway, a small smithy on his left and more of the low cabins to his right, with a square box of a structure directly in front of him, the palisade wall rising strong at its back.

More than a cabin, this; Judge Pike had himself a proper courtroom. Gabriel shook his head, half-amused. Some judges rode circuit, same as the marshals, and some set up shop in places where marshals and folk could find them easy, but few of them felt the need to replicate the formalities of Law elsewhere. It didn't apply the same here in the Territory.

But Gabriel wasn't going to deny the tendril of anticipation he felt, seeing the scales carved below the marshal's Tree over the doorframe, even though he was there only to witness, not prosecute. But when he heard yelling coming from within, all humor dropped and he knocked the door open with his hip, knife out of its sheath and in his hand before wiser thought could prevail.

LaFlesche was the one yelling. Another woman, younger and slighter, looked like she was the target. The judge was standing between them, trying to keep the peace.

Isobel. Where was Isobel?

"It wasn't my fault! She just . . . collapsed!"

Those words reached Gabriel at the same instant he saw Isobel stretched out on a bench, her arms placed over her stomach, unmoving. Another figure hovered over her, holding a cloth, and he realized with a sudden sharp sinking pain that the dun-colored fabric was marked with blood.

"What happened."

His voice cut through the yelling, a razor against skin, and a dread silence fell. His boots made a heavy, muffled noise against the plank floor, accompanied only by the exhale and inhale of the others in the room as he reached Isobel's side.

"What happened?" he asked again, taking the cloth from Tousey's hand and dabbing gently at the red stream still flowing from her nostril. Her eyes were closed, her skin clammy, and the throb at her neck was too quick for his satisfaction.

Had he only just been thinking he could be rid of her? He eased the fury rising and waited for someone to answer him.

"We're not sure," LaFlesche said. "She went with Lou here to look at the wardings. And something happened there."

"Nothing happened! She came and looked, and she asked me a few questions, and then she fell over." Lou sounded distraught and more than a little afraid. Gabriel could almost feel sorry for her: getting on the wrong side of people who could bring in two magicians without obvious harm to themselves must be terrifying.

Tousey had taken a few steps back when Gabriel came in, hovering just out of reach, his gaze flickering between them all. Poor bastard had been thrown headfirst into the brambles of the Territory; Gabriel wasn't sure he'd have been anywhere near as calm, were their conditions reversed, but he didn't have time to coddle him now.

"What questions?" he asked Lou, forcing his voice to stay even, the way he'd once questioned witnesses prone to emotion.

"Don't remember; something about how old they were? And then she went all pale and pitched forward, I swear it."

He risked looking away from Isobel to take in LaFlesche and the judge. "I didn't feel anything flicker in the wards," Gabriel said. "But this isn't my town; I might not've. You two?"

LaFlesche shook her head, sucked her cheeks in before responding. "No. But we were already in here when it must have happened."

Judges' quarters were sigil-warded, same as a marshal's badge-house and—he realized suddenly—the lockhouse. Had his being close to Possum's work kept him from feeling trouble when it reached out?

"She didn't even touch them; I don't see how—"

"Touch?"

"The bones." Lou took in his expression, then turned to look at the judge as though for support, but he shook his head, as confused as she by his reaction.

"Your wards are set in bone?"

"Well, yes. We saw no need to—" The judge stopped and looked at LaFlesche, as though expecting her to explain, but she merely shrugged.

"The wards were a gift," Lou said, her voice quavering. "From the natives who lived here at the time. I told her. We've used 'em ever since."

The judge nodded. "Way I heard the story, there wasn't much choice. To not use them would have given insult."

Gabriel was putting pieces together, and he didn't like the shape of any of them. Trusting your safety to someone else, someone else's long-dead-and-gone . . . it made Gabriel's skin crawl, but he supposed out here, deep in the winter, you had to trust someone. And it seemed to work for them.

But it would explain why Possum wouldn't show him what he'd done, why nobody here seemed interested in news from the rest of the Territory, and maybe why Isobel's poking at the wards had caused them to strike back—the devil's mark on her might have been seen as an attack or insult.

Or it could be something else entirely; he didn't know. Couldn't know until Isobel woke up.

"Iz?" He patted her cheek gently, brushed a fingertip across her neck, testing the heat of her skin, the throb of her pulse, then lightly touched her closed eyelids to see if there was any reaction at all.

She stirred restlessly under his hand, then sneezed, turning her head away from him.

"Hey, there." He sat back on his heels in relief, slipping his hat off and placing it on the floor next to him. The trickle of blood from her nose was only a drop now, and he cupped the side of her face, turning her head gently to look at him.

Her eyes were half slitted, as though the dim light from the lamps hurt them, but she seemed to be tracking and aware.

"Welcome back."

"The wards . . ."

"Yah. Do you know what happened? You fell . . ."

"Bones." The word seemed to exhaust her. "Their wards . . ."

"Tribal warding. So I heard. Is there a problem?"

Was there a problem that the Devil's Hand needed to deal with, he meant.

She closed her eyes, then nodded once.

"Blast and tarnish." Magicians and American interference, shaking ground and unhappy natives, a vicious haint, and now this . . . He was remembering why he rarely rode this far north, beyond civilized behaviors. "Is it on fire?"

A hesitation, then a single shake of her head. They had time to deal with it. He combed his fingers through her hair, loosened from its braid, and said the very last thing he wanted to tell her just then.

"Iz. I think one of the magicians woke up."

Her eyes opened, that forthright stare filled with such exhaustion, he almost told her not to bother, that they could deal with this without her.

But they couldn't.

There was nothing, then faint, muted noises, like listening from under a heavy blanket, voices from far away and downstairs. Then Isobel was vaguely aware of the flurry of activity around her, the voices clearer, urgent, and she was being moved, being lifted, a blanket over her shoulders she didn't need, and a mug in her fingers that she didn't want.

The liquid in the mug was warm, though, and when she sipped the broth, she found that she was starving.

"Slowly," Gabriel warned her when she would have drained the mug. "A sip at a time."

She nodded and took another sip, blinking as her vision cleared. Plank floors, worn smooth underfoot. Four walls around them, also plank; a large room, almost a hall, unfamiliar and yet—

She realized with a sudden shock that the room reminded her of the main room back in Flood, early in the morning before the tables were set up, the floors swept clean: that same sense of a space waiting to be used. The sensation was so strong, she found herself looking for the boss, flaring her nostrils to catch the warm, familiar smell of spice and whiskey and smoke that always accompanied him.

Gabriel's scent filled her nose instead, and an odd, acrid tang of something metallic. She raised the hand that wasn't holding the mug and touched under her nostrils. Her fingertips came away stained pink.

"Nosebleed," Gabriel told her. "It's stopped now."

His voice sounded strained, and she worried that he had hurt himself again, wanted to tell him to take off his jacket and shirt so she could check his bandaging. It had only been . . . how long since he was injured? Her thoughts wouldn't focus; she couldn't remember. Days . . . weeks?

"My head hurts." It came out as a whimper, and Isobel cringed in embarrassment.

"The broth will help," Gabriel said. "It will be all right."

She couldn't remember what had happened. Where were they? What had—

A voice caught at her, and she looked across the hall. Two men sat on a bench, enough space between them to tell her they did not want to be there, took no comfort from the other, making her aware of how close Gabriel sat to her, his arm draped over her shoulder, and how much comfort she took from that.

The shorter of the two men looked up, scowled at her, and a *click click click* of bootheels coming down stairs was her memory and she knew who they were: the strangers who had provoked the magicians, then called false insult against them. They were here in Andreas and—

"The magicians!" She tried to stand, but Gabriel's arm turned into an immovable weight, keeping her still.

"Easy, Iz."

"You said they were waking." She could feel her blood rushing, skin prickling, urgency driving her, but was unable to slide free from his hold.

"One. But the lockhouse can hold them for a little while longer. Drink the broth; you're going to need to stand up and be presentable soon."

Isobel knew that voice, knew it would be useless to protest. Despite his warnings, she drained what remained of the broth in one gulp, grimacing at the silty, overly salted dregs at the bottom. Broth for blood, Molly used to say when one of them had their cycles. She thought about telling Gabriel that, then decided against it. He was skittish enough when she bled; no need to remind him of it. Men were awkward that way.

She blinked down into the cup, feeling the warmth slowly creep back into her flesh, aware that she was thinking foolishly, that Gabriel was right; better she sit and be still a while longer.

"Maître Isobel."

She looked up as the man approached. Old, balding, a shirt buttoned to his neck, neatly darned at the elbows . . . Judge Pike, she remembered. He'd met them at the gate, and then . . .

"No, don't you stand," he reassured her. "Marshal LaFlesche has already given her word; all I'll be needing from you is why you say these men have brought false claim, and there's no need to be formal about it with only us here. You being who you are, your word will be enough."

Isobel blinked at him, then looked at the marshal standing a few paces behind. The older woman shook her head once: she hadn't told the judge anything. But she'd said she was of Flood, and he'd mentioned the boss, not her. . . .

Isobel bit her lip. When she'd first left Flood, she'd thought the name alone would make people look up to her, give her some kind of power. Now, months of travel from home, that name elicited the respect she'd craved, and she didn't trust it.

She wasn't fool enough not to understand why. This far out, the boss wasn't even a name; he was a figure, faceless and powerful. All they needed to know was she came from Flood, and she had authority. Her word would hang these men.

The Americans had given false witness, whether they'd understood that or not. Everyone in the Territory had to abide by the same rules. But she would give them fair telling.

She straightened her back and lifted her chin, putting the now-empty mug into Gabriel's hand, as though she were making her evening report to the boss, telling him what she'd seen, what she'd observed of the players at the table, the loiterers along the bar.

"My mentor and I were riding north along the Road when I was called to witness."

No need to say she'd been alone and asleep, or that the whisper hadn't been a dream-call, not truly; explaining all that would take more strength than she had, with what she had yet to say.

And the whisper itself . . . Her thoughts of that, her dizzy, impossible thoughts, the sensation of something replacing herself with itself, she'd keep to herself. For now.

"We first encountered a homesteading, where the residents told us of the earth shaking, that there was a . . . something wrong, further north. That the ground shook and the animals fled."

Had this been the boss, she would have told him of the sadness Jumping-Up Duck had described, had told him about the way they had seemed afraid of what was happening, the sorrow and anger they had described. But such things had no place, no weight in what this man must judge.

"Following their guidance, we rode further and came to a valley where . . ." She hesitated, suddenly wishing for the mug to be back in her hands, to give her something to hold on to, clench her fingers around. Instead, her fingers dug into her palms, feeling the cool lines of the sigil on her left, the warm, unmarked flesh on her right. "Some terrible medicine had been worked there," she said finally. "A circle of power, a trap set . . . and death."

So far, nothing she had said had made the judge react; she did not know if that meant her words matched the marshal's or he simply had the ability to keep his thoughts from showing in his face or body.

There was no need to tell this man what the magicians had drawn back to half-life, or that the dead lingered as a haint, tainted with madness, bound within the earth for eternity. No need to speak of the torment they lingered in, that shook the valley with their pain. There was nothing his knowing could change, nothing his judgment could heal.

That was her burden to carry, not his.

"Magicians built that trap—and died in it," she went on, and was gratified, selfishly, to be able to read the surprise in the way his eyes widened ever-so-slightly.

"A *duel* caused the quakes?"

Duels—one magician setting themselves against another—were not common, but they were not uncommon, either. They preyed on each other the way wolves preyed on deer, and woe to the soul caught up in their storm.

Isobel had survived such a storm, though as much through luck as wisdom. She knew firsthand what a magician could do, and what two magicians might do, if they took their battle outside a crossroad.

If you see a magician, run. It was advice meant to keep ordinary folk alive.

"Not a duel," she said quietly. "They were not waging war against each other, but together."

The judge spluttered before he regained his words. "You're mad."

"I wish I were," she said. "But I speak truth. Five who died, and two that we know of who lived."

Seven was strong medicine. Territory medicine. Seven calls from an owl meant someone would die. Gabriel had taught her that.

She thought of the owl she had seen, the one that had led them to the marshal, and something cold stroked her bones. There was nothing to say to her that it had not simply been a bird, disturbed from its slumber, hunting by day. These things happened. But Isobel had grown up in the devil's house, and she knew better than to presume. The wapiti guarding the valley, the owl leading them to the magicians . . . spirit-animals with impossible, contradictory advice, and whatever had happened to her in those hills that left the lingering taste of smoke and silver on her tongue. If she could only *remember*.

None of that mattered now. She focused instead on shaping the right words, clear and concise.

"And these men . . . I cannot speak to the how or why, but they were in that valley. They admit to attempting to influence the acts that happened there. That the magicians may have tried to kill them after cannot be proven"—though it was likely, and a pity they didn't succeed—"but that it was without cause is blatantly untrue; whatever happened in that valley, they were part of it. And that they do not speak of that part, their culpability, makes their claim of insult nothing save falsehood."

The words poured out of Isobel now, and the relief she felt as her mouth moved was akin to slipping into the hot water of a bathhouse. Her mouth, her tongue, her throat forming the words, her breath pushing them out, but the words themselves came from deeper than she could reach, drawn not only from her thoughts or the sigil in her palm but the heat curling up along her bones.

She was the devil's gaze cast over the Territory, the great and the small alike. But something else looked through her as well.

"And that is your observation?" The judge had listened to what she said, showing no more emotion after that single slip, waiting for her to say that yes, that was her observation, and be done.

"It is my observation and the judgment of the Devil's Hand."

She had not meant to say that, had not opened her mouth to say it, and yet the words came, falling solid as stone into the room.

The twitch in the judge's jaw was the only sign she had that her words affected him. She could not override his decision, whatever it might be. This was not a matter for her—for the boss—to decide. But she had just confirmed his suspicion that the Master of the Territory was watching.

She had grown up under the boss's eye, his hand a comfort on her shoulder. It was difficult for her to remember that to some, he was mysterious, unknown, unpredictable. Frightening.

And now, to everyone here, so too was she.

To give the judge credit, the twitch and the flicker of his eyes was the only sign he gave, then his face shuttered again, unreadable.

"Mister Kasun?"

Gabriel slid his arm from around her shoulders and stood up. She was so accustomed to seeing him on horseback, or sprawled on his kit once they made camp, that she could have picked him from a crowd a hundred paces away, and yet the man in front of her suddenly seemed a stranger. Gone was the casual slouch of his shoulders or the easy way he placed his boots, like he knew the ground would rise up to meet him. This man's boots were planted solid on the floor, his hands clasped behind his back, chin up and hair slicked back out of his face.

"I was not privy to certain details Isobel observed, nor the means by which she determines truths. However, I have observed her in detail over the past months and will place my word that she speaks the truths as she observed them."

The judge sniffed once, not entirely displeased. "Eastern advocate, are you, boy?"

"Trained for it, sir. Not currently practicing."

There was some joke there that the two men got—three, from the snort that came from the States' marshal still sitting on the bench across the room.

"And you give your word on her."

"As her mentor, yes, your honor, I do."

Gabriel had never had cause to give his word before a Territory judge before, although he'd seen it done, when he was younger: the settlement he'd grown up in had been fractious enough that a judge had made a point of stopping by twice a year to settle things before they got out of hand. Those had been noisy affairs, yelling in two or three languages, depending on who was before the bench, and usually ended with a round of drinking that would inevitably start the next round of arguments.

It was quiet in this bench-hall once they'd finished giving their observations. The judge had not retreated to his quarters, as Gabriel'd half-expected, but rather leaned against the far wall, his eyes hooded, occasionally rubbing his bare scalp with one hand as though to stimulate his thinking.

The road marshal paced, her bootheels a steady, sharp slap against the planking, then a pause as she wheeled, and the *slap slap slap* again. He wasn't sure if it was soothing or prone to drive him mad if she kept it up much longer. The woman who'd gotten Isobel into trouble, whatever her name was, had disappeared at some point. A wise choice—it may not have been her fault, but he couldn't hold her blameless, either.

Next to him, Isobel was watching the Americans. They were sitting still, not looking at each other, a marked distance between the two of them. The judge had spoken to them, quietly, before he heard from the marshal or Isobel, but if they'd spoken since then, Gabriel hadn't noted it. Then again, he'd had other things to worry about.

Her nose hadn't started bleeding again, and her voice'd been steady when she spoke, no stutters or hesitations, but the memory of too-cool skin and too-fast pulse haunted him.

"What happened out there?" He didn't look at her, and he didn't feel her shift to look at him.

"I don't know. It's still hazy." Her voice was soft but certain. "Lou showed me a ward post. They were . . ."

"Native work, yeah." Mayhap his original thought had been true, that the foundation had taken insult at the Devil's Hand come too close into things that didn't concern him. Mayhap that's all there was to it, his deeper concerns baseless.

"They used bones."

That was a new one to him, but it didn't surprise him overmuch: bones had strong magic and remembered for a very long time. Likely even forever. "You touched them?"

She bristled under him like a cat splashed with water. "I did not. They were . . . I can't *remember*. But there was something about them that . . ."

Her voice trailed off, and he slid his arm back over her shoulders, not pulling her closer but just to reassure himself that she was there, that she was upright and breathing. The memory of her laid out on the bench, her nose bloodied and her eyes vague, still made him feel ill, but his responsibility was to teach and support her, not coddle her.

"Whatever you felt, you didn't like it?" Her skills were still raw but there had been nothing wrong with her judgment, and if her gut was reacting like his, the odds were high something *was* wrong.

Her breathing steadied a little, and she leaned in toward him. "Lou couldn't feel them. She can't feel her own boundary-wards. She said that not many of 'em here can."

That surprised him—usually, you went into the wilderness, you found more folk with the touch, not fewer. Insular, he thought again. Incurious. He'd give pure silver to speak with some of the younger ones, those out working the field, see if they were the same. "But they were working?"

"Yes. They were . . . alert?" She wasn't asking him, he thought, but testing the word for herself. "Awake. They were awake, and that . . . that didn't seem usual. So, I tried to listen closer."

Of course she had. Gabriel swallowed a rebuke, knowing it was at least partially his fault, and waited her out.

"They were layered, old over older. And I could hear this . . . noise. Like a hive readying to swarm."

She stopped, swallowed, the noise of it loud in his ears. He waited, gaze fixed on a spot somewhere between the drop of the ceiling and the rise of the wall, where some discoloration of the planking made it look as though there was a hole. It was easier to speak when you could pretend there was no one listening; he had spent a few nights like that, in a starlit camp, speaking things that could only be said to the fire, the ashes of your words gone cold and scattered in the morning, never spoken of again.

"And I didn't touch them, but I almost did, Gabriel. I reached out, and then the world went dark, and . . ." Her left hand flexed and clenched, resting on her lap as though it didn't belong to her at all. "They burned me, Gabriel. The bones, the oldest bones. When I reached out to them."

"It was warning you away?" His fears returned that the old medicine left here had taken insult by her arrival. The settlement was non-native now—the devil held dominion. But the wards might not realize that . . . They needed to talk to Possum, and this time the man would be more forthcoming.

"I don't know," Isobel was saying in answer to his last question. "I don't think so. But I don't know." Her face scrunched in concentration and distress. "There was something they told me, something important, and I can't remember . . ."

Her wording eased some of his fears—"told," not "warned." "Leave it be," he told her. "It's easier to remember when you don't actively dig at it." He rested his right hand over her left, still tight-clenched. "Is this telling you anything?" The sigil, he meant.

She glanced down, and an expression he couldn't read passed over her face. "No."

"Then leave it be for the nonce. There's only so much you can pack on a mule and then it's got the sense to kick off the weight. You'd best be at least as smart as a mule."

She looked as though she were about to argue, pulling in breath to speak, but they were both distracted by movement at the other end of the hall, the judge pushing himself away from the wall, shaking down the line of his coat and fixing his vest, the image of a man about to make a pronouncement.

Isobel had never understood fury, whiskey-hot rage that made her stomach roil and sparks crackle in her skull, until the judge told them his decision.

"You're as mad as they!"

"Iz . . ."

Isobel shook off Gabriel's calming hand, turning to stalk after the judge as he paced the width of the hall. Behind him, LaFlesche looked nearly as unhappy as she felt but said nothing.

"You can't simply—"

His voice was weary but firm. "They've done no injury by the Law that I could hold them, and I've no authority to bind such as they for anything less. The magicians go free."

"They attempted—" She clamped her jaw shut when he swung around, raising one finger to her, warning her to cease interrupting.

"Whatever they attempted, it's no business of ours. Magicians are creatures outside the Law, outside the devil's claim, and unless they've wish to involve themselves"—and his expression showed he thought little of the odds on that—"then they are to be on their way as soon as they are able."

And not a moment too soon, his tone conveyed.

Open the door, unlock the wards, and allow them to saunter away. . . . Isobel could understand his reluctance to keep them within the confines of the town, but to simply wash his hands of what that meant?

"The Law is the Law," he said. "Magicians are neither mine nor yours to control. You will release them, and they will go. And we will all hope that they do not decide to take offense at your treatment of them."

She lifted her chin and stared up at him. His gaze met hers evenly, with neither a flinch nor an apology.

She could defy him. She could demand he . . . do what? Hold the magicians forever? Kill them? She knew that they came back from that as often as not, having seen Farron torn apart by a summoned spirit and then reappear not days later as though it had never happened.

Isobel tried to rein in her fury. Judge Pike was correct, as little as she liked it. The magicians had done damage—immense damage—but the Agreement did not cover them; the Law did not apply to them. Like all other creatures of the territory itself, they were unto themselves.

She thought of the buffalo she had seen, slaughtered by these magicians for their blood and hide, for the strength they carried, and left to rot without dignity or respect. She thought of the promise she had made— the promise Something had accepted—and her heart ached to think that she would fail in that.

But there was nothing she could do.

We tell you nothing you do not already know.

She was sworn to the Master of the Territory. His limits were her own. Weren't they?

Listen, Hand.

If she could remember what the wards had told her, if she could remember . . . Why couldn't she remember?

"Isobel?" The judge was expecting her to back down, to accept his authority in this matter.

"And what of those who incited them?" She swept her gaze to the two men still waiting along the far wall. The scout was busily staring at his boots. The marshal looked back at them, a resigned patience all she could read.

A swell of sympathy surprised her. She too had been sent out unprepared. But she'd been given Gabriel. This man had been given a snake-faced scout who didn't have the courage to face his consequences.

The Territory didn't care.

"Paul Tousey. Jedediah Anderson. By the word given of Isobel née Lacoyo Távora and Gabriel Kasun, confirmed by the word of Marshal LaFlesche, you have been observed falsely claiming insult. The punishment for that is severe. However, since those you insulted are not within the purview of the Law and have not chosen to act on their own behalf, we dismiss those observations."

The scout looked up at that, a gleam of hope lifting his shoulders.

"Notwithstanding," the judge went on, "you have also been observed by Isobel née Lacoyo Távora in the act of inciting damage to the land of those who have kept peace with us, who have lived by our Law as we live by theirs, according to the terms of the Devil's Agreement."

"And that means what, exactly?" Tousey stood, his pose similar to Gabriel's earlier, his shoulders straight, hands clasped behind his back. She wondered if that was a thing they taught men, across the Mudwater, in the East.

LaFlesche spoke this time. "It means that you have given insult."

The scout made a noise, a sharp, cut-off bark of a laugh. "It means they're gonna kill us. Or give us to the savages to kill, or eat, or whatever it is they do. Fine, then, old man, get on with it. Quit yapping at me."

"Anderson, shut up," the marshal said, and then turned to address the judge, his tone dry as wood. "And may we speak in our defense? Or do our voices carry no weight under your law?"

"You have a defense that amounts to more than causing mischief?" The judge's voice was equally dry, his hands tucked into his pockets, elbows loose, hips and knees straight ahead, not turned out the way

Gabriel and LaFlesche stood, or hip-cocked the way the boss leaned, casual as a coiled snake. Or the scout, who remained slumped, his shoulders rounded in resignation.

Isobel was suddenly brutally aware of her own body, how straight her back was, her right hand clasping her left, thumb pressed into her palm. She could feel a bruise on the side of her knee where she'd fallen, and another on her shoulder, the smell of blood and sweat still too strong under her nose. She wanted a bath, and a bed, and a warm meal that had no beans in it, served at a table, with a chair under her backside, not a saddle or dirt.

"Acting under orders of your government will not save you," Gabriel said from behind her, a caution that seemed to spark something ugly in the other man.

"You've no government for me to be in contrivance against." The marshal's skin was sallow in the lamplight of the judge's bench, and the hollows under his eyes deeper than merely exhaustion, the look of a man already dead, who simply hadn't realized it yet to lie down. "I am, at worst, a goad, a match. If there was nothing to set alight, I could do no harm."

Something shimmered, hot and angry, in Isobel's bones. But she thought it was not directed at the marshal himself.

What? she asked it.

Listen, Hand.

"You admit that you were sent here to cause harm." The judge again, his voice calm as though they were discussing the turn of a card, something of significance but no particular urgency. He shifted, though, his body turning to keep Tousey in full sight, suddenly a potential threat.

"Not to cause harm, no. To observe. To note. To report back. Discovering two . . . magicians mid-battle was pure chance, and we—"

"You interrupted a duel?" There was surprise in the judge's voice then, surprise and astonishment that they were still alive after that, much less able to affect anything.

Tousey raised his glance to the daub ceiling, then shook his head, the resignation of a man who saw no more point in arguing, convinced he was the only rational soul left among the mad. "I saw two men circling each other, chanting nonsense. Andersen told me that they were magicians, men who had some power in this land, that they did not kowtow to your . . . devil. I thought they might be useful to cultivate as potential allies."

Isobel pressed her thumb harder into her palm, forcing herself to listen not only to the words but what snaked underneath. Fools die. The first thing a child learned in the Territory. But Tousey had not died. Not a fool, then, or his luck had been stronger than his foolishness.

Luck was medicine of a sort for some. A man with luck could beat the devil with his own cards.

"And what did you use as bait to entice them to listen to you?" Gabriel's tone tore her attention away from the marshal; she had never heard his voice that cold, not since . . . not since that first day on the Road, when they'd encountered a posse who'd looked at her wrongly.

He was angry at the wrong thing, the wrong person. She knew that, but she didn't know *why*—or who.

"What does it matter? You've already judged me and measured the rope."

Gabriel could move like a ghost cat when he chose to. Tousey and he had seemed evenly matched, but the rider had him up against the far wall, a hand wrapped around his neck, before any of the others could react. "What. Did. You. Use?"

"Mister Kasun." The judge's voice wasn't as cold as Gabriel's, but it carried a distinct chill. "This is my bench, if you please."

She could see the muscles bunching under the back of Gabriel's shirt, but then, slowly, they eased, and he released the other man, stepping back just enough that he could still lunge again, easily. She couldn't read most people from behind, but Isobel had spent enough time riding behind him to learn Gabriel front and back. He wasn't angry. He was afraid.

Of what?

"There is no rope," the judge said, stepping forward so that Gabriel had to take another step back or be pushed aside. "That is not how it works in the Territory."

"What, a knife? A bullet? Or was Anderson right; do you turn us over to the savages?" Tousey didn't spit the word the way Anderson had, but it still tasted sour in the air, anger and fear and disdain mixing with the lingering smell of sweat and blood to make Isobel's stomach churn with upset.

"We would be well within our rights to do so," the judge replied. "Your actions caused them direct harm, and this would show them that we took that harm seriously."

"Well, that's just lovely," Anderson muttered, still sitting on the bench. He hadn't so much as flinched when Gabriel attacked Tousey, slumped against the wall, still staring at his boots. "We'll end up stretched on poles and shucked into stewpots, then. Tell them where you got the damned idea, Tousey, and maybe they'll kill us outright instead. That'd be a better fate."

The American's jaw clenched, the muscle in his jaw twitching hard enough to make his eyes squint half-shut. "I was told, if I encountered a magician, that the only thing they respected, the only thing they coveted, was power . . . and the only thing they wanted and didn't have was freedom." He exhaled, his chin lifting not in defiance but an odd sort of . . . pride? "I was authorized to offer them passage across the Mississippi if they so desired—"

"You are mad." Gabriel's voice was flat, brooking no dispute.

"The United States Government—"

"Has no idea what they were offering. And you—you told them what? That they would have free range there? What would they have to give you first?"

"To bring down the boss." Isobel knew she was right, felt it in her bones. "That was it, wasn't it?"

Tousey's gaze flickered sideways. "That was not in my orders."

"No." She stepped closer, but where Gabriel had attacked, she slid, winding herself around him, until there was barely a handbreadth between them. Rosa taught the new girls how to do that, to distract and set a man back on his heels when he got too rowdy. If you could confuse them, she'd said, you could control them.

Isobel knew she wasn't Rosa, didn't have the swing of hips or perfumed hair, in her worn traveling dress, her hair a mess, stinking of blood and sweat. But his breath caught and his gaze flicked down at her, then away anywhere else, discomfort writ in his face. She refused to allow sympathy to soften her, pushing forward, her hands flat on his chest, the flesh under her skin pulsing with that flowing, hot power.

She could *feel* his heart beating under her hands, feel the quickly indrawn breath, the panicked scurrying of his thoughts, wondering what sort of witch she was, suddenly realizing, remembering that it had not been Gabriel who had bound the magicians but her, that she was the dangerous one. . . .

She stepped back, her hands pressed together, palm to palm, touching fingertips to her mouth.

"He was told to offer them whatever it took," she said, not looking away from his eyes. "If they could bring down the boss, make people doubt his ability to keep them safe. It was an open pot with no limit. With that much of a lure . . . they were willing to work together to achieve it."

She tried to imagine it, seven versions of Farron, agreeing long enough to not try to destroy one another to gain greater power. . . .

Yes. Enough of a lure, and they would. And they would not stop—would not be *able* to stop and consider if the bait were true or empty, the way LaFlesche's crossroads trap had been empty.

We tell you nothing you do not already know.

"But they couldn't hold it, could they. It wasn't only that what they were trying to do was too powerful . . . they turned on each other the moment they had the ancient spirit in hand."

The churn in her stomach worsened, disgusted by the thought of what must have followed, the raging madness of the spirits, of an ancient being thrust back into flesh only to be trapped once again, of the frothing, possessive madness of the two surviving magicians the judge was determined to let loose back into the Territory. All because of this man.

No. A chill settled over the heat in her bones, and she could see the threads that wove to make the cloth, one pattern overlaid on another. The Americans were fools, but they were not the ones to blame.

Isobel turned her face away, the hall suddenly too close, the air filled with the memory of burnt flesh and soured blood, rage and loss. The magicians had killed the buffalo for power, betrayed the Territory with their greed. Everything the boss fought to keep in check—they'd ripped open.

She could sense Gabriel near her, the feel of him like running water, easing the press of rage. She opened her eyes, forcing herself to observe, the way the boss would expect, to give nothing away.

The judge was speaking again—to Anderson and Tousey, not her. "Acting on behalf of a foreign government, to create dissent and trouble within the Territory." The judge pursed his lips, shook his head. "Your own words, your own admission. That seems clear enough, however a fool's way you chose to do it."

The marshal's face was still again, his body likewise. "And the punishment?"

"Had you foolishly chosen a settlement to stir, we would have ridden you back to your border and pushed you, naked as a babe, back to the trouble that spawned you. But it was not us you gave insult to."

"Tolja," Anderson spat, still slumped against the wall. "They're gonna hand us over to the savages."

"Would you rather I chose the mágicos to punish you?" the judge asked, his voice coolly amused. "Creatures of madness and whim?" He turned back to Tousey. "The Kohogue or the Sutaio, they might kill you, they might keep you, but you are a warrior, and while you were foolish, you have not behaved dishonorably. They would treat you with respect."

The look he gave the guide suggested that the judge didn't expect so much on Anderson's behalf.

"You will be given shelter here overnight. In the morning, I will request the presence of the elders of the nearby tribes. They will say what your fate may be." The judge stepped back to his bench and rapped once on the wooden surface with a fist-sized mallet.

Someone outside must have been anticipating that signal, because the door opened and a shadow filled the doorway even as, in the corner of her eye, Isobel saw LaFlesche step forward, the silver wrist-cuffs dangling from her hand.

Anderson must have seen the cuffs too, or like a cornered animal sensed the trap, because he lashed out, coming off the wall like a storm, head-butting LaFlesche hard enough to send her staggering backward, his left arm swinging up and slapping into her torso.

Isobel saw the glint of metal, heard the sharp gasp of indrawn breath before the road marshal dropped to her knees.

A fight had broken out in the saloon once, when the boss wasn't there. Someone had gotten too familiar with one of the girls against her wishes, and Iktan had stepped in. The man had thought that because Iktan was old, he wasn't a threat.

That fight had been fast, over before she was even aware it had started. But this time she saw all of it as though every motion were slowed down, her heartbeat taking forever to go *thump-thump-thump*. The tang of blood reached her nose, and Gabriel lunged past her to tackle Anderson, Tousey diving for the man's legs and yanking them back, the judge yelling something garbled over her head.

It took forever to happen, a hundred counts in one beat of her heart, and then Isobel moved, with each step her heels clicking on the planking, cutting through the noise of the scuffle and the yelling like thunder cutting into a storm, crouching next to the wounded marshal and pulling her upright, searching for where the wound had been made, where the blood was coming from.

It all snapped back, and then things moved too quickly.

"Stupid son of a bitch." LaFlesche's face was pale, but her eyes were bright with anger, even as her hands pressed against her abdomen, trying to staunch the wound. "I didn't think to check for an arm sheath; thrice a fool." She rasped once, a harsh sound deep in her chest. "Is it bad? I don't want to look; if I look I'll likely faint, and the judge will never let me forget it."

"Let me see. Come on, let me see." Isobel coaxed her hands away, gently. More blood soaked the cloth of LaFlesche's shirt, accompanied by the smell of shit and urine. She pulled her own knife from her belt and cut the cloth away as carefully as she could.

"How bad?"

"Bad." Worse than bad; Isobel caught a glimpse of something pink and pulsing under the wound: the source of the smell. The knife had been yanked out so hard, it had tried to take her insides with it. "Gabriel!"

She could hear the noise of the fight going on behind her, though she couldn't take her eyes away from the wound, pressing her hands against it as though to stop the bleeding through sheer willpower.

"Boss, help me," she said despairingly. "Please."

Then Gabriel was there, his hands over hers, pressing down, and the marshal started to swear, the shock wearing off and the pain setting in. "Son of a bitch, oh damn Anderson you quivering pustulent sack I'll— oh!" LaFlesche arched away from their hands, cursing fit to curl Isobel's hair, and she looked at Gabriel, hoping he would tell her what to do.

He shook his head side to side, forehead creased, his eyes sorrowful.

"He cut you something fierce," Isobel said, surprising herself at how light her tone sounded, as though she were talking about a broken leg, something that might heal. "Please tell me there's a curandero in this town; otherwise, we'll have to rely on me for the stitching, and mine are never as neat as they should be."

That got what might have been a laugh from the marshal, a gasping, dry noise. "I still got a nose, girl. I can tell when my gut's been ripped open. Your finest hand won't do much save make me pretty for the night birds."

Gabriel's lips pressed tight, his hands still holding torn flesh in place. "Can you . . ." His eyes asked the question his mouth couldn't complete. Isobel pressed her hand down harder against the wound, letting her palm slip against the slick surface, not flinching from the unpleasant texture.

"Iz?"

She felt the pulse of flesh underneath stutter, then begin to slow.

"I'm sorry." She wasn't sure who she was saying it to, Gabriel or the woman dying under their hands. "I'm so sorry."

She had been warned before she left Flood: the Left Hand did not carry mercy but judgment.

There was no bench observance for murder committed in front of witnesses. The knife, a viciously sharp skinning knife, light enough to be overlooked and slid up a sleeve, had been clenched in Anderson's hand, slicked with blood, when they finally wrestled him down to the floor, still flopping like a fresh-caught fish.

Tousey had been the one to subdue him finally, they were told, with a boot to the neck of his former companion. The US Marshal was solemn-faced now, his shirt bloodied, standing off to the side, nearly forgotten as judgment was carried out. The small sounds of a blunderbuss being primed were too loud in the air, the crowd who had gathered to watch quiet save for their breathing and the rustle of their coats as they shifted. Somewhere in the distance, a dog barked and birds called, and farther off Isobel thought she could hear the lowing of cattle, but then the tamping rod was inserted, and the faint clicking noise seemed to overwhelm all else.

Anderson stood, sulkily defiant, scowling at his executioner. "Didn't mean t'kill her," he said, given the option to say last words. "But I'll be damned if I'll be handed over to savages."

"You'd be damned either way," the judge said, and nodded to the man with the blunderbuss. A square block of a man, he raised the gun to his shoulder, braced, and pulled the trigger.

Isobel closed her eyes, the echoes of the shot knocking against the walls of the town until it faded back into silence, the smell of black powder chasing the tang of blood from her nose.

"It's done," Gabriel said.

They laid the marshal to her rest after sunset, when the winds were still and the bright blue points of the Eagle barely visible in the darkening sky, the moon's circle dimmed, as though it, too, grieved. The same thick planked wood they used for the walls made up the platform, higher overhead than Gabriel could reach, wide enough to rest two bodies side by side. There were thick gouges in the supports where something with claws had stretched, but they went only halfway up; Gabriel's people had encaved their dead, and even then, burrowing scavengers had made their feasts. Back east, he'd seen, they buried the bodies whole and never looked at them again.

Dead was dead, he supposed, and the dead cared not for flesh. But the thought of a body decomposing below ground, locked in a wooden box, made his own flesh crawl. Time enough to be interred once your bones were clean and warded.

She had been washed and dressed in clothing from her packs, her sigil repinned inside her lapel, the silver resting over her breast, her hair washed and left loose, a heavy leather band placed over her eyes. She rested on a fine woven blanket, her arms stiff at her side, her weapons and saddle next to her on the platform.

When they took the ladder away, the judge stood there, half-lit by torchlight, and looked up at the platform.

"She was not a friend. She was not my family. I did not know her well. I cannot speak for her, but there are none here who may better, and so I must. I never heard it said she made a promise she did not keep, or gave insult where none was earned, nor was she cruel or petty. And she was gentle when she could be. More than this I cannot say."

Someone else should speak for her, Gabriel thought. That alone was not enough of an epitaph. But they were far from any people she might have had, and he could not think of anything; he had not known her either.

"She did not deserve this death."

Isobel, standing beside him, her voice low and steady.

"She did not ask for this death. And yet, the day she took the Tree into her hands, the day she pinned the sigil to her cloth, she chose this death." A brief gulping swallow, so faint only he could hear it. "To walk the road of justice. To cleanse the road and make it safe for all. Those are the oaths they make. I did not know this marshal, but I rode with her. She was strong and honest, and saw clear where others perceived shadows. She died in service of the Tree. The Territory honors her for that."

There was weight in her words, warm in the cool night air, and in the silence afterward, he felt her hand reach for his own, fingers curling for comfort and reassurance. Gabriel squeezed once, and then they turned around and followed the others back along the narrow trail, through the gate, within the safety of the palisade walls, leaving the dead behind.

In Flood, when someone died, there was a gathering in the saloon after. The tables were put up, and the boss hosted the first round, and even though no one mentioned the dead person's name, it was almost as though they were there, until morning came and it was time to bury the bones. Andreas was more solemn, or perhaps it had been because the marshal was a visitor, a stranger, and they could not bring themselves to care.

It made Isobel wonder where she would die, if there would be anyone there who would know enough to speak for her.

"Stop that," Gabriel said.

"What?"

"You're thinking on your own death. Don't. It comes when it comes, where it comes, and that's the only certainty we have."

They'd been given a small cabin for the night, two rooms, with a square chimney in the center for heat, the same plain wooden planking they'd seen elsewhere. The beds were covered with blankets woven with colored bands of different widths, like Gabriel's, only unfaded, and feather-stuffed pillows that had Isobel immediately wondering if she could possibly shove one into her pack when they left. Gabriel had put his kit on one bed and dropped his jacket over the single straight-back chair. "The dead are dead," he added. "Let them go."

She didn't know how to do that but nodded and followed him out the door.

They'd been invited to eat with the judge and his wife, a square-faced, solid woman with skin a shade lighter than her husband's, her curls the color of pewter, her eyes surprisingly blue. Their children were grown and working land just southeast of the town, she explained, but she was too old and lazy to wield a hoe any longer.

Looking around the cabin, simple but neat as a pin, with walls carefully chinked against winter winds, braided rag rugs on the plank flooring, and neatly sewn curtains over the windows and door, Isobel suspected that neither of their hosts had ever spent a slothful day in their lives.

They did not speak of judgment, nor the man closed in a room awaiting his own punishment in the morning, nor the two still unconscious and warded in the lockhouse; Gabriel and the judge exchanged news of the Territory and beyond, of people and places Isobel had never heard of, and she, defaulting back to the girl she'd once been, stayed quiet, opened her ears, and listened for what wasn't being said.

They had not felt the quaking of the earth. The conversation touched on it, briefly, and then moved on: they were not aware that it had been worse, that game had fled the area, that people beyond their walls suffered.

She remembered what Lou had said, about so many here lacking the touch, and wondered if that lack of concern were connected or coincidence. You did not ask where someone came from or why they'd come; no more so could she ask if they could feel the Road, the wards, the Territory itself around them. She could not ask why the people here did not seem to *care*. But not knowing made Isobel uneasy in ways she could not explain.

The sigil in her hand remained cool, the whisper absent. But—despite judgment—the day, the events, did not feel finished.

Gabriel, across the table from her, wiping the gravy from his plate with the last of a bit of bread, seemed to have no such discomfort.

She pushed at the feeling the way she pressed on the sigil in her palm, gentle, steady pressure, but nothing shifted underneath. There was nothing wrong here save her feeling of wrongness.

Trust yourself, Gabriel had said.

"If you'd care to," the judge said as his wife cleared the plates from the table, "we've a bathhouse you might make use of. I remember . . . Well, there comes a time when sloughing off all you've been carrying with a dose of hot water is just the thing."

"You go first," Isobel fiddled with the napkin on her lap, the cloth rough against her fingertips. "I . . . need some air."

Neither man questioned her, although the judge's wife gave her a considering look over her shoulder from where she was scraping dishes into a wooden barrel, as though wondering what sort of woman would pass up a bath when offered.

A woman filled with power, and none of it her own.

Andreas might be a bustling town in the winter, when all its residents returned within the walls, but tonight, with the warmth of summer hinted at in the night air and the weight of the day's events lingering, it was quiet as a boneyard. Some doors were still open, lights visible through windows, but save for an old man smoking a pipe, she saw no one as she walked. The moon was entirely absent from the sky, allowing the stars to shine all the more brightly, as glittering as the cut glassware Iktan washed so carefully every night behind the bar.

A longing for the saloon, for Flood, clawed gently at her. When the boss was distant but ever-present, when folding linens and serving drinks were the routine of her day and helping to unload a wagon was the excitement, when the only things she'd ever seen die in front of her were chickens, and once a dog that'd been kicked hard by a horse.

When she didn't know the stink of disease, of blood, of death, when it lingered on her hands. When she didn't feel something *else* whispering in her bones.

Isobel's steps took her past the stable where their horses and the mule were, and she hesitated a moment, thinking to go in, rub her hands against that smooth, warm, living flesh, feel grassy breath on her hair, lean her face against the mare's neck. Instead, she moved on until she came to the lockhouse.

The man Gabriel had said maintained the wards, Possum, was not standing guard, but she did not think he was far away. She breathed the night air, letting her eyes rest on the sigil on the doorframe. The paint was black, but shimmered as she looked at it, as though saying hello—or "stay away." The protections on the walls and roof kept her from touching her own wards, wrapped around the magicians to keep them still, but she thought they remained intact. But that uncertainty might be the source of her unease.

"Are you awake?" she called out, standing next to the door. "Are you aware?"

There was sound of something—someone—shifting. She touched her left palm to the door, asking the wards under the sigil to let her see.

They resisted: she was not the one who had laid them; she had no sway over them. Isobel felt a flash of irritation: she would accept the earth's refusal of her, but not this. The devil's sigil was not greater than the Tree, but it was no less, either.

Kneeling, her skirt tucked under her legs, Isobel placed her palm instead on the ground. It was night-chill and dry, and she remembered the feeling of the valley, where she had been cut off from the bones, cut off from the Road.

Choose, the spirit-animals had told her. Was this what they meant? She hesitated, unsure, then she pushed down, feeling the now-familiar dizziness and disorientation as the bones reached up, drawing her in and spreading her thin.

The Road sang to itself, miles distant. Closer, rock grumbled and shifted, cool water trickled and pooled, steam gathered, constant pushing and pressing, building and breaking. All the Territory, as close as her fingertips. Isobel was tempted to linger within, tempted to go deeper, to look backward, to see if she could reach the damaged circle and the power constrained within.

She resisted; she dared not disturb further the spirit or the madness trapped with it. All she needed to know was what waited on the other side of the door in front of her, quench the sigils that flared like a forge as she approached, warning caution to all flesh.

Her breathing rasped in her throat, heart too large to rest within her ribs, thumping to escape. She felt as though she had a fever, skin too tight over bones too warm, the world colorless but too sharp, as though the shapes might cut her eyes if she gazed on them for too long. She could break the wards if she chose to. Sliding from the roof and walls, shattering at her touch, ripping the Tree out by the roots.

She shook her head violently, to rid herself of that thought, and her braid knocked against her shoulder, the feathers braided there tickling her chin, as though familiar fingers stroked her skin, gentle, gentling.

Calls Thunder, the dream-speaker who had gifted her with those feathers. They'd had no great meaning, no significance, Broken Tongue had said. Just . . . feathers.

A gift, Gabriel had said.

She exhaled, reaching up with her free hand to touch the feathers, flicking the braid back over her shoulder, feeling it settle against her back, feeling her spine elongate, a snake stretching itself full length in the dirt, a ghost cat leaping, a Reaper hawk spreading its wings, rising into the sky, the proud line of the wapiti's neck, prongs limned by sun and moonlight. A thing of the Territory. A thing that belonged to the Territory.

Something settled within her, smooth and heavy as stones, and her heart slowed, *thump-thump-thump*, then *thump-thump, thump-thump*, until she could breathe again. The rage disappeared; the power remained.

Her left hand dug into the ground, the sigil burning like a coalstone. Power. Responsibility. The lesson she'd never quite learned: be careful what you ask for, for the devil will give you exactly that. What a magician did was none of the devil's concern. Until she decided it was.

Show me, she told it. And it did.

One magician had woken, and consumed the other, taking all he was and leaving a husk of flesh and bone behind. Restless, roiling; power still contained behind the wardings, but slowly, carefully, craftily they were being scraped away from inside, layer by layer unraveling.

Bones are strong, but the wind will not be contained.

Isobel sat back on her heels, her skirts covered in dust, and breathed.

Magicians were creatures of the Territory. Like the Reaper hawk or the buffalo, or the waters rushing down from the hills to feed the prairie grasses, or the stone spires rising toward the sky. The eight winds owned them; they answered to nothing less.

But an owl had led her to them. Spirit of the winds, omen of death.

The boss waited in Flood, shuffling decks and turning over cards, watching and manipulating, piece by piece, the Right Hand to succor, the Left to . . . to what?

The great elk had told her to deal with the intruders, to be the knife the devil had sent her to be. The Reaper hawk had told her to walk away, to leave the valley, to survive. Both were creatures of the Territory, but they counseled her at odds.

But the snake, what had the snake said? *We tell you only what you already know but will not let yourself hear.*

She had been sent out, not kept. She had set foot on the dust roads, had heard the beat of the buffalo herds in her own blood, felt the scream of a Reaper hawk in her bones, breathed the resin-filled air of the mountains and drunk the dark, cool waters, dug her fingers into the grit and loam . . . felt the whispers of the earth itself in her own bones.

All her confusion, all her uncertainty came from that. She should never have listened to that whisper, should never have allowed it within.

And yet, had there ever been another choice? Had the boss *intended* for her to have no other choice?

The Left Hand was the knife in the darkness, the cold eye. The ease she could offer was not to heal but to ensure no further harm. Isobel pressed her left palm back to the dirt.

The magician inside was restless, tightly twisted; it knew she was there but considered her no threat, not now. She had crept in through the bones, drab-colored and dry, and what threat could earth be to something born of the wind?

The calm amusement she'd always felt in Farron's power was absent here. No humor, no affection, nothing to soften the madness that seethed, needing more without any hope of satiation, no Law, no limits. Only hunger. Only greed.

Her hesitation disappeared. Isobel placed both hands palm-down on the ground, stretching so that she lay flat on the ground, her face pressed into the dirt, nails digging past the crust, the smell of it in her nose, the taste of it in her mouth; she was the ground, she was the stone, she was the water trickling deep within. And then, faint, soft, the brush of wind, there and gone.

There was no Isobel. The flesh becomes dust, the bones become stone, the blood becomes wind. The touch of the devil on her palm spreading into every speck, curdling her, thickening and softening, hardening and changing. An instant of dropping dropping too far and rising too fast until a sharp wrenching sensation and there was nothing but a narrow pinprick, nothing but a single intent, sharp-edged silver coin turning and turning as it spun through the air, landing in the shadow of a crossroads filled with rage and despair.

Not enough. She was not enough, not against this.

Open, Hand.

She opened, unthinking. And then, agony, her body seizing, sinews contracting, bones crunching, blood steaming from skin, skin burning, lungs collapsing, and the rush of rain-wet wind wrapped around her, the hot agony of molten silver shoved into her, welcomed into her veins as though it'd been formed there, then the taste of mud and sulphur coating her tongue, and slowly, slowly, Isobel returned, curled on the ground outside the shack, and when she opened her eyes, a man sat next to her, sharp nose and red-rimmed eyes and grizzled grey hair loose and tangled.

"That's done, then," he said, patting her shoulder awkwardly, as though to offer comfort. "It's done with ya, for now, and he's done with the bath and looking for you. Go. I'll deal with this here."

She had no idea who he was or what he meant, but she had no strength left to ask or argue.

PART SIX

WAKE THE BONES

Gabriel dreamed of death.

He stood in the middle of a creek bed, dry and mud-cracked, the sun cold and heavy on his bare shoulders, and knew that he should not turn around, that the night bird waited for him.

Not for you.

"That doesn't make it better." His dream-voice was higher, lighter, the voice of a child, not a man. That was how the dreamspace saw him, Old Woman Who Never Dies had said. Foolish but teachable.

Be careful, Two Voices.

He was always careful. Too careful, Old Woman had said that, too, in a tone that said it wasn't a good thing, not like a hunter was careful but like a coward.

Gabriel had never denied it.

"Do you have a message, or is this a thing I needs must learn on my own?"

He was alone in the middle of a dry creek bed, the water and fish long since fled, the sky blue-white and sunless, and then he was awake, a too-soft bed cradling him, and Isobel's soft snoring across the cabin the only noise he heard.

❧　❧　❧

Sleep never returned. Gabriel finally gave up, pushing aside the covers and reaching for his boots.

Isobel was curled up with the covers pulled to her nose, her head shoved half under the pillow. He suspected he hadn't looked much better: after weeks on the road, sleeping on bedrolls and using their packs as pillows, even lumpy, musty beds were a gift. But the sticky remnants of his dream, coupled with the events of the previous day, left him feeling too restless to remain.

When he stepped outside of the cabin, stretching the creaks and aches from his back and shoulders, the morning air was cool enough to make his eyes water. Traveling the plains had made him soft, unused to the bite of mountain air even in early summer.

They'd been given a cabin toward the center, near the common green. The air smelled of pine and sap and meat cooking somewhere, making his stomach grumble. He needed coffee. And breakfast. With luck, Missus Pike would be willing to feed another mouth, since the town had no saloon or dining hall.

Walking back toward the back of town, where the judge and his missus lived, Gabriel realized that unlike any other town he'd ever been in, there was no hammer of anvils or clatter of wheels breaking the morning's silence, no voices raised in argument or muttering against chores. Of itself, that was nothing to be concerned about: Andreas was, as they'd said, a half-empty town during planting. But as he came closer to the judge's home, he heard the quiet buzz of voices, the unmistakable tone of panic.

That was enough to warn him, even before he saw the small crowd gathered outside the bench, the judge in the middle, already dressed and looking stern.

Yesterday had been bad enough; Gabriel didn't want to consider what could have happened overnight. He thought about waking Isobel up, then decided that if nobody had come to roust them, this wasn't their problem. Let the girl sleep.

But he was here, and it didn't seem as though he'd get breakfast until this was settled.

"Judge." He cut through the crowd with an apologetic nod and a tip of his hat, but for the most part, they gave way without complaint. "There a problem?"

It was obvious there was, but Gabriel was simply a guest here now. All the judge need do was say that was handled, or nothing was amiss, and he would be able to turn away with a clear conscience.

"The magicians," the judge said, turning a sour look his way, and Gabriel's soul went cold for an instant, before realizing that if they'd broken the wards, the judge *would* have woken them, violently and with a great deal of noise.

A flickering memory of his dream, *be careful,* and he braced himself for what might come. "What happened?"

"That's an excellent question," the judge said, still sour. "Micah, tell him what you told me."

"We went in the morning, to check and offer 'em water. 'Cause we assumed they needed to drink." The other man said it almost as a question, wringing his hands and speaking down to his boots. Without seeing his face, Gabriel couldn't guess his age, but his hands were thin and age-spotted, not Gabriel's first choice to send to care for two madder-than-most magicians. "Only, when we got there and had Possum open the door . . ." The speaker looked up then, grey eyes wide and terrified, and younger than his hands would suggest. "It was like some beast got in there. Got in there and tore them up but good."

Gabriel's hunger turned to a cold curdling in his stomach. Breakfast be damned, his dream be damned: he wanted out of this town. Whatever had happened when Isobel touched the ward post had been bad enough, but for her to then see the marshal die under her hands, to not be able to save her . . . She was only a girl, for all that she was asked to carry. She shouldn't have spent last night washing cold blood off her hands and out of her clothing. She shouldn't have to see this. . . .

The judge turned back to him, the wrinkles in his face deeper than they'd been even a day before. "I'd not ask this of you, rider, but it would be days before another marshal could be summoned, and if there's something hunting within our walls, we need to know now, not after more are dead."

Unspoken but clear: anything that came hunting magicians was nothing any of them could stand against.

Nothing except Isobel.

Gabriel bit his teeth against that knowledge, the urge to flee battered by responsibility, obligation. But the dead were already dead. He would let her sleep until he knew more.

The inside of the lockhouse had a dirt floor rather than the planks he'd seen elsewhere, and no furniture or windows, the walls—lit by pale morning light coming in through the open door—covered with sigils and scratchings laid over each other, some carved, some painted, some old and some brightly new. But the walls were only a distraction from what lay on that dirt floor.

"River have mercy," Gabriel breathed, then gagged, the smell too much in the enclosed space. He backed out, breathing into his sleeve in an attempt to block it out. "I've seen bear maulings prettier than that."

"The last time we had a bear inside the walls, it was a half-grown cub the children smuggled in," the judge said, his face no better than Gabriel's, a faded blue kerchief held against his nose and mouth, "and we had to deal with the mother trying to knock the gate down. That mistake has not been made again."

Another time, the story would have amused Gabriel. But with the memory of bodies torn and strewn about, he couldn't even muster a smile. "Then what?"

He knew, even as he asked the question. It was possible that a beast or man might kill a magician, especially one that was already bound. But both, within the wards? There was only one thing Gabriel could think of that could do that to two magicians. Another magician.

"Tousey said they came on two magicians in a duel and recruited them, and then five more. All accounted for. But if they reached one and he decided not to participate, didn't want to play with others . . ."

The judge considered his theory. "He might have thought they were easy prey, with the máitre's bindings on them."

One of the people who'd followed them from the judge's cabin and gathered outside the hut while the judge and Gabriel investigated, asked. "And got to them how?"

"Does it matter?" Gabriel eyed the woman: younger than most, pale-skinned and leaning heavily on a wooden crutch. That would explain why she wasn't working a field—and possibly the look of distrust that seemed etched on her face, as though she expected everyone she met to lie to her. "Trust me, trying to think on what magicians can and can't do will keep you awake in the small hours. Best to be thankful they chose to destroy each other and not us."

Except they might have chosen exactly that, if what Tousey said was true. If they thought it was in their best interest to turn on the Territory in exchange for riper pickings . . .

No. This, all of this proved that no magicians could work together, not even for a wanted goal. They were too mad, would turn on each other from instinct and need. Even Farron, for all that he seemed fond of Isobel, had warned her that a moment's faltering on her part, and he would not be able to resist, like a fox in a hen yard. And that had been a magician in full control of himself. One touched by the madness Isobel described?

"You think we need to increase our wardings?" a third voice asked. Gabriel couldn't pick him out of the small crowd, but it didn't matter; they all looked the same just then, as though Gabriel had begun speaking Hollandic—the words might be familiar, but the meaning escaped them. That was the problem with settlements, he thought. They became accustomed to things *working* and stopped thinking about *why* they worked that way, just blindly following along. . . .

Gabriel thought of Isobel laid out cold and bleeding on the bench merely from having touched one of the ward posts they all took for granted. "I think whatever medicine could reach through what you have already, there isn't anything anyone here could do to stop it."

Isobel, his thoughts supplied. Isobel might.

Might. Would try, if she knew. And might fail.

He was not her guardian. He should go wake her, tell her what had happened. Let the Hand decide what to do.

He stood just past the doorway, his back to the shredded bodies, and did none of that.

"All right, enough," the judge snapped when someone else tried to ask another question. "There's not a thing for any of you to do here, unless you're volunteering for cleanup?" He waited, but when no one volunteered, he waved his hand irritably. "Then get, all of you." He waited until they began to disperse, then called out, "Possum!" The hut-keeper ambled over from where he'd been crouched by the door, his eyes redder than the day before, his hair and clothing just as tousled and grimy.

"Anything to add to the conversation?" The judge's voice was just as sharp, but there was a level of respect that hadn't been there before when he spoke to the others, and Gabriel wondered if there was more to Possum than he'd realized.

"If'n I did, I would have told you." His gaze flicked back and forth between the two men, and Gabriel wished Isobel were with them so he could ask her if the ward-maker was lying.

"All right. Do you think you'll be able to clean that mess up?"

"Not enough that we'd ever be able to use it again," Possum said readily. "Not so much the blood and guts as what was done to 'em." He sucked at a forefinger, then added, "Living silver done that. Likely have to burn it down and build anew, maybe even dig up the floor, depending how deep it went."

Gabriel went still and cold.

"Take what you need to make it done," the judge said, as though he had no understanding of what the old man had just said. "If anyone gives you grief, send them to me."

Possum grinned at that, showing blunt yellow teeth. "Ain't no one will give me grief, and you know it. Even if they do feel summer-dumb." He gave Gabriel a mocking salute, then ambled past him, pushing the rider aside to reach the doorway, and disappeared inside.

"He's as mad as a magician." Possum couldn't have said what Gabriel had heard. He couldn't have.

"Not nearly, but . . . he's always been a special one, from the day he was born. But without him, we'd have a harder time of it, keeping the wards intact, so allowances are made."

The judge took Gabriel's arm, pulling him gently away from the lock-house, leaving Possum to do his work unobserved. Most of the crowd had faded away as well, and Gabriel could hear the previously missing sounds begin, noises of a living town going about its day.

"Did you hear what he said?"

"What, about having to burn the hut down and build again? Yeah, that'll be a hardship, but I'm thinking we got off lightly after—"

"No." Gabriel interrupted him. "About the living silver."

"Living silver is a myth, a story natives tell, to explain things they don't understand. I told you, Possum's a special one; he believes things like a child. But he's a fine maker, and I suppose the two may happen together, yes?"

"It's not a myth."

"Oh, come now . . . ," the judge scoffed, then sobered when Gabriel did not laugh. "You're serious?"

"The miners believe it."

"Oh, well, miners." The judge waved a hand as though to dismiss the entire breed.

"And so does the devil."

The judge placed a hand over his mouth, drawing it down into a fist resting at his chin, his eyes gone distant. "Impossible," he decided. "Even if such a magic exists, which I'm not saying it does, we've little enough silver here among all of us, and all of it forged and still. No, that was only Possum being Possum. I won't worry about it."

Gabriel bit his tongue rather than speak the words he was thinking. Silver was a tool, forged and smithed into useful bits, be it a buckle or a button or the coins they carried. But the deepest, most powerful veins? They were more dangerous than a dozen magicians and thrice as unusable. Simply putting pickax to a vein could be enough to destroy the mine itself and everyone within it.

But the judge was right: there were no mines here that he'd ever heard tell of, and living silver could not be shaped or formed to carry anywhere. The judge was likely right: Possum was the sort who'd lead you by the nose for amusement if you let him.

"—about then, I find myself envying you the Road, I don't mind admitting." The judge had still been speaking; Gabriel tried to make it seem as though he'd been listening. "And speaking of which—" The judge looked up at the sun just now rising over the eastern wall. "Time we wake our remaining prisoner and send him on his way as well. You'll be there?"

And that, Gabriel surmised, would close the book on this matter for the judge. One prisoner executed, one condemned to his fate, two magicians dead—but since he saw no threat to any of his people, the matter was of no further concern.

The worst of it was, Gabriel could not bring himself to blame the man. That was how the Territory worked: you honored the dead and you warded their bones, but you did not linger with their memory.

But Gabriel, for all that he knew better, for all the warnings he'd been given, couldn't let go so easily. Only two things could destroy a magician: the wind they took their power from or another, stronger magician. And if a wind had taken back its medicine, there would not have been a lockhouse left standing to be blood-splattered.

A duel, one against two, and the two lost; the winner unknown but filled with the power they'd stolen, a powder keg of madness ready for a match to ignite.

The people of Andreas could pretend this didn't affect them, that someone else would clean the mess. Gabriel traveled with the Devil's Hand and had no such luxury.

Isobel wasn't quite sure where she was when she woke. There was a bed underneath her and a warm coverlet above, and a feather pillow under her head rather than the hard leather of her kit.

Then memory hit her: magicians, the frantically beating wings of the ancient spirit, the marshal's death, molten claws of something beneath her skin . . .

She sat up and shivered in the cool air, her bare arms prickling. It might be nearly summer, but she suspected it never reached the warmth of the plains this far north.

She had been warm the night before. Had burned from within, her bones limned with liquid heat, opening to . . .

She closed her eyes and breathed out. *Survive*, the Reaper hawk had told her. Isobel thought if she remembered too much of the night before, she might not.

Gabriel was nowhere to be seen, the blankets pushed to the foot of his bed, his boots missing. It was ridiculous to feel abandoned, alone: he'd likely gone to use the privy or find breakfast and would be back soon enough.

Isobel rummaged in her pack for her comb and toothbrush and powder, then dressed. On a whim, she dug into the bottom of her pack to find the shawl she remembered folding and placing there so long ago, back in her room at the saloon. It was dark blue and fine-woven, a birthday present from when she turned thirteen, one of the few things she'd packed simply because it was pretty. She pressed her face to the soft wool now, remembering green felted tables and sawdust, whiskey and soap, fresh bread and brimstone, and all over it, running underneath it, the familiar-comforting tobacco smoke and bay that meant the boss had been near.

After so many weeks of horse, leather, and woodsmoke, those

once-familiar scents were strangers, and that thought made her eyes water before she dashed the dampness away, draping the shawl over her arms the way Marie had taught her, and went in search of Gabriel.

The judge's house was open but empty, neither judge nor his wife nor Gabriel to be found, and Isobel had no idea where to look next, her lack of direction allowing uncomfortable thoughts to creep past her ear, trying to find their way to her eyes, to make her remember.

She drew the shawl more closely around her shoulders, wishing she had simply put on her well-worn jacket, and tried not to think at all.

"Excuse me?" She raised her hand, oddly tentative when she saw a group of three, two men and a woman, walking toward her. They paused on seeing her, as though they'd forgotten there were strangers in town, then the woman smiled—tightly, nervously—and said in a voice softer than her face, "How may we help you, dear?"

"I'm looking for my mentor? Gabriel Kasun?"

Something shifted on their faces, echoing the woman's nervous smile, and Isobel's nerves tightened. "Do you know where he is?"

He was, it turned out, checking on the horses. Uvnee and the marshal's pony had been let out into the small fenced yard, and the mare whickered when she saw Isobel coming, hoping for a treat. She rubbed the mare's nose fondly, then went into the shed, looking for Gabriel. He was checking Steady's hooves while the mule was busily chomping down on something out of a wooden trough set along the far wall.

Other than their three and the marshal's pony, there was an elderly brown mare who likely had been retired from heavy work, resting in the shade, and the two brown dogs keeping her company.

"I would have thought they would have more horses," she said when Gabriel and Steady both raised their heads to see who had come in.

"The others are in use," Gabriel said, going back to work with a hoof pick. "Not that they have many—they kept 'losing' them to raids."

"Raids?" Isobel was confused. "I thought they were on good terms with the local tribes."

"They are. I suspect that's how they kept it that way." He finished checking Steady's hooves, tossing what looked to be a small pebble to the side, and leaned against the horse's side as she gave the mule a hand to sniff in greeting. "Gives them something to brag about and argue over when they get together. Pride's important to a warrior. Stealing horses has become an honored tradition."

"Gabriel." She could read him too well. He was talking the way she was not-thinking, to keep something at bay.

"The magicians are dead. Something got through the wards last night, early this morning, and killed them." His words were sharp, dropping into the air like knives, slicing at her, opening her.

"What?" Her voice was faint, hollow, echoing the faintness inside her chest, something fluttering faintly in distress.

"This morning, when they opened the wards to bring them out. That's all they found."

"Are you certain?"

"Saw it myself, Iz. Wards were intact, magicians were dead. Mind, I'd say fair riddance to the both, but it makes me worry what else is out there now, more powerful than the two of them, and mayhap just as mad."

Isobel could feel her brow crease, a hard tic twitching in her cheek, and she schooled herself as though she were facing the devil across the card table, refusing to let anything slip free. "Are you sure they didn't destroy each other once they woke up?"

"Not unless it's normal for them to rend each other limb from limb and leave only bloodied bits and bone behind," Gabriel said. "And it's not, so far as I've ever heard."

Isobel turned her face back to the mule, smoothing a hand over its soft nose to gain time to respond.

"Isobel."

He was asking her what to do—not mentor to student, but rider to Devil's Hand.

Survive. No whisper, no memory, this, but common sense.

"They're likely far away from us by now," she said. "If whatever did this meant to strike at us, it would have already. Farron said magicians have much cunning but little patience."

"'And blown by the winds from which they take their names,' yah, I remember that. So, we've no fear, leaving this town in our dust?"

"I see no reason why it should return." Her voice shook a little, and she firmed it by the end, willing her words to convey confidence without allowing for further questions.

To her relief, he only nodded. "The judge has asked us to carry word of the marshal's death. He'll write up whatever report's needed; we only need take it with us."

With the mail chain broken until the post rider recovered from the flux or was replaced, it was the least they could do. And Isobel couldn't deny she'd a fierce need to leave this town and its high walls behind and never return.

"So, we can leave?"

Gabriel hesitated, and she braced herself. "We . . . You should be there when they hand Tousey over. As witness."

As the Devil's Hand, he meant. As witness.

They went back to the cabin they'd been given, repacking their kits in silence. A fresh pitcher of water had been left, along with a covered tray holding a corn mush that tasted better than it looked, and what might have been half a small pig, roasted to crackling perfection and cooled so you could eat the strips with your fingers. Isobel might have wished for coffee, but the water was fresh and cool, and sufficed.

She didn't think being more alert for what was to come would help, anyway.

There were four natives outside the judge's bench, as though they had been waiting there forever and would wait forever again with equal ease. Isobel was still learning what Gabriel seemed to read easily as breathing, but even she could tell that the quillwork on the moccasins on the older man with two silver braids was a different style from the beading on the vest of the younger man next to him, dark head bent as he listened to what the first man was saying, and the other two, standing at a respectful distance, had shorter hair and broader features, and their leggings and moccasins had no visible bead or quillwork. At least three tribes had sent someone to speak for them. The same three who had followed them here? Likely.

There were two settlers lounging nearby also, younger and bulkier than most of the people she had seen so far, sun-dark, and she thought maybe the judge had called in aid from the nearest fields, although the scene appeared peaceful enough.

She had a passing thought that had he taken such care earlier, the marshal would not have died, but she and Gabriel had both been there and the marshal had died anyway. Isobel had been able to scrub the blood from under her nails but could still feel it when she rubbed her fingertips together, unseen in the whorls of her skin.

The older man with the braids looked up as they approached, and stopped speaking, but he did not acknowledge them. Following Gabriel's lead, Isobel paused at a distance and stood, waiting.

Then the door to the bench opened, and the judge came out, followed by Tousey. He was bareheaded and disheveled, having spent the night in his clothing, but he walked easily, without visible shame or fear.

The four warriors stood, somehow seeming to come together even though they did not move closer, as the judge and Tousey came to them. Gabriel put his hand on her arm to stop her from joining them.

"This isn't our trouble," he reminded her. "We're only here to watch."

The silver-haired elder eyed Tousey up and down and then up again, then reached forward to poke one gnarled finger into his shoulder. "You are the one who caused the ground to shake?" Disbelief was clear in his words.

"He brought the idea to the wind-taken," the judge said. The elder ignored him, staring steadily at Tousey, who seemed to almost smile, briefly. Isobel thought that for the first time, he looked like a man who knew his place and what was expected of him.

"My name is Paul Tousey. I am a United States Marshal, sent here to engage with the individuals known as 'magicians' in order to determine if they might be useful allies for my government." He glanced to where Isobel and Gabriel stood. "It is my considered opinion that they are not, and the results of that contact are . . . regrettable."

The elder stared at him, then nodded once, as though he'd understood every word. "We will take him."

And that was that, near as Isobel could tell. The two younger natives came forward, slipping a horsehair rope over Tousey's head but not tightening it; it seemed a reminder, some ritual of parole more than an actual restraint. But before they could lead him off, he said something to the judge, who gave a sharp nod and made a hand motion. They dropped the end of the rope and let him step away.

Coming toward them, Isobel realized.

"You've lived in the States." He was speaking to Gabriel, not her.

"I have."

Even with a rope around his neck, the skin of his face rough with exhaustion and whiskers, the marshal had a certain air to him now, an assuredness that was not boastful. He nodded, as though Gabriel's words confirmed something.

"I would ask you a favor, one I will, regrettably, be unable to repay. If you would, send word across the river to my superiors. Inform them of the events of the past few days. I would prefer that my fate be clear rather than left open to interpretation."

"You don't want them to think you deserted."

Tousey gave a wry smile and a shrug. "In the event of my death, my family will receive my pension. Otherwise . . . Will you do this for me?"

There was a pause, and then Gabriel nodded. "I will do this for you."

Isobel looked between the two of them, feeling as though she'd come late and missed something important. But she had a more urgent question whispering in her mind just then.

"Do you think they will send others, despite your failure?"

Tousey looked at her then, his eyes clear, and sad. "I am certain that they will."

Someone coughed behind them, and he took a deep breath, then exhaled. "I will not offer you my hand; we were not friends. Farewell. I do not think we will meet again."

"The road turns on itself," Gabriel said, "and we never know where we may end or who we may see there."

Tousey did not smile again; she thought perhaps he had no more smile left in him. "Very well, then. If so, I hope that we may begin as friends in a less inopportune time."

Isobel watched as he walked back to meet his captors, then allowed the four to escort him away. "What will happen to him?"

"It depends on which tribe gets him," Gabriel said. "For three different tribes to come, either they all felt aggrieved by his actions, or—"

"Or?"

"Or they want to know what he knows." Gabriel's mouth pressed into a thin line. "Magicians aren't the only ones who might think to benefit from powerful allies, Iz. The Agreement is old, but it's not unbreakable. On either side."

Isobel stared at him.

She thought of the buffalo, slaughtered for the power in their blood. Of the great, ancient spirit trapped by greed. Of men far away, poking and poking at the Territory, promises carried on threat of hellfire, or sweet-milk promises that only make your stomach bloat.

She thought of the whisper waking her from sleep, and the way the devil studied his cards, every hand he dealt, and a man who walked to his fate without flinching, though someone else sent him there.

And she thought again of the buffalo, hooves pounding heartbeats against the ground, of cards falling on felted tabletops, of the look in the Reaper hawk's eye.

Survive. Protect.

She pulled the shawl more tightly once again, although she felt too warm, not cold.

"We need to go back to the valley."

It might have been proper to stay until the marshal's bones were reclaimed and safely interred in the boneyard, but neither of them had any desire to stay, and it seemed the town had no desire for them to linger either. The town of Andreas might live by the Agreement, but Gabriel did not think that they had been particularly comfortable with the close-up reminder of it.

They left the marshal's pony in the stable with the old mare. He'd thought about taking her—a tough little road horse like that would be wasted pulling a plow, but when Isobel looked at her, then looked back at him, he'd shaken his head.

"We've no need for her. They can let her be stolen at some point, make a nice gift to some young warrior."

She'd only nodded. He hadn't added that he thought the reminder of the marshal's death would be an extra burden on shoulders that already bore too many.

No one saw them off as they rode back through the gates, the judge having made awkward farewells immediately after the American had been handed over. It was just as well, Gabriel supposed. "Lovely to have visited; sorry about the dead marshal and shredded bodies we left behind" wasn't the best repayment for hospitality, and if only Gabriel understood how close they had come to a potential border incident with a foreign power . . .

He didn't regret agreeing to carry the marshal's message. Tousey's family deserved that much peace. But Gabriel wasn't sure how he would word it, who he would send it to, without explaining how he came to be there—without making himself seem more useful to them than he had a desire to be.

And they would see him as useful; there was no escaping it any longer.

As preoccupied with his thoughts as he was, Isobel was worse. She had been stiff as they saddled the animals, and even now her fingers were too tight on the reins, making Uvnee tense as well; her shoulders were stiff, and she didn't look around, taking in any last memories of the town the way she had every other place they'd left, but stared ahead, her expression grim.

He watched her from the corner of his eye as they rode down the dusty trail away from the palisades gate. Slowly, her shoulders eased a bit, the reins lowering, but her expression remained somber, her eyes distant. He breathed the warm air, feeling the weight of blood and too-close quarters washed away by the smell of grass and water, the sun warm overhead, the distant feel of water sliding through stone deep below them, and waited.

He waited until her legs softened around the mare's sides and her mouth eased, and she smiled when a gold-and-blue butterfly chased itself around the mare's ears before flitting off into the grass.

"You killed the magicians, didn't you."

He had chosen not to watch her as he spoke, keeping his gaze between Steady's ears, watching the soft brown flesh twitch back and forth, pleased to be back on the road as well. Her laughter might have sounded true to someone who did not know her.

"You can't kill a magician. They just . . . come back. Remember?"

He had almost missed her impudence, in all this, and chose to consider its return a good thing. He took two breaths, waited four soft clops of Steady's hooves, before he looked over. Her fingers hadn't tightened on the reins, and her body remained open and calm. Her braid was curled over her shoulder, the feathers braided into it fluttering as she moved with her mare, the two of them practically one beast, the way a proper rider should be. Her profile, shadowed under the brim of her hat, showed no hint of a smile, but neither was she frowning, and when she felt his gaze on her, she turned and met it, square and unafraid.

She had spent her childhood at the devil's knee; he couldn't bluff his way past her. So, he took a different approach. "You were not pleased with the judge's decision to let them go free."

"Neither were you."

"No. I wasn't. But I had no ability to prevent it. To prevent them from doing as they would once they were free." His throat was dry, and he reached for the canteen slung at his saddle, taking a long swig before going on. "You stopped them."

"Were you the one who told the Americans to approach magicians?"

Her question was so quiet, he almost didn't understand the words, or the intent behind it. "What? I—"

"That letter that was in the waystation box for you. It came across the river. Good paper, ink that didn't fade. The boss uses ink like that, and pays well for it. So, someone with money. Over there, you said, money means power." He saw her shoulders rise in a slight shrug. "I'm guessing that people with that kind of power aren't that different from magicians. They want more. And . . ."

"And the Territory, to certain people, reeks of power, both the money kind and . . . other," he finished for her. "Yes." He could lie to her, but he would not.

"Why?"

That hadn't been the question he'd half-expected. The devil understood power, manipulated the desire for it to match his own intentions, whatever they were. But then, the devil stayed in his town, at the center of his web, and wove the strands he needed. His Hand strayed further, saw more.

Gabriel knew from experience that more was often confusing.

"Back in Patch Junction, you said that people who wanted things from the States, who tried to bring what was there here, that they were fools. You said that April was a fool for yearning after those things."

April had been a fool—not for wanting the things civilization could bring, but for not understanding what else they would bring with them. He had the flash of a dry, cracked riverbed, a cold sun, and rubbed one hand against his leg, feeling sweat that had nothing to do with the heat of the day.

"My letters were to a friend. Someone I trusted. What he did with the things I told him could not have given injury." He had passed along nothing of the devil, nothing of magicians, only tales of long rides and small towns, of ten ways to cook beans and the pleasure of the open skies, compared to the cramped quarters of Philadelphia and Boston. Even if such things had been shared . . . No.

"Are you certain?"

It would have been kinder if her voice were accusing, angry, rather than curious. Accusations and anger he could counter, deflect, defuse.

They rode without speaking after that, birds calling and insects singing, and the occasional relief of a doe and fauns lifting their head to watch them ride past, until the weight of it all pressed too heavily on him. He had shared nothing untoward across the river—and he had not shared everything that came back to him. He had thought—had decided—that it was nothing to do with him, no matter of his, what games others played in distant places.

He had been wrong, and the fact burned in his gullet like rotgut. The snakes had warned him, over and again: enemies and friends would tangle and be confused. Be careful, Old Woman had said. Even Graciendo had warned him indirectly; the old bear had known that traveling with Isobel—with who she was—would endanger him, claw at his refusal to give in, drag him into the very involvement he had run from.

Not of any thing she would do or say, but simply by being what she was . . . and him being what he couldn't help but be.

The Territory had never let him go.

The moment he had looked into those eyes and offered, on a whim, to mentor the potential he saw there, he had been found.

"The letter you carried. It was from that friend. He heard a thing that worried him, and he spoke of it to me, I think to ease his mind, to somehow pass word along into the Territory the only way he knew how."

Gabriel had spent years in the States, pretending to fit, making himself fit, but he'd never been able to let go, either. Abner had known that before he had. Had not been surprised when Gabriel packed up one night and boarded a coach, not stopping until he hit Saint Louis. The letter hadn't been guilt speaking; it had been a warning.

"The new president, Jefferson. He's a smart man, ambitious. And he's been given authority, given funding to send a mapping expedition into the Territory. Maps are a kind of power too, Iz. They change the unknown into known, and once a thing is known, it can be taken."

She was listening to him, chewing his words. "And something like that, an expedition, it would be allowed. They'd pass the Mudwater unmolested. The boss wouldn't even notice it, because it's not military, not force. Like the monks."

The Spanish monks, who had been chasing down an unholy magic unleashed by their masters. The magic itself had carried no intent; the monks had not cared about the Territory, only themselves. There were holes in the devil's protections, holes that her boss did not seem to care about.

Or wasn't aware of. Gabriel wasn't sure which thought unnerved him more.

"Only way to stop them would be to shut the border entirely." He swallowed, and Steady shifted underneath him, dancing sideways, picking up on his discomfort. He stroked Steady's neck to calm the horse, trying to imagine that, the inevitable and likely immediate results of such an act on the devil's part. "He'd have to shut all the borders." Allowing settlers from all three borders meant no one nation could claim insult—not the Spanish crown nor the British, not the Americans. Nor the French, although they seemed to care little for what happened here, the trappers and woodsmen who remained so well-mingled with the tribes, he suspected they thought themselves other than French. If he didn't shut all the borders, the ones who were affected would take that as excuse. The Territory standing alone was a potential prize yet to be won. The Territory possibly allying with another nation became a threat.

"He can't," Isobel said, and she had that tone again, telling him that although her mouth shaped the words, the *knowing* came from another source entirely.

He didn't know if it meant the devil couldn't because it would cause more problems than it solved, or if he couldn't, quite literally.

The why didn't matter, only the end result: the Territory remained open for Jefferson's handpicked spies to continue poking into it, causing trouble they were entirely unprepared to understand, much less survive.

Gabriel didn't need a spirit-dream to tell him who would be tasked to deal with the results.

"You could leave." Her voice was small but solid, and he had the uncomfortable thought that he might as well have spoken his thoughts out loud. "I'm not sure what's considered usual for a mentorship ride, but I'm reasonably certain this isn't it."

That surprised a laugh out of him, and he took a swig off his canteen to buy himself time to answer.

Guilt alone didn't explain it. Nor duty—he had little enough of either, and she knew that.

He remembered the dream of a cracked creek bed, the cold sun, and further back, the fish swimming at his feet, passing over him as though he were not there. He remembered the snake's hissed amusement, and Old Woman's frown, following him every step deeper into the very thing he'd sought to escape.

Isobel had been confused by the wapiti and Reaper hawk giving her conflicting advice. He'd been dealing with that since he'd returned from the States, Graciendo telling him how to remain apart, while Old Woman's teachings followed down into his dreams.

He could do both. He could remain himself and still be Isobel's mentor properly. He simply had to make her understand.

"All my life, I wanted nothing but to leave. I wasn't a farmer; that was clear from the beginning. My siblings were born with their hands in the dirt, but I . . . It wasn't for me. When my parents agreed to send me East, for schooling, I thought it was the beginning of my true life, my real life. I was sixteen, a man, and the world lay at my feet."

"But you didn't like it there."

"The city . . . There were so many people, even in my classes, it took me months to walk through them and not flinch. But the things I learned, the things I heard, saw . . . I made friends there, friends who had plans, wanted to shape the world. I thought I could be part of that too, in my own way. But the Territory is possessive, Isobel. It will let us go only so long.

"I fell ill. Soul-sick. I barely made it to the Mudwater before collapsing. If it weren't for the Old Woman . . ."

He had told her some of this, but only some: she had no need to know of the weeks he'd spent recovering, too weak to move, too weak to not listen as the Old Woman poured stories into his ears, waited by his side while the dreams came. "Most folk who live on that side of the river, they plug their ears and blinder their eyes. They don't want to see there's a difference between the banks, don't feel the way things change. But the folk who cross back and forth, the ones who work the waterways . . . They know. They knew they had to get me back across, soon's I was strong enough."

"And you were angry about that."

"Furious. I raged as best I could, being weak as a newborn babe. I cursed and I swore, and then I learned new words to better curse. But that changed nothing. The Territory had decided where I would belong.

"But it couldn't claim me, either. Not if I didn't let it."

He waited, but Isobel didn't ask.

"And you kept in touch with your friends there all this time?"

"It's part of how I resist. How I bite my thumb at it." He reined Steady in, blocking Uvnee from walking on. "But I swear to you, Isobel

Devil's Hand. I did nothing with intent to harm the Territory, or those within."

She studied him, her face blank, her eyes flat under the shadow of the hat's brim, and something flickered in those dark orbs, a trick of the light.

Then she looked away, and he could tell himself it was nothing.

"Why do you think it wouldn't let you go? Is it like that for all of us?"

"I don't know. And no—some come and go without issue. I've no idea why I'm so fortunate."

She let the bitterness pass unremarked. "But you were here, and you were in Flood on my birthday and thought to offer me mentoring."

He could see where she was going with that, even blindfolded in the mid-night. "I don't believe in fate, Iz. We make our own choices."

"Yes. And your choices led you there, on that day." That suddenly, the blankness was gone, her face still somber but her eyes holding that familiar sharp spark of life, as though she'd finally bested him. "And that road led to this one, and this particular mess."

He moved Steady out of her way, pressing his heels into the gelding's side. "Wouldn't be anywhere else."

Much to his dismay, he meant it. Even though she had never answered his original question.

Which of itself was answer enough.

Her heart had nearly stopped when Gabriel asked her, blunt as a bullet, if she'd killed the magicians. The words had coiled in her throat, but instead she had turned it back on him, pushing her own questions until he had no choice but to retreat.

She had known some of it before, half-told stories and confessions, a life left on the other side of the border, threads of it still tying him there. But the idea that leaving had made him so ill, that had been new. Disturbing.

She looked at the sigil in her palm, tracing the thick black lines and curves with a delicate finger. There were times she'd swear she could feel them, like a scar, but the skin was smooth under her touch now, the loops as familiar as her own breath.

And now, if she let it, she could feel that warmth in her bones, imagine the white traced with faint, glittering strands of silver.

Purest fancy. And yet.

Something moved within her. Something that did not carry the scent of the boss's cigar or his whiskey.

Had she ever had the option to leave? If she'd left Flood behind her, followed her parents across the Mother's Knife into Spain's arms, or taken passage across the river into the States, or headed into the far north with the Métis, into English-held lands . . . Would she too have been driven back, sooner before later, ill and broken?

Had the choice she made been no choice at all?

And if so . . . had the devil known?

They made camp well before nightfall, choosing a spot on the bank of a wide creek, surrounded by scrub and berry bushes. They moved around each other smoothly, settling and grooming the horses, building a fire, settling their packs. The hum of insects was loud around them, and she spotted a pair of rabbits nearby, eyes wide at her before they decided she was no threat.

Somehow, the thought of trapping something held no appeal tonight. She picked a hatful of berries instead.

Among the supplies they'd taken on was a loaf of fresh bread that had been taunting them with its smell all day. Isobel cut two large slices off of it, then placed them on a flat rock she'd set just next to the fire, and left them to warm, while Gabriel cleaned the berries and added them to the meat he was simmering in the tripod pot. They'd not stopped for a mid-day meal, and Isobel's stomach had been too upset with nerves to want any of the dried venison she carried, so even though she didn't feel hungry, the tightness in her stomach reminded her that she would need to eat now.

They had another two days, at this pace, before they were back at the valley. Another two days before she had to face the haint—and its keepers—again.

Gabriel finished what he was doing, then sat back on his haunches and studied her until she felt the urge to check if she had a smudge on her nose or a leaf in her hair.

"So, what's the plan?"

She almost laughed at that, except it wasn't funny in the slightest.

"Isobel. Do you have any idea what you're going to do once we get there?"

He sounded so much like Marie just then, for all that his voice was so much deeper, she broke into giggles. And once she started, she couldn't stop. Hiccupping, painful giggles that formed deep in her belly, pushing up through her chest and into her throat, causing her to bend over and wrap her arms around herself, trying to make them stop.

Then warm arms were around her, drawing her against a broad chest, and the weight of something against the crown of her head, barely audible words of comfort against her ear.

"It's all right. It's all right, Isobel. Let it out. It's been a horrible few days, hasn't it? I know, it's all right, there's nobody here but us, you can cry, it's all right."

Slowly, the storm inside her wore itself out, leaving an aching emptiness behind. Her back ached, and her nose was snotty, and dinner had likely burned itself, but Isobel couldn't bring herself to move just yet.

"I don't know what to do." The words were muffled against his chest, her hands fisted between them, nails digging into the flesh of her palms. "I don't . . ."

She knew what needed to be done. She thought she would even know how to do it once she was there. But she didn't want to. "I'm tired, and I'm sore, and I don't want to be this person anymore."

The admission was torn out of her, scraping her throat raw, making her cringe at the sound. She'd made a Bargain, she'd inked the pen with her own blood and bound herself to the boss, and once on the Road, she'd bound herself to the Territory somehow, and she didn't regret it she truly didn't but she was so *tired*.

She didn't realize she was saying all of that out loud until too late. Horrified, she pulled away, opening her left hand—wincing at the ache in her knuckles—as though afraid that the mark there would have disappeared, that her words would somehow be enough to break the binding.

It was still there: thick black lines looping twice, an open circle curling around it. The devil's sigil, pressed into flesh, and she traced the cool lines with the forefinger of her other hand and let out a sigh that ended with a painful hiccup.

Black marks, not silver. She took some comfort from that. She could see the boss, rage at him. He was *real*.

"Here." Gabriel dug awkwardly into his jacket pocket and pulled out a kerchief. It wasn't the cleanest linen she'd ever seen, but she used it to wipe her eyes and then blow her nose.

"Keep it," he said, and she was able to giggle, real humor this time, even as she scrambled out of his lap, trying to reclaim a few shreds of dignity.

"Better?"

"Yes. No." She sniffed, but her nose was too clogged to smell anything. "Did dinner burn?"

He glanced at the fire. "It's fine. Go walk it off. Take the mule. Mules are good for this sort of thing."

"What?" He was making no sense.

He made a sweeping gesture with his arm. "Go, walk. With the mule. Trust me."

Isobel wasn't sure which one of them had gone mad, but she got up, brushing the dirt off her skirt, and went to gather the mule.

Flatfoot had been comfortably grazing, but when she slipped her fingers into its mane, tugging gently, it followed her without complaint.

Past the berry bushes, the ground was mostly rock and sagebrush. The sun was sinking but still high enough for Isobel to see clearly. The bugs zipped and sang around her, a stick-bug leaping nearly across her nose when she startled it. In the distance, she heard foxes yip, and she thought of the rabbits she had seen earlier, wishing them luck and fleet feet, to stay uneaten. A bird perched nearby and sang at them, liquid sounds broken by sudden chirps.

Another day's travel and none of this would surround them; the land would slowly become empty, sorrow and anger turning it barren.

The mule made a deep groaning noise and pressed its weight against her side. She slung an arm over its neck and leaned back. It smelled terrible; dirt and dung and musk, but even the terribleness of it was familiar. Comforting. One long ear flicked backward at her, and he whuffled, this time more contentedly.

Gabriel had been right, as usual. This helped.

"Who knew you would be useful," she said into one furred ear, and the mule snorted at her, then tried to eat the feathers in her braid. By the time she pulled them away, the longer one was slightly soggy, the edges badly ruffled.

She smoothed them as gently as she could, trying to reshape them flat, then held her braid up for consideration, letting the afternoon light catch glints and colors in them she'd either never seen or forgotten about.

They had been a gift, an acknowledgment that she was . . . what?

Touched, Lou had said. Touched by the Territory. Something shifted inside her at the thought. Trapped by the Territory, bound to it . . . but she hadn't *wanted* to leave.

Her fingers brushed over the feathers, wondering if she had been doing the wrong thing wearing them every day, or if she should have left them in while she slept, or if she was meant to burn them when they became ragged, an offering back to the winds. . . .

"Would it be so much," she said, as much to the world around her as to the mule accompanying her, "for things to be explained rather than feeling as though the world's watching me try to figure it out?"

Flatfoot flicked his tail at her, as though warning her to watch what she asked for, and Isobel held her breath. She wasn't sure if she wanted an answer or not, but when no snakes or hawks or deer dropped in with useless advice, she exhaled in relief.

"When I get back to Flood," she told the mule, "the boss and I . . ." Her voice trailed off and they wandered on in silence. She might like the idea of demanding more information from the devil, but she wasn't fool enough to think it would happen. She knew he cared for her, cared for all of them, but he was still Master of the Territory, and she was in his service.

And if he had not known, if this thing happening to her were none of his doing or planning . . .

She had agreed to whatever had been asked of her, even if she hadn't known it at the time. Be careful what you ask for, because the devil will give it to you.

"Isobel." She turned at the sound of her name being called, surprised to realize that they'd wandered so far from the camp. The sunlight was beginning to fade, the small flames of the fire rising above the grasses, casting the surrounding dusk a shade darker. The smell of cooked meat caught a tendril of breeze, wafting toward her, and suddenly, she was starving.

Gabriel didn't say anything when she hugged the mule around the neck and sent it back to join the horses, then sat down at the fire, only handed her a plate.

"We're being followed."

She hadn't expected that, but she supposed it wasn't a surprise: they'd been followed to the town; it would make sense they'd be curious where they'd go next.

She took a bite of her dinner, then asked, "How many?"

"Not sure. Maybe only the one? Whoever it is, they're good enough I doubt I'd be able to catch them out. But stay alert; our luck's bound to turn at some point."

Gabriel scraped his plate with his fingers, sucking the juice off them with satisfaction. Having fresh meat that they hadn't had to catch or skin was a rare pleasure on the road, and the lamb had been particularly tasty. She finished her own, then thought of going back into the valley, where living things had fled, and the last bite tasted sour in her mouth.

"Those buffalo . . ."

"The herd you found?" He rubbed the scruff on his chin, scowling at her in a way that, if she didn't know him, would be frightening. "We burned the hides we found. It wasn't enough?"

"I don't know. How can it be? I promised them I'd do what I could. But there isn't anything I can do, is there? They're already dead; I can't make their lives less wasted. Their blood was used for . . . for a terrible thing, and I can't make it right—"

"Isobel. Stop." He stretched out one leg and kicked her gently in the shin. "You're right; there's nothing you could do. You were there too late, and even if you had been there . . ." He picked up his own plate, then hers, once she indicated that she was finished, and put them aside for washing. "If you'd been there, you'd be dead now, Iz. You'd have tried to stop them and you'd have failed. And you can't take the entire chain of events on your shoulders, because, well, you just can't. People—even wind-mad magicians—make their own choices, wise and foolish, and there's nothing you or I or the devil can do about that.

"If it makes you feel better, when all this is sorted, we'll go back and burn the bones. That way they can return to the dust properly."

She exhaled, a little shaky still, half-expecting something to happen, something to speak or appear. But she was alone inside her skin. "When this is sorted."

"And speaking of which. How are we to accomplish that?" His foot remained pushed up against her leg, and it reminded her of the way Flatfoot had leaned against her before. The thought made her smile, even though there was nothing amusing in what she was about to say, and she thought that smile might look a bit like the boss's when he was particularly unamused.

"I haven't any idea. I'll make something up when we get there."

Gabriel had made his bed up that night with Isobel's words rattling between his ears, aware for the first time in years of every rock and root under his bedroll, the rough leather of his pack under his cheek, and every noise and silence of the night, until finally the stars dimmed and he was able to sleep.

They were both up before the sun lifted over the hills behind them, casting pale red rays over the higher mountains directly ahead.

"We could always . . . go back."

"To Andreas?" The look Isobel gave him made it clear she thought he'd lost his wits.

"To Flood."

Her face went flat, only the fluttering blink showing her surprise.

"That was what you had wanted, wasn't it? To go back to Flood?"

"To make sure you were healed properly," she said, going back to saddling her mare. "You're moving well now. I saw you hadn't rebandaged the claw marks; they're scabbed up cleanly."

"Iz."

"So, there's no need to ride all the way back there, and you were correct; it would have been foolish anyhow, so—"

"Isobel!" He couldn't recall the last time he'd raised his voice, and certainly not to a woman. Mayhap back when he was young and still living with his sisters . . . "Isobel," he said more quietly, seeing that she had paused in her actions, arms frozen in place over Uvnee's nose, the bridle half-on, her back straight and too stiff. "There's no shame in asking for help. You're just one woman; we're both just . . . If you think this is too much for us to manage, then there's no shame in handing this over to the devil. It's—"

"No."

"All right." He swung up into Steady's saddle and waited for her to do the same with Uvnee, tucking the edges of her skirt under her legs and adjusting her hat before picking up the reins again. "Onward and upward and on to glory, then."

They'd gone barely ten paces from their campsite before he nearly tore his shoulder out of its socket trying to grab the carbine and load it while also reaching for his boot knife. The conflicting instincts slowed him down enough to realize that the shadow at their shoulder wasn't a maddened magician, a ghost cat, or another irritatingly useless spirit-animal, but the elder Isobel had half-mockingly named Broken Tongue.

"Grandpapa," he said finally, hoping that his voice was calm enough to be polite, switching to French with an effort. "We did not expect to see you again."

The old man sniffed once, with unmistakable emphasis. "I did not think you to be fools."

"I am a fool traveling with a woman."

"You say the same thing twice."

Gabriel was not going to translate any of that for Isobel, riding on his other side. She seemed to have taken the old man's reappearance more calmly than he had, or maybe he'd simply missed her reaction. Or, he thought, at this point Isobel had gone beyond surprise or dismay at anything. That was not a comfortable thought.

"Tell him we go to cleanse the valley," she said, looking up along the path they'd been following, rather than at either one of them. "If it is possible."

Gabriel explained that, hoping that the elder would not ask him how she meant to accomplish such a thing when she had failed before. This might well get him killed, but it wasn't as though he couldn't die any number of ways otherwise. All flesh failed, and every story he'd ever been told of those who wished otherwise ended badly.

Grandfather walked with them without speaking after Gabriel told him what Isobel meant to do. It would have been rude to interrupt his thinking and equally rude to speak to Isobel before the elder had indicated he was finished, so Gabriel contented himself with studying the landscape in front of them, trying to determine where their trackers were at any given moment, wondering if they were part of Grandfather's tribe or another group, and very carefully not wondering what would happen when they rode through the entrance to the valley again.

"Je sais ce qu'elle est maintenant. Est-ce qu'elle le sait?"

I know what she is now. Does she?

When he looked to his side again, the old man had disappeared as silently as he'd arrived, with neither Steady nor the mule, moseying along behind them, so much as twitching an ear in reaction.

He was not fool enough, though, to presume that they were alone now. The old man was keeping an eye on them, had likely been doing so ever since they first came to the valley.

Gabriel wasn't sure if that was comforting or made it all that much the worse.

He wiped his forehead and replaced his hat, refusing to give the old man the satisfaction of seeing him look around.

"What did he say?" Isobel asked finally.

"Nothing of use."

"Of course not." She pulled the brim of her hat down over her face and slumped in an exaggerated fashion in the saddle. "Native or spirit or . . . when a magician gives more answers than the rest of you, what's the use?" she asked, loud enough that anything with sensitive ears could hear her from twenty paces back. "Fine, then. Let them leave us be, and the devil won't have to look in after them in turn."

As indirect threats went, Gabriel had to admit that should be a particularly effective one.

She knew that Gabriel was watching her. The boss used to do that too, then he'd sit back in his chair and light the cigar he never smoked, watching the pale blue plume of smoke twist and turn in the wind, or he'd open a new deck of cards and shuffle them against the dark green felt of the card table, spreading and rearranging the cards like they told him something new each time, waiting to hear what she would say.

But where once she would have looked anxiously at the boss, hoping to find some clue as to what she should do, some approval that she'd made the right choice, now she sank deeper into Uvnee's saddle, wrapping the reins comfortably around her right hand, feeling every patch of her body, where it pressed into the saddle wrapped around Uvnee's body, where the warming air touched her skin, where the sweat trickled under her hatband, sliding down the back of her neck, the occasional ruffle of breeze against her skirt, her boots now comfortably broken in, no longer chafing against her unmentionables or causing blisters on her heels.

The familiar rocking motion of Uvnee's walk was as soothing as folding linens, the repetition allowing her to move her awareness away from herself and outward, that sense of the Road below her no longer requiring the touch of ground directly. The push-away she'd felt before, the refusal that had left her feeling oddly hurt and uncomfortable, was not here; the bones allowed her to reach out, using them to spread herself further, though it felt more difficult here, as though she pulled a laden wagon behind her, weighing her movements.

Ahead, the Road faded into mist and shadows. Isobel felt an urge to push into it, but that was not her immediate concern. Aside, behind: that was where the stranger-eyes watched, more than just the old man, their regard a tactile sensation here, sharp pricks of attention tapping at her, hail on the window or rain on a creek, impossible to deflect.

Attention, focused. Aware of them. But nothing else: no anger or hunger, no fear or worry. No emotions, no distractions; merely a sensation of follow-watch-follow-watch.

More than human eyes watched them.

Isobel blinked, suddenly solidly within her own bones and flesh again. She swayed forward, wrapping her free hand in Uvnee's mane, feeling the coarse strands against her skin, the smell of leather and trail-sweat and sun-warmed air and grasses and dirt in her nose. She tilted her head back to the sun, opening her mouth as though to drink it all in.

Next to her, Gabriel rode closer than usual, ready to catch her if she became too dizzy to ride. She could feel him watching her, although his own attention seemed focused ahead of them, constantly scanning the rock face and brush for something that shouldn't be there. Maybe he was waiting for the old man to appear again, or a Reaper hawk to land in front of them. Or the ground to shake suddenly, or any of a handful of things that could very well happen. Again.

"We've gone into sacred ground and come back down again," she said. "And now we're going back. They're watching to see what happens to us."

"And to think I could have stayed home as a child and been a farmer," Gabriel said dryly, not asking who watched or how she knew.

"Or stayed out of Flood entire as an adult and been none the wiser," she retorted. "If fate did not force you to ride into the devil's town and offer to mentor one of his workers."

"No, that was purely my own folly and good fortune," he agreed. The urge to throw something at him came and passed, luckily for him, as the only things close at hand were her canteen and her knife.

"Tell me a story." At the very least, that would distract her from where they were heading and what she would have to do once they were there. . . .

"About what?"

"Demons." Of all the things to suggest . . . but demons, at least, were not their problem here. "How many are there? Where did they come from?"

Gabriel shrugged. "How many peaks are there in the Mother's Knife? How many buffalo in the northern plains? More than anyone has ever counted, possibly fewer than we think. Nobody's ever seen anything but a full-grown one; we don't even know if they spawn or appear full-blown out of a winter's sneeze."

"You don't have any stories?" It was a challenge: Gabriel had stories for everything, gathered over the years.

"Some say they're the children of the living silver who came to the surface but were so disappointed in what they found here, they turned around to go back, only to find the gateways had been closed, leaving them trapped on the surface, growing dryer and dryer with every year.

"Another story says that the first demon was born of wind and stone, and raised by the night bird to help it scour the bones, but it refused to limit itself to the dead, and so the night bird cast it out, breaking it into a hundred hundred pieces."

"None of that is comforting."

"None of them were meant to be."

They rode the rest of the day without discussing demon or magicians, what Isobel hoped to do once she returned to the valley, or what had happened back at Andreas. Gabriel made her practice dropping from the saddle at a trot, until her toes were sore from landing, and then, lacking other distraction, she taught him how to braid the rough strands of Steady's mane into a credible plait. They paused at the spot where they'd made camp before, although Isobel refused to believe it was the exact same spot until she kicked up the still-fresh char from their fire pit as she was setting down her bedroll.

"You need to look more closely," he said in response to her glare at the fire pit. "The ground will tell you whatever you need to know, if you look and listen properly."

The thought that she still had more to learn should have been depressing, and yet Isobel found a measure of comfort in it. If she was still ignorant, it was because she was still Isobel, not . . . something else.

She rubbed at her forehead and crawled into her bedroll before the night was fully dark, determined to not think at all about anything.

But sleep that night was fitful, despite exhaustion. Isobel finally gave up, moving to sit by the remains of the fire, watching the stars wheel across the sky above them, the faint glimmer of a crescent moon barely visible for their brightness.

In the shadows, Gabriel's soft rumbling breath was almost a snore, counterpoint to the sleepy rustlings of the animals, and the soft noise of the night-hunters in the air and on the ground around her.

It all felt familiar, comforting . . . safe. But Isobel could feel the storm caught within the bones, the closer they came to the valley, and she knew better.

The first sign of trouble came the next morning, when they reached the narrow climb into the pass that led to the valley, and the mule decided he wasn't going back. Long ears flattened back, eyes rolling, and gums pulling back from flat teeth in a clear threat to bite anyone who tried to pull him forward. Flatfoot lived up to his name finally, digging in and refusing to move.

"That beast's smarter than us both," Gabriel said. He had picked up a length of twig as a switch but seemed loath to put it to use, reluctant to punish the animal for not wanting to do what none of them wanted to do.

The horses waited patiently; they might be no happier, but they were willing to trust where the humans led, at least for now.

"If we leave him here, the odds that our belongings will still be here when we return?" She firmly believed that they would return; she had to believe that they would return.

Gabriel huffed, running the back of his neck as though it pained him. "There is no honor in stealing from someone trying to help you." But he pitched his voice so that it carried past the two of them, lingering in the mid-day air.

Isobel let a few breaths go by, but nothing sounded in response. "He's your mule," she said, "and most of what he carries is yours too."

"We can shift the most essential supplies to the horses. The rest will be safe enough until we return. And if we don't, he's too smart to let himself starve here."

It was a quick matter after that to unload the mule as though they were preparing to camp for the night, then sling several of the packs over Steady's broad hindquarters. His tail twitched, but he allowed the indignity, as though aware it would not be for long.

The leather satchel with the salt stick and her journal, Isobel slung over Uvnee's shoulder as she mounted. She had not yet written down the events of Andreas, had not yet noted the names of the dead, and that knowledge was a bruise, tender and sore, until she could remedy it. But there had been no time then, and this was no time now.

Gabriel left the rope halter on the mule but undid the other straps and bands, giving it a roughly affectionate scritch on the poll before turning away and swinging up into Steady's saddle, the gelding living up to his name despite his own clear unease.

The mule let out a low noise, as though it were confused about what was happening, watching as they walked the horses toward the pass. When Isobel looked back, half-turning in the saddle before they passed out of sight, the mule was still there, watching them go.

The narrow path and sudden drops seemed somehow less unnerving this time through. Isobel was unsure if it was familiarity or she was simply too tired to care. Then, she'd thought only to put distance between her and the haint, thinking that the wisest thing.

There was nothing good waiting in that valley. Nothing she ever wanted to see again. And yet, here they were.

She waited for Gabriel to tell her that she didn't have to do this, that they could ride back down to the plains, continue on their way, following the route Gabriel had laid out, not the pokings and proddings of a whisper.

He said nothing.

Her mentor was practically slouched in his saddle, reins held loose in one hand, brim of his hat pulled down over his eyes, shading the afternoon sun from his face. Every inch of him spoke of casual comfort, as though he were half a breath from falling asleep, but she could feel the tension in him; he wanted to go through that passage even less than she did.

She looked down at her hands, the right holding Uvnee's reins, the left palm down on her leg, moving restlessly against the fabric of her skirt. When they reached the next town, she was going to dump all her skirts, all her unmentionables, into a vat of steaming water and boil them until they were clean again, if she had to sit in her shift to do it. Then she was going to refill the vat with even more steaming water and boil herself until she felt clean, from her toes to her scalp.

And then she was going to make Gabriel do the same.

"I wanted this," she told herself, the words barely carrying past her lips. "I chose this. Even if there never was a choice."

The boss always said all he did was deal the cards; how someone played them was up to them. But once you picked up the cards, you played or you folded.

She thought, probably, a Hand wasn't allowed to fold.

She flicked Uvnee's reins and pressed her legs against the mare's side, moving her into the passage, trusting that the others would follow.

The sense of foreboding grew as they reached the plateau and started down again, the itch on the back of her neck intensifying, so when the heavy beat of wings overhead came, she was already primed to duck forward, wrapping her arms around the mare's neck in case Uvnee took it into her head to bolt.

Other than a full-body shudder, though, the mare kept to a walk, and when Isobel brought herself back upright, it was to see an owl staring at her from an outcrop on the rocks to her left.

She could not swear that it was the same owl that had led them to the marshal and her captives, any more than she could swear that that had been the same owl that had startled her as they broke camp several nights before. But she could not convince herself it wasn't the same, either.

In daylight, she could see the slight clouding of its golden eyes, but its gaze seemed sharp, head tilting to follow her movement until she came alongside its perch.

"Well?" she asked it, too tight-wound to be polite. "If you've advice, you'd best give it now. I may be too busy later. Or dead."

Somewhere, weeks' travel distant, Isobel thought she heard the boss laugh.

In front of her now, the owl lifted its wings, great banded feathers spread wide, and launched itself off the outcrop, swooping down before gaining height, leading the way into the valley.

"I'm not sure if that was advice or not," Gabriel said, his voice dry as wood, "but it seemed reasonably clear."

"And about as useful as dust," Isobel muttered, but followed the bird out of the passage and into the afternoon light of the valley.

The meadow, when they reached it, looked much as they had left it, although she thought the area of dead grasses had grown. The presence that had been there was faded; no corner-of-her-eye shadow or sense of menace lingered underfoot.

But she did not believe it was gone. And other than the owl—that had disappeared, she noted, checking the sky overhead—there was still no sign of life anywhere in the valley. Even the constant annoyance of flies gathered around the horses' eyes and haunches was obvious by their absence.

She slid down from Uvnee's saddle and pulled the satchel with her. The salt stick had been worn down to nearly a nub, fitting easily in her palm now. She reached past it, past the leather-bound journal, to the bottom of the pack, where one other item rested.

The etched stone that she'd discovered earlier, still wrapped up in the torn stocking. The feeling she'd had, that it had been left there by Farron for some reason of his own, still lingered.

She could not say why she took it out now, why she had not left it along the trail, thrown it into a creek and let running water have it. Gifts from magicians were to be avoided as much as magicians themselves. But he might have known she would need it, somehow. Or it might have been utterly random and useless, a foolish prank from a madman.

Gabriel might have told her to lose it. So, she had not told him.

"How many magicians are there, wandering the Territory, do you think? As many as buffalo?"

"Buffalo don't feed on each other," Gabriel said, sliding down out of Steady's saddle, his gaze still sweeping around them, looking for something, then returning to her. "And magicians seem to breed slower. Far fewer than even a single herd would be my guess. Fewer than all the settlers from Clear Rock to Poll's Station."

She had no idea where Poll's Station was or how many lived between those two spots.

"What is that?" He'd seen the stone in her hand. She turned, opening her palm to show it to him but keeping far back enough that he would not think to take it from her. She felt a stirring possessiveness toward it, or perhaps a wariness: if it was a magician's making, it was likely dangerous and certainly unpredictable.

"What is it?" he asked again.

She closed her fingers around the heft of the stone again, almost expecting the sigil in her palm to react to it somehow, but nothing happened. Making a decision, she shoved the stocking back into the bag and kept the stone with her.

If it was Farron's making, maybe it would be useful.

"Isobel." Gabriel's voice was stern but curious. "What are you up to?"

"I need to release the angered spirit, and clear the magicians' medicine from where it is trapped."

"You couldn't before."

"You can't kill a magician," she said, agreeing with him. "That was the problem. And, maybe, the answer."

He took off his hat, running a hand through his hair, then down along the side of his cheek, all signs he was nearing exasperation.

"Isobel."

"You can't kill a magician," she said again, feeling her way through it. "And they . . . they brought the ancient one back. Why and how?"

"Blood medicine," he said. "Buffalo are powerful."

"Blood—and hide to wrap it in. Territory medicine. The buffalo's medicine and the medicine of this place, sacred ground, all strong. Too strong. And magicians refuse to die down.

"It's not a haint, Gabriel." She felt some of her worry, her fear, crack through her voice, and tamped it down again. "That's why I couldn't set it to rest. The Territory trapped it half-alive, and now it can't let go. It doesn't know *how*."

"If you break it free—the magicians will be able to re-form somewhere else?"

Isobel shrugged; they had seen Farron do something similar, but she did not know enough to say what would be done. The magicians she had dealt with . . .

She remembered little of it, as though something threw a drape over her memories. But she did not need to know how; if she was in truth the devil's silver, meant to cleanse what had been fouled, then like silver, she did nothing of her own willing but rather what she *was*.

And if she were something else . . .

"Iz?" He'd seen something change in her face. "What is it?"

"What am I?"

He'd not been conscious of it, but the moment the words came out of her mouth, Gabriel knew that he'd been waiting for that question.

"You're Isobel of Flood. Isobel of the Devil's House. Isobel Left Hand. Isobel of names yet to be earned. We're none of us who we were when we began, Isobel. That's the point of taking the dust roads."

"That wasn't what I meant." She shifted uneasily, looking down at the stone in her hand as though she'd forgotten she held it, then shoved it into her jacket pocket. "Back in town, those magicians. I stood outside the cabin, I looked at the sigils, and I knew that I couldn't allow them to go free. Not the way they were, not *what* they were." Her eyes wouldn't settle on him, shifting right, then left, always at an angle, never looking directly at him. Her hands were shoved into her pockets, her body braced as though expecting a blow. "You said . . . you said they were torn apart, bloody. I never touched them, Gabriel, I never even saw them, but I did that. I did that to them, something *in* me did that to them, and I don't remember it."

A breeze touched the tendrils of hair that had escaped her braid, and the tips of her two feathers danced lightly, even as the air cooled the sweat the sun had raised on his skin. He thought a cloud might have passed across the sun, although the sky had been pale blue all day, but he didn't dare look away from her, even for a second, to check if the weather had changed. It wasn't storm season; they should be safe enough for now.

"You made a decision, and you carried it out." He didn't like what he was about to say, but it was his responsibility to say it. "Sometimes those decisions, those things, will be ugly. That you didn't do it with your own hands? Doesn't make it any less your responsibility any more than it wasn't the judge's responsibility when he had a man executed, for all that someone else primed the shot.

"So, you take responsibility. Could you, in any conscience, allow the magicians to be released, despite the fact that they had committed no wrong under the Law?"

"No." There was no hesitation, no doubt in her voice. "The madness, I could feel it in them. They had no control; they didn't *want* control, only to consume. They would have gone after anything that fed them—anyone with even the slightest hint of power, and they would have gone after the weakest first."

Someone like April, her girlhood friend they'd met in Junction, whose touch was to grow things green and bright. Or Devorah, any rider; anyone who could touch the Road could feel the bones beneath their feet. Or even himself: Gabriel might resent and resist, but he knew what he was, what he could not escape. His water-sense would mark him, no matter how slight.

The things that made them part of the Territory, he thought, and wondered why he'd never thought that before, so obvious and yet invisible.

"They would have gone after anyone with even a scrap of power. I couldn't let them. But"—and there was the thorn in her heart, the crack in her chest; he could hear it, see it in her, and his own chest ached for her—"if I am the cold eye and the final word . . . what is there to stop *me*?"

"Nothing, save your own sense of where to stop."

That brought her up short: she had been expecting him to say something else, mayhap tell her how to limit herself, or some secret, but he had none, had no answer save what he gave her.

"You are the devil's eye, Isobel. What do you see?"

She stared at him finally, and then turned away, looking out over the expanse of grass, the clustered line of trees, the rise of the hills and mountains around them, and then back to him. Her eyes were nearly all pupil, like a cat's in candlelight, and he felt the urge to remain still and make no sound.

"Infection," she said finally, her voice heavy and slow. "Things ooze where they should be solid, hot where they should be cool, cold where they should be warm, soft and brittle as it eats into the bones, and the bones cannot hold, even as the spirit cannot break free. Poison, seeping into everything. If it were a wound like yours, I would slice it open and wash it until your blood ran clean."

His hand touched the scar on his side reflexively. It was healed now, only giving him the occasional twinge, but he could remember the pain he'd felt those first few days, when every breath made him wonder if he would ever rest easy again, much less ride.

"But the left hand is not the giving hand," Isobel went on. "If I do this . . ."

"You're afraid you'll hurt the spirit, do what the magicians couldn't?" He wanted to scoff, to tell her that a single mortal couldn't do more than an impossible banding of magicians, but then he remembered the scene inside the lockhouse, the bodies torn and strewn across the hard-packed ground, and was uncertain.

"This is not part of the Agreement, Gabriel. There are none under the devil's protection who are harmed here; the men who did this have been punished, either by death or worse, and the ancient one is not mine to interfere with. This is . . ." Her voice slowed, grew more strained.

"This is not the devil's due, nor were those magicians. And yet I carried out that sentence, without hesitation, as though . . ."

The ground swelled underfoot as she spoke, a rumbling he could feel with his skin, and behind them Steady let out a ringing cry, part defiance and part fear, even as the hills rising above them shook hard enough to cause, in the distance, the crashing sound of a rockslide.

"No." Her eyes were wide, her face ashen. "No—"

She wasn't speaking to him, he realized even as Isobel picked up the salt stick and threw it at him. "Ward yourself and the horses," she told him. "And stay there."

She grabbed the fabric of her skirt in both hands and hitched it, then took off at a dead run for the center of the valley, going three quarters of the way across before stopping as though she'd hit a wall, spinning around, and collapsing to her knees.

A heavy wind slicked through the valley, low along the tops of the grasses, the ground shuddered, unruly, and the blue sky overhead seemed a distant, peaceful joke. He ground the salt between his palms and tried to draw a warding circle, but the wind scattered the grains faster than he could pour them. Giving up, he stuck the salt stick between his teeth, wincing at the bitter, sharp taste, and ran for the horses, grabbing their reins and bringing them close together. If he could, he would have sent them back through the passage, but he worried that a rockslide there would be deadly for all three of them.

Better to stay here, as far from rocks or trees as he could, and pray the ground did not open up and swallow them—or Isobel.

And then the world broke loose.

The moment Isobel had dropped to her knees, her palm down on the ground, she felt slapped between two impossible weights pressing the air from her lungs, the strength from her limbs.

"Please." She wasn't sure what she was asking for, or who, but the word was all she could squeeze out. "Please."

They did not listen, could not hear her. The wind picked up, nearly knocking her sideways, the grass sharp-edged and harsh against her hands and face. Her hat was knocked clear off her head, only the leather cord under her chin keeping it from blowing away, digging into the soft skin there until she jammed it onto her head again, defiant as though to tell the wind to keep its hands off her and hers.

She didn't hear it laugh; that had to have been her imagination.

She turned her fingers downward, nails digging past the grass into the dirt, all her weight pressing into her palm until her arm and shoulder ached with it, doing her best to ignore everything but the knowledge of the sigil on her palm and what it meant, what it meant she was, what it meant she was required to do.

"Please," she said again, asking the barrier that met her to allow her through, the way she had moved past bone and stone and warding, to reach the magicians within the hut. The valley shuddered under her, the disorientation outside and around her as well as within, as though she were trapped in a fever rather than the fever being under her own skin. The spirit raged; she could feel it, this close, as though she'd grabbed a heated poker, no, something hot but spiked, a handful of gooseberry vines or a cactus pad that wriggled and fought within her grasp, and each wriggle sent another rumble through the bones as they pushed back, pressing that rage flat in an attempt to calm it.

"That won't work." She was unsure if she spoke the words or merely thought them, unsure if the barrier she sensed was aware enough to even know she was there, much less hear her. "You're doing more harm that way, can't you see?"

It was useless; the bones knew only the bones, knew only the earth they were buried in, the deep slow movements and the sudden cracks; the barrier was there to protect itself, not those who lived above.

She thought of the elk's advice and the Reaper hawk's. To save herself, to do what she had been sent out to do. To leave the bones to themselves, to meddle in it.

The Agreement gave the devil dominion over those who came into the Territory but not those who were of the Territory—the tribes, and those born of the bones themselves, the creatures of spirit and medicine. And not the magicians, who came from outside but gave themselves over to the winds.

But what of the Territory itself? She could feel it spreading out under her hand, though they were far off the Road here, in this deserted hollow, the cool fire of stone and bone rising from below to tower overhead, everything resting just so, and she thought again of Gabriel's story of the Black Hills. Too large, too strong for even the devil to comprehend. He thought to control this?

She bit her lip until she felt blood in her mouth, her thoughts hurt as badly as the burning thorns, prickly discomfort that made her shy away.

You know. The whisper, molten threads, no longer outside but within, running through her bones. *The Master of the Territory saw what you are, but we have the greater claim.*

She lifted her hand to her mouth, smeared the blood there across her palm, mixing with soil on her skin, the bitter taste of dirt on her tongue. The Territory had been given into the devil's keeping, and she was of the Territory by birth and touch and claim; she could do what the devil could not.

Living silver, wrapped in her bones.

Magicians could not die, a spirit pulled back to being could not fade; the fury it felt would last a thousand and a thousand years, until nothing lived in this valley, in these hills, anywhere for a day's ride or more, spreading over time. If they released it . . .

That fury would scorch the ground, burn dirt and rock, turn water to steam and every living thing to ash. But then it would be free, and the damage would be contained, the land—the people—beyond this valley safe.

Gabriel. Her stomach dropped. No warding could protect him if that happened. She should never have let him come with her if she'd thought it through, if she'd thought at all.

Another rumble, this one stronger, more violent, and she swayed on her knees, feeling the beating of massive, invisible wings below her, and curled around it the shadowed tendrils of something else, thick and clinging, reeking of *want* and *need*.

The magicians who had died here were not destroyed; they lingered by the power of their own desires, and for the first, for the truly first time, Isobel understood why they were told to run when they encountered magicians.

They had no care for anything save power, not even themselves. They would willingly spend their very blood and bone to become something greater. Would willingly destroy the world below them to achieve what the winds contained. Just as the ancient spirit would destroy everything to be free.

Isobel pulled her palm from the ground, her other hand scrabbling for the knife at her side. The silver along the handle and edge no longer gleamed in the sunlight, tarnished to a dull black just in the time since they'd ridden into the valley, just the same as the silver band on her little finger.

"Tell me something useful," she muttered to it. There was no need to toss silver here to know that something was wrong, something was dangerous, and not all the silver they carried on them was enough to clear the way.

Living silver. Living silver clears all things.

She laid the edge of the knife across her palm and drew a line deep into the flesh until blood welled, rising up to the black lines embedded into her palm. She dropped the knife into the grass and slammed her hand down onto the ground again, the dirt under her fingernails and pressed into the whorls of her fingertips mixing with the blood running down her fingers, aching pain driving from her palm up into her arm, coiling around her elbow and up into her shoulder, her neck, and down her spine, spreading throughout her body until all she could feel was the ache. When the ground trembled underneath her again, as though trying to buck her off its skin, she shoved all of that down, the ache and the pain, the blood and the fear and *need* she felt, to feel the ancient one move freely, for the magicians to disperse into the winds, for the land to settle back onto its bones and be calm once again.

She was the Devil's Hand, the cold eye of justice, and she would do what was required to keep the Territory whole.

And if that meant destroying everything within this valley, she would do so.

"But it doesn't have to be," she told it. "Let it go." Neither a command nor a plea: a suggestion, a better way. "Trust me."

The bones wavered, and she felt the warding crack and splinter. The spirit howled itself open, the tattered remains of the magicians fell away, and the spirit broke free.

There were no words to describe it, nothing in Isobel's thoughts that could contain it, save the dismay that even a brace of magicians had thought to control this, the air above them filled with a presence that made clear the form she had sensed before was barely the shadow of its shadow: endlessly stretching wings, and eyes and claws and elongated head, the rattling scream of a tornado above her, the wind no longer laughing but howling with outrage. Immense, ancient, powerful as only the long-dead become, fed on the blood of the Territory and the flesh of the winds. And she, petty and puny, daring to—

"Not me!" she screamed at it. "It wasn't me!"

It had consumed them, consumed their power, stuffed it greedily into its maw and swallowed them whole. But not enough. Never enough. The shreds that had clung to its wings burned in the air, burned the soil down to rock with its rage, and the ancient spirit searched for the others, a thousand red-faceted eyes, a thousand bloody talons ripping through her, until it reached the core.

She braced herself on hands and knees, her eyes closed, head bowed, until the whisper curled outside her ear, opened itself up, and flowed.

An endless current, unfolding from the earth, tumbling on the winds, a respite of silence within the storm. Isobel was there, held by the current curling out from within her, but the whisper looked past her now, Isobel only the container, and whatever occurred, occurred far beyond her understanding.

And in that nub of silence, the storm moved, the endless wings lifting, the red eyes looking elsewhere, the grass around her burnt to the ground, thick smeared clumps of soot filling the air, but her own skin untouched, her clothing ashes on her flesh, only the knife, the silver shining clean, remaining.

One heartbeat. Another. Then the faint clack of grasshoppers, somewhere grass still remained. And then, overhead, the long low call of an owl, hunting as the sun slowly slipped over the mountains to the west.

And then the sound of her own breathing, as she realized she was still alive.

She let that rest for a moment, feeling her heart beat, too fast and too loud, the breath in her lungs too harsh for not having moved, the lack of weight pressing at her. She lifted her bloody hand from the ground, then pressed it back again, wincing at the sore flesh on dirt but feeling only the soft familiar dizziness of the bones deep below, the Road distant but *present*. The barrier was gone; the valley had been abandoned.

"Gabriel?"

Something harsh and warm draped over her shoulders, and she reached up to touch it—a blanket, familiar, her own blanket from her pack, and equally familiar hands wrapping it over her arms, a shaking hug engulfing her and the blanket, soft, harsh breath mingling with her own as he held her like a child, and she, dry-eyed and unutterably weary, stared out at the burnt expanse of the valley.

Justice is done, the whisper said, and was gone.

"I want a nice, quiet week in a town," she said. "Just a week. Maybe two. Can we do that?"

"Yah." He shook, and it took her a moment to realize it was from laughter. "Yeah," Gabriel said, "we can do that."

It was late even by a saloon's standards, the bottles closed and dishes washed, the felt tables covered by sheets, chairs stacked and floors swept, the larger lamps trimmed and closed for the night. Marie walked across the main floor, her slippered feet and skirt making soft sounds in the air. The scent of bay oil and whiskey lingered over a fainter, more pervasive smell of tobacco and brimstone, and she followed it to the far wall and the faint indentation of a narrow door set into the wall.

He was within; she knew that the way she knew everything that occurred within the saloon, within Flood itself, from the river banks to the outskirt farms, and she thought, briefly, to leave him to it, to retire to her own bed and wait for him to speak to her instead.

"Come in," came the response before she could decide.

She placed her hand against the wall, and the door swung open. She wondered each time she entered what would happen if she were not granted permission, if the door would still open or no, but had never felt the need to test it. If she were not wanted within, she would not enter.

There were no windows in this room, no desk, only a sideboard with a crystal decanter of whiskey and the remains of supper on a tray. The walls were light brown wood, smooth-hewn and polished by time and use, three of them set with lamps that cast no shadows, while one was covered by a map, a fine-grain calfskin larger than any calf ever grew, etched with careful black lines and lettering.

His back was to her, hands resting on his hips, his attention on the map. He had shed his jacket during the evening, his hair slicked back and dark against the starched whiteness of his collar, his shirtsleeves rolled to the elbow.

The map was still for the first moment she glanced at it, then a patch of yellow faded to pale green, a thick black line thinning, a shadow of pink darkening to red. In the upper left corner, new lines formed, spiderweb-thin, a dark, ominous blue.

She waited, but no further shifts occurred.

"You worry." His voice was rich and dry, and the face he turned to her was marked by wry amusement, all white teeth and smooth brown skin. For once, his amusement did not sit well with her.

"I always worry." She was his Right Hand, tasked to ensure that those who came to him were seen, heard. If something was happening, something that affected the House, troubled him, she needed to know.

Unless, the thought came on the heels of the first, it was not a thing for the Right Hand to know. Unless it was a matter for the Left Hand.

She glanced at the map again, but—as ever—it was too much for her to take in, too much to look at for too long.

"It's nearly dawn. Even you need to sleep eventually."

It was an old joke between them, decades old, and his smile softened in acknowledgment before turning away from the map entirely, moving across the room to pour a measure of whiskey into two glasses, offering her one.

She raised her glass to the light, admiring the reddish-brown liquid before taking a sip. It warmed her mouth and burned in her throat, honeyed fire with the kick of a full-grown mule.

He drank his portion quickly, seeming barely to notice it, and that worried her where nothing else before had. In all the years she had served him, he had always been driven, noting each and every thing that occurred within his domain, but he was also a creature of his comforts, and for him to treat Iktan's finest with such disregard . . .

"It's coming, isn't it?"

He went still, his long-limbed body somehow coiling with threat, a snake about to strike, before relaxing once again. "It's always been coming, Marie."

Knowing he was aware of her study, she watched him, seeing the dark strands of hair shade to fox-red, the skin fade to parchment-white, the bones of his face shift and yet somehow always remain instantly recognizable, those golden-brown eyes that saw without judging, weighed without devaluing.

"What do we do?"

"Do? The cards have been shuffled and dealt; now all I may do is wait to see how they will be played." He lifted his hand not holding the glass and spread slender, agile fingers, palm up, as though waiting for something to be placed within.

"And if it all falls to ruin?" He had seen the potential in young Izzy, had given her a shape to grow into, waited until she chose it of her own will and desire. But potential and shape were not enough.

He refilled his glass and turned back to the map. Dismissed, unanswered, Marie left the office, closing the door softly behind her.

She had been a woman grown when she came to Flood, desperate to trade her burdens for ease, her pain for numbness. There were days she wished he had refused her Bargain, had sent her to deal with the pain as others did. And yet, even now, she could not imagine being anyone save who she was.

But the Right Hand was simple, overt. The Right Hand was kind.

The Left Hand was none of those things. She could not afford to be. Not if she was to prevent what was coming.

ACKNOWLEDGMENTS

First and foremost, every employee and volunteer at Yellowstone National Park, for taking care of one of our most valuable resources—the wilderness from which we've carved our home. This book would not have been possible without all you do, and my life would be far poorer without those experiences. The National Parks are our past, and our inheritance.

For information and inspiration:

The staff at the Seattle Public Library, Central branch. Particularly the kind folk who help me navigate the Spiral.

Dr. Geoff Abers, Cornell Geological Sciences, who knew I was picking his brain, but not for what purpose.

And also the geosciences department of Skidmore College, ca. 1989, for coaxing a liberal arts major into the sciences in the first place.

Jeff and Carolyn of Green Creek Inn, Wapiti Valley, WY.

Bill Cody Ranch, Shoshone National Forest, WY.

The entire damn town of Cody, Wyoming.

For support above the call of duty or friendship:
Karri Sperring, Fran Wilde, April Steenburgh, Jaym Gates, Barbara Ferrer, and Lewis Pollak.

Team Inevitable Innuendo, for year-round insanity checks.

And of course, my copyeditor, Richard Shealy, for being the final filter for the details of the Devil's West, even when they were (intentionally) inconsistent—but they were *consistently* inconsistent, RS!

Extra acknowledgment:
The nursing staff at New York-Presbyterian. You were kind to us at a time when nobody is at their best, and I probably didn't say thank you enough.

Inevitably, I will forget someone, including people who have continued from the first book, helping me build the Devil's West into something real and living. It's been a very busy year, and I spoke with a great many people, scooping up details and color as I went. But trust me, I think back on your contribution with gratitude!

ABOUT THE AUTHOR

LAURA ANNE GILMAN is the Nebula Award–nominated author of the Vineart War fantasy trilogy. She has also dipped her pen into the mystery field, writing the Gin & Tonic series as L. A. Kornetsky (*Collared*, *Fixed*, *Doghouse*, and *Clawed*). You can find her at lauraannegilman.net and on Twitter at @LAGilman.